# NEW ALBION SUNSET

LUMINARE BOOKS BY L. WADE POWERS

## NOVELS

*The Home*

*The Party House*

## SHORT STORY COLLECTIONS

*Falling In Love and Other Misadventures*

*Confronting the Boundaries*

# NEW ALBION SUNSET

### Drake's Lost English Outpost in North America, 1579

a novel and a history by

## L. WADE POWERS

New Albion Sunset
Copyright © 2020 by L. Wade Powers

All rights reserved. This book or any portion thereof may not be reproduced or used in any manner whatsoever without the express written permission of the publisher, except for the use of brief quotations in a book review.

This is a work of fiction, and the characters are derived from the imagination of the author. With the exception of recognized historical figures and events, any resemblance to actual persons, living or dead, is purely coincidental.

Printed in the United States of America

Cover Design by Claire Flint Last

Front: The *Golden Hinde* and *Northern Venture* in the Pacific Northwest. Painting by Simon Kozhin, 2007, www.kozhinart.com.

Back: Three Rocks at the mouth of the Salmon River, Oregon.

Luminare Press
442 Charnelton St.
Eugene, OR 97401
www.luminarepress.com

LCCN: 2020914031
ISBN: 978-1-64388-558-2

*For Erik and Leslie*

*Dread not the uncharted waters, fear not the unfamiliar.*

*Let your imagination take you to the heights and depths.*

*Let the oceans roar and the clouds whisper.*

*It was all made for you.*

# Table of Contents

*Acknowledgments* ... xi
*Preface A Voyage from Fact to Fiction* ... xiii
*Major Characters of New Albion Sunset* ... xviii

1. Farewell to New Spain ... 1
2. Northward Bound ... 17
3. Northern Contact ... 31
4. Northern Explorations ... 44
5. Nova Albion ... 65
6. The *Northern Venture* ... 86
7. Southward Bound ... 103
8. Shipwreck ... 124
9. Stranded at Three Rocks ... 143
10. Drake's Anchorage ... 162
11. Ne-Chess-Nee ... 169
12. Into the Valley ... 184
13. The Great River ... 197
14. Historical Epilogue ... 212

*Appendix 1: Essays to Document New Albion Sunset* ... 221
*Appendix 2: Reference Chronologies* ... 233
*Appendix 3: Geographical Considerations* ... 255
*Appendix 4: Further Reading* ... 261
*About the Author* ... 269

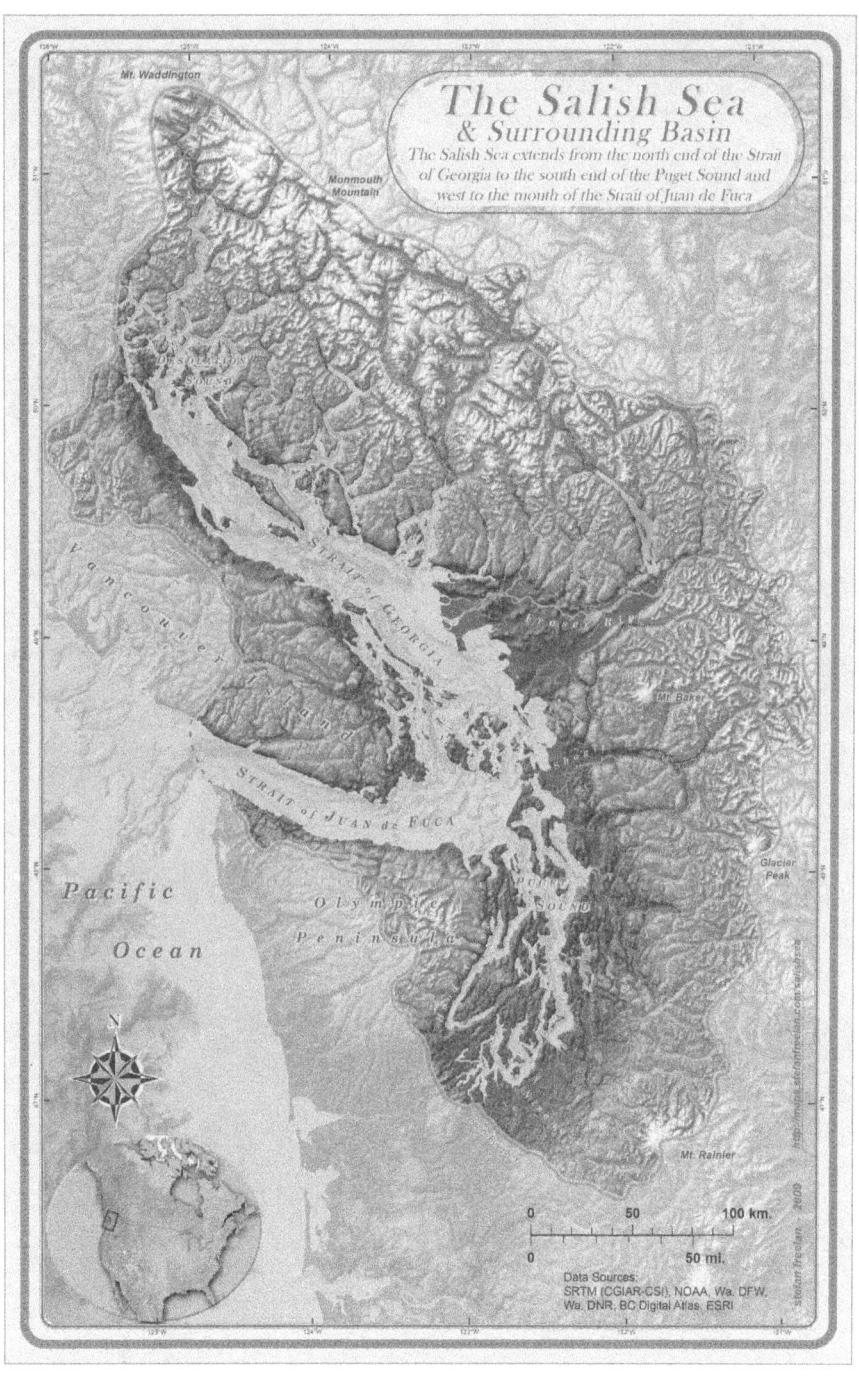

Relief map of the Salish Sea and surrounding basin. By permission of Stefan Freelan, Western Washington University, 2009.

# ACKNOWLEDGMENTS

The vast majority of fictional works do not derive entirely and solely from the imagination of the author. Historical fiction imposes greater restrictions on inspiration and requirements for collaboration. Francis Drake and his lost harbor mystery first arrived in my universe as a friendly discussion with two of my Oregon Tech colleagues shortly after the turn of the millennium. Fred Garland, Bob Rogers, and I challenged each other with our knowledge, and ignorance, of the Pacific coast and the possible location of Drake's anchorage. Together with our respective spouses, we explored the Marin Peninsula and the nearshore waters of Tomales Bay, visited Drake's Estero, and satisfied ourselves that we wouldn't stumble on something important that others had overlooked.

The website presence of Bob Ward in Newport, Oregon, resulted in a visit to his house. He graciously shared his research and belief that Whale Cove, south of Depoe Bay, was a site, if not *the* site, of the historical landing. We looked at maps, visited the cove, and walked into an area of the nearby woods that holds remnants of a protective stone wall. His enthusiasm and encouragement fed the fires of my curiosity, leading to other searches in the literature and at possible harbor sites. Bob also alerted me to the suspected presence of a historically significant barque buried at the mouth of the Salmon River, just north of Lincoln City. Although it was told in secret at the time, he subsequently revealed the location as he sought funds to recover the ship.

Gary Gitzen in Wheeler, Oregon, had written a number of books promoting Nehalem Bay and nearby Neahkahnie Mountain as landmarks associated with the 1579 landing. He described stones with markings, recovered from the area and now located in the Tillamook County Pioneer Museum, as part of the supporting evidence. Following my visit with Gary, I had the honor of writing the introduction to his 2008 book, although I repeated an error that Drake's "connies" were otters instead of muskrats. Bob Ward graciously notified me of the misidentification. A number of books and websites have presented other additions to the mystery, but I acknowledge the online blogs and postings of Oliver Seeler from Albion, California, and the 2019 book by Melissa Darby. Thanks to Stefan Freelan at Western Washington University for permission to use his beautiful relief map of the Salish Sea where so much of this story takes place. Although it and the illustrations in the appendices are rendered in gray tone for the softcover edition, the e-book and limited hardcover editions display them in their full glory. Dan Hawkes at the Klamath County Museum prepared several maps for the appendices. The route maps were initially suggested by Bill Johnson, a faithful friend and critical reader who has long encouraged my completion of this project.

My gratitude to Simon Kozhin, a talented Russian artist, for the use of his painting as the cover illustration. The original subject was the *Golden Hinde* and a smaller ship, possibly the *Marigold*, sailing through the Strait of Magellan, but he graciously permitted me to recaption it for use in the present book.

As always, I find support from family and friends. My wife, Alla Vichurina Powers, a research librarian and partner without peer, and Norman Brady, Jr., an amateur archaeologist and well-read critic, provided invaluable feedback and encouragement. William Cook, a fellow writer and unflinching critic, provided continuous help with the English language. Special thanks to John and Eva Lund and to Chris Castor, friends who read what I write and help me revise. Thank you one and all.

Once again I give my sincerest thanks to my publisher, Patricia Marshall at Luminare Press, and her great staff: Kim Harper-Kennedy, Claire Flint Last, Jamie Passaro, Nina Leis, and Melissa Thomas. You help make the dream take shape.

PREFACE

# A Voyage from Fact to Fiction

WHEN AND WHERE DID THE FIRST TERRITORIAL CLAIM OF England occur in North America? Before going to the Internet, divert your attention from the Atlantic coast to the Pacific. Before Roanoke (1585) and Jamestown (1607) were established in Virginia, an English mariner, Francis Drake, landed on the West Coast and claimed a large area for Queen Elizabeth. He called it Nova Albion after an ancient designation for his homeland.

The circumnavigational voyage Drake commanded from 1577 to 1580 has been documented, analyzed, and subjected to endless speculation for over four hundred years. It is an adventure story without equal—the account of a bold privateer in the service of the Queen (the English view) or a villainous pirate (the Spanish view) at a time when England was emerging from its insular isolation to challenge the might of Spain's western empire.

Despite the wealth of information detailing Drake's daring raids, one episode remains mysteriously absent from contemporary accounts of the voyage. Original sources, including depositions of crewmen aboard Drake's ship, indicate the *Golden Hinde* sailed from Mexico to the northwestern coast of America, possibly as far north as southeastern Alaska. Details of the northern Pacific voyage are sketchy in the original source material: *The Fabulous Voyage*, part of *Principall Navigations* (1589) and in *The World Encompassed* (1628). The latter is based, in part, on the official journal of Francis Fletcher, the ship's chaplain. Other contemporary accounts and maps constructed after the voyage are contradictory, suggesting Drake's expedition reached maximum latitudes of 48°N to 42°N and sought anchorage at 38.5°N. Modern analyses of these maps and the few surviving documents have led to varying interpretations of the reasons for sailing to the Pacific Northwest and the exact location of the land named New Albion.

One reason for the deceptions and omissions is obvious. England needed to open up a trade corridor with the Far East, Cathay (China) in particular. Hoping to find a navigable northwest passage connecting the Atlantic to the Pacific, it would allow the English to bypass the Spanish gauntlet of South America and the treacherous Strait of Magellan. The other route to China—around Africa and across the Indian Ocean—was lengthy and arduous and faced opposition from Portugal.

A major focus of speculation among sixteenth-century mapmakers and explorers involved the proposed Strait of Anián, which some thought connected the North Sea (North Atlantic), Arctic Ocean, and Sea of Mangi (North Pacific). The semi-mythical passage may have received its name in relation to Ania, a province of China mentioned by Marco Polo. In any case, numerous sixteenth-century mapmakers included the strait on their maps (see Appendix 1). Various explorers from England and other countries attempted to discover and claim the passageway. Despite their failures, belief in the Arctic route continued for at least two centuries. It is interesting to note that current climate changes in the Arctic have resulted in just such a passage.

If Drake's 1579 venture into the North Pacific reached the opening to what is now named the Strait of San Juan de Fuca, positioned between present-day Washington State and British Columbia, did they believe they had discovered the passageway known as Anián? If so, did Drake and his officers attempt to establish an outpost along the northwest coast and hold it until reinforcements could arrive and create a permanent fortress and settlement? If all this were true, would the English want the

Spanish to know that they had found a way to circumvent their southern defenses?

Is the following novel historical fiction? There are a number of historical fiction subgenres, including alternate histories and historical fantasy. They vary in degree of authenticity with regard to known events, places, and people. Some serve to entertain, with no pretense to a factual basis. Other novels use a strong foundation of research, but the narrative must still engage the reader and add flesh to the historical skeleton. It isn't always easy to delineate the boundary between fiction and fact, and this in itself can add to the intrigue and appeal of a story. What is history and what is reliable fact, especially when set in times before documentary media were readily available? We know a fair amount about what occurred during Drake's voyage—with the exception of the New Albion events. What has been published about the encounters between Drake's crew and various Native Americans is contradictory, speculative, or outright erroneous. Some of the "expert" analyses in modern times may have been deliberately altered or suppressed for local commercial purposes (see Darby's book for a review of the California controversies).

Historical nonfiction is always subject to some bias and distortion, reflected in the often-quoted adage that "winners write the history." Take any contemporary event and dissect the reports and essays that are offered from different points of view. On the contrary, it is comforting to realize that fiction is created primarily from the author's imagination. It may be shaped and molded by commonly accepted facts but need not be unduly constrained by them. The following story is not documented—it is a fictional account of what might have happened from the time Drake and his crew left Mexico and before they made their way across the Pacific and Indian Oceans and returned home to Plymouth, England, on 26 September 1580. *New Albion Sunset* relates the fate of twenty men who were left behind to initiate an outpost for England.

In this novel, there is something to offend everyone from California armchair historians who claim the mystery is officially solved to Oregonian and Canadian proposers of alternate views. I borrowed freely from all of them. Spoiler alert! If you are a student and defender of the traditional views on Drake's voyage, this story might not correlate well with your preconceptions. I have employed character names based on historic documents and credible monographs (see Nuttall 1914). Most of these are recorded in history as names only, with little description or detail of character or background. Some are known by surname only and a few by first name only. Others I simply invented.

In telling their story, I have mostly avoided using dialogue that corresponds to English of the late sixteenth century. Consider it to be a translation of a language that is mostly lost to us in modern times, surviving in the works of Shakespeare and other writers of the time but not necessarily reflecting the expressions and everyday speech of sailors and crewmembers of Drake's expedition. I also tried to be sparing with nautical terminology and did not identify the locations other than by latitude readings or with names Drake and his officers may have proposed at the time.

The five short essays in Appendix 1 are intended for readers who wish to explore some of the controversy about Drake's anchorage site. Two historical chronologies in Appendix 2 provide timelines to place events in context. Appendix 3 includes a list of contemporary geographical designations along with latitudes and references to the novel. Three maps show the routes, and the major places are identified by number so the reader can visualize where the events occurred. For historical purists, and those simply curious about the mystery, the conspiracy if you will, there is a list of resources in Appendix 4.

The lost colony of New Albion is a fascinating story without the fiction. I consulted these references and many more while creating the story, but "true" determination awaits further investigations, including the recovery of a Nicaraguan barque made of teak or ironwood buried under several feet of sediment at the mouth of a river on the Oregon coast. Read and come to your own conclusions. Bon voyage!

L. Wade Powers<br>
Klamath Falls, Oregon<br>
August 2020

# MAJOR CHARACTERS OF
## *NEW ALBION SUNSET*

| | |
|---|---|
| Francis Drake | Admiral of the fleet that left Plymouth, Captain of the *Pelican / Golden Hinde*, but often referred to as General Drake. |
| John Drake | Cousin of Francis Drake, 17 years old, cabin boy and illustrator. |
| Thomas Drake | Youngest brother of Francis, general seaman and council member. |
| Lawrence Elyot | Gentleman, amateur naturalist, and council member. |
| Francis Fletcher | Anglican chaplain, keeps official and secret journals of the voyage. |
| John Gallawaye | Lieutenant, second in command of the *Northern Venture*, member of the New Albion Company. |
| Chrystopher Hals | Gentleman, council member, and former captain of the *Northern Venture*. |
| William Hawkins | Gentleman, experienced mariner, nephew of John Hawkins, and council member. |
| Christopher Hayman | Commander of the *Northern Venture* and member of the New Albion Company. |
| Tomas Moone | Assistant to Drake, commanded the *Benedict*, enthusiastic Protestant. |
| Nazario de Morera | Basque pilot, boarded ship in England, secretly a papist. |
| Emmanuel Watkyns | Gentleman, selected leader of the New Albion Company. |
| George Cooke | Young musician, member of the New Albion Company. |
| William Crowley | Seaman, gifted as an impromptu interpreter. |

| | |
|---|---|
| DIEGO | Drake's black personal assistant and a freeman. |
| FRANCISCO | A black man freed by Drake from a ship off Peru. |
| NICHOLAS FRANCONI | Assembles pinnaces, member of the New Albion Company. |
| RICHARD GRAYE | Experienced soldier, member of the New Albion Company. |
| LITTLE NELE, THE FLEMING | Experienced steersman, member of the New Albion Company. |
| MARIA | A black woman freed by Drake from a ship off Central America, the only woman aboard the *Golden Hinde*. |
| MARK | A young black freed by Drake from Guatulco, Mexico. |
| PETER | A black man freed by Drake with Maria and Big Tom, a member of the New Albion Company. |
| TOMAS (BIG TOM) | A gigantic black man freed by Drake with Maria and Peter, a member of the New Albion Company. |

CHAPTER 1

# Farewell to New Spain

The *Golden Hinde* and a smaller barque enter the quiet harbor of Guatulco on the Pacific coast of New Spain on Monday, 13 April 1579. Only a small merchant vessel lies at anchor, its crew enjoying siesta. The small dock and adjoining village are quiet and the streets nearly deserted as preparations are underway to celebrate the Holy Week before Easter. A light breeze, barely enough to ruffle the banner hanging in the central plaza, brings little relief from the early-afternoon heat, hot and dry enough to be summer, but that will come later. The deathly quiet is not disturbed as the ships drop sails, coast to a stop, and set anchors. Men gather at the rail of the larger ship to maneuver a smaller launch, or pinnace, over the side.

Francis Drake, captain of the *Hinde*, orders the pinnace ashore with twenty-three men armed with harquebuses and swords. The English crewmen are eager to engage their enemies one last time, if only to provide an additional dose of humiliation, before they leave the Spanish empire of the Americas. The few buildings that comprise the harbor settlement offer little promise of valuables, but there is always a need for fresh vegetables and water.

The town's mayor, Gaspar de Vargas, mistakes the ships and the approaching rowers for his countrymen. He ambles toward the shore to extend his official welcome to increasingly infrequent visitors. The mayor, or *el alcaide*, realizes his mistake as the boat draws closer. They pull the pinnace onto the sandy strip and jump out, yelling curses and brandishing their weapons. After storming the beach and firing random shots in the air, they run up the main and only street as the surprised population, a few Spaniards and several Indians, scatters and takes refuge in their houses or outside the settlement.

Drake's orders are to search the village and confiscate any items of value. "Be sure to pay your respects to the local church, the largest building, for it will be the best source of precious metals and fine adorning linens." He remains aboard his flagship while the shore party thoroughly vandalizes the church and removes money, gold chains, chalices, and rich cloths that had served as altar coverings, canopies, and garments. One determined sailor, a burly hunchback, removes the heavy church bell from its tower. Closer inspection reveals it to be an alloy of bronze with not enough silver to justify melting it down or taking it to the ship. However, its desecration reminds the Spanish regional authorities that Her Majesty's subjects have paid one more call to the western coastline of the Americas.

Tom Moone, the *Hinde's* first assistant and one of Drake's most loyal crewmen, breaks down a heavy wooden front door and enters the luxurious house of Francisco Gomez Rengifo. He is the *encomendero*, the local holder of a royal title to land, and has become the richest man of the immediate region. Rengifo is also entitled to commandeer and use local native labor to help accumulate wealth for Spain and himself. Moone confronts the terrified man who is on his knees and ready to plead for his life. Rengifo doesn't speak much English and Tom knows only a few words of Spanish. No problem. The burly sailor grins while the much smaller man trembles, holding his hands in front of him, clutching a rosary. Tom relieves him of the money and gold chains with which he was trying to flee. As an afterthought, Tom picks up a large, wooden crucifix and smashes it against a table. Splinters fly across the room, and one shard lands in the kneeling man's hair.

Moone laughs at Rengifo. "You may well be upset, for you are no Christian. Only idolaters worship sticks and stones." He thinks about grabbing the rosary from Rengifo's hands, but joyful shouts from outside the house alert him that the marauders are departing for the pinnace. With a final snarl, he grabs Rengifo by the arms, hauls him to his feet, and marches him out the door and down the street to join the others with their ill-gained prizes.

It isn't the first time that Tom and a few more zealous Protestants have demonstrated an unnecessary inclination to destroy religious artifacts and insult their captives. When the few secret papist crewmen aboard the *Hinde* observe or overhear Tom and others bragging about these exploits, they cautiously suppress their resentment. It is, however, duly noted by several, including a Basque pilot named Nazario Morera. The returning crew brings with them seven captives: the local priest, the landowner Rengifo, a judge, a Spanish visiting official, and three Negroes who were on trial for attempting to burn the town. The captives sit on the deck and are watched by several of the soldiers among the crewmen. They are not bound or mistreated in any way, consistent with Drake's usual disposition of prisoners. Food and water are made available to the Spaniards as they ponder their fate.

The next day, Drake has an afternoon meal prepared and invites four of the Spanish captives to join him in his cabin. Because it is Holy Week, the priest and judge refuse, but Rengifo and the Spanish visitor relent and eat at the captain's table. The black captives are fed on the deck with the crew.

After dinner, Rengifo casually examines a copy of Fox's *Actes and Monuments* on display in the cabin. Also known as the *Book of Martyrs*, it has illustrations of Englishmen being burned at the stake as infidels by the Spanish. The priest starts to caution his friend about looking at the infamous drawings, but seeing Rengifo's interest, Drake turns pages in the large tome to reveal additional tortures. The general makes it clear he will not harm his current captives, but he takes pains to remind them that he has not exhausted his desire to revenge past wrongs suffered at their hands. During dinner, Drake indicates his intentions to his "guests." He will sail north to Acapulco and burn the town and any ships in the harbor. It is not clear from his threats whether he actually plans to attack or simply to create a diversion, but the captives later report his words to the Spanish authorities, including the viceroy of New Spain. Later the same afternoon, the general takes possession of provisions aboard the cargo ship in the harbor.

In the meantime, El Alcalde Gaspar de Vargas eludes capture and escapes during the raid, running to the larger and official village of Guatulco nine miles to the north. Not a trivial feat, for he is in his late fifties and boasts considerable girth. There he sends an urgent dispatch to Viceroy Martin Enriquez, warning him of Drake's presence. He also mentions the presence of a pilot aboard the invading vessel, one N. de Morera identified by some of his men. In response, the Spaniards at Acapulco prepare for further English raids by assembling a militia and crewing three vessels with more than two hundred men.

On Maundy Thursday, two mornings later, several crewmen go ashore for fresh water. After they return, Drake sets the captives free. One of the blacks, a thin and energetic eighteen-year old named Mark, asks to join Drake's group. Mark has observed four other blacks aboard the ship who are apparently free to move about like any other crewmember. The young man speaks some English along with the Spanish of his previous owners.

In a sudden move, Drake places his Portuguese navigator, Nuño da Silva, onboard the deserted cargo ship—surprising, because da Silva has been cooperating with Drake ever since his capture in the Atlantic, even adopting some of the Englishmen's religious practices. The navigator speaks excellent English, and it appears to all that he is Drake's willing ally and able assistant. Before releasing da Silva, Drake carefully tutors him about an alternate plan for returning home. Instead of the trans-Pacific crossing to the Moluccas he freely announced to earlier captives, Drake indicates they will first attempt to find the fabled Strait of Anián, the Northwest Passage, for their return to England. Da

Silva dutifully repeats this to the Spanish authorities later, but evidence of the pilot's complicity in Drake's raids weighs heavily against him and they refuse to believe the story. Drake's motives for instructing da Silva to inform the Spanish remain private. Although he and his gentlemen officers discussed the possibility of returning to England by a northern route, he does not consult them about revealing it to the Spanish.

Knowing much about the tactics of his enemy, Drake believes they will interpret the story as a false lead, an attempt to disguise his return trip by the way he arrived through the Strait of Magellan. It must have been an effective subterfuge, because the viceroy sends couriers south to warn ports and to man ships to intercept El Draque, the dreaded English pirate.

---

THE *GOLDEN HINDE* AND THE SMALLER BARQUE ARE READY TO sail on Good Friday, 17 April. After a brief morning service, General Drake announces that the barque previously captured off the Nicaraguan coast will forthwith bear the name *Northern Venture*. The crewmen and gentlemen applaud the naming, and a bottle of Madeira is sacrificed across the bow for the occasion. More than one sailor and soldier realize the significance of the designation. The rumors are true! They will seek a shorter route home. Furthermore, the successful discovery of the mysterious passage will enhance the reputations and fortunes of all.

Not everyone is overjoyed at the imminent departure. Francis Fletcher, the expedition's chaplain, reflects on the start of a dangerous voyage on a holy day. It is one thing to be at sea on Good Friday but something else to sail outward. His pleas to the general to reconsider are met with determined eyes and harsh words.

"Do you think the Spanish will wait until the priests give their blessings? When word reaches Acapulco, the seas will be filled with ships and cannons in hot pursuit. No, we go now with favorable winds and tides to put distance between us and the evils of this papist empire. Trouble me not with your superstitions, Priest. Say farewell to Nova Hispania!"

Fletcher walks away dissatisfied. He is in turmoil, his obedience to the tenets of faith set against his loyalty to his military commander. *Another strike against God. For what purpose is da Silva left for the Spanish to torture? My general appears to be a man of faith and charity, yet he displays acts incompatible with Christian practice. I admit I am fond of the tall, handsome Portuguese pilot. He learned English quickly as we crossed the Atlantic to Brazil, and he showed sincere curiosity about Protestant practices. I believe the man is ready to convert. His cooperation with the general and experience at sea is invaluable.* Admittedly, da Silva had never navigated the South Sea or the vast stretches of the Pacific and Indian Oceans, but to Fletcher, that seemed a poor rationale for casting him loose at Guatulco. Other freed Spanish captives would no doubt testify about da Silva's overt alliance with Drake, putting the man in jeopardy. *Why did the general go through so much trouble to convince the pilot they would attempt to find the fabled passageway? Why not keep it secret or, better yet, mislead the Spanish to think that Drake will sail south and attempt to return the way he came?*

Fletcher is no longer privy to the general's immediate objectives or ultimate plans. He can only speculate on perplexing questions that elude satisfactory answers. The good chaplain has become a naïve bystander, witness to the devious ploys of an experienced military leader, but he is unable to reconcile what he sees with what he believes.

---

WITH WATER AND PROVISIONS SUFFICIENT FOR ABOUT FIFTY days, the *Golden Hinde* and the *Northern Venture* sail westward from the Mexican coast, leaving New Spain to venture into the Pacific Ocean's calm waters. Their first need is to put distance between themselves and the anticipated pursuit from an Acapulco fleet. They will seek higher latitudes to use the westerly trade winds that will guide them to their second but most important objective. In the meantime, hundreds of leagues of open sea await. Drake and his crew have ample time to reflect on the successes and tragedies that have thus far accompanied their voyage from England to the Americas.

The erstwhile religious leader of the expedition, Fletcher meditates by candlelight in a corner of the aft deck. Only twenty-four years of age but ordained as a priest of the Anglican Church, he resigned his position as rector of a parish in London to assist Drake in preparations for the mysterious voyage. He is intelligent and observant and has traveled to Spain, Russia, the Mediterranean, and the Levant. In addition to providing spiritual guidance and leading religious observances, he maintains a journal of the expedition, an account that will be shared with financial sponsors and with Queen Elizabeth. This is in addition to the official rutter, or log of the ship, kept by Francis Drake, captain of the *Golden Hinde* and admiral of the five-ship fleet that departed England in 1577. The crewmen more commonly refer to him as General Drake or "the general." Fletcher wryly reflects that his leader has almost as many titles as the Queen herself.

The chaplain has secretly started a second journal, an unofficial account of the events to which he has been an unwilling witness. While writing, he keeps the official journal at hand to conceal the secret manuscript. The sea is gentle, and only a puff of wind is present to partly fill the sails or disturb the candle's flame. General Drake and most of the crew are asleep, and Fletcher sits alone with pen and paper.

*Friday, 8 May 1579*

*I care not for the new status of our general. He usurps my spiritual authority and now conducts religious services and prayers as if he was ordained to do so. It began with the ungodly execution of Thomas Doughty in Patagonia, a man doubtlessly guilty of carelessness and arrogance but a gentleman of deep and abiding faith and a colleague of our patron, Sir Christopher Hatton. Thomas and the general enjoyed mass and dinner the evening before the sorrowful day, seeming as friends in arms, yet despite my protests, the general pressed for the unfortunate man's beheading. Afterward, the atmosphere aboard our ship darkened, and my service has since been reduced to that of a mere acolyte. I fear for the soul of our general and the success of our voyage.*

The candle flickers slightly, and Fletcher lowers his pen. His thoughts turn to home and the people, his friends and parishioners, left behind. Despite the dangers and narrow escapes encountered, he has never doubted he would return unharmed and wiser for the experience. Much about his current charge—the crew of the *Hinde* and the year and a half he has sailed with them—has been pleasant and exciting, every bit the adventure he had hoped for and dreamt about. The financial success of the voyage is not in question for Drake or his crew. They raided town after town along the South American coast from Chile to Peru. They seized several ships and their valuable cargoes and thoroughly humiliated the Spanish in their heretofore uncontested Pacific monopoly. The capture of the *Nuestra Señora de la Concepción*, more familiarly known as the *Cacafuego* (shit fire), guaranteed financial remuneration for their sponsors in England. The Queen will be pleased and her treasury replenished. In addition, Drake gained no small measure of revenge for the loss of his comrades and ships at San Juan de Ulúa in 1568, an affair sullied by the treacherous breach of a negotiated truce with the Spanish.

However, the chaplain is deeply troubled by the moral conflict that now permeates the voyage. He and most of the crew were recruited under the pretense that Drake's flotilla of five ships was bound for the Mediterranean, ostensibly for purposes of trade at Alexandria and other ports. The soldiers and armaments were standard protection from the pirates operating on the high seas, especially off the coast of North Africa. When the general's intentions concerning the Spanish Empire and the New World became apparent, Fletcher realized that a major part of their mission was to harass and plunder. His secret journal continues.

> *As a devout protestant, I should feel no regret about relieving the Catholic Church of its ill-gained riches. Their cruel exploitation of native peoples in the name of Christ cannot be justified, yet are we more righteous in our cause? Killing and stealing are sins regardless of who or for what reason. Will I be able to reconcile what we fight against with what we are? In his favor, the general has shown mercy toward his captives. Rich or poor, he has spared those who have surrendered, and he has freed from the Spanish a number of Negro slaves. Yet I cannot and never will forget the day at Puerto San Julián when Mr. Doughty met his end at the general's insistence. May God have mercy on their souls.*

The trouble started in May 1578 during their anchorage in Port Desire on the Patagonian coast (Argentina). Thomas Doughty, one of several gentlemen aboard, had several times challenged Drake's authority and demanded that a deputy be named in case something should befall the admiral. There had been several incidents during the trip across the Atlantic in which the gentleman had shown poor judgment toward the crew. Most troubling were reports that Thomas, a former friend of Drake and the representative of one of their sponsors, Sir Christopher Hatton, had been spreading rumors and gossip about Drake himself. Unfortunately, Thomas was accompanied on the voyage by his brother, John, and several friends. He was liked and respected by some members of the crew.

At one point, Drake assigned Thomas to the smallest ship in his fleet, the *Christopher*, but placed him under Captain Gregory, a man who had no love for Doughty. After a violent argument between Drake and Doughty on 17 May, the general had Thomas tied to a mast on the *Pelican,* Drake's flagship before it was renamed, where he was humiliated for two days, being released only to eat and sleep. The talk got uglier, and Fletcher overheard that throats would be cut before the voyage was over. With signs of a mutiny brewing, Drake could no longer afford milder measures against the arrogant gentleman who considered himself the general's social better.

The Drake fleet arrived at Port San Julián on 20 June 1578, farther south on the Patagonian coast. It was the same harbor that hosted Magellan in 1520 when he executed one of his Spanish captains and several crewmen for mutiny. The site appeared to be cursed. A skirmish with the local natives on 22 June resulted in the deaths of two of Drake's crewmen, including the ship's surgeon.

On 30 June, Drake organized an inquiry into the behavior of Doughty. The combined crew of the fleet gathered around Drake. Thomas was flanked by armed guards, and everyone fell silent as the general addressed him. "Thomas Doughty, you have sought by diverse means and as hard as you can to discredit me to the great hindrance and overthrow of this voyage, besides other great matters I have to charge you with. If you can clear yourself of these charges, well and good. You and I shall again be very good friends. If not, you deserve to die. Say now by whom you will be tried."

The prisoner, for such he now was, smiled at the gathered audience and said clearly, "Why, good Admiral, I will be returned to my country and there be tried by Her Majesty's laws."

This bold rejoinder placed Drake in the precarious situation of continuing with Doughty's likely attempt to take over the expedition or to abandon the venture and return to England, a failure financially and militarily.

Drake fixed him with a steady eye. "Nay, Thomas Doughty. I will impanel a jury to inquire into the charges."

"Then I hope you will be sure your commission is sufficient." Again, Doughty smiled. His friend and lawyer, Leonard Vicary, had prepared him to answer the charges.

"You may be sure my commission is sufficient."

"I pray you then, let us see it. It is necessary for it to be shown."

Drake didn't have written proof of life-and-death authority over his crew, but he decided to bluff. "Well, you shall not see it. See how full of prating the desperate fellow is, my masters. Bind his arms. I do not feel safe with him unbound."

They bound him while Drake appointed a jury of forty men led by John Wynter, captain of the *Elizabeth*. One after another, witnesses testified of Doughty's threats, accusations, and bribes to influence the crew. In response, Thomas calmly indicated they were words spoken either in anger or in jest and not meant to be taken for action.

Ned Bright, one of the senior mariners, stepped forward with a new charge. Doughty had confided in him during the early planning for the voyage. Thomas had told Ned that Drake was of little consequence. Furthermore, he might need to promote his own leadership, displacing Drake. Doughty told Bright that he was in the confidence of Lord Treasurer Burghley, the chief advisor to Queen Elizabeth. Lord Burghley was firmly opposed to any intervention with Spain or Portugal, and it was understood that the Lord Treasurer would not be informed about the upcoming voyage through their territories. Nonplussed, Doughty affirmed that Burghley indeed knew about the real mission.

Drake jumped from his chair and shouted, "No, he has not!"

"He has," said the prisoner in a manner serene and composed.

"How?"

"He had it from me."

In Drake's mind, this public admission amounted to treason. The backers at court, who did not include Burghley, were instructed to maintain the highest secrecy to prevent Spanish spies from learning about the true purpose of the voyage.

"So, my masters, what this fellow has done! God will have all of this treachery known, for Her Majesty gave me special commandment that of all men, my Lord Treasurer should not know it. See how his own mouth has betrayed him."

As presiding judge and prosecutor, Drake expertly maneuvered the jury of laymen with no legal training or stomach for the politics of far-off London. He stated his position as if he was an experienced barrister, appealing to the crew's loyalty and their need for a leader to see them safely home. He compared a homecoming of failure to one in which they would achieve success, every sailor and soldier returning with enough riches to become a gentleman. A few gentlemen seated in the front row smiled but away from Drake's notice. Drake summed up by saying, "I do not see how this voyage can continue if this fellow is allowed to live. Well, my masters, what do you think? If you say that Thomas Doughty is worthy to die, hold up your hands."

All forty men, some reluctantly, held their hands up. Although Thomas was found guilty of mutiny, he was cleared of treason. The general announced that the prisoner would be executed by beheading, a gentleman's death, two days hence. Doughty didn't flinch when he received the verdict. Instead, he suggested it could be commuted and he might be put ashore with a gun and rations. Drake replied that he couldn't risk the possibility of Doughty revealing his plans to the Spanish.

Wynter suggested that he could keep the prisoner in irons aboard the *Elizabeth* until they reached England, where he could stand trial. Wynter was sympathetic to some of Doughty's views, and although he had also voted for a guilty verdict, Drake believed he couldn't trust the two of them together. He refused to consider it further and declared the trial over.

On the morning of 2 July, Drake and Doughty met on the foredeck of the *Pelican* and took communion together. Fletcher heard Doughty's confession, but the man declared himself before man and God to be innocent. He knelt beside his general, and together they took the sacrament. They had been friends in England before the voyage, and it was an emotional moment for both men. For Fletcher, it was nearly unbearable.

The men shared a midday dinner in the captain's cabin. Doughty toasted to the success of the continuing voyage, and Drake toasted to the darker journey Thomas would soon undertake.

After their meal, they were rowed to a small island in the bay where the fleet's members stood in a square around a large block of wood. Before continuing, Doughty asked Drake if he could have a few words in private, so the two walked along the shore. A few minutes later, they embraced and returned to the block. Fletcher would always remember how the condemned man knelt to the block and calmly told the executioner to strike clean and use his sword with care.

After Doughty passed into eternity, there was a long silence. Drake needed to quell any regrets or sympathy for the mutineer. "Lo, this is the end of traitors." He shouted it out to the assembly, but many lowered their heads, not sure that justice had been fully served. They would later refer to the small islet as "The Island of Blood." Thomas was buried on the island, detached head and body facing northeast toward England. Fletcher invoked a final blessing for his soul before the crew returned to the mainland.

The next few days were dark, morale at its lowest. The weather was terrible, and many members of the crew favored turning back. They would soon be facing transit through the notorious Strait of Magellan, and solidarity was paramount. On 11 August, Drake gave an impassioned plea to the assembled crews, asking for loyalty and effort. For the first time, he made it clear that he was the only authority and that order and discipline would rule for the remainder of the voyage. Before departing for the strait, Drake ordered a new designation for the *Pelican*. It would henceforth be known as the *Golden Hinde*, a reference to Sir Christopher Hatton's coat of arms. The relationship between Thomas Doughty and Hatton was well known, as was the friendly relationship between Hatton and the Queen. Would the tribute be enough to protect Drake from charges of murder later in London?

---

PUTTING PEN AND PAPER ASIDE, FLETCHER RECALLS THE LAST few months of their odyssey. He is unsure about the changing morality of their mission. Are they on the Queen's business or have they indeed become pirates, looters on the high seas?

Despite the unknown fates of their missing sister ships the *Marigold* and the *Elizabeth* in the Strait of Magellan and the loss of a few crewmen during skirmishes ashore, the *Golden Hinde* had pushed ever northward up the coast of South America. The captured Spanish money, gold, silver, jewels, and other valuable items filled the 140-ton ship to a capacity that threatened their continuing voyage and return to England. An opportunity to seize a forty-ton barque off the coast of Nicaragua provided Drake with an additional ship for the precious cargo, more provisions, and room for several Negro slaves who had been freed by the Englishmen. The smaller ship was also capable of exploring shallower bays and rivers and avoiding the risk of the flagship running aground. Although Drake expressed his regrets to the barque's captain, Rodrigo Tello, he felt he had no choice but to commandeer the boat for his immediate needs. In exchange, he gave Tello an assembled pinnace and put Tello and his men to sea, retaining one experienced pilot and his charts from the barque. The pilot, Alonzo Sanchez Colchero, was a veteran Pacific navigator from the Acapulco-Manilla route and a valuable asset to plan the next stage of the voyage. After making needed repairs on the *Golden Hinde* at the small island of Caño and fortifying the barque for the open sea, the expedition continued northward. Drake still hoped to be joined by one or both of the ships he had left in the strait.

One more score at sea awaited Drake's crew as they entered Guatemalan waters. A merchant barque carrying fine porcelain and linen en route from Manila to Panama, owned by a Spanish nobleman, Don Francisco de Zarate, was encountered and captured on 3 April 1579. After a few days, Drake released Zarate and his crew along with the previously captured pilot Colchero but retained two of Zarate's pilots with their charts. Colchero had proved recalcitrant, and Drake was happy to be rid of him. In addition, Drake freed and welcomed on his ship two Negro men, Tomas and Peter, and a Negress named Maria. Tomas, later to be known as Big Tom, was enormous. He measured seven feet and five inches in height. Fortunately for everyone, he was cheerful and worked hard. He could speak some Spanish but mostly talked in a Caribbean patois that only a couple of the other blacks could easily comprehend. Fletcher noted the difference in the former slave's status in his journal. *A Negro slave is now a black free man.*

Fletcher feels uneasy about the presence of a woman aboard the ship, and most of the crew is in agreement. Near the bow, well out of earshot of the priest, two crewmen discuss the young black woman, and a third man overhears them in the darkness.

"Bad luck, for sure," comments Tom Moone. "Nothing good can come from this." Tom is never reluctant to pass on his beliefs about the mysterious rules of the mariner's universe.

Andy McGuane laughs. "Aye, Tom, but she is a comely one and a comfort to the eye. Better than watching your hairy butt." Andy is freckled and red haired—a gunner aboard ship and a soldier with a caliver, a light matchlock musket, when ashore.

"What would a bloody Scot know about comely?" says Tom, lying back against the starboard rail. "You must be thinkin' about your highland goats, lad. No fit women in that desolate place."

"Ah, some of them goats be better companions than many of your weak, milky English lassies from what I've sampled." Andy pauses as if in thought. "A wee bit of thigh might work for some of the gentlemen aboard, that being their privilege, but not for the likes of thee and me, you can be sure."

"Nay, Andrew, the general would soon lose all control of his ship should the common crew be fightin' over one maid, if maid she be."

Georgie Kershaw listens as he sits beside the foremast. He is only nineteen, and it is his first time at sea. Strong of arm but not overly endowed in mind, he works as a general laborer and assists the chaplain in church services, although his role has declined as General Drake assumes much of the religious protocol. He serves as Fletcher's eyes and ears, quietly reporting on the moods and mutterings of the crew. This helps the chaplain identify troubles and concerns before they became a greater problem in the confined quarters.

Tom looks at him, and Georgie lowers his eyes. Most of the crew is aware of Georgie's confidences with the priest, but they don't regard Fletcher as a threat. Many of them regard the young priest in a favorable light, although more than one seasoned mariner considers him naïve and gullible. During the past few months, the strained relationship between Drake and the chaplain has been increasingly apparent. Some support the general's need for discipline, but others are uncertain. All of them admire Drake's tenacity and bravado, but they are less enthusiastic about his arrogance. "Authority goes with the captain," say some. "Would you expect less?"

Fletcher muses on the relationships among the crew. The dozen gentlemen aboard are mostly privileged, belonging to families of power and money. They volunteered to make a name, if not a fortune, from the voyage. Most of them admire Drake's leadership as a capable sailor and excellent navigator, but several resent the fact that he is no gentleman of birth. Francis Drake is the son of a poor country parson who rose to his standing with the Queen because of daring deeds and apprenticeship under well-known seamen such as John Hawkins. He has also benefited greatly from the patronage of others who have access to the Queen's court.

The murmurs are discreet and shared among only a few, but the Doughty affair disrupted the good spirits and loyalty expressed at the onset of their journey. After the execution, Drake's impassioned plea for unity included the charge to forego class distinctions between gentlemen and sailors, exhorting those with soft hands to pitch in with the common chores to work besides the laborers for the good of all. Drake's youngest brother, Thomas, was included at the officer's table but worked as a sailor among the general crew, setting a good example for others. Nevertheless, solidarity was advice that was halfheartedly acknowledged and only when necessity prevailed.

CHAPTER 2

# Northward Bound

The first leg of the journey due west into the open ocean passes without incident. The boredom of routine ship chores and sailing across a monotonous blue expanse replaces the excitement of exploration, land raids, ship battles, and the capture of treasure in quantities heretofore unimagined. For most of the crew, when not busy mending lines, scrubbing decks, preparing food, and keeping watch, the days are filled with waiting and gossiping. There are many things to discuss while huddled together out of earshot of the officers and gentlemen.

Some express their dissatisfaction with the officers, not uncommon on any ship, but there are exceptions to their resentment. The general's seventeen-year-old cousin, John Drake, serves as a cabin boy and companion, but he is also a talented artist and produces drawings of the coastlines, harbors, and important recognition features of their travels. He draws plants, animals, and portraits of indigenous natives they encounter. Most of the crew feel well disposed toward the enthusiastic blond lad who is short of stature like his cousin Francis.

Lawrence Elyot, the ship's amateur naturalist and one of the dozen gentlemen aboard the *Hinde*, especially admires John's illustrations. Lawrence encourages the boy to publish a folio of the birds, mammals, and plants they have encountered, and he promises to provide an accompanying text when they return to England. However, more than one sailor regards the slim, blond man who collects birds and butterflies to be worthless at sea, another mouth to feed without contributing honest labor or military expertise, but then that opinion applies to many of the elite officers, some of whom serve as nominal captains of various ships in the fleet. They eat at the captain's table and sleep on trundle beds in the large dining cabin under the aft deck, but the actual responsibilities for the ships remain with the masters, boatswains, and pilots of the various ships.

The crew holds in high regards only two of the other gentlemen aboard the *Hinde*. John Martyn of Plymouth has been a courageous member of exploratory shore parties and was wounded at Mocha by Indian arrows the previous November; he still carries the scar. The second is Thomas Drake, the youngest brother of the general. He has a sense of humor and often refers to his brother by the Spanish nickname. "Don't let the Dragon hear that, for he shall be sorely displeased," he tells a disgruntled crewmember. Both smile to reassure each other their breaches of conduct will not be reported. Because Thomas works alongside them as a sailor, it is easy to overlook his privileged position with the gentlemen. The crew also respected Thomas Flood, one of the two ship's surgeons, but he was captured and slaughtered by the Indians on Mocha during the confrontation that wounded Martyn. The chief ship's surgeon, Robert Winterhey, died in Patagonia at the hands of natives.

Although not classified as a gentleman, the steward of the *Golden Hinde*, William Legee, is well known as a jolly fellow who always has an encouraging word for the officers and common crew alike. Short and a bit robust, he often intervenes when a sailor's frustration grows beyond what the captain and company might tolerate. Although he would later lose an argument over a piece of gold treasure and fall out of favor with the general, he consistently serves the crew of the *Hinde* well.

---

Two hours past sunrise on 15 May, after sailing some 500 leagues (about 1,400 land miles) westward, the ships catch a fair wind and turn their course north by northeast. The mood of the crews brightens considerably, and the vessels close within hailing distance so news can be shared between the twenty-two men manning the *Venture* and the sixty-eight individuals aboard the *Hinde*, including eight boys under the age of sixteen, five black men, and the black woman, Maria. The ships make rapid progress, aided by the northwesterly trades and good weather. A few late-spring storms provide additional fresh water, and occasional successes with trailing lines add fresh fish to the pantry.

On 3 June 1579, Fletcher writes in his official journal they have sailed some 1,400 leagues since leaving Mexico, and their position is now about 42°N. The temperature drops rapidly, and the winds from the northwest increase during the night. The next morning, Thursday 4 June, an icy deck and lines greet the crew as they awake. Those sleeping topside were aware of the sudden change in weather—the bitter cold penetrates every bone, making each step and hand movement a torment. The winds steadily increase during the day, filling the sails but causing much misery among those exposed. Intermittent frozen rain makes surfaces difficult to traverse and footing hazardous. Fletcher comments that it now takes six men to accomplish what had previously taken three. Morale suffers. A few men openly suggest they should turn back toward warmer climes before the frozen sea swallows them. Others have their doubts but defer, as if they have a choice, to the determination of their general. Despite the weather, most of the crew responds favorably to Drake's words of divine providence, quoting scripture and urging the men to give everything for the glory of the Queen and the enterprise. He also informs them that if they find the northern passageway to the North Sea, it will greatly shorten their journey home. Fletcher does his part, circulating among the crew on the *Hinde* and calling out encouragement to those on the *Venture* when the winds permit, urging them to stay the course.

Stay it they do though the cold becomes extreme and the crew's despair increases until they reach an estimated latitude of 49°N on 17 June. Overcast skies make latitude readings unreliable or impossible. By this time, some food provisions are running low, and water, although partly replenished by rainfall, is also rationed. Fletcher prays constantly, alternating between pleas for a break in the bitter weather and the discovery of land—any land. For the first time in his life, the young priest begins to question not only God's mercy but His existence.

---

"Land ho!" comes the cry from the lookout aloft, and several of the crew rush to the bow and starboard to verify the call. It is difficult to make out the dim shape of the mountains ahead—fog lies about them like a thick winter blanket, and the peaks barely project from the shore layer, but it is their first sight of land since leaving Guatulco in mid-April.

"There she is, just like the general predicted," offers Tom Moone, hanging over the rail, not sick but grinning at their good fortune.

"Aye, let us pray that this land will provide a suitable welcome for the likes of us," answers his sidekick Andy. All are hopeful but no one assumes an uncontested landfall.

The ships turn eastward to approach a coastline of low, forested plains and hills dusted with snow. From time to time, the crew can discern larger, snow-covered peaks in the distance. The vessels align and near the coast side by side, the *Venture* on the port side of the *Hinde*. The wind howls like a banshee as the ships search for a cove or harbor. Voice communication is impossible, and Drake decides not to send a boat in the rough seas to the *Venture*. He hoists a small flag on the bow that indicates to the barque to follow the *Hinde*. The ships turn to the southeast and run along the shore. The wave action and projecting rocks discourage any thoughts of closer contact.

After passing several narrow inlets surrounded by high cliffs, they come upon a broad, shallow sound. The *Hinde* heaves to as the *Venture* passes her and prepares to enter. For the first time, the smaller ship exercises the advantage of its shallower draft to find suitable anchorage. A yellow flag is hoisted aboard the barque as she proceeds along the port-side cliffs, taking soundings as she goes. The larger vessel waits for the flag to descend, indicating that they can proceed. As the crew watches anxiously from the *Hinde*, the *Venture* lowers her flag, furls sails, and drops anchor. A few minutes later, the *Golden Hinde* lies in place beside her. The sheer cliffs provide shelter from the unrelenting northwest wind. There is no beach or shore access near their anchorage, but there appears to be a shallow slope and beach farther along the shore. Although many of the men strongly desire to set foot on land, they decide to wait out the bad weather.

That night, the officers gather in Drake's cabin to discuss their next move. The *Hinde* is leaking again and needs to be careened and caulked. The barque might also need attention, but that is less certain.

The general sits in his usual position at the head of a long table. A modest repast lies before him and the assembled gentlemen. Red wine fills their glasses, as is their custom in the late evening. Drake's cousin, John, is to his left, and his brother, Thomas, sits on his right. Absent from the original company of gentlemen leaving Plymouth are John Doughty and his late brother's friend, the lawyer Leonard Vicary. Both men are free to roam the ship, but they sometimes eat apart from Drake and the gentlemen, mostly at their own insistence.

Gregory Cary—a kinsman of Lord Hundson, the Queen's cousin—speaks first. He is never shy about offering his opinion whether graced by knowledge or not. "This climate is displeasing, Captain. I believe it will do little to improve the morale of our crew."

Drake acknowledges him with a glance but says nothing.

William Hawkins speaks next. He is the nephew of John Hawkins, a mariner Drake apprenticed with in the Caribbean during the 1560s. Drake is also a second cousin of John Hawkins. William readily volunteered for Drake's expedition and is known to have the general's confidence in all matters relating to the voyage. "I would remind everyone of how close we approach our ultimate objective: discovery and possession of a northern passage. Not only will it ensure a rapid return to Her Majesty and England, but it will be a just claim to enduring fame in the annals of history yet to be written."

"Well spoken, as always." Francis Drake surveys the table, his eyes resting on each man for a moment and letting the implications of William's words fully register. "In the morn, if the winds and this accursed fog should abate, we can search for a suitable cove to reprovision. If our chaplain could favor us with a prayer to the Almighty for the same, we might be graced with the ability to make repairs to our hull and inspect that of the *Venture*." A prolonged gaze at Fletcher indicates he is to do as bidden.

Fletcher is mildly surprised at the general's request. *Is this a reprieve from two months of disgrace and disregard?* The chaplain bows his head, and the company does likewise. "We beseech you, our Lord and Savior, to whom we offer our thanks for deliverance on this foreign shore, to provide further guidance as we complete this mission in your name and under your protection. Bless this crew, one and all, and bring to us your wisdom for the decisions we undertake." He raises his head briefly and lowers it to continue. "Provide good vision and fortune to our captain, general, and leader, Francis Drake." Fletcher looks up to see the slight smile disappear from the general's face. *Cannot harm to rebuild and maintain whatever good relations remain possible.* He sits up and lowers his hands as several men say amen and lift a glass.

Thomas Hord continues the discussion. He is a practical man and often assumes the role as one of the group's clear thinkers and leaders. "We have time before the summer winds turn in the lower latitudes. If we cannot find a navigable passage within the next month or so, we can sail west with most of our treasure and crew. This will…"

"Most of our treasure? Most of our crew? Thomas, why wouldn't we take all of our men and one woman back to England?" The question from John Chester, son of the ex-lord mayor of London, produces smiles and muffled snickers. Drake's lack of amusement quells the distraction.

Hawkins answers. "Discovery of a passage is not adequate in itself, or have some of you forgotten? We previously discussed establishing an outpost, a modest colony if you will, to hold the territory we claim for the Queen. Sovereignty over this land is greatly enhanced by occupation. We will need several men to remain here or there, wherever it may be, to build a fortress and negotiate with the natives for trade and other," he looks around the table, lingering on the chaplain, "favors and services."

"That hasn't gone as well as we might have wished, has it?" asks John Martyn, one hand resting over the scar on his neck, the one he will carry as a memento from Mocha for the rest of his life. "Until we meet them, we won't know if they'll prove hostile or friendly. Our recent history does not favor the latter."

General Drake clasps his hands in front of his chin, peering at a spot over and behind the men opposite him. He takes his time before speaking, building the tension and commanding the moment. "So noted. As Mr. Hawkins has clearly indicated, once we determine we are near or in the passage, we will need to establish an outpost. I have given the matter serious contemplation, especially during the quiet days following our departure from New Spain. I propose a name for this land and its possession for England. We are sufficiently distant from the Spanish incursions to the south. Although they pompously claim all shores and adjacent lands touched by the Pacific Ocean, they will not reach this far north before we reach England and register our stronger claim. Any outpost should be safe from their predations until our return, even if we must complete the lengthy circumnavigation westward. I propose we name this land, to be later delineated, Elizabeth Land in honor of Her Majesty and our countrymen." He unfolds his hands and looks around the cabin.

Smiles and nods of approval respond to his announcement. Gregory Cary raises his glass. "Hear, hear to Elizabeth Land, the

Queen's claim to the New World, and the Spanish be damned." All hoist their glasses, including Chaplain Fletcher, who possesses no love for the papist Spaniards.

---

THE NEXT MORNING, THE WINDS SUBSIDE, BUT THE RAIN FALLS in heavy sheets, and visibility has not improved significantly. The nearby beach proves untenable. Led by the *Venture*, the ships pull anchor and move cautiously along the coast, continuing in a southeasterly direction. It isn't possible to get an accurate sighting for latitude, but they estimate from the time elapsed that they are approaching but have not reached 48°N.

The sudden appearance of a large, eastward-trending opening into the rugged landscape produces an enthusiastic response from everyone. The night shift rouses from sleep to greet the dramatic passageway penetrating into the interior but obscured by the low-hanging fog. As the bow points eastward, men without immediate duties line the starboard railing to look with with pleasure at the shoreline delineating the south side of the entrance. "Aye, this be a portal for sure," remarks one of the seaman, staring at the broad waterway. Several agree as the ships prepare to explore the entrance.

They slowly approach the dramatic southern cape, the *Northern Venture* leading the way, making frequent soundings. The *Hinde* trails by several ship lengths. The depths are more than adequate for the draft of the bigger ship. A bottle collects seawater as they progress, and one of the sailors tastes it for saltiness. Fresh water is present, and an outflowing current opposes the ships and the prevailing northwesterly winds. These are not good signs for an expected oceanic passageway, but the width and depth of the channel encourage them to penetrate farther eastward. As the morning fades into afternoon, the fog lifts somewhat, but the continuing cold and the dark shore add an ominous presence that has many muttering and praying. Despite prevalent superstitions and sailors' inclinations toward pessimism, there remains hope they have at last reached a decisive destination.

Francis and John Drake share a different perspective on the stern deck. While the general becomes increasingly convinced they have found the fabled passage and that it is clearly navigable, the young artist is busy making sketches that accurately depict the shapes and positions of shoreline features for future reference.

The chaplain quietly steps up and positions himself at Drake's left hand. "Is this it, the promised passageway?" he says, still not daring to hope it is so.

Drake turns and bestows a warm smile on him for the first time in two months. "So it may be, Mr. Fletcher. Maintain your prayers for deliverance and a speedy voyage home."

"Yes, the thought has never been far. The men will surely welcome this as a sign of God's mercy and blessing."

"Many of them appear uneasy at the appearance of such a rugged coast. Although it resembles much of what we saw in the Strait of Magellan, I sense that the weather will be much more favorable. Go among them and reassure all that this is what we have sought. It means a return to our shores in weeks rather than months. It also signifies we have accomplished far more than we could have dreamed. If the passage proves true, we shall plan for a feast of celebration and thanksgiving within the week. Our Sunday services will be robust with our gratitude."

Fletcher nods but says nothing more, knowing the general will likely perform the pronouncements and rituals—once again relegating his chaplain's role to that of an accessory. He steps back and turns to circulate among the crew and offer encouragement as instructed.

They pass slowly up the waterway that is almost a straight path east by southeast. The shores show traces of snow here and there, and the thick forest is overshadowed by tall, whitened peaks. One mountain to the south in particular seems to dominate the landscape as if it is a throne from which pagan northern gods might be watching their progress. From time to time, they glimpse the rolling back and tail fluke of a large, dark whale and schools of smaller gray whales. On one occasion, two porpoises ride the bow wave of the *Hinde*, much to the delight of John Drake and several of the younger boys. "Good luck there be for us," shouts one of the sailors. Large numbers of seals occupy rocks and islets along the shore, including some very large and noisy ones that are strange to the crewmen.

---

THEIR FIRST SIGHT OF LOCAL INHABITANTS COMES ON THE morning of 21 June. The ships round a prominence on their starboard, revealing a broad inlet with a gentle sloping shoreline and beach. Across the water, several large, ornate canoes move rapidly toward them, each holding about twenty men with oars dipping in synchrony.

"Mother of God, what now?" mutters William Crowley, the first of the deck crewmen to spot the oncoming natives. He gives a shrill whistle, and several others gather at the rail to gawk while the general alarm sounds and several soldiers rush onto the deck with harquebuses. The muskets are readily available, but the powder and shot has to be distributed from a locked container by the boatswain, Thomas Blacolar. They don't have time to don mail or armor, but they crouch behind the railing, guns ready for the approaching canoes.

The general exits from his cabin accompanied by William Hawkins and Diego, his black assistant. Diego is an imposing sight—six feet four inches tall and dark chocolate in complexion, a Panamanian Cimarrone who had helped Drake during a tense confrontation with the Spanish at Nombre de Dios in 1572. When freed by Drake, he returned to England and has been a part of Drake's personal retinue since. Now he serves as Drake's paid personal aide and often accompanies him when danger threatens. The three stand back from the aft deck railing, observing the canoes that gather off the starboard side.

The natives ship their oars and stand, most holding long spears. A few in each boat possess bows, and each warrior, for that is what they are, has an arrow notched and poised for use. Each man wears a breechcloth and has a cape-like fur about his shoulders, leaving his chest exposed. The temperature is cooler than most men would find comfortable, but the natives appear to be at ease with minimal clothing. A tall man more elaborately dressed in long furs and a conical hat made from thin, wooden slats stands at the bow of the closest canoe. He calls out to the men aboard the *Golden Hinde*, chanting in a lyrical tone to bless them or curse them—the recipients are not sure which. The armed *Hinde* crewmen, now possessing powder and pellets, remain hidden behind the railing. The *Northern Venture* stands farther offshore about two hundred yards up the strait from the *Hinde*. Neither ship is anchored, but drifting is minimal near the inlet.

After a few minutes of animated calling, the leader, if that is what he is, folds his arms and sits down. The warriors do likewise as they relax their grip on spears and bows. They wait without speaking, keeping their eyes on the ship. Several direct their gaze at Diego, whose physique and color differ from the pale men around him and must be startling to behold.

Drake signals to the man who spotted the natives first. "Mr. Crowley, attend me here, if you please."

William leaves his place at the rail and climbs the few steps to stand in front of his captain. "Aye, sir, what service might I render?" He already knows what the captain wants. His ability to communicate with native tribes has served them well in the past. He can't speak at any length or in depth but by means of signs, and as a quick learner of crucial phrases and words, he is the best interpreter they have.

"Determine their intentions to the best of your knowledge. If friendly, arrange a meeting for the purposes of gifts and trading. Assure them we mean no harm." Drake turns to Hawkins for his input.

Hawkins nods at Crowley. "This is too far north for them to have had misadventures with the Spanish. Unlike some of our previous encounters, we shouldn't expect them to be hostile, but take nothing for granted. I estimate there are several hundred armed men near enough to board. We will keep our harquebusiers ready in case."

"Aye. I'll go back to the rail and make signs of peace." He glances at Diego as he turns to descend to the main deck. *Maybe he will impress them enough to hold off any untoward moves against us. Pray God it be so.*

The men above deck are cautioned to move slowly and remain silent as Crowley negotiates a peace with the natives. Their lead canoe nears the *Hinde* to within a few arm lengths, and the spokesman, as he is later identified, stands again. Crowley leans over the rail, his arms hanging over the side to indicate he is unarmed, about fifteen feet above the native's head. They signal and speak for more than an hour. Hawkins goes below deck, but Drake and Diego remain at the stern to watch Crowley and the warriors in the canoes. It seems surreal to Drake and his crew: hundreds of men silently waiting while the two talk quietly, most of it by gestures.

Finally, the chief sits down, and the canoes turn and paddle for the sandy shore of the inlet. Crowley pulls back from the rail, noticeably exhausted, and makes his way back to the captain.

"Perhaps a bit of real ale, not the sickly sea beer, would suit you at this time, Mr. Crowley." Drake reaches out his right hand to steady his ambassador. Diego turns and descends to the galley to fetch a mug of the undiluted amber.

"They call themselves the Kwee-dich-chu-atx or something to that effect," says Crowley. "I may have convinced them we mean no harm, but the truth may be in the later telling. They return to their village, which lies in the forest beyond the beach. They wish us to attend a feast in our honor, and they would be pleased to meet you, our chief."

Drake smiles as Diego returns with a mug of ale and hands it to Crowley. "When would this feast occur?" asks Drake.

Crowley takes a hearty swig. "At the height of the sun tomorrow, if it please Your Excellency. They will have an honor guide to accompany us from the beach to the village."

Drake scratches his chin thoughtfully. "How many in the honor guard?"

"I am sorry, sir. That was not revealed."

"How many of them do you think will be at the village?"

"From the size of the group that greeted us in the canoes, I would guess there may be several hundreds, but I don't know if women and children will be present or if all the warriors will be invited."

"We will have our own honor guard equipped with swords and muskets and... with Diego." He smiles up at the black man who is stoic and seemingly unconcerned about another foray into the wilds of the New World. Neither of them has forgotten the nineteen wounds Diego suffered from the native attack at Mocha, but fortunately, most were superficial.

Crowley finishes the ale, mumbles thanks, and walks back to the harquebusiers who are dispersing. Four of them remain at watch for any signs of deceit or return. The *Venture* moves toward the *Hinde*, and both drop anchors side by side about one hundred yards from the beach. Hawkins believes that distance will give them adequate warning of an approach by canoe. Chrystopher Hals, appointed temporary captain of the *Venture*, crosses to the *Hinde* with two of his officers for supper with Drake and the gentlemen, followed by a strategic session on how to proceed on the morrow. Fletcher later notes in his private journal that it was a heated debate.

Lieutenant John Gallawaye sits at the left side of Hals. He and Lieutenant Christopher Hayman serve as officers on the *Venture* and join Drake's table to participate in planning for eventualities that might arise from the meeting with the inlet tribe. Gallawaye had talked with William Crowley after the ship-canoe discussion, and he is especially interested in attending and observing the local inhabitants. Previous meetings with natives during the voyage were brief and sometimes violent. This is the first time the expedition will attempt to negotiate a long-term relationship with indigenous peoples, an advantage if they hope to occupy an outpost and later establish a settlement in the region. Any help they can secure in repelling Spanish incursions will be an added bonus.

The lieutenant is thirty-one, has flaming red hair, stands six feet tall, is well read, and unmarried. He understands and speaks Spanish well enough to interpret and has travelled to France, Portugal, and Italy. Previous ocean trips taught him navigation, and he has an interest in natural history. Although assigned to different vessels, Gallawaye and Lawrence Elyot quickly became friends. In addition, Francis Fletcher instructs him in simple church protocols so John can provide limited religious services to the crew of the *Venture* when they are at sea.

The mood of the after-dinner discussion is hopeful but cautious. Several gentlemen maintain fears of what might occur once Drake and the others reach the village. The treachery at Mocha is mentioned several times, but Fletcher supports Drake in the attempt to parlay. Thomas Hord and William Hawkins suggest measures to respond if the situation turns hostile. It is a calculated risk but one that needs to be made. The last word, as always, rests with the general. Drake asks for a show of hands to proceed, but no one doubts that his mind is already set. The vote is unanimous to accept the tribe's invitation.

CHAPTER 3

# Northern Contact

The morning dawns warm and bright, the sunlight reflecting from the glassy surface of the inlet. Even the strait shows barely a ripple, and banners hang limp from masts and yardarms. Both ships are beehives of activity as men prepare for the departure of the shore party. Two pinnaces are ready to transport the general and his honor guard to the village ceremony. Only a few gentlemen accompany him—the others remain aboard the ships with instructions to sail if the event turns tragic. Twenty well-armed soldiers, guns primed and ready, form the military segment. No one has delusions about how effective their protection will be if hundreds of warriors attack. Diego will walk at Drake's side. One of the officers suggests the landing party include Big Tom, the giant freed slave. He has a gentle disposition and is a hard worker, and he is well liked by the crew but understands only a few words of English. Although speaking won't be necessary in the shore party, Drake declines the suggestion, not knowing what reaction the black goliath might induce in the natives or vice versa. The chaplain attends to elicit divine support, and Crowley serves as interpreter, although everyone understands that translation will be slow and imperfect. John Gallawaye is granted permission to watch and learn, in effect becoming an apprentice interpreter.

As a precaution, the pinnaces will return to the ships and ferry an additional company of thirty armed crewmen to the beach. If it should be required, they have instructions to burn and hack holes in the native canoes to deter pursuit or attempts to board the ships. The sound of gunfire from the village will constitute the critical signal for action by the beach contingent.

Thomas Drake asks to accommodate the village party, but Francis refuses, telling him to look after his cousin, John. Francis has already lost two brothers during earlier expeditions in the Caribbean. William Hawkins is left behind to captain the *Golden Hinde* if needed, and Chrystopher Hals is appointed second in command. Emmanuel Watkyns and Christopher Hayman are designated as officers on the *Northern Venture,* and they remain aboard the barque with twenty other men.

As the crew makes final preparations for departure and is boarding the pinnaces, they observe a number of natives emerge from a forest trail and slowly move toward the shoreline. The natives appear to be unarmed, which provides a small measure of relief to Chaplain Fletcher as he stands in the bow of the *Hinde* evoking blessings for the men about to go ashore. Crowley is at his side, his lips tight and eyes squinted against the reflected sunlight.

Crowley grunts and remarks in a slow drawl, "I count about two dozen of the bastards, but there may be more waiting in the shadows. Guess we won't know until we get there. I can see some of their canoes protruding from the bushes." He turns to look at Fletcher, who is still beseeching the Almighty. "You might want to save some of that for the village and pray that we're not on the menu." With a short bark of laughter, Crowley joins the line of men descending into the first pinnace.

The two launches, fully loaded with men and gifts of linen, knives, and English silver coins, pull together toward the shore. The men received communion earlier that morning—several indicated they were prepared to die and left letters for their loved ones with those remaining onboard. Fletcher wonders if the dramatic change in weather is a good omen. It is the first rain-free day they have seen in over a week. The two pinnaces touch the beach at almost the same moment, and the men wade onto the sand and form a line in front of Drake, Diego, Fletcher, Crowley, Gallawaye, Hord, Martyn, Elyot, and Cary. The latter four gentlemen had volunteered enthusiastically to accompany Drake. Elyot indicates he relishes every opportunity to inspect flora and fauna wherever they land, but he is cautioned to remain close to the group and not go off chasing butterflies. Thomas Hord is given the responsibility of responding to any imminent threat. He will give the command for the soldiers to fire if Drake is unable to do so.

It is only after they disembark that it occurs to Drake they don't know exactly where the village is or how far from the beach. *Odd that I neglected that essential point in our preparations. A few yards or a few miles?* Drake turns to Crowley and whispers, "Mr. Crowley, do we know the distance to their village?"

Crowley lowers his head and replies in a soft voice, "Not far from what I could gather, which I admit wasn't much. Maybe a short walk, a few minutes."

"Let us hope that is so." Drake turns to the men assembled around him. "Look sharp and confident with no fear in your eyes. The trail appears narrow, so we will have several of you in front and several to follow." He nods at Hord to take charge of the deployment.

During this time, the natives stand silently to one side, although several of them stare unabashedly at Diego. He seems especially impressive next to the Englishmen who, like Drake, are mostly under six feet tall. With few exceptions, the natives are also short in stature. Crowley motions to the Indian he thinks is in charge, indicating they are ready to follow. Martyn, Cary, and Elyot carry the gifts in three bags. The soldiers keep their hands free, and the burden keeps Elyot from wandering off to explore nature.

Half of the natives start across the beach for the trail, and as Drake and his men follow, the remainder of the natives fall in behind. Drake's men have been warned to remain alert and not speak unless necessary. The tension is palpable, and everyone understands the next hour might prove critical not only for the success of their venture but for their lives.

Aboard the *Hinde* and *Venture*, the men watch as their general and his party disappear into the dense foliage. Their vigil will not end until the group returns and is safely aboard. George Kershaw, the chaplain's informal acolyte, speaks aloud to no one in particular, "I can say a prayer for them." He looks around, not sure that he has the right to make such an offer.

"You go ahead and do that, Georgie boy. You pray as hard and long as you want," one of the crewmen says with a smile of encouragement. Several others nod in agreement.

---

The walk to the village requires ten minutes. They duck under low-hanging branches and traverse a short incline, gaining fifteen feet of elevation from the beach. The group emerges into a sizeable clearing to face several dozen large buildings made of cedar planks. Most of them are elevated on short posts, and smoke rises from rooftop exits on most of the structures. A large bonfire holds center stage in the clearing, and a number of men wearing elaborate furs are gathered around it. The leader they saw the day before in the canoe sits to one side of an older man dressed elegantly in furs and adorned with a large necklace of seashells. He squats on a hide blanket between two large whale ribs that form an arch above his head. Other whale bones appear on structures and along a pathway that leads from the village to the right.

The native escort in front of them parts, forming a line to the assembled gathering. Drake's front guard walks through the open space and takes up positions interspersed with the standing natives. Drake, Diego, and Crowley step up to within ten feet of the sitting leader and what appears to be his council of older and younger men. Gallawaye remains behind with the rest of the group but in position to see what transpires.

Francis Drake is only five feet five inches tall, but his boots and a feather-tipped hat present an image to impress. He wears the bright colors of a uniform befitting the Queen's ambassador to the New

World, and his bright, reddish-blond hair and beard contribute to the spectacle, none of which is lost on the natives during this first encounter with white men. Diego is no less splendid as the big man beside Drake. His tight britches emphasize his muscular thighs. A cotton blouse left open down the middle exposes sculptured abdominal and chest muscles. The short sleeves display his dark, brawny biceps and lower arms. He appears to be the very embodiment of a warrior.

Crowley steps forward, greets the council with signs, and introduces Drake as his chief. A few of the native council appear surprised, as if they expected the black man to be the leader. As he introduces himself, Drake's rear guard forms in a circular line behind Drake and the gentlemen. The remaining native honor guard closes behind Drake's men, effectively sealing off the path to the beach.

Fletcher casts about nervously. *No quick or easy escape now.* He looks around the clearing and spots a few women and children on the periphery, well away from the fire and assembled men. Based on what they saw in the canoes the day before, it seems that many of the native men are in attendance. There are forty to fifty around the fire and the twenty or so warriors in the honor guard. He can't discern any weapons, at least not any in plain sight or within close reach. There is no extraneous talking or movement—the scene is one of quiet expectation.

Several women carrying hides appear from a building behind the chief, and they place these on the ground around Drake's men before withdrawing. An Indian of fifty or sixty years stands and makes motions for the white men to be seated, which they do. He appears to be the spokesman for the tribe rather than the man who greeted them from the canoe. The blankets are deerskin pelts, and each man has one to himself. The native honor guard remains standing.

Crowley calls for the three bags of gifts, and these are presented one item at a time to the spokesman. With much ceremony after receiving each gift, the spokesman turns to the chief but hands it to the man from the canoe. This man piles the gifts in front of himself, but the chief appears pleased and occasionally examines one of the gifts for several minutes. When the knives are presented, the spokesman distributes them to each of eight men who sit to the left of their leader.

From the building behind the native council, three braves laden with furs step out. They set these in front of the spokesman and withdraw. The spokesman picks each fur up and hands it to Crowley, with a few words describing the animal and its merits. Unfortunately, Crowley isn't able to understand these praises to the animal spirits. Crowley passes the skins back to Drake's company. Each man, gentlemen and soldier, receives a pelt of varying size.

Remembering the fascination that some South American Indians had with regard to hats, Drake had ordered an officer's naval hat be included in one of the gift bags. He gives this to the spokesman. The man holds it up to the sun and laughs, seemingly delighted. He turns and hands it to the chief. The man stands, removes his conical wooden cap, reaches for the naval hat, and puts it on his head. He looks at Drake's hat, points to it, and then points to the one on his head, laughing. Many of the other men join in, and the event terminates the solemn formality of the ceremony.

Crowley, Drake, and Diego are invited to move closer while facing the chief and his council. Fletcher remains farther back with the other gentlemen and watches as Crowley enters into an elaborate series of signs and signals with the chief's spokesman. Occasionally, each man confers with his respective leaders.

After an hour of intense conference, women emerge from a nearby building with wooden platters of food that they serve to the conferring group. Additional food is brought for the rest of Drake's party and soldiers. The native honor guard continues standing in silence as if guards at a funeral. The comparison does not amuse Fletcher.

Venison is prominent, but other roasted animals are presented, most of which Fletcher can't identify. *Perhaps our naturalist will help me provide names later*, thinks the chaplain. The natives drink clear water from hollow clay pods. At first, Drake's men are reluctant to drink it. Water aboard ships is notoriously foul and often leads to dysentery and other severe illnesses. Rum, wine, and beer are the preferred drinks, although fresh rainwater is a suitable alternative. There are three types of nuts, some gourds, onions, other tubers, and a lot of fish. One in particular is tasty. It has reddish flesh with a flavor very different from the usual trout. Although fish like it can be found in the waters of home, especially in Scotland, many of the *Hinde*'s crew have never tasted it. There are piles of mussels, clams, and other shellfish. It seems to the visitors that this tribe lives among a veritable storehouse of foods. When most of the meal has been consumed, a last course consisting of a rich meat with abundant fatty material is served. Later, Crowley explains that this was whale meat, and the tribe is particularly proud of its prowess as marine hunters. Special canoes are designated for the purpose in addition to the war canoes the crew saw earlier.

The party lasts about four hours, and it concludes when Crowley indicates to Drake and the others that enough has been said. The chief stands, opens his arms, and utters a few words. The council stands and files out of the clearing, leaving most of the other men sitting beside the fire. The rear native honor guard moves aside, indicating that the trail is available. Drake and his party rise and assemble as before, and they follow several natives down the trail to the beach. Each man still maintains vigilance, never forgetting the treachery experienced on Mocha after what seemed a friendly encounter.

---

ABOARD THE *HINDE*, A CREWMEMBER GIVES A SHOUT, "THEY'RE coming out, lads. Launch the boats." The two pinnaces leave the *Hinde* and *Venture* and pull onto the beach a few minutes later. The natives gather around to inspect the craft, especially the oars. They attempt to ask Crowley about them, but their language skills are not sufficient, and he is understandably exhausted from the lengthy conference.

The crew and soldiers push off and make their way to the two ships. The pinnaces return to pick up the beach contingent of soldiers that has been silently standing by. The men returning from the village proudly show their furs as they board the *Hinde*. Fletcher presents his to John Drake, who waits anxiously by the rail. "For you, son. I am sure there will be many others for us to acquire before we leave this land, but I don't fancy them for myself."

Dinner that night for the officers and gentlemen is raucous. The Madeira flows freely and is accompanied by French brandy and lilting tunes from the four musicians. Everyone is in a gay mood, prompted by the success of the afternoon meeting with the natives. After a few nervous maneuvers and formalities, the ceremony proceeded better than the Englishmen could have wished. The accompanying soldiers attend their own celebration on the aft deck. Although the mood is celebratory, caution remains in force.

Usually an optimist among the crew, Chaplain Fletcher is quick to remind others of their past miscalculations. Guards posted on both ships are instructed to keep a sharp outlook over the inlet and scan the shore for the approach of any craft. No one underestimates the potential threat from a multitude of armed and physically endowed warriors.

Crowley sits as a guest of honor at the captain's table. He is called on frequently to relay bits of conversation for the benefit of those at the luncheon as well as those who were absent. He invokes laughs when he describes the wide eyes and open mouths of the warriors when they spotted Diego. "Probably thought he was one of the black hounds from hell itself." Usually present but silent at the council gatherings, Diego remains stoic. Drake smiles and raises a glass when the occasion demands but says little, allowing the others to share their impressions. Everyone around the table knows it is time to make decisive plans and take advantage of the day's achievements.

The general stands without a glass in hand, and silence replaces the noise. Crowley starts to rise, but Drake places a hand on his shoulder and motions for him to stay. "You will be needed during the next several days with the present inhabitants of our new land and many others we might meet. You will be our ears and tongue, Mr. Crowley."

"Aye, sir. I serve at your pleasure." He sits.

The general turns to his chaplain. "Father Fletcher, you have said little at our table this evening. Do you have thoughts you would care to share about our new friends on shore?"

Fletcher looks up from his reverie. He has been content to share the good company and high spirits and had not thought of voicing his opinions. He pauses to gather his thoughts. "Friends? I believe we might be prudent to hold our judgment a while, Captain. Although their laughter when you presented the hat provided good evidence of their nature and I believe their intentions may be honorable, they could be a formidable enemy if the mood should change for the worse. I took the liberty of examining one of their canoes, if you can call it such, when we returned to the beach. They appear solid and seaworthy, if I can be a judge of such. Men who hunt whales and other goliaths of the sea should alert us to be cautious, perhaps even respectful, of their potential."

Drake gazes at the men around him. "As you are all surely aware, the good pastor and I have not always agreed on events that have occurred during our voyage. Tonight he speaks true, and his words should be heeded by all. Let us be hopeful but remain prudent. Now, let me summarize what Mr. Crowley has been able to determine from today's conference with the Muh-kwa." He notices smiles and puzzled looks. "The name they call themselves is beyond our ability to imitate with facility, so Mr. Crowley requested a shorter form. Their spokesman suggested a name the tribe across the strait has for them, and they take no offense if we use it.

"First, they accepted our gifts and gave us items of value in exchange. We have agreed to prepare a small feast for their council members, two dozen in all, on the beach tomorrow. Unfortunately, we will have only one woman to provide service, and I have recruited Maria, along with our steward and a few of our sailors, to help in this regard. The meal will fulfill our obligation of exchange, and most important, we will be regarded as friends and allies from this time on.

"We indicated that we wished to sail farther up the strait to determine how far it continues. Mr. Crowley, please correct me if I misspeak. They indicated many hours of water travel to the east followed by a northerly turn for several days. This provides us with additional reason to hope that the long-sought passageway does indeed lie before us.

"We were asked if we wished for an escort to lead us forward, but we declined. They assured us that should we return, we would again be welcomed as brothers of the sea. They expressed their regret that we would be soon departing. Do any of you have questions or wish to share thoughts on this and the next few days ahead?"

Many at the table voice congratulations to William Crowley and the great service he has rendered. The chaplain gives a blessing for the day and the morrow, and the men disperse to their quarters. Captain Drake sits down as all but his brother and cousin depart. He picks up a wine glass, still half full, downs the contents, sighs, and looks at John. "Be prepared with pen and paint, for now we begin the real journey, perhaps the most important one anyone has ever undertaken. We shall prepare a record that will amaze the most cynical of men at court. One that will entrance the Queen herself."

John grins, and Thomas puts his hands on his young cousin's shoulder. Although John will remain short in stature like most of the Drakes, he has shot up several inches during the voyage and is rapidly maturing. Thomas thinks, *Will John's parents recognize the stripling youth who left Plymouth two years ago? For that matter, will any of my friends or family recognize me?*

---

The black people aboard the *Hinde* include Maria, Diego, Mark, and Francisco. Big Tom and Peter serve aboard the *Venture*.

All were freed from the Spanish at one time, and all have been given their unconditional freedom by Francis Drake. Maria and Diego share a small alcove next to the captain's quarters. Despite the fears some men hold about a woman aboard a ship on the high seas, most are not reluctant to cast a lascivious eye in her direction. Whether it is the serious countenance of Diego, her guardian and some assume her paramour, or the stern words of warning from the general that she is not to be molested or harassed in any manner, the crew keeps a respectful distance. Some begin to regard her as an enhancement, a living figurehead for the *Hinde*.

Though the only female among dozens of men, Maria has taken to life aboard the ship as if she has been born to sail the seven seas. Other than brief bouts of vomiting during the first days away from shore, she makes herself useful as a member of the crew, helping in the galley, mending clothes, and offering a smile and cheerful word in broken English when the occasion arises. She dresses modestly in a skirt to her ankles and exposes no cleavage, giving no reason for the men to step out of line.

The night descends as a thick fog engulfs the inlet and strait, creating a dark shroud between the *Venture* and *Hinde*. Periodically each ship sounds a bell, and the other answers to indicate all is well. Drake sleeps in fits, waking at times to revisit doubts about the coming day and whether it will prove to be as productive and gratifying as the day just passed. He is not alone in his uneasiness. The other men—gentlemen, seaman, and soldier alike—share his discomfiture and hope the morrow will not see a reversal of their fortune.

---

The next day proceeds as expected. The stores of the *Hinde* provide a midday meal on the beach. A smaller gathering than at the village is served salted pork and beef. The natives eat slowly, not accustomed to the heaviness of the dry meat and the gravy with which it is served. This meal brings the expedition closer to an empty larder, but the crew expects to being able to restock the pantry from the abundant wildlife ashore. Maria causes a sensation among the natives, especially the few tribal women in attendance. More than one native man gazes at her with obvious desire. She has a lighter complexion than Diego and the other black men, and her facial features are not vastly different from many of the native women.

That night, following the second and final gathering of Drake's party and the Muh-kwa elders on the inlet beach, Fletcher writes in his secret journal.

*Monday, 23 June 1579*

*It all goes well by the grace of our Lord and Savior, praise be to him. There was much to eat both from our provisions and additional items served by the natives. Once again, women emerged from the forest to lay food before us while smiling shyly. The women were especially curious about Maria, and they made signs to Mr. Crowley to ask if all our women were dark like her. William indicated they were not, that his wife from far away was as fair as the sunshine. This produced additional amazement on their part. Compared to the day before, there was little formal conference. The mood was festive, and the few warriors who attended mingled freely with our soldiers.*

*We brought no guns, but several of our men had swords. The natives inspected these and were delighted when one of our officers, Mr. Watkyns, used a sword to cut several bushes away from the ground. Mr. Crowley indicated that the natives harvest shellfish from the tideline with sticks. The general brought them a new shovel and showed them how to use it for digging large, long-necked clams when the tide recedes. In return, the chief bestowed on our general a handsome shield decorated with many eagle feathers.*

*We returned to the ship as the sun was setting behind the point but still with light to prepare for tomorrow's departure.*

> *There remains the problem of leakage and the need to careen both ships while the weather holds. Mr. Hawkins asked if the present inlet would be suitable, but the general replied that he didn't want to impose on the goodwill and hospitality of our new friends more than necessary, and the work would take many days. Without saying so, he inferred the task would render us vulnerable for some time, and he preferred to complete the work on an isolated or uninhabited beach.*

Lieutenant Gallawaye is temporarily assigned to the *Golden Hinde* so he can confer with William Crowley on communicating with natives. Crowley has learned from the Muh-kwa that a number of common words and signs exist among many of the tribes of the inland coastal waters, and he shares this knowledge with the lieutenant. John is an eager student and quickly assimilates much of what Crowley has acquired despite the fact that his local exposure is limited to three days with one tribe. The need for others to have interpreting skills has been apparent to Drake, Fletcher, and others.

John spends the evening contemplating his future. An incident on the beach that day keeps returning and haunting him with its simplicity, brevity, and innocence. One of the Indian women, perhaps more a girl than a woman, caught his eye several times as she served food. No words were spoken, and their romantic interchange comprised only a brief smile, but it was enough to plunge the navigator into dreams and schemes of an exotic liaison. He is no stranger to the boudoir but has never pursued an affair with serious intent. However, years away from the fair gender has produced a realization that his longing is more than mere lust. He finds himself yearning for the touch, the embrace of a soft skin, and the murmur of a voice beside him. It has been too long.

CHAPTER 4

# Northern Explorations

---

Flags raise on the *Golden Hinde* and *Northern Venture* to signal the synchronous weighing of anchors—sails hoist and unfurl a few minutes later. As they move away from the inlet and up the strait, a large number of Muh-kwa gather on the beach. Several war canoes are afloat but stand well off from the ships. A moderate breeze shakes the canvas aloft, and there is little time for the sailors to look back at their recent hosts.

In the captain's cabin, Francis Drake, his cousin John, and two other men gather around a table displaying a large piece of parchment. John has drawn an outline of the strait's opening from the Pacific Ocean that indicates the large peninsula south of the strait, the bay with the Indian village, and the coastline opposite. Hernán Perez and Nazario de Morera, two of Drake's navigators, make measurements and calculate distances as the *Hinde* sails eastward. Although neither has been to the Pacific Northwest or through the East Indies, their accumulated experience in sailing difficult waters and skills at plotting charts are much needed. However, the general is regarded by all, including himself, as the principal navigator.

"Our native friends indicated we would reach a bend in this waterway turning to the north." The general briefs his navigators on what they know so far about the inland shorelines. "From what Mr. Crowley could determine, we will see it before sunset. They also talked of many islands in the middle of this strait where it turns. There are additional inland waters and islands south of the turn. It seems we have an inland sea before us. We need to find a convenient harbor protected from storms but with a beach suitable for careening. Both ships will need scrubbing and caulking. Preparations are in order for what might be a difficult passage in the northern waters ahead. After that, we can determine where to explore."

Both pilots know sufficient English to understand the general. Perez is Portuguese and more fluent and communicative than Morera. Nazario boarded the *Hinde* at Plymouth and helped navigate the coast of Brazil and Argentina. A Basque who is often given to bouts of sullen silence, he is competent and his skills compensate for his lack of social grace. After leaving Guatulco, he has become increasingly despondent and complains of being ill. He is not alone.

Many of the expedition's company are not in their best health, and a number of the men display the characteristic gum redness and malaise associated with sailor's disease (scurvy). Perez is well aware of the condition and the preventative measures that his countrymen have taken to lessen its impact on their oceanic travels.

He urged Drake to acquire fresh fruits and vegetables while in Guatulco, but they didn't stay fresh for long in the mid-Pacific tropics, and most of the fruit was quickly consumed. Some of their vegetables lasted longer. They loaded berries, onions, and other greens at the Muh-kwa inlet. In addition, a tea rendered from pine bark and needles was offered to Drake's officers during their last beach luncheon. Perez recognized the curative properties of the tea and indicated that a supply of the needles should be taken onboard and the tea given to those suffering the worse from the malady.

The remedy particularly interests William Hawkins, who witnessed many sailors falling prey to the disease in the Caribbean. Drake earlier rejected the dietary remedies and was convinced by Perez only after the ship's physicians, Richard Winterhey and Thomas Flood, were killed by natives at San Julian and Mocha Island, respectively. Neither of the good doctors subscribed to the pilot's knowledge of curing sailor's disease, but Drake has little reason to object without their presence. The natives showed Crowley how to soak the needles and bark in hot water overnight and drink the tea soon afterward.

Nazario de Morera's private demons have less to do with illness and more to do with religion. He was aware that Drake, his gentlemen, and most of the crew were Protestants before he joined the expedition in Plymouth. He has not disguised his faith from the others, but he makes no attempt to pray outside of the ship's Sunday services. He carries but does not display a rosary. The rampage in Guatulco, including the desecration of the church, resulted in his pronounced social withdrawal from the crew. He considers the general generous and merciful, but like many of the other outspoken infidels, at times Drake is blasphemous and profane. On other occasions during the voyage, sailors and soldiers have destroyed sacred artifacts and ridiculed the true Church and its followers. He understands the general's hatred of the Spaniards, and he has no great love for the New World conquerors, but he gradually realizes that he is an accepted member of the company only because he keeps his faith unspoken and unpracticed. There are a few others aboard who also hold to the Catholic faith, but they invariably keep their beliefs private.

Morera has no doubts about Francis Drake's skill as a navigator and military leader—it has been demonstrated fully and dramatically numerous times. In his opinion, however, the *Golden Hinde* does not merit the same respect. It leaks often, and the hull requires frequent scraping and caulking. In the past, they were fortunate to find suitable locations to careen the ship, but prospects in the northern passage seem less probable. The shores are rocky, and ice is expected in these latitudes. If they can find a suitable beach before beginning the unknown transit, hopefully before winter comes calling, the route might be short enough to reach England before another overhaul is required. He is tired of the voyage and the behavior of his shipmates and dreads the longer trip across the Pacific if the northern route doesn't materialize. He fervently hopes it will.

John leaves the cabin and climbs to the aft deck with sketchpad in hand. He continues to illustrate coastal landmarks on both the northern and southern shorelines. Under the supervision of the pilots and Drake, he uses a method of triangulation with sun angle to estimate the distance they travel, which is corroborated by a pine log towed with a knotted rope. A following fair northwest-by-north wind propels them at about six knots. The opposing current remains constant and becomes noticeably less salty as they make their way east in the strait.

Shortly before sunset, the strait widens to the north as predicted. The coastline is rugged, especially on the northern shore, as they round a cape and change course to north by northeast. That evening, they lose some wind due to the intervening land mass, so they angle easterly toward a number of islands, some large and many small. The ships drop anchor while still in moderately deep water.

After the evening repast, Drake consults with his council, the captains of the ships, and the pilots. "Gentlemen, this appears to be the northern waterway we were informed about." His eyes move around the table, measuring each man's response. "With good fortune, we may be close to discovering the western entrance to our long-sought Anián. We will cross this water, what appears to be a broad inland sea, and explore the eastern shore for outlets. We will also seek a beach to make repairs to the *Hinde* and inspect the *Venture*. If all is well, our ships can separate temporarily to increase our chances of discovery. Does that seem reasonable to all of you?"

The general doesn't always ask for advice unless a military action is imminent. A few nods greet his announcement, but there is little to debate.

Morera remains silent, but Perez comments on the islands ahead of them and the need to proceed carefully in uncharted waters. As before, the *Venture* will lead the way to sound for shallow reefs and look for rocky outcrops. Later, Captain Hals returns to his barque and communicates the general's plan to the crew of the *Venture*. Fletcher's journal entry that evening is one of excitement and hope.

*Friday, 24 June 1579*

*Morale runs high and with good cause. We have been blessed with fine weather and smooth seas. The mountains rising from the land on all sides are magnificent, as if they were beds of heaven on which the angels recline. The air is sweet with the smell of pines, and even a casual look into the waters reveals an abundance of fish. We have seen a number of whales in the strait that some of the crew have been referring to as Drake's Passage. He disavows this, wishing to wait until we determine where it leads. Along the rocks on the northern coast, we espied a number of large herds of seals that the local natives hunt for fur and food. We were given a few fine examples of these pelts by our recent hosts. Most of the company is looking forward to our anchorage in the next day or so. Only a few of them had the opportunity to leave their ships while we were at the inlet. Careening is a difficult task, but all are looking forward to walking on land for the first time in over two months. May God bless and keep us and continue to guide us on our way home.*

The sun barely breaks the eastern horizon as the ships get underway, still tracking northeast by east. After leaving the islands behind, they cross an expanse of water toward a low-lying shore into which several streams and a large river empty. Catching a fresh northwesterly, they make good progress along the densely wooded shoreline with the *Venture* in the vanguard. At midday, a small headland appears before them, jutting southwestward and enclosing a small bay. Once again the ships close so Drake and Chrystopher Hals can confer and agree on the next move.

"The bay before us is small, but there is a protected beach," observes Hals.

"Are there any signs of inhabitants?" asks Drake.

"We saw a bit of smoke earlier, but it has since disappeared. I see no canoes on the beach. Perhaps there is activity on the other side of the point."

The general considers this for a moment. He is anxious to get the *Hinde* anchored and careened, for the leakage has increased noticeably during their passage up the strait, yet he wants to be sure they won't be disturbed. "Let us sail pass the point. If all is well, we can return and make camp. A few extra leagues won't be such a delay as to forego prudence."

The ships continue along the coast. There are only a few scattered rocks projecting near the shore; the deep water provides assurance of an easy passage. An hour later, they face a larger bay that also has a prominent point projecting southward. Noting the large beach and headland, they pass its chalky, white cliffs and continue for another hour to sail by the outlet of a large river with several branches forming a flat delta. Beyond that, they encounter additional white cliffs and dunes bordering a shallow inlet. Tom Moone remarks to several men on deck that sections of the shore resemble the white cliffs of Dover, reminding all of how far from home they are.

The *Hinde* signals to the *Venture*, and again they close and confer. Drake shouts across to the *Venture's* deck, "We make for the last large bay, Mr. Hals. Proceed us in and sound as you go."

"Aye, Captain." Hals cannot contain the grin that acknowledges the long-anticipated order.

An hour before sunset, the ships maneuver around the headland, drop anchor in the large bay, and stand well off from the beach. Dark shadows on the eastern side of the point obscure its shoreline. Only the eastern beaches in the distance reflect some light. They appear to be deserted.

Rotating sentries are posted on both ships. Captain Hals and Lieutenant Hayman join General Drake and his gentlemen for dinner and are entertained by the four musicians. They drink malmsey (Madeira) and secke (a Canary Islands dry white) wines and consume a sumptuous meal that makes up for a modest midday snack. The food stores would be depleted if not for provisions provided by the Muh-kwa, but these will need to be restocked in the days ahead. The gathering is jovial with much humor evident. John Fortescu of Devon, the son of the Queen's wardrobe keeper, reads poems that include limericks of bawdy content.

Afterward, all eyes turn to the general, who has smiled and toasted but said little during the evening's festivities. "Gentlemen, we have arrived, but as to where, we do not yet know. We should take this moment to give praise and ask for such blessings as we might deserve. Chaplain Fletcher, if you please."

Fletcher rises, lowers his head, and invokes the Lord's favor. He doesn't speak at length, but he dares to entertain some hope for the expedition and for himself. *Perhaps the anticipation of accomplishing our objective has restored matters to their proper place,* he muses. As he glances about the cabin, even John Doughty, the brother of poor Thomas, seems in high spirits. Although John often dines with the other gentlemen and is free to move about the ship, he has been kept under close watch and is the only crew member not permitted to leave the ship since the tragic execution in Patagonia.

Lieutenant Gallawaye, still assigned temporarily to the *Hinde*, has made good use of his time with Crowley. He memorized much of the native jargon Crowley acquired at the inlet but needs practice to effectively communicate. He hopes to rectify that during their next encounter with local tribes, wherever and whenever it happens.

---

FRIDAY MORNING DAWNS WITH A SLIGHT BREEZE AND FAINT fog, but the first light before sunrise reveals a dramatic panorama they missed the evening before. As the crews of the ships rouse and look west at the eastern shore of the point, they see that the beach is occupied by several camps. Drying racks filled with fish, beached canoes, and temporary tent-like structures are numerous. Both vessels spring to action as general alarms sound, and armed men quickly assemble along the rails facing the shore. Hawkins, Hord, and the general stand on the aft deck surveying the quiet—all too quiet—shoreline. They detect no movement. It is as if a busy and populous encampment that stretches for over a mile along the shore has been hastily abandoned. Only puffs of smoke from one or two pit fires and from one wooden plank house near the point closest to them give evidence of current or recent occupation.

"Looks like we stumbled into the midst of a fishing village," remarks Thomas Hord, cradling a musket. The ships are far enough off shore to compromise visibility.

William Hawkins spots natives moving along the forest line toward the point. "Another reception? Let us hope this be as agreeable as the last one."

Drake has not finished dressing, and he shivers in the morning cold. When Diego comes to his side, he asks the black man to fetch him a coat and find Crowley. "Send him to me without delay."

People slowly emerge from the shrubs and trees onto the sandy beach. Most are adult men, some armed with spears and bows. They line up at the water's edge and look out at the ships. Fletcher tries to imagine their amazement at finding two large, strange objects in their bay. Would they be curious and welcoming like their neighbors to the west? The Muh-kwa had not warned them about specific tribes or dangers in this part of the inland sea, but everyone knows that communication is less than perfect.

Diego retrieves the general's coat and Mr. Crowley. One look at the bank is enough to remove the interpreter's last traces of sleep.

"A chance to earn more ale, Willie." Hawkins laughs.

The men on the ships need not wait long. They observe several canoes being readied, men climbing aboard them, and paddles being lifted. They count almost a dozen of the slim wooden craft launching within a few minutes of each other and steering toward them. The boats are not as robust as the Muh-kwa canoes. As in the earlier encounter, armed soldiers crouch behind the *Hinde's* rails, and word passes to the sailors and others looking on to

51

remain calm, smile, and make no sudden movements. The *Venture* lies twenty yards off the starboard side of the *Hinde*, farther from the approaching canoes. Diego stands beside the general as Hord, Hawkins, and Crowley assume a midship position on the port rail to greet the natives.

Fletcher notes that their dress, or lack thereof, is similar to that of the Muh-kwa. Some of the men have a breechcloth but lack anything above the waist. The few exceptions wear a pelt or woven cape about their shoulders. As they near, the priest counts three individuals, in different canoes, with conical caps constructed from cedar bark.

The closest canoe pulls to within a few yards of the *Hinde* and stops. The man in the bark cap stands and begins chanting. Crowley waits patiently while the native gives an oration that lasts thirty minutes. From time to time, the men in the closest canoes voice a short call: a prolonged "oh" repeated three times. During the long monologue, Drake and the others notice men, women, and children gathering high along the top of the headland. Occasionally, the wind brings the sounds of chants from this group. The beach is now a busy scene of natives walking about, tending fires, and working at the fish racks. As the sun rises, it is apparent that both ships missed the presence of the settlements, for there appear to be more than one, during their initial passage by and return to the broad bay.

On the *Golden Hinde*, Lieutenant Gallawaye watches the scene unfold. He joins Crowley near Drake and several others as the orator finally sits. Crowley begins a series of gestures toward the native, who indicates that he recognizes the interpreter's signs. He stands again, and the canoe draws nearer. The men exchange a few words with accompanying movements of their hands and fingers. The standing man turns to face his men and raises his arms in the air. They give a brief shout, and the canoe turns to head for the shore, followed by the other canoes. The chanting from the hilltop becomes louder as the natives beach their canoes.

Crowley and Gallawaye announce to Drake that it has gone well. "I could still stand a bit of suds, be it though only midmorning and

I hardly broke a sweat," Crowley growls. Grinning, Diego wanders off to fetch a mug while the general clasps Crowley on the elbow, congratulating him once more for easing their way with the local inhabitants. Drake asks Hawkins to call for Captain Hals to join them on the *Hinde*.

A meeting on the flagship occurs shortly after their midday meal. The officers agree on sending a shore party to test the Indians' willingness to continue friendly relations. They prepare bags of gifts, and an armed party is readied to accompany Francis Drake, Fletcher, Hord, Hals, Crowley, Gallawaye, Diego, and Big Tom. Peter also joins them so the giant black can understand instructions while ashore. If their reception goes smoothly, the shore party will assess the beach for the best spot to careen the *Hinde*. Hawkins is left in command of the *Hinde* and Christopher Hayman in charge of the *Venture*. John Gallawaye realizes that his chance to practice the language, a local trade jargon called Chee-nook, is at hand.

The reception proves a grand one by any standards. As the two launches row toward the beach, a large crowd of natives gathers a few yards back from the waterline. In front of the group stands a tall man who is middle-aged and regally dressed from shoulders to waist in an otter skin cape. Unlike the other prominent natives, he doesn't wear a conical cap but has an elaborate headpiece made of feathers. Gallawaye recognizes eagle, egret, and woodpecker plumage among others. The faces of several men of his entourage are painted in red, black, and white. Except for the few men wearing pelts and breech clothes, most of the men are naked save for a strap around the waist that holds a knife or some other object. The women are naked from the waist up, and the children have no clothes at all.

Francis Fletcher isn't shocked—he has seen a fair amount of naked inhabitants during their trip around South America, but he is surprised that the natives of this settlement, like those at Muh-kwa, exposed to a climate that remains cool during the summer, can so readily forego clothes. Nights and winters must be unbearable. Only later would he learn that clothing and footwear for all, including the children, will be donned when the snows come.

The greeter in the feathered headpiece gives a long welcome, part speech and part chant that is punctuated with answering calls from the men in the crowd. The women and children remain silent. The feathered leader moves to the side, and the spokesman from the canoe steps forward to speak with Crowley, joined by Gallawaye. The conversation of several minutes is accompanied by gestures and pointing in different directions. As the three confer, Crowley occasionally pauses to inform Drake and his men on what is said.

"There is more than one tribe at this place. The local group, the ones who live in this bay and the two bays south of here, are called the Sem-iah-moo. One of their chiefs is the one in the feathered hat, but they have several chiefs. He is in charge of the summer fishing camp. They are joined by two tribes from the south and one tribe from the north, from the large river delta we sailed past yesterday. They share this bay every summer and are willing to share it with us as well. They have many questions, but I haven't yet provided answers."

Drake looks at Fletcher and Hord, but they say nothing. Diego and Big Tom stand behind them, and both men receive intense attention from the Indians. Drake faces Crowley as Gallawaye looks on. "Answer their basic questions, assure them of our peaceful intentions, and ask them if we can use the beach east of here to fix our ships. Ask them if we are permitted to fish and hunt away from their camps. Determine if they are on friendly terms with the Muh-kwa. If so, let them know we are also friends. If not, say nothing."

Next to Drake, Fletcher makes mental notes of all that transpires. Crowley nods and speaks again with his counterpart.

Some of the natives began to disperse, but most remain gathered around the group on the beach. No weapons are in evidence, and the armed soldiers with Drake remain relaxed and in the background. Aboard the two ships, the vigil is silent but intense. At the distance of half a mile, it is not easy to discern any specific actions, but the lack of movement indicates calm and progress toward a peaceful resolution.

After talks between Crowley, Gallawaye, and the native spokesman conclude, Drake motions for Diego and Big Tom to retrieve the bags of gifts from the *Hinde's* launch. Several of the warriors move backward as the blacks lay the bags down and open them. Thomas Hord and William Crowley pass out a number of beads and silver coins to the nearest natives. Drake delivers a knife each to the spokesman and the chief, which they receive and examine. Crowley cautions them about the fine edge, running one of the blades across his finger to show them a few drops of blood.

"Another mug of ale, heh, Mr. Crowley?" remarks the general.

"Aye, all for Queen and England, sir."

The agreements finalized, the white men are invited to tour the fishing camp on the following day, and gifts are exchanged. Most of the native presents consist of woven baskets and clay bowls painted with motifs of sea creatures, some of them resembling fantastic monsters. They give the visitors various rushes and herbs, but whether these are medicinal or intended as food is not initially known. They present clusters of feathers to Drake's officers and gentlemen—these are apparently important. Lawrence Elyot examines them and recognizes many of the feathers from shorebirds such as herons and egrets while others are from eagles, hawks, and ravens.

Fletcher is adamant about providing clothes to cover the natives. Although the women wear a short skirt made of hemp or rushes, the priest believes their naked breasts will incite lust in the hearts of the ordinary crewmen.

"Just the common crewmen, chaplain?" Fortescu laughs. "We gentlemen are not mortal or human, you say, that we don't notice a teat or a shapely hip? What of our general? I suppose he has no eye for it, only for the haunches of the *Golden Hinde*."

Fletcher frowns as several of the officers and crew gather around him. "Save your witticisms for the captain's table, sir. All men, even your humble servant, can be aroused to unseemly passion by an innocent display, but it is our Christian duty to educate the pagans and enlighten them to our ways."

Chrystopher Hals smiles in a kindly way as if to a younger, more naïve brother. "Enlighten away if you must, dear priest, but let us not break our legs in haste to cover nature's most beautiful delights." The *Northern Venture* captain is usually reserved in such observation and comment, but he is met with a chorus of "aye" and "amen."

---

ON SATURDAY MORNING, 27 JUNE, THE *HINDE* AND *VENTURE* pull anchor and move closer to the beach at the north end of the bay, about two miles from the headland. The barque, with a shallower draft, edges closer to the beach and assumes a broadside position with the *Hinde* standing parallel. By midday, the woods in front of the ships have been scouted and reports sent back to the *Hinde*. There are trails and evidence of campfires, but no villages or natives appear to be present. Long ropes are brought from the *Venture* and tied to the masts and bulwarks of the *Hinde* to bring it as close to shore as depth permits. The arduous task of transferring ballast, much of it in the form of silver and gold, plus cannons and iron stores, to the beach begins.

Although they remain a prudent distance from the summer fishing camps of the natives, Drake orders the construction of a low wall as a nominal fortification and to contain and secure the contents of the flagship. Remembering a hat that had been stolen by an ambitious Indian in Patagonia, Drake posts three guards near the cache for rotating sentry duty. Other laborers gather stones from the nearby woods, and the two masons aboard ship direct their placement in the wall. Men with axes and saws walk into the forest to harvest trees for construction of some simple huts. After the *Hinde* rolls on its side, the temporary structures will be used to distribute meals and serve as sleeping quarters. However, the three Drakes and most of the gentlemen sleep on the *Hinde* until it is ready to tilt. Although unbound, John Doughty remains a virtual prisoner aboard ship, and he will sleep aboard the *Venture* with the others while the *Hinde* is careened.

---

THE SUNDAY SERVICE ABOARD THE *HINDE* LASTS TWO HOURS. After Fletcher's prayers, hymns are sung, and Captain Drake addresses the crew. He reminds them of the long trek and their many successes, including the shares in treasure they will receive in due time. He acknowledges their difficulties, the need for discipline, the long days at sea, and the recent bitter cold. He tells them they can be proud of their endurance and survival. There is comfort in fellowship, and they have already surpassed the expectations of their sponsors and others in England. Hawkins leads the men in a self-congratulatory cheer. Mark joins the other blacks in the moment of celebration, something he never experienced on a Spanish ship. After a closing prayer by the chaplain, the day begins in earnest.

After three days, unloading is sufficient to haul the *Hinde* to port and lean at a thirty-five-degree angle, exposing the starboard hull and keel. Men in two pinnaces work the side, scraping barnacles and other encrustations, smoothing the wood, and caulking cracks with fresh pitch. A boiling pot on the beach maintains a steady supply of the tarry residue. Inside the hull, others work to dry and caulk the interior.

The *Northern Venture* has fared better. The seams hold tight, and only minor repairs are necessary from inside the hull. During this time, natives gather on the beach to watch the activities. With Gallawaye's help, Crowley answers questions about the ships, but he carefully avoids any mention of where they have come from, other than the strait, or where they are going. The crewmen aren't sure about an answer to the last question themselves.

---

THE GENERAL'S COUNCIL GATHERS AROUND A BONFIRE ON THE beach the third evening ashore following the tilt of the flagship. The group eats roasted venison brought in that morning from the scouting party. Baked fish and clams are distributed among the crew members relaxing nearby. The land and sea are indeed bountiful, promoting a sense of satisfaction and high spirits as Fletcher and Drake had hoped. They discuss sending the barque north in the strait to search for continuation or discovery of an eastward passage.

"No need to wait for the *Hinde* to finish repairs," says William Hawkins. He has a mug of beer in one hand and a roasted deer leg in the other. "We will be right busy with our good ship for another two weeks before we can reload her. Why not send the *Venture* north in the meanwhile? She can return and guide us to our passage home when we're ready to sail."

Gregory Cary offers a rejoinder. "I'm not so sure splittin' our forces be the best of plans. We may yet run into some of the tricky bastards. Our cannons can't be easily moved on the beach. The *Venture* can offer a broadside if they come pourin' out of the forest. It seems, in my humble opinion…"—this draws laughs from the group—"that a couple of weeks out of all that we have been through can't make a great difference." Cary doesn't need a pint or two to give voice to his thoughts. He has already quaffed three and is looking toward a fourth.

In contrast, several of the gentlemen are ready to return to the Pacific and sail for home as originally planned. A few of the council with close contacts at court note the obligation to repay the expedition's financial backers. Others point out the length of time they have been away and that the crew was recruited for a voyage of only a few months to the Mediterranean. The majority of the council favors a return across the Pacific if the northern passageway is not discovered. The naturalist Elyot and soldier George Martyn voice support for exploration at their present site. There are many inlets and possible waterways that haven't been probed, and the strait is still open ahead of them. There are also the waters south of them as they were informed by the Muh-kwa. When they made their turn north to their present location, they spotted open seas and numerous islands off the starboard stern.

Drake ends speculation about the multiple plans of action raised. He declares that the rest of the discussion will focus on what to do with the *Northern Venture*. By common agreement, especially by those who had sailed her, she is not appropriate for a trans-Pacific voyage, much less the continued trip through the Indian Ocean, around Africa, and back to England. With its propensity for leaks, the *Hinde* is not a certainty but has weathered many thousands of leagues of open ocean. Once across the Pacific, there will be places in the East Indies to careen and caulk.

"What about her cargo?" asks Gregory Cary. Everyone knows he is referring to tons of silver and jeweled ornaments still aboard the barque. The *Hinde* is loaded to maximum capacity, and they will need every bit of space for the additional provisions to see them to the Moluccas. Then there is the crew; the barque carries between twenty and twenty-four men, and there is not sufficient space for them and the provisions they would require aboard the flagship. If the Northwest Passage can't be found, the ship, its men, and additional treasure will need to remain in the New World.

"Not necessarily a bad thing in itself," ventures John Chester. "If all of us cannot return, those who remain become the first English residents of this new land, further bolstering our possession. They set up the outpost, hide the silver, and continue friendly relationships with tribes in this area." John is one of the merchant gentlemen especially interested in establishing a trade route between England and Asia. He has been privy to many of the discussions to seek the necessary and convenient northern access. It is still his hope that both ships can return to England by the shorter route, but that does not necessarily eliminate the need for a small settlement to maintain a territorial claim.

Usually hesitant to join in the council discussions, Thomas Drake speaks next. "If we do need to leave men here, others can return to fortify the outpost by coming across the Pacific and bringing more soldiers and merchants for eventual trade with Cathay. In the meantime, the *Venture* and its crew can continue to explore the coastline for our northern passageway." Most of his observations are communicated in private with his brother, but tonight he seems inspired to participate. His cousin, John, catches the excitement of the decision to return home and the possibility of establishing a formal presence in the new land. He waits to address his special request to the general in private.

"Who would stay and who would go?" asks Hawkins. He looks around at the council, pausing on each face. There has been some drinking during their supper, but all are relatively sober, and the question produces a level of somber introspection. Several are quick to offer reasons why they have to return to England and pursue businesses, family affairs, and politics. Most of the gentlemen are there for experience and fortune—none thought of becoming pioneers or long-term residents of this mysterious continent. "We'll need to ask for volunteers. First, who will take command of the *Venture*?"

Although not a formal member of the gentlemen's council, Christopher Hayman is invited to join them in the discussions. He stands and announces he will gladly take charge of the barque if a more qualified captain doesn't come forth. Although many eyes turn toward Captain Hals, he declines, so the general approves Hayman's command of the ship, promoting him formally to the rank of commander. His first official duty is to request John Gallawaye as his second-in-command. "The lieutenant is bright and good with pen and paper, and I believe he is making fair progress in learning the local languages."

Drake nods his assent. "I believe Mr. Gallawaye to be without a spouse. If he is willing to remain with the *Venture* and possibly remain here, your selection is approved."

Emmanuel Watkyns, a merchant from Devon and one of the gentlemen of the council, volunteers to be the leader of the group when not aboard ship. He entertains high hopes they will find the Strait of Anián and desires to help establish the first settlement in the new land. Furthermore, he hopes for favorable treatment by the

Queen for future commercial enterprises. A devout Lutheran and unmarried, he is an excellent choice to remain behind if it becomes necessary. Of medium build and quick of mind, he has gained a reputation for compromise and good will. Many of the crew, including the gentlemen, address him by his nickname "Manny."

Drake smiles. "This is a heavy decision, Mr. Watkyns. You might want to sleep on it."

"Or at the very least wait until you've quaffed a few glasses of malmsey," offers Cary.

Several gentlemen around the table laugh, but many are visibly relieved when Manny steps forward, resolving them of the responsibility to do so.

Watkyns indicates he is committed to the enterprise. Several other names are volunteered, some skilled workers and others good soldiers and sailors. Drake asks Francis Fletcher to consult with each of those named to see if they might be prepared to stay. The chaplain can offer them a larger share of the silver they are to safeguard as additional payment for their sacrifice. Fletcher and Hawkins promise to secure the rest of the outpost party the next day.

That still leaves the question about when to send the *Venture* forth. The general stands before them, the fire at his back. It gives his red hair and beard a fiery aspect as he rotates to face each of them in turn. "You all make valid points. We do need to be cautious and patient. I believe a compromise is in order. After the *Venture* helps reposition our flagship for the second hull scraping, we let her go north for several days. With God's blessing, she may discover the passage we seek and return without delay. That would render our discussion about leaving men behind as an option but not a requirement. If they are unsuccessful, we can continue explorations for a week or two or make the decision to leave some of our countrymen, as discussed. Mr. Hawkins, when you interview the crew for the *Venture*, please inform the volunteers that they may need to remain here until we return. A duration of up to two years, possibly longer." He pauses. "Gentlemen, how say you to that?"

Murmurs of "let it be so" and "aye, well thought" along with nods of approval provide the token and expected confirmation. Further discussion will be needed only if someone raises a critical objection and all recognize the seriousness of the moment. This will be the first time since the capture of the barque that the two ships separate. The disappearance and presumed loss of the other ships in their fleet weigh heavily on each man. If successful, the *Venture's* mission will change the course of history as well as decide the scenario for proceeding with the expedition. There remains the possibility that fate will dictate another outcome. The *Venture* might encounter disaster along the uncharted shore—Drake's expedition might never see the ship or her crew again. Therefore, it is essential to provide the ship with skilled crew members without depriving the *Hinde* of those critical for her survival and navigation.

Hawkins suggests that Morera be assigned to the *Venture*, leaving Perez with the *Hinde*. Drake has reservations about the pilot's willingness to communicate with other crewmen, but he agrees to consider the suggestion. The talk turns to William Crowley. Thomas Hord asks, "Would Will be better used aboard the barque in case they meet natives or here with us, to continue his good work?"

Drake is sitting, knees crossed in front of the fire and letting the gentlemen have their say. William Crowley is eating and drinking with the sailors at another bonfire farther down the beach.

"This would have been a perplexing dilemma, Mr. Hord," answers John Martyn. "His value in dealing with our native friends is not to be dismissed, as we have seen several times during our journey. However, if Mr. Gallawaye agrees to join Commander Hayman, I believe the outpost group will be well served." He looks around the circle of gentlemen and is met with smiles and affirmative nods. "I also propose we have Big Tom enhance the frigate's crew. If they can't talk to the natives they encounter, perhaps they can scare the bloody hell out of them."

Francis Fletcher listens carefully to the exchange. He rarely says anything at the council meetings unless called upon, but this time he rises to his feet and looks toward the general. "I believe Mr. Martyn offers a useful suggestion. We can ill afford to lose Mr. Crowley. The short venture by the *Venture*," he smiles at his cleverness, "should not require a landing, but if they do meet with difficulties, John Gallawaye is skilled. Tomas can be an asset for his appearance and strength. His friend, Peter, might accompany him to facilitate communications." The chaplain sits as the others nod and signal approval.

Drake stands. "Good words all around, gentlemen. In a week or so, we will swing our good ship about and make lines fast to complete the careening. At that time, we will see our barque off with the men who have volunteered." He leaves unvoiced the question that several men share but keep to themselves—what if they don't obtain a sufficient number of volunteers? "Mr. Hawkins, will you see to the rest of the proposed crew and make sure they have sufficient arms and extra supplies in case there be a delay in their return?"

William rises. "Aye, General, as you wish." He, Fletcher, and Christopher Hayman walk away from the fire to inform the pilot, the giant black, and the other crew members of their proposed assignment. A few of the gentlemen remain around the fire eating, drinking, and holding a lighter discussion, some of which focuses on the comely native women in the village they have recently departed and in the multiple fishing camps on the headland.

"Since we already have one woman aboard, perhaps we should bargain for a few more," offers John Chester.

"And put poor Mr. Legee out of a job?" replies Manny Watkyns. "We already have people to serve our meals."

"You damn fool, that isn't what I had in mind for the fair lasses, but you probably wouldn't know about that, would you?"

William Legee, the steward, grins and regards John and Manny. "Gentlemen, if it please you, I would be happy to sit on my arse for a bit. Not that I mind serving you your fare, but I'd not mind a bit more leg to view until we make ready for the voyage home."

Laughter and good humor are evident along the beach while Francis, John, and Thomas Drake make their way to a tent by the water. They will be up at sunrise with much to do. Before retiring, John approaches his cousin, Francis.

"Sir, might I accompany the *Northern Venture* when she sails? I could continue my depictions of the coastline and assist Señor Morera with his charting duties."

The general puts his hand on the lad's shoulder and answers in a low, gentle voice. "If we were assured of the outcome, your offer would be well received, but they will be far removed from safety and any assistance we can provide. You will have an opportunity to map and illustrate the coast when we join them. In the meantime, I would like you to do something similar while we are here. This seems a fair harbor, one that might provide good future use. Go with two of our soldiers to the top of the bluff, and prepare a perspective view of this place, one we can present to the court on our return."

John smiles and bids goodnight. Although disappointed about not joining the barque's exploration, he will render a map and draw the bluffs and beach areas as requested.

The following day, Hawkins and Fletcher interview half of the combined crew of the ships and draw up a list of the designated crew for the *Northern Venture*. Besides Watkyns, Hayman, Gallawaye, and the pilot Morera, the proposed crew of twenty-one includes one of the *Hinde's* musicians, George Cooke, several sailors (William Haynes, Thomas Grige, Richard Morgyn, Little Nele the Fleming, Thomas Martyn, and John Deane), soldiers (John Cowrites, Luke Adden, Thomas Cuttyll, and Richard Graye), and general laborers who will be handy at building an outpost if needed (Nicholas Franconi, William "Old Bill" Whyte, Francis Caube, and Chrystopher Huntsman). Several of the men double as sailors and soldiers, and most are employed with construction chores while on land. The blacks, Big Tom and his friend Peter, are requested to join the exploratory group. The former evokes comments from several of the crew. "He can build an outpost single-handed." "An army all by himself." The *Northern Venture* crew comprises twenty-one men, not all of them true Englishmen, Drake notes.

CHAPTER 5

# Nova Albion

Two evenings later, Francisco and Maria sit next to Diego on a rock near the waterline. The waves gently lap the shore, and the sunset produces a soft, orange glow across the sand and into the conifers behind them. Diego has been quietly contemplating the ocean and enjoying the company of several patrolling plovers nearby.

Francisco and Diego became frequent conversants after the young man was liberated from a ship north of Paita, Peru, in February. Both are Cimarrones and share common experiences from when they were slaves in Panama. Francisco was sold to Gonzalo Alvarez and served aboard his coastal trader for two years. When Maria was introduced to the *Hinde* in April, Francisco took an immediate liking to her, and it was reciprocated. General Drake's admonition against crew fraternization with the young woman also applied to the blacks. Diego was her guardian, and they were allowed a common sleeping space, but he was prohibited from pursuing amorous adventures with the attractive lass. Drake made it a badge of honor, seconded by Fletcher, for the woman to remain safe from molestation. Unknown to all except Maria, she had already suffered that fate at the hands of her former owner, Don Francisco de Zarate.

She started to suspect she might be pregnant in early May while they were still in quiet, mid-Pacific waters. She was ill several mornings, but no one, including herself, had reason to believe that it was anything but seasickness. Her previous life at sea existed only on Zarate's merchant ship, mostly sailing in quieter coastal waters. Francisco also suffered several days of motion sickness during their initial outward journey from Mexico, but Maria missed two menstrual periods, something the twenty-two-year-old had never experienced. Now in her fourth month, there was no doubt. Her bulky clothes revealed nothing to others, but she could see her flat belly had begun to swell. The aches, cramps, and occasional nausea could no longer be regarded as change in diet or motion sickness. She confided in Francisco, telling him the only man she had laid with was her Spanish owner. The black man in his mid-twenties became the surrogate father and her consort, despite her guardianship by and proximity to Diego.

The trusted assistant to the general listens without comment or interruption as Francisco confides what Maria has told him. She sits to his left, head down and her shoulder against Francisco's side.

"What should we do? Maria will give birth before we return to England. Can it be possible at sea or aboard ship?" Francisco pleads their case to the one person he believes might be willing and capable of helping them.

Diego regards Maria who still has not said a word. He has grown fond of her. She is quiet but cheerful and has been a good companion during their strictly platonic relationship. He was previously married to an Indian woman in Panama but left her and his Central American life behind when he joined Drake. He easily understands Francisco's desire to protect the pretty, young black woman and possibly win her favor for the longer term.

Diego answers in a deep, gentle voice. "I don't believe the *Golden Hinde* is a proper place for a young mother, much less a nursing infant. There will be loose talk about the identity of the father. I have heard ugly rumors about her being a comfort, kept for the convenience of the officers, possibly for my captain. I know these to be false, for his heart in this matter is pure, and he enforces the same for his gentlemen." He looks into Maria's eyes. "None would dare touch you, but the sailors know nothing of this and will believe what they wish. They wish you could be theirs."

Maria looks up at him, alarm written on her face. "Please, Señor Diego. I did not wish to have this baby, especially not by such a man as the Zarate, a selfish evil one who showed only lust and no love for me or for the others aboard his ship. He treated Peter with much cruelty. If had not been for Tomas, I don't believe Peter would have survived."

Diego reaches across Francisco and touches her lightly on the shoulder. "We will work out something, I promise. It would be too cold for you here, so you should stay with us until we decide our route. If we can reach England from here in a few weeks, you can return with us. If we must take the longer route westward, we will find a safe place for you and your companions to stay." He looks at Francisco. "May I relate this to our leaders, Francis the general and Francis the priest? I will pick an appropriate time, but it should be before her condition becomes apparent to all."

They assure him they will abide by his judgment. Relieved to have an important ally at their side, Francisco and Maria walk slowly back to a larger group standing and sitting around one of several bonfires on the beach. Diego remains on the rock, meditating about the affairs of man, whether at war or at peace, facing life and death. He has learned much since joining the daring buccaneer, yet the adventure promises evermore to unveil mysteries and secrets. Maria's condition is but the latest and, he is certain, not the last.

---

THE CAREENING PROCEEDS AND ON 13 JULY, A MONDAY, IT IS time to turn the flagship around to scrub and caulk the port side. Once again, the *Venture* uses her leverage to bring the *Hinde* over while the tide is in, leaving it exposed at ebb tide. The men are about to begin the day's labor when canoes appear along the south border of the inlet. Like the earlier reception, the dozen or so craft move swiftly toward them. All the occupants remain seated until they are within fifty yards of the *Hinde*. Soldiers are summoned to positions along the beach, and a pinnace is made ready to intercept the canoes if necessary.

The canoes row swiftly pass the ships and stop a few yards from the beach. Accompanied by Diego and William Crowley, General Drake steps to the waterline to greet the arrivals. A relatively young warrior who is muscular and semi-naked stands and raises his hand. He speaks for several minutes, but as in earlier encounters, no one knows what he is reciting. Gallawaye joins Crowley, and they employ the gestures and words they have learned. After several minutes, the warrior indicates he understands.

"They are from a village south of our harbor but are related to some of the natives who fish here," Crowley says to Drake. "They have other villages scattered inland from here, some only a mile or two away."

Drake scowls and turns abruptly toward Crowley. "Despite our patrols, we didn't see any evidence of them. Were there no fires, no smoke?"

William makes more gestures and points at the surrounding forest and headland. The warrior points at the *Venture* and imitates the flapping motions of a bird with his arms.

"I may be mistaken, sir, but I think they put out their fires when we passed their village. From what I gather, it is located between the small bay we first passed and this one. We have been watched since we landed, but many of their people are afraid of us and our big canoes with wings."

Several warriors who are sitting but holding spears stare intently at Diego. They measure his size as they scan him from head to toe and, like the Muh-kwa, compare his skin color to the white men around him. Big Tom is out of sight, working inside the hull of the *Hinde*. Most of the soldiers have gathered behind the general. Some have muskets ready, but all are in relaxed postures as instructed while negotiations are in progress.

After conferring with William Hawkins and Thomas Hord, the general asks Crowley to welcome the natives to the beach. Crowley relays the message to the warrior and the warrior signals to his men. They paddle away from the beach and return south the way they came.

"Why were his people afraid of us but the people here were not?" asks Drake.

"It seems that fierce raiders from the north occasionally visit, kill some of the men, and take a few women and children as slaves. Their village was attacked last year at this time."

Thomas Hord turns toward the general. "To the north, he says. Should we send the *Venture* in that direction with twenty men and a few arms?"

Crowley interrupts. "These men will return tomorrow along with others of this area. We'll have a chance to find out more about the fierce ones. They call them Latch-Quill-Tak or something like that. They live in the northern lands and on the great island across the strait."

Drake's eyes open wide. "Island? The land across from us is surrounded by water?"

"Apparently so, sir. It is a large one inhabited by a number of different tribes. It seems that some are friendly and others not. We will need to speak at some length with our hosts to identify the differences."

The general and his council come to a unanimous decision that evening to delay the departure of the *Venture* and prepare for the expected second visit of the southern villagers. Although there is no indication of hostility from this native group, the Drake crew has not been invited to the village, and there is no definite plan for the next meeting. Crowley believes they will return, but with whom and what will result are open questions. Drake, Hawkins, and Hord have added concerns about the tribes on the other side of the strait and to the north. They instruct Crowley and Gallawaye to make every effort to learn what they can.

---

THE NEXT DAY DAWNS BRIGHT WITH ONLY AN OCCASIONAL PUFF of cloud—the wind is gentle and the strait waters calm. The return visit occurs shortly after noon. Work is underway on the *Hinde* but with greater urgency. The crew of the *Venture* stands on alert and has two cannons on the seaward side readied as a precaution. The news of other hostile tribes in the strait increases the need for military vigilance, but Drake and many of the professional soldiers in the crew feel more comfortable under such conditions. It has been several months since their last skirmish. Although no one desires hostilities, preparation brings a welcome and familiar sense of discipline that replaces passive waiting.

Canoes appear from the south the same time a group of natives files from the forest line. They gather near a sand embankment that forms the landward edge of the beach. None of the newcomers are recognizable from the canoe group that visited the day before or from the fishing camp on the headland. Gallawaye remains at the waterline with several of the men observing the approaching canoes. Drake, Crowley, and a number of soldiers intercept the other natives at mid-beach. Crowley steps forward and exchanges gestures with three of the natives in the vanguard. The three apparent leaders have animal pelts draped around their shoulders. All the others wear simple loincloths, and most are naked from the waist up. One who is older than the others sports a double-stranded necklace of tooth-shaped seashells. He listens as the other two exchange signs with Crowley, occasionally nodding or speaking with them.

Francis Fletcher is nearby, taking in as many details about the meeting as he can. Later, he prepares accounts of the Indians at Nova Albion that comprise a fanciful amalgam of fact and fiction. It is neither the first nor the last time he is cavalier with the truth in his "official" account of the voyage. Although perceptive and well meaning, he is prone to misinterpreting actions, especially the motives of the natives during their interactions with the white men.

The natives in the canoe join the group on the beach. After several minutes of discussion, William indicates that the southern natives are receptive to their presence but still in awe and uncertain as to what or who the white men represent. Both groups depart, but Crowley indicates they will return with their chief in a few days.

Fletcher is the first to interrogate the interpreter. "Do they think we are gods from the sea?"

"I'm not sure. They might think we be departed souls of their ancestors come to visit, like a haunting. Our white skins might make it look like we are dead. They took special notice of the blacks they saw. I wonder what they would have made of Tom." The giant has still not showed since their first reception on the point. Diego suggests he be kept in reserve in case they need him for something special but doesn't elaborate on what he has in mind by "special."

"Should we prepare a welcoming feast for our important visitors?" asks Hawkins. By this time, several of the gentlemen have gathered around Drake as an impromptu council. "We've managed to stock fresh game and fish, although we are still a bit short of vegetables."

Drake responds. "Not yet, Mr. Hawkins. I think we'll wait and see what develops. We can arrange a feast afterward when we know how many to prepare for and what is at stake. We should continue work on the *Hinde* and finish the fortification in case we need to defend the beach and our ships until we get the flagship raised and ready to sail." The general turns to his right. "Mr. Hord, until further notice, double the number of guards deployed, and urge them at their peril to remain alert. I will not have our new friends slipping past us at their leisure and without sufficient warning to affect an adequate defense." He glances around at the circle. "Are we in accord?"

The necessary preparations are instituted without delay: extra sentries, teams to cut and trim trees, and workmen to gather additional stones. Fortunately, the woods contain a number of limestone outcrops and other stones that the masons from the *Hinde* easily gather and shape. The resulting wall is three to four feet high and provides enough barrier for three dozen men to deploy along and crouch behind.

During the weekend, Nazario de Morera, selected to pilot the *Venture*, becomes increasingly depressed and complains of stomach pains. He has been in a sour mood for several days and makes it known to anyone who will listen that he is unhappy about being assigned to the barque. Morera knows that his best chance for survival is to remain with the *Hinde* for the time being. His intention is to desert before the ship sets sail across the Pacific.

Drake consults with William Hawkins and the chaplain. "What's this all about, Mr. Fletcher? Why is Nazario in such a state?"

"He believes himself ill and is complaining of bellyaches. He also tells me that this cold air is not to his liking, and he wishes to go no farther north."

"He won't be traveling that far north, only a couple of days or so. Have Perez provide him some of his magical tea. It seems to work for the dispositions of the others."

Hawkins regards the general and the chaplain. "Sir, if I may be so bold?"

"Speak, Mr. Hawkins. You know I always appreciate your good counsel."

"A disgruntled pilot might not be in the best interests of the *Venture's* mission. Since Mr. Gallawaye is an accomplished navigator, has experience as a pilot, and has some ability to communicate with foreigners, I suggest we relieve the Basque of his assignment. We best deal with Señor de Morera while close at hand." Hawkins doesn't need to remind them that Nazario is a Catholic. Fletcher and Drake are aware of the fact, but the Spanish pilot has never given any overt indication of disloyalty or rejecting the Protestant services aboard ship.

Drake thinks a moment and turns to the chaplain. "Inform Morera that he can remain with us, but keep a close watch on him. In the meantime, have him take the tea treatment."

Fletcher nods and goes to find Perez.

"Unless we replace the pilot, twenty men will man the Venture," states Hawkins.

Drake replies, "That should be sufficient for such a short journey."

By that evening, the roster of the *Northern Venture* has been finalized. Drake and the gentlemen eat and sleep aboard the *Ven-*

*ture*, lying on hides strewn on the open decks. Most of the sailors, soldiers, and the three blacks remain on the beach not far from the two pinnaces. Fletcher takes the opportunity to update his journal.

*Tuesday, 14 July 1579*

*Our schedule for exploration to discover the fabled passageway has been disrupted. We may be blessed with a favorable response by our new hosts, but the general, with wisdom I freely acknowledge, has taken precautions to defend our tenuous position that are necessary until our flagship can be righted and reloaded. This will require another week or longer even with extra shifts hard at labor. No one complains, as everyone from gentleman to slave, even the serving boys and musicians, is aware of the present danger and our vulnerability. I pray we enjoy the same success as before and that we may continue the search for which we have traveled thus.*

Wednesday morning arrives without fog as the sun rises over the eastern mountains. Work resumes on the *Hinde* and in the forest on the fortifications. The smell of hot pitch, transferred from shore to the side of the *Hinde*, wafts over the encampment, extinguishing the smell of grilled meat, a most welcome accompaniment to the biscuits and porridge that comprises most breakfasts at sea.

"They'll need and appreciate the extra food for what lies ahead," remarks Will Hawkins, and no one disagrees. The obvious blessing is the weather. It is mild and ideal for hard labor, especially for the scrapers and caulkers who are exposed to the sun on the outer hull or are inside the claustrophobic interior.

Big Tom sweats like a rainstorm inside the ship, but he is used to hard labor and inspires dedication to the task by those around him. From time to time, his deep baritone voice echoes throughout the hull with a boisterous shanty. No one understands the words, but Peter tells them it is a chant that black slaves used to sing when working on ships in the Caribbean. Extra water is made available for the interior hull workers, although one crewman jokes that all they need do is stand next to Tomas to get all of the water they need.

As the sun approaches its zenith, a horn sounds from one of the outer sentries. A second horn repeats the warning a few minutes later from a guard closer to the beach announcing the approach of a native party. A short blast indicates a slow, nonaggressive group; two blasts warn of a potentially hostile encounter. The fortification within the forest is nearly complete, and several soldiers pick up pikes and harquebuses to stand along the low wall. Trees have been removed behind them so they can be seen from the beach and the ships. Most of the *Hinde* and *Venture* crews are ashore and assemble around their general. Big Tom is in plain view.

The natives emerge slowly from the woods, walking along the trail in a stately fashion, heads held high, stepping carefully and looking forward. First comes a group of two dozen warriors who are mostly naked. Some wear a thin belt apparently made from a strip of hide or sinew around their waist. Strings with shells are attached to it, and some carry knives in sheaths. Several men have pelts across their shoulders, most of them made from the skins of the coney-like animals (muskrats) the white men commonly encounter in the marshes. All the men have painted their faces in white, black, and red. None carry additional weapons. Other natives look down on the scene from hills farther along the beach.

As the natives approach, they began to chant in a repetitious melodic fashion, and several of the lead men start dancing, hopping around in a circle on the sand. Other men who are more elaborately decorated with feathers stuck in their long, black hair appear on the trail. Most of them display double braids tied in the back, wear breechcloths, and have larger deerskin furs about their shoulders. The newcomers move to the forefront as the first men part to let them through. They come to a halt ten yards from the general and his councilmen, who remain motionless, flanked by soldiers with pikes and harquebuses.

William Crowley and John Gallawaye prepare to greet them, but yet another group of Indians arrives. One man carries a cane of black wood four feet long. He is followed by a large man with a knitted cap covering his dark hair. Interwoven through the knitting are plumes of birds and an array of seashells, especially those resembling teeth. He is dignified in posture and movement.

The staff carrier stops before the general and begins a long oration peppered with dramatic gestures and signs. This continues for twenty minutes while the general and his men wait patiently, never looking away from the orator. From time to time, the other natives utter a prolonged "oh" similar to the sound the group on the beach made during their first day at the bay. Otherwise, the Indians are silent and immobile. The chief, for that is what he appears to be, looks on as the ceremony continues and surveys the crew gathered behind the general. When the staff carrier finishes, he steps back but remains in front of the chief and two flanking warriors.

Drake signals to Crowley, and he moves forward. He is visibly sweating despite the cool breeze blowing in from the inlet. Gallawaye stays at Drake's side. William signs the usual peace gestures, announces his name, and introduces the general. While this is taking place, more men gather behind the native group. A number of women appear behind them. They are also naked from the waist up, although many wear shoulder pelts open in front to expose their breasts. After several minutes, the staff carrier motions for Crowley and Drake to sit. When they sit, the chief, his two bodyguards, and the staff carrier do likewise. No pelts are provided, but the sand is soft and warm.

During the conversation, which lasts for another hour, gifts are brought forward and presented to the general. Some are bunches of feathers tied with string. More common are the reed baskets and bowls, most of which contain herbs, dried fish, and other foods. In exchange, Drake has Crowley give them linens, shirts, and coins. Fletcher's clothing is meant for them to cover their nakedness, but none of the Indians use them for such. Later, the chaplain finds most of the clothes and linens hanging from poles or used to swaddle babies.

After the talk, the native men rise, signal farewell, and withdraw. The chief, his guards, and the staff carrier lead. As the men and women leave the beach, they chant but never look back at the white men waiting for Crowley's report. If the natives notice Big Tom or the other blacks at the edge of the assembled crew, they give no indication.

As protocol now dictates, William Crowley is presented with a fresh mug of ale to wet his throat and help him compose his report to the council. He drinks, smiles, and downs the rest of the mug, releasing a resounding burp while wiping his mouth and beard on his sleeve. "I believe we are in agreement, sir. They welcome us to their land and wish to visit with us during the days to come. We have also been invited to visit their largest village a mile up the trail from here tomorrow at noon." He glances over his shoulder, and a plume of smoke can be seen rising from the purported village location.

Drake turns to Thomas Hord and William Hawkins. "How many days before we can reload the *Hinde* and be ready to depart?"

"I make it six more days to finish the repairs and three days to place all things aboard," replies Thomas.

"That will put us at the morning of the twenty-fourth of July, a Friday," adds William.

Hord looks around at the council. As most of them are present, he believes it is a good time to resolve unfinished business. "Should we dispatch the *Venture*? Do we dare send them before the *Hinde* is ready, and if so, should they sail north?"

Drake renders the executive decision without delay. "Let us retain the crew we selected and prepare our barque to make its exploratory probe northward. If there are no untoward behaviors from our native hosts, we can send them on their way after we visit the village tomorrow. If they succeed in finding a likely passage, they are to return, and we will follow them. If not, we will decide whether to establish an outpost here or at some point south along the outer coast."

## New Albion Sunset

Drake addresses Hayman, Gallawaye, and Watkyns. "Gentlemen, it is understood that when you sail forth, you will keep a prudent distance between your ship and shore. You will be alert and ready to repel any would-be boarders. If Mr. Gallawaye can negotiate safe passage through their waters, all the better, but make every attempt to refrain from going ashore. You will be provided with sufficient food and water for ten days. Make plans to sail on Saturday, and return here by noon on the twenty-third. If we need to sail together to the outer coast, we will leave here the following day. If we decide to establish our outpost here, the *Hinde* will still sail on the twenty-fourth.

"Although this is the plan that was discussed and agreed upon, it should be well understood that other courses of action are possible. If the passage is present and navigable, the *Hinde* and *Venture* will return to England together. If passage via a northern route is not feasible, the *Hinde* will sail to the coast and prepare for the longer circumnavigation across the Pacific Ocean. The *Venture* and its crew will remain in the present location or, more likely, follow the *Hinde* and establish an outpost along the Pacific coast but well north of Spanish detection and interference."

Hawkins has a troubling thought as he regards Hayman. "Suppose the barque is unable for one reason or another to return to us. Not questioning your experience or abilities, Commander, but we need to know the nature of our response."

Hayman answers the master seaman, "No offense taken, Mister Hawkins. A clear course of action should be known by all."

Drake ponders the question before answering. "If the weather be fair, I would expect the *Venture* to travel no more than two days north before turning back, passage or no passage. Providing two extra days for mishaps or unforeseen delays provides an allotted time of six days from when the *Venture* leaves. Therefore, the *Hinde's* scheduled departure requires the barque to return by the following Thursday. If no contact results, we will sail for the outer coast by noon on Friday. If they do not return by then, they will be on their own. If they survive the mishap or disaster that delayed them, they will need to establish whatever they can of a fortified outpost and wait for our return. That can be here in the inland sea or on the ocean coast. It will be at least a year before we reach home port. Provided we can muster the support for our return, and if we need to sail back across the Indian and Pacific Oceans, it might be as long as three years before we bring relief." He looks at Hayman for comment. "Does this timeline seem unduly harsh, Mr. Hayman?"

"No, sir. I understand the need for you to be underway. You also have peril in your path. The *Golden Hinde* and crew is rightly your primary concern and responsibility. The *Northern Venture* will be mine." His eyes are steady.

The council is satisfied with the plan. Although not as satisfactory as all would have liked, it is the only reasonable one under the circumstances.

---

Displaying high spirits, Tom Moone chats with several of his mates. Drake is nearby, observing the careening with his brother Thomas. "It must be a good sign, lads," grins Tom, "to see those bright white cliffs up the coast. If I hadn't known it, I would have sworn we were off our own merry coast. Not as high as the cliffs of Dover, but it's a bit of England for the eyes, for sure."

"My thoughts exactly," responds Andy McGuane. "Almost brought a tear to my eye. Now if there had been a bit of the highland in view, I might have been sobbin' like the drunk I know you to be."

Thomas Drake looks at his brother. "Do you think that is a coincidence? The cliffs are white. They must contain some of the same chalky limestone as those on our shore."

Francis experienced a similar reaction when he saw the cliffs during their earlier brief trip up the strait. The exposed outcroppings were prominent, especially when lit by the afternoon sun. Whether by luck or providence, he decides the white cliffs might provide a further rallying point for the expedition. He faces Thomas.

"What say you to a different yet significant name for this place, this harbor and the surrounding land? What about Albion to mark the white seaside and a reminder of our country's ancient namesake?"

Thomas regards him with surprise. "Didn't we propose to christen this country Elizabeth Land?"

"Yes, when we first entered the seaward passage and before we saw the interior. I believe that Albion—better yet, Nova Albion—will more aptly describe the landscape and commemorate its future connection with England. We will name the strait and perhaps one or more rivers or bays after Her Majesty. Nova Albion shall appear on an inscribed plate to mark our presence." A brief consultation with his council affirms the designated name.

That afternoon, Drake and Hawkins instruct the chief metal worker aboard the *Hinde* to cut and inscribe a rectangular metal plate, several inches in height and a few more in width, to serve as evidence of the English claim to the uncharted lands as Nova Albion.

---

THE NEXT DAY AT MIDMORNING, DRAKE, THREE OF HIS GENTLEmen, and several armed soldiers follow two warriors up the trail from the beach and into the forest. Lawrence Elyot, eager as always to observe the landscape and its attendant fauna and flora, totes a bag of gifts. Fletcher is in the group, prepared to take note of the village, and Crowley and Gallawaye attend as interpreters.

The Semiahmoo village is similar but not identical to the Muh-Kwa settlement. Although not nearly as grand or permanent in appearance, it is substantial. The rectangular houses consist of cedar planks. Some dwellings are rounded and constructed of hides stretched over frame poles to form a cone with a smoke hole at the top. People sleep on reeds or hides on top of platforms attached to the inner periphery. They store baskets, nets, and other materials on shelves above their beds and store firewood below the platforms. One larger building is reserved for the chief and his immediate retinue.

The visit goes well, gifts are exchanged, and Crowley indicates that the relationship between the tribe and the white men appears well founded. Only one shadow pokes its head above the sea of tranquility. According to the interpreter, the tribe is under the impression that the white men are there to stay. They have no knowledge of plans for the *Hinde* to depart and no idea about the arrival of other white men in the future. Drake decides not to enlighten them on either score.

Crowley inquires at length about the tribes to the north and west. The elders acknowledge the need for caution, and a few show alarm when William indicates that the smaller ship plans to sail up the strait to investigate the waterway. The Semiahmoo offer to send a few warriors with them, but Drake politely declines. He does not want to complicate operations aboard the barque or be responsible for the natives' safety.

---

Friday dawns again without fog, a bright clear day. The work on the *Hinde* is almost complete, and reloading is anticipated within a few days. Drake assembles his men at midafternoon on the beach, save a few outlying sentries. An imposing post stands near the forest edge, cut from a medium-sized fir, sized to ten feet in length, and erected the evening before. It rises in front of a four-foot embankment and well back from the highest visible tide line.

Thomas Cuttyll stands next to the general, holding the tin-bronze-lead plate in his hands. Inscribed on it are the name of Her Majesty, Queen Elizabeth of England, the date, Drake's claim to possession of a land to be known as Nova Albion, and the general's name. At Drake's signal, Cuttyll affixes the plate to the post with a spike. William Hawkins holds out a silver sixpence bearing a crude likeness of the Queen's image in profile. This is attached to the plate with an additional spike. A small flag with a St. George's cross hangs limply at the top of the pole. General Drake announces the claim for England over the land before them and extending in all directions for several hundred leagues. In a clear, loud voice, he tells the assembly, "Let this be for after known as New Albion to the glory of Her Majesty, Queen Elizabeth." It requires less than three minutes to attach the plaque and coin and say the few words that, in the English view, establish a North American presence. After George Cooke plays a solemn tune on his flute, Drake requests a blessing.

Francis Fletcher walks to the post, turns to face the crowd, and speaks in a clear voice, invoking God's assistance and continued guidance on their expedition. He mention the sacrifices made by members of the crew, avoiding the name of Thomas Doughty. He prays for the crews of the *Elizabeth* and the *Marigold* from who they still have no word. Finally, he asks for God's care of the crew of the *Northern Venture* in their forthcoming exploration. The crowd voices amen, several soldiers and sailors lead three cheers for New Albion, and the assembly disperses.

A large group of natives, including women and children, watches from the top of the neighboring highlands. A small group of warriors stands apart from the white men on the beach and observes the ceremony with silent curiosity. Crowley knows there will be additional questions to answer. Fletcher will later write in his official journal that the natives have freely surrendered their sovereignty to the English general, making him their high chief. In reality, Drake knows the natives have no idea of land ownership, much less the notion that it can or should be given to foreigners, whether they are gods or mortals. However, the rites serve a purpose, as all ceremonies do. The crew is heartened by this symbolic show of effort made and sacrifice rewarded. The physical presence of flag and coin represent pride and payment for the hardships and tragedies suffered, and they help to validate the promises and future labors that will come. The other significant effect of the ritual is the noticeable increase in energy that characterizes the last few days of work on the flagship and, after the *Hinde* is righted, the reloading of cannons, supplies, and the majority of the treasure.

After considerable deliberation, the council decided on the night before what to do with the thousands of pounds of silver bars, coins, and plateware on the *Venture*. Some of the ornate silver that had adorned wealthy Spanish tables and churches was included in the stores of the *Hinde* for return to England, but the flagship could not carry most of the metal that had been transported by the barque. Since the *Venture* would be searching for the passage in uncharted waters, it will be safer and less cumbersome if it is not fully loaded. After a full meal, much wine and further discussion, the plan materialized and Francis Drake approved it.

While Drake and his party visited the native village on Thursday, a crew prepared an area near the forest edge. Several guards maintained a perimeter so native eyes didn't observe. Twenty yards past the beachfront tree line was a natural partial clearing containing two medium-sized boulders. Workers placed these on each side of the clearing to mark its location. They carefully removed bushes from the clearing and dug a large pit in the sandy soil several feet wide, four yards long, and seven feet deep. The *Venture's* silver was stacked on a broad sheet of sailcloth and tied at the top. After lowering the treasure into the hole, they filled it with sand and carefully smoothed it over. They scattered the brush and bushes about the clearing and dispersed the extra sand along the beach. No natives appeared while they worked, and by late afternoon, the task was complete.

The claim pole erected Thursday evening was placed so that its afternoon shadow marked the direction of the clearing in the forest beyond. The pole will still point between the two stones even after the shadow shifts direction with the changing seasons.

---

By nautical time, 19 July begins at noon on Saturday rather than at midnight twelve hours earlier. Although Fletcher maintains his diary in civil time, the official rutters are kept by the clock of the seas, starting each day at high noon. Most of the crew of the *Northern Venture* gather on the beach before a pinnace. A few of the sailors are already aboard the barque. Big Tom stands proudly next to Commander Hayman, smiling at everyone around him. Peter is beside him, ready to communicate between Tomas and the crew in Spanish, although the giant now understands and speaks several phrases of English. Diego and Maria offer smiles and waves, wishing them good fortune.

Drake and Hawkins chat with Christopher Hayman and John Gallawaye for a few minutes, and several sailors and soldiers make their farewells to their comrades. Although the trip is designed for four days total, it seems to many they are preparing for a much longer voyage.

Friends surround the New Albion Company, as they are now designated, to congratulate them or commiserate, depending on their view of the departure. Although all of the barque's crew had volunteered, some did so under peer pressure, others only for the promised bonus of silver, and others for personal reasons they were reluctant to reveal. Three of them are closet papists who are relieved to be free from Drake and his chaplain. One of them has become enamored of the native women in the Muh-kwa village and hopes to return and bargain for a wife. Several of them anticipate poor futures when they return home. Their best chance of earning a living has been with Drake's adventure even when it was disguised as a Mediterranean trading mission. Whether they return or forge a new life in a new land is more a matter of convenience than a viable option for success.

Morera has his own thoughts on the matter. He silently vows never to set foot on the deck of the barque again. He has no delusions about crossing the Pacific with the *Hinde*. He knows the Drake group will need to make landfall at least once more to store provisions for the long open-ocean crossing. Late summer or early autumn will be better weather for venturing across the expanse, past the time for the typhoons that rage in the western waters near Filipinas. He will make his move at the appropriate time and place.

One last time, Drake reminds Hayman and Gallawaye that the *Hinde* will sail west for the Pacific and prepare for the long crossing to home if they don't hear from the *Venture* by noon on the twenty-fourth, the following Friday, becoming the twenty-fifth at noon. The general speaks in decisive terms. "We'll make one last provisioning stop for a week or two along the coast wherever we find a snug harbor. We will stay north of 40°N if possible to avoid any galleon that might be coming from Manila. By mid-August at the latest, we should be on our way to the East Indies. God willing, we expect to see you before Thursday, and if the news is what we hope for, we shall be sailing to England together."

"After we dig the silver up," laughs Gallawaye.

There is a slight smile on Hayman's face, but the general displays not a trace of humor. "May that be our fate. If not, it will be your mission to survive and keep the treasure and the Port of Nova Albion secure until our return. If you cannot return to or remain at our harbor, may God guide you and keep you wherever you find yourself. You will not be forgotten." They shake hands, and Fletcher, standing by with a prayer book, pronounces the final blessings as they climb aboard the pinnace. There are cheers from the crew on the beach and those aboard the *Hinde*. A number of natives have gathered. Crowley has informed them the smaller ship will be leaving and returning, but he makes no mention of the plans for the *Hinde*.

The pinnace and its men board the barque. The crew lines up at the rail to wave farewell, and the anchor is raised. A half an hour later, the *Northern Venture* rounds the western headland of the bay and slips from view. John Drake walks up the trail to a bluff overlooking the beach and harbor, sketchpad in hand, accompanied by soldiers. He watches the barque making its way along the eastern shore of the broad strait as he sits down to produce a perspective sketch of their fair harbor.

During the next several days, the Indians visit the encampment. They come in smaller numbers, and every three days, they return with gifts similar to what they bestowed before. Some of the women attempt to talk with Maria, but she isn't able to do more than smile and occasionally accept a basket. Crowley gives her a few coins and beads with which to reciprocate. The waiting game for the return of the *Venture* is on.

CHAPTER 6

# The *Northern Venture*

⎯⎯⎯∞∞∞⎯⎯⎯

The *Northern Venture* sails past the point of earlier exploration as Gallawaye records the outlets of rivers, islands, and bays along the eastern shore. One of these, a broad delta with several large and small islands, seems promising, and the barque enters the inlet. It lies in a north-by-northeast direction, but within twenty miles, the bay narrows and the river, for such it is, begins climbing into the bordering mountains. By evening, soundings indicate that no further progress will be possible. They drift downstream for two hours before casting anchor, not wishing to risk a collision in the dark.

Christopher Hayman and John Gallawaye confer in the captain's cabin. Watkyns joins them but has little to say about navigational decisions. All express disappointment that the broader strait continues in a decidedly northwest direction, but for how long? They discuss the large river they passed on the first day in the strait and on this day.

"It also runs eastward and it's wide, but the current flows strong. Must be another mountain-fed stream, not a passageway," observes Hayman.

"I agree," says Gallawaye, nursing a glass of port. "We shouldn't waste time or effort on these. We can sail at dawn and continue up the main strait until dusk, making note of likely openings. That will give us time to explore one or two of the best possibilities before returning to our harbor."

Big Tom and Peter relax and talk on the open deck where they have pitched their bedding. "I like this place. I feel good here, maybe to stay," says the giant. "Find me a brown woman and have many kids. Go fishing forever." He laughs from his belly, a good-natured sound that bellows and is enhanced by the broad smile of a face that greets each day with boyish enthusiasm.

Peter chuckles, enjoying the company of a man who holds no bitterness about his past. "You think there be women for me, Big Tom?"

"Women? You want more than one?" Big Tom produces another hearty laugh. "Sure, why not? There be plenty just like for the white men. They take whatever they want. We be like them."

"You really gonna stay? Just like that? Even if we can go to England with the other ship?"

"I don't know. Maybe. Maybe they need some people to stay behind and protect the land. Save it for the Queen. Maybe save it for the general." He gives Peter a sly grin. "Maybe save it for Tom and Peter."

"It could be very cold here, Tomas. Diego told me this now is the warmest time. Maybe too cold for you and me."

"Maybe we need deer or bear skins to wrap up our bodies. Maybe we need many women to stay warm."

---

The next day, a Sunday, brings heavy cloud cover blowing from the west. After Gallawaye leads a brief shipboard service, they are underway. It rains steadily for the first two hours after sunrise, and the sea turns choppy, but full sails speed them on their way up the strait, still tracking northwestward. There are other inlets and islands, but none of the openings seem to offer hope for a waterway to the north or east.

Manny Watkyns watches the barque's progress from the midship starboard rail. He talks to Hayman and Gallawaye frequently and dines with them but stays out of their way when the ship is under sail. He is friendly and open with the crew, and the relationships

87

between the barque's officers and the others are informal. Despite the uncertainty of what they will find, Manny is at ease. With each day, his confidence in the expedition increases, and he sees himself as an integral part of the new English territory. *Watkyns of New Albion. It has a nice touch if I do say so myself.*

By midmorning, running with a moderate northern current, they pass along the east side of a long island or peninsula, they aren't sure which, also trending in a northwest direction. There are additional mainland inlets. All but one appears to be shallow or an obvious river outlet. They enter the deepest inlet and record its depths, but within a few miles, the opposing flow indicates it too is a river. They turn about, exit the inlet and continue in the narrow channel between the mainland to their east and the wooded land to their west. At noon, the latitude reading indicates they are approaching 50°N when they clear the northern tip of what is now seen to be an island. Once again they have a view of the larger strait to the west. Ahead, the broad passage to the north appears to be a cul-de-sac, blocked by land. They approach what appears to be the terminus of the strait. Off their portside, a narrower passage continues in a northwest direction. There are several bays and inlets, interspersed with islands big and small, to the north and northeast.

Hayman and Gallawaye discuss their options as gentle afternoon breezes blow across the deck. The anchor has not been dropped, and the barque is drifting slowly toward the north and into a large bay several miles across.

Gallawaye scans the horizon in all directions. "The channel on our portside may be navigable, but its direction leads us away from our objective. The large bay at our bow allows us to maintain a prudent distance from shore." During the day, they spot occasional plumes of smoke on both the eastern and western shores of the strait. They have no way of knowing if these represent hostile or potentially friendly tribes, but the waterway is their primary mission. Find it and return.

With a few hours of daylight remaining, they enter the large bay and proceed toward a smaller bay at its northeastern end. The water becomes shallower, but there is no strong opposing current. Perhaps they have finally discovered a waterway that isn't a river. Numerous islands are scattered about the shores. The *Venture* continues in the same direction until the pending darkness dictates a halt for the night. They drop anchor several hundred yards from both shores and post two guards for each shift. The moon is less than a quarter phase, and fog obscures the little bit of light it might have provided.

The next morning, they lift anchor and sail deeper into the mainland, pleased to continue the general northeast trend. Directly ahead lays a point of land, probably another island, with channels forking to the left and right. Another decision. Gallawaye expresses a desire to try the right fork, but Hayman points out increasing sediment and a detectable current, signs of a river mouth. "The channel to our left is broader, and the northwest direction might hold only for a short distance. If it proves to be false, we can return to your preference." Hayman gives his second a reassuring pat on the shoulder to indicate that his authority to lead is not meant to be dictatorial.

Gallawaye shrugs and smiles. "Every road is an unknown, so let us investigate and pray we have found the right one, whether it be left or right." He smiles at his wordplay.

After two hours of careful sailing and sounding, the channel turns north and continues for several miles before assuming the hoped-for northeast vector. They have been blessed with good weather, and their noon reading indicates they have reached 50.4°N. Speculation by many cartographic authorities placed the Strait of Anián at anywhere from 44°N to 68°N, so they know their present position is not unreasonable with regard to expectations.

"Do we dare go farther?" asks Gallawaye. He and the commander stand on the aft deck surveying the high, snow-capped mountains around them. They can see the channel a mile ahead curving to the north, but it is broad and exhibits only a slight opposing current. It is midafternoon, and a decision whether or not to return will need to be made soon.

Hayman is not convinced they have found *the* northern passage. "If we bring the *Hinde* to this place and it is a blind end, another mountain river, it will greatly delay their Pacific crossing and return. I doubt the admiral will be overly pleased if this proves to be false."

"True, but the decision will not be ours. We can report what we found without conclusions or recommendations. We don't know that this is the mysterious strait, but we can describe what we have seen and learned. It may be that General Drake will continue with his plan to depart as scheduled but leave us to continue further exploration here or elsewhere along the coast." Hayman acknowledges the wisdom of Gallawaye's advice, and they decide to swing about and return to the Port of New Albion.

Acting as pilot, Gallawaye has been sketching the eastern coast of the mainland and the islands and channels of the inlets as they sail north. He consults with the appointed leader of the New Albion Company. Although Manny leaves the navigation decisions to the two men in charge of the *Venture*, he readily agrees to their decision to return to the harbor.

Proceeding south in the channel, they approach the island that had marked the northeastern turn. At this critical juncture they make a navigational error, one they will long remember. They are no longer taking soundings but have swung to the starboard, preparing to tack across the channel to the eastern shore. As the order to turn reaches Little Nele at the whipstaff, the barque lurches and comes to a sudden stop. The slight downstream current pushes them farther into a sandbar bordering the western bank on the passage. They are only twenty yards from the shoreline, which is mainly wooded but includes a short stretch of exposed beach.

"No time to lose, men. Launch the pinnace," orders Hayman. John Deane and Richard Morgyn, accompanied by Big Tom and Peter, drop the pinnace over the side and climb in, intending to help tow the ship out from the bar. Using a sturdy rope, John and Richard pull the bow of the barque back and away while Tom and Peter row with all of their combined strength. The slight current helps once the ship loosens from the sediment and begins to drift downstream, but the bow once again digs into the bar. The pinnace swings back to the starboard side to pick up additional men to row and use poles to push against the shore. Exhausted from their efforts, Deane and Morgyn climb onto the barque.

Richard Graye, one of the highly competent soldiers with a harquebus, stands guard on the shoreline. He is joined by several other soldiers, and they alternate between the hard work of trying to move the barque and remaining alert.

There is no sign of people, but Commander Hayman is uneasy. It is already late in the afternoon, and they had hoped to be out of the bay system and back in the strait well before nightfall. "We have been strongly cautioned about going ashore, but we have little choice. I know we have three days to return but I don't want to tarry any more than necessary." He looks at the lieutenant, but Gallawaye appears lost in thought and doesn't reply.

The men continue their labors, and the barque slowly begins to display movement. Aided by Thomas Martyn and Francis Caube, Big Tom and Peter give a shout as the *Venture* begins to float off the bar. They join Luke Adden, John Cowrites, and Richard Graye on the beach and start for the pinnace twenty yards from where they were working.

A scream pierces the air, and dozens of warriors burst from the woods with clubs and knives. There is no hesitation in their charge toward the stunned white men standing a few yards from the pinnace.

Walking in front of the group and carrying a harquebus, John Cowrites attempts to bring it to his shoulder, but he is overwhelmed in an instant as two natives fall on him, pushing the hapless soldier into the sand while clubbing him viciously about the head. Richard Graye orders the men into the pinnace, priming his musket as the natives advance, now stalking rather than rushing at them. Caube reaches the boat first, clambers to the stern, grabs an oar, and faces the attack.

Richard Graye is able to get off a shot that hits one of the warriors in the chest and knocks him backward. Whether it is the smoke, the loud report, or the unexpected result of a strange weapon, the natives pause to look at their fallen comrade. This gives the men the precious moments they need to reach the boat and grab oars. Martyn stays in front of the boat with a drawn sword to buy time as the men ready to push off. Four other men, including Big Tom and Peter, are still engaged with the natives.

The two unarmed blacks are fighting hand to hand a few yards from the boat, protecting their right flank. The giant has his right hand around the neck of a brave who recklessly charged him with a club. Using his left arm, he clubs the attacker's head, and a loud snap is heard. Tomas drops the Indian, his neck twisted at a grotesque angle. He is prepared to take on another when Peter lets out a cry and drops to his knees, a bloody gash across the right side of his face. Another warrior with a black stone knife is standing over him, ready to strike again. Tomas jumps over Peter and knocks the Indian back but not before suffering a slash to his left shoulder. Enraged, the black falls upon the brave and smashes him in the face with his right fist, breaking his skull. Tomas picks up the knife with his left hand and turns. Seeing that Peter has crumpled to the sand, he grabs him with his right arm and half carries, half drags him to the boat.

Richard Graye and Luke Adden retreat toward the launch using swords to fend off five natives who recovered from the novelty of the gunshot. A second shot from Martyn in the boat thunders across the beach, and one of the five natives falls to his knees, clutching his stomach. As the other four hesitate, Graye turns and runs toward the pinnace. Luke, a burly Irishman with years of military experience, is not as fast or fortunate. A club thrown from some distance catches him on the side of the head, and he sinks to his knees, his sword pointed at the four facing him. They jump around the sword, dispatch the dazed soldier, and run toward the boat, yelling as they advance. Gray climbs into the boat as the oars strike the water and the pinnace pulls away from the beach. The natives line up along the shore, wade in to their waists, and yell with their hands over their heads.

As they make their way toward the *Venture*, the crew can see the bodies of their two companions on the beach. At the moment, there is no way to retrieve them or give them a proper Christian burial, another grim reminder of the disaster at Mocha in the South Sea.

Chrystopher Huntsman is repairing a sail line aboard the deck when he hears the first gunshot of the skirmish. He calls to his mates, and they witness the brief but violent action that follows. There is no time to man the cannons, nor are the guns aligned with regard to the warriors on the beach. As the pinnace approaches the ship, they make ready to help the men board. A few minutes later, they haul the pinnace on deck. Some of the men have a few scrapes and minor cuts. Big Tom has a deeper cut from the stone knife that remains in his possession. The shiny, black knife has an extremely sharp edge and is a lethal weapon by any measure. The big black's concern is not for himself, however. Peter lies bleeding profusely from wounds across his neck, face, and left temple. He is barely conscious as they carry him to a raised platform on the deck and lay him on a large pelt, one of the gifts from the Muh-kwa. Big Tom kneels beside him, tears in his eyes as he holds his friend's smaller hand gently in his big fist. George Cooke tries to comfort Tom, but John Gallawaye crouches beside him and is able to say a few words that the giant understands.

A few minutes later, Hayman, Gallawaye and Watkyns stand at the rail, facing the beach. The natives have gathered in a cluster and are slowly moving back to the forest's edge. They pick up their own fallen fellows, but the white men remain where they dropped. It is early evening, and fog is beginning to descend as the air cools.

"Do we risk going back for Adden and Cowrites?" asks Manny.

The commander thinks a moment. "Not yet, Mr. Watkyns. Let's see what the bastards do next. We don't know how many of them there might be. If we arm the men with muskets, we might be able to hold them off long enough to get our boys." He looks over at Peter and the men gathered around him. "We have no one skilled in treating the wounded. John Cowrites was the only other man among us who had a trace of the healing knowledge. The poor black is in God's hands now."

As the natives disappear into the forest, the commander faces his men on the deck and announces his decision. "If we see no further signs of the natives, we will return to the beach in a short while. This time we will not be taken by surprise, and we will recover the bodies of our shipmates, our friends. Even Mr. Crowley would not have been able to forestall this sudden, violent assault. Perhaps we have been naïve and spoiled by the benevolence of our earlier welcomes in the Muh-kwa and Semiahmoo villages. Now we must do what needs to be done here and rejoin the company of the *Hinde* without delay."

The sun descends toward the horizon while the crew prepares to go ashore and makes the barque ready for the journey back to the outer strait. No natives return to the beach while Thomas Martyn and Richard Graye keep watch. A few minutes later, an armed party of fifteen pushes off in the pinnace, leaving Big Tom and George Cooke to guard the ship. Neither one wants to leave Peter alone.

They row quietly, conversation curtailed and their eyes scanning the forest boundary. There are only seven harquebuses available, but all are primed for firing. Each man also has a sword and a long knife. They beach the boat and carefully step ashore. Holding their harquebuses at the ready as they walk toward the body of Luke Adden, they confirm that he is dead. Three of the men without muskets pick up Luke's body and bring it to the launch. They return to the rest of the men standing between John Cowrites and the beach embankment, pick up his body, and lay it in the boat beside Adden's corpse.

"Let's get the hell out of here," remarks Hayman as they climb into the pinnace and put oars to water. None of the natives reappear during the few minutes required to retrieve their shipmates.

"We can give them a proper burial at the Port of New Albion. The first of our kind to die in this land," says Gallawaye as they near their ship.

"May they be the last," adds Little Nele.

The evening ends as the sun lights the tops of dark trees and distant mountains. The present serenity belies the violent tragedy of two hours earlier. In silence, they bring the pinnace and the two bodies onto the deck of the ship.

The first thing the returning group encounters is the death of Peter. Big Tom sits in a corner, head down and his face wet with tears. He is neither fierce and formidable nor the jolly black giant. He is inconsolable.

George shrugs and faces the commander. "Sir, poor Peter has passed on, God save his soul, and poor Tomas, he will die of a broken heart if we neglect him to it."

The bodies of Cowrites and Adden are placed next to Peter. Hayman and Gallawaye are considering their next move when a loud shout from the bow breaks the silence. "Canoes approaching from downriver, Commander, many canoes!"

The men rush forward to the port rail to witness a sight that none wished to see. At least twenty canoes are spread across the passage and heading their way. Each canoe contains a dozen men armed with spears—some may have bows. It is difficult to discern details because of the distance and growing darkness, but the objective of the arriving party is not in doubt.

"All hands to the ship. Get us under way," cries Hayman, an order that needs no repetition. Each of the crewmen—sailor, soldier, or general laborer—knows his role, and they quickly raise the anchor and unfurl the sails. Little Nele takes the whipstaff, and the barque begins slowly moving toward the approaching canoes. There is no other route to safety. They will need to ram through the assault and fend off any natives who attempt to board. At the same time, they must dodge incoming spears or arrows, for they can now see that several of the men in each canoe are so armed.

By the time the canoes are within range with the native's weapons, the barque is well underway. The rope ladders have been withdrawn, and several men stand by to repel any would-be boarders. Thomas Cuttyll and Nicholas Franconi are ready with muskets, but they aren't required. The ship pushes past the screaming and gesturing natives. It receives two spears and a few arrows into the hull, deck, and main mast. None of the missiles hit the barque's crew, and the ship passes the small flotilla quickly and moves to the fork in the channels where they had decided to take the fateful left turn. When they glance back at the beach where they were attacked, they can barely discern the natives standing at the water's edge.

Emmanuel Watkyns stands at the middle of the aft deck out of the way of the working sailors. It gives him time to reflect on how close they have come to total disaster and to renew his admiration for the competent leadership of Commander Hayman and Lieutenant Gallawaye. *All the men showed courage and responded decisively. General Drake and his council chose well. We are still alive. However, we can't be sure we have located the critical passageway. It might still be up here somewhere—one of these inlets or an open sea beyond the northern land mass we observed yesterday. As we were warned, these lands are occupied by a fierce people not disposed to let us intrude, even in passage. Now when we return to the port, it will be my turn to display courage and leadership. We will need to survive, possibly for several years, in our harbor in the south, wherever it may be. Fortunately, we appear to have good allies in the natives of the bay where we staked our claim. We will no doubt need them. The immediate task at hand is to return to our bay before the* Hinde *sails. Barring other mishaps, we should have adequate time.*

Relief fills the hearts of the crew as the *Northern Venture* sails south down the inlet to the wide, yet-unnamed strait. It is an ignominious and sudden end to their dream of glory: being the first to challenge the Spanish in the heart of their Pacific empire. Now they are reduced to fleeing for their lives, hoping to rejoin their companions and eventually return home. The downriver trip is hampered by a steady headwind as they tack toward the shallow bay at the head of the strait. Night falls before they can clear the passage's outlet and reach the strait proper. They anchor well off from either shore and post four sentries for each shift. The moon is a waning sliver, and an incoming fog hampers visibility.

"This climate be damned," exclaims Gallawaye as he joins the commander for a late-night snack. "The more I see it, feel it in my bones, the less I want of it, New Albion or not."

"It seemed better at the harbor, but this is still summer." Hayman pauses. "I think. Maybe everything is reversed on this side of the world. Maybe we are turned upside down and don't know it."

Gallawaye smiles, knowing that the length of day doesn't lie. Still, he wishes for a more temperate locale, especially if there is any possibility of remaining for an extended time. He has decided to suggest they relocate farther south, well apart from detection by the Spaniards but removed from the coastal fogs and bitter cold winds that have plagued much of their travel in the northern latitudes.

"We will still be on the back side of Labrador, wherever our Ships Land be situated," Hayman notes, using the designations that circulated among the general's council before New Albion was proposed. As if reading his lieutenant's mind, he adds, "I would prefer a warmer setting for our outpost if it comes to that. We can still explore the waters south of our port. Who knows—perhaps we will find our fabled passage there." He smiles at his second-in-command, happy to have his company rather than the morose pilot Nazario. "By the way, why did you volunteer to come along?"

"I'm not as sure now as I was then. I was sober, I remember that. I thought we would find the northern passageway we sought. It was a chance to see something new." He thinks about the attack and the loss of three men. "I will always see those two lying on the beach and Peter dying in Big Tom's arms. It wasn't what I had in mind, sir."

"Forget the sir, John. Despite my title, you are every bit my equal and a lot better as a navigator. I regret that you had to witness what happened today, but I am very pleased to have you aboard."

A knock on the open door announces Watkyns' arrival. He sits with them, holding a bottle of wine. "Not too much, gentlemen. I know we all need to maintain clear heads for the coming days, but I thought a drop or two would help ease the pain of the day's events."

Hayman rises and retrieves three cups. "Indeed, sir, it will be most welcome. I am always pleased to have you join us." He pours wine for each, and they enjoy a brief toast and sip the secke as they discuss the day. There is no blame to cast, no recriminations—all share in the responsibility for the common tragedy.

As they finish the dry white liquid, it occurs to John that his prayers for good keeping that morning were not answered. *Have I found disfavor among our heavenly protectors?*

---

THE NIGHT FOG IS A HARBINGER OF THE DAY TO COME. THEY can barely determine that the sun has risen over the eastern mountains. They can't see the peaks, the bay in front of them, or either shore. If a canoe were twenty yards off their side, it would be invisible. The wind is almost absent, a slight breeze that barely flutters the English flag.

"I suggest we pull anchor and drift with the foresail until this fog lifts or we reach the broader strait," says Gallawaye. The remark comes after a light and hurried breakfast. The men form a circle on the middeck, awaiting instructions.

"Make it so," the commander answers. "Hoist anchor. Mr. Martyn, keep her steady toward the south. I want lookouts at each side of the bow to be watching for rocks or shore."

Thomas Martyn mans the whipstaff, commonly known as the whip. It is connected to the tiller below deck through an opening called the rowle, that in turn connects to the ship's rudder. It will be over two hundred years before the ship's wheel, so prominent in many depictions of large sailing ships, is invented. It requires a sturdy arm, such as that of Martyn or Little Nele, to handle the stubborn steering control. Martyn is thirty years old and an experienced mariner who says little and does not have many friends among the crew. Despite this, he is valuable as a sailor and soldier and adept with long bow and arrow and with a pike. His secret has always been a mortal fear of the savages they encounter. He fully realized this only after the attacks in Patagonia and Mocha Island. Even the meetings at Muh-kwa and at New Albion did little to relieve his fears. He always suspects an ultimate betrayal or treachery from the natives. One primary motive for volunteering to join the barque was the possibility of fewer encounters on the way home. Like Watkyns and many others, he thought they would be ensuring a shorter and safer passage to England.

Unable to deploy their main sails, the barque drifts with the slight current downstream and enters the strait just before noon according to their clock. They still can't see the sun, and as they turn south, they face a head-on current. The wind picks up a little in their favor, and with it come heavy, rain-laden clouds that bring sheets of water across the deck and add to the misery of everyone aboard. The three bodies have been covered with a tarp and lashed down. The winds increase as they approach the long island, and they experience increasing difficulty in handling the ship. Little Nele, their best steersman, takes over at the whip. He is big and strong and knows how to swing the pole about as needed.

It isn't enough. While they skirt closer to the western side of the mainland than they wish, a large rock appears off the starboard bow. One of the crewmen shouts a warning that is barely heard above the howling wind that is now almost gale-like in force. Little Nele pulls hard on the staff, and the ship lurches to port just enough to avoid the obstacle. This brings them into shallow water, and the ship grinds to a halt in the soft silt.

"Not again in two days! What the hell, the bloody hell." Gallawaye raises his fist to the dark sky, close to damning the God he so fervently worships. He exclaims, "Satan be gone. It is you who plagues our endeavor. Take your evil schemes with you to the bowels of hell." A grumble of thunder answers his entreaty, and the rain falls harder and colder.

The strait exhibits moderate tidal activity, and, fortunately, they struck land at low tide. A few hours and a few feet of water rise later, the ship moves off the bar and is ready to sail. The rain eases along with the wind, and the sun sets as they near the southern end of the island. Not wanting to risk another mishap, Hayman decides to anchor in deep water and make their final run in the morning. With two and a half days remaining before the *Hinde* departs, he calculates they should make the port and rendezvous with adequate time to spare.

---

THE NEXT MORNING DISPLAYS ONLY A BIT OF FOG THAT BURNS off by midmorning while they are under sail. Little Nele is the first to detect the slow response from the rudder. Using a whipstaff and tiller never produces an instant response in steering a ship. The lighter barque, at forty tons, is able to affect only a 12° turn, but the Flemish sailor can tell the difference in handling. The grounding must have broken something, although he can't determine how badly. They are running mostly before a northwesterly breeze, and no tacking is required until they approach the harbor, but then a sharp cut to port will be needed. The only alternative is to make a large, sweeping circle into the bay that is clumsy at best or untenable if they don't start and time the approach correctly.

Gallawaye examines the coastline charts he sketched on the way north. He estimates they are forty miles from their destination. At their current rate against the current, it will be nine or ten hours before they can enter the harbor. That still gets them in by late evening or, if forced to stop for the night, by early the next morning. He informs Watkyns and Hayman of his calculations, much to their relief.

About midafternoon, Martyn has relieved Little Nele at the whip. He shouts to the deck below, "We've lost her. We've lost our rudder." He is swinging the whip back and forth, and there is obviously little resistance. With no steering, the ship begins to blow toward the mainland shore. There is a large inlet on their portside—the river delta they observed and decided to forego days earlier. Directly ahead is the land projection and headland north of the harbor, twelve miles in length.

"So close and so damned far," mutters Watkyns as the crew reduces sail, trying to slow the drift eastward.

"We still have time. We can do this," intones Gallawaye as if speaking to a cathedral audience.

The ship nears the shallows of the inlet and, for the third time in as many days, grinds to an abrupt stop on the shore. The weather is calm; the crew is not. All share angry words and scowls. Gallawaye, Martyn, Little Nele, and Big Tom launch in the pinnace. Little Nele dives below the surface to inspect the rudder. In the meantime, Franconi, Huntsman, and Whyte, with Hayman, check the tiller and connections to the rudder and whip inside the hull. Little Nele emerges from the water, shaking his head as he found nothing underwater in the way of damage. A shout from the deck calls for the pinnace to return. The problem is a broken coupling between tiller and rudder, something that can be repaired by Huntsman, the carpenter, and Old Bill Whyte, the rope maker and cook. This comes as a rare bit of fortune, as it is much easier to repair while the barque is afloat. It will still take time to fashion a new coupling and replace the broken one. They start immediately.

The *Northern Venture* is almost within sight of the harbor entrance if she stands farther out in the strait, but from where they lie on the shore, it lies behind the cliffs and land mass before them. The cliffs are low but bright pinkish white in the setting sun, an irony not lost on the crew as they wait for Huntsman and Whyte to finish. It is a more difficult task than first surmised.

"If I had the shop and materials on the *Hinde*, this would take but a few hours," remarks Chrystopher. He is covered in sweat and taking a brief break from the hold where he has been laboring by candle most of the night. "I can probably get it fixed enough to get us around the point and headed for the harbor, but I can't guarantee how long it will hold or how well the *Venture* will perform."

"Do what you can, Mr. Huntsman. It is all we can ask," Hayman looks around at the crew gathered on the deck, "of any man." He and the others are concerned that time, which seemed adequate earlier that day, is deserting them. Huntsman and Whyte continue to work the next day.

Thursday night, the twenty-third, Hayman has a somber discussion with Watkyns and Gallawaye. "We can probably reach the *Hinde* tomorrow if we put a few strong rowers in the pinnace. The current is against us, but we can deploy a sail if the winds cooperate." He looks at Gallawaye. "If the harbor is only twelve miles away, they could reach it in a few hours. Once alerted, the *Hinde* can delay a few hours until we can reach them or they reach us."

As they attempt to reach a decision, Huntsman enters the cabin and announces that they have finished the repair, although he is less than satisfied with it. It is well into the night, and the idea of launching the pinnace with essentially a bare trace of moon is to no one's liking.

"We will have several hours of sunlight," Hayman observes. "The tide is coming in during the morning, and if we can get underway, we should be able to catch our flagship before she leaves the harbor and is out of sight." They agree and prepare for an early-morning launch of the pinnace to assist in an all-out effort to free the barque.

The sun has not yet emerged from the mountain tops, but first light has all hands scrambling. The tide is rising, and the barque shifts a bit but holds fast to the bottom. Aided by the strength of Little Nele and Big Tom at the oars, several men in the pinnace attempt to move the ship off the shoal. It is slow work, and they force it free by late morning. The crew hurries aboard, and the sails are made ready as the *Venture* begins to move toward the strait. Anyone looking up at the blue sky can see noon has arrived.

CHAPTER 7

# Southward Bound

---

While the *Venture* sails the northern strait, final preparations are made on the hull of the *Hinde* before reloading. Fletcher and others have time to observe aspects of the local native culture. Led by three natives, the priest, Thomas Hord, John Crowley, John Drake, and Lawrence Elyot walk along the cliffs of the strait's eastern shore and descend to the Sawassen camp at the southern branch of the large river delta. The white men watch with amazement as natives deploy two canoes, aligned in parallel, across the stream. They stretch a woven net between them and dip it in the water. It quickly fills with salmon, and they drag it ashore while two other canoes take their place. Other natives employ spears and arrows to snag fish closer to shore. Some of the older boys adeptly catch them with bare hands. Crowley speaks to one of their Semiahmoo guides and confirms that they use the same methods, but the guide says the parallel canoe technique is not widely practiced by other tribes along the strait.

Fletcher and Crowley interview one of the Semiahmoo shamans. They learn about the tribe's special reverence for the dead and the role of bones as symbols of power and access to the spiritual world. Crowley isn't able to understand everything, and the shaman seems reluctant to reveal some of his knowledge, but they understand that the departed are often lonely and always hungry. Therefore, it is necessary to talk to one's ancestors, feed them in special ceremonies, and continue to honor their memory. This is partly to assure that the living will be granted access to the underworld when they die. There are many taboos about children being kept away from funerals because they are susceptible to being stolen by the spirits. Food is not to be eaten outdoors at night because hungry spirits gather. Many of the other related tribes throughout the straits, from the Muh-kwa in the west to the Euclataws in the north, share these beliefs.

Bones are also an important prop in one of the gambling games played at large gatherings. The game called "slahal" involves teams of players who guess the number of marks on two pairs of deer knee bones. The teams and witnessing individuals gamble vigorously on the outcomes, and the gatherings involve singing, drumming, and clever insults of opposing players.

Salmon have spiritual significance. When they make their spring and summer runs upstream, they represent undersea people who have transformed into fish. Children carry the first catch of the year to a ceremonial feast where all the villagers eat some of the flesh. The fish bones are carefully returned to the sea to assure a bountiful harvest the following year.

Fletcher is unsure about how much of the native belief systems to record. On one hand, he enjoys the richness of the culture and his chance to be among the first to report details of it. However, he is troubled by the pagan beliefs that these people embrace, and he does not want to assume responsibility for spreading a false religion. Even his secret journal would be contaminated with such notes, so he foregoes writing about much of what he learns.

Francis Drake and his company take note of the changing weather in the north. All hope for the safety of the *Venture*, and the chaplain redoubles his efforts at prayer. Most of the heavy rain and stiff winds don't reach the harbor of New Albion, but the crew can observe dark clouds and occasional lightning flashes from their headland observation post. The natives appear to ignore the distant weather as they finish their summer fishing activities. A few of the distant tribespeople have already broken camp and journeyed south.

As the *Hinde*'s day of departure draws near, a few gentlemen ask if they shouldn't delay sailing for an additional day or two. Whether feeling compassion for their fellow travelers or a simple desire to know if they have found the passage, a number of the crew are also uneasy about the designated date. The general assures the dissenters that the *Venture* crew, his New Albion Company, is aware of the dangers, and they are prepared to finish building and manning the outpost if they don't arrive in time from their northern trip of discovery.

John and Thomas Drake talk quietly on the beach some distance from other ears. John shares some of the doubts about leaving as scheduled. Although a Pacific crossing and completed circumnavigation holds the promise of exciting adventures and fabulous sights, he maintains concern for the crew of the barque. He entertains a continued interest in sailing aboard her and hopes he will have the chance to illustrate the fabled Northwest Passage on their way home.

"Thomas, your brother will not relent from his determination to sail south tomorrow?"

"I don't keep my brother's counsel, John. You should know that by now. If his gentlemen have not been able to dissuade him from his plans, it will come to pass. Like you, I serve at his pleasure. No more than that."

John nods but maintains a sense of glum resignation. He knows he can do little once the general decides on a course of action. To waver now might be seen as indecisive or, worse, weakness on the part of their leader.

Thomas reaches out and touches John's shoulder. "Don't despair, cousin. We are witnesses to history regardless of the *Venture*'s fate. We will also have a share in the riches we have so skillfully removed from the hands of the Spaniards. Have you thought about what you will do with yours?"

John stares at the water lapping on the shore. "I intend to return to the sea. I will purchase a ship or a share in one and indulge my fancy for travel and adventure." His eyes make contact with the older man. "Maybe I will find a way to come here to New Albion to be a trader and defender of the enterprise."

Thomas smiles. *The Drake family and near relatives seem destined to roam the world, but not me. My share will go toward a quiet country estate. Raise a few animals, find a good wife, and have children. No surprises.*

---

ON FRIDAY MORNING, CHAPLAIN FLETCHER PRESENTS A BRIEF sermon and blessing for the approaching departure on the beach. The general addresses the assembly and praises the courage of the New Albion contingent. They have not heard from the crew of the *Venture* but still hope for their safety and a reunion, even if it occurs several years in the future. He offers encouragement to the crew of the *Golden Hinde*. Their mood is somber but optimistic. He tells them they will explore the outer coast south from their seaward entrance to the waterway that some of the gentlemen are calling the Strait of Elizabeth. They will spend a couple of weeks at a good harbor to prepare for the voyage home. Drake promises he will return to New Albion with several ships and supplies, settlers, and replacements for those who wish to go home. He will keep his promise of compensation to all survivors of New Albion. Their fortune in buried precious metal helps guarantee the promise.

They receive the message well. Why would the general or any of the gentlemen with a stake in the seized Spanish treasure abandon these riches to a primitive land? It is only a question of time. The Spaniards are far away and presumably without a clue that the two ships have made landfall so far north.

A large group of natives gathers on the beach and along the headland as William Crowley signs to their chief that they will sail away as the smaller ship did. As the message is relayed to the natives, many show signs of distress and moan with a slow chant. Some of the women shriek and cut their arms and chests as if someone has died and these were the last rites. Fletcher notes the outcry and interprets it as mourning for the sea gods that are deserting them.

Mr. Crowley isn't so sure. He tries to explain to the chaplain that any departure of friends or family is subject to a similar emotional display by the women. However, even he is alarmed at the intensity of their demonstration. He fails to make the natives understand they will return some time in the future.

An hour before noon, the sentries are recalled from the headland. No sign of the *Venture* has been seen. Crowley makes his farewells to the spokesmen from the tribe as their chief stands apart, stoic and aloof. Finally, the last pinnace leaves the beach and rows smoothly toward the flagship.

A favorable wind blows at noon, and with flags flying brightly in the sun, the *Golden Hinde* eases out of the broad harbor into the strait. Although still Friday by the civil calendar, it is now 25 July in nautical days—the Day of Saint James, the patron saint of pilgrims and fishermen. Although a traditional Catholic feast day, it is also honored by the Anglican and Lutheran churches, but without prayers to saints.

It doesn't take long for the ship to leave the harbor behind them. Two hours later, they are sailing among the large islands they passed a month earlier. The eastern point of an island to their west presents a large colony of sea lions and thousands of nesting seabirds. Although the crew loaded adequate provisions before leaving Port New Albion, eggs and seal meat are not plentiful at the harbor, and the fishing camp natives had first access to the latter. As they pull around the sharp point of land, they observe a long beach and protected cove. A party of twelve launches the pinnace, goes ashore, gathers eggs, and kills dozens of the large sea mammals. By midafternoon, they are again under sail, heading south and passing other large islands to their east.

The cooks fix a grand feast late that afternoon for the officers and crewmen in honor of Saint James Day. Usually the midday meal is the largest, but shipboard and expedition duties require flexibility. The gentlemen decide to name the island from which they procured the eggs and meat. "Saint James Island, what else?" remarks Francis Fletcher.

Francis Drake indicates to his young cousin to make it so on the maps and in the rutter. The chaplain also takes note that it is the first time during the voyage that a location has been named after a biblical figure. Full and happy yet sobered by thoughts of the fate of the New Albion Company, they anchor for the night at the eastern end of the Strait of Elizabeth and the beginning of their westward leg to the Pacific Ocean.

---

THE *VENTURE* PULLS ABREAST OF THE HARBOR TWO HOURS after noon. As they enter, it is apparent that despite their most fervent hopes and prayers, the *Hinde* has sailed. They are on their own. The beach is deserted, but smoke rises from fires on the headland in the direction of the two closest villages: one behind the forest and their claim and the other south of the harbor. They know the flagship has a head start of a couple hours, but the *Venture* is lighter and can tack west in the strait more efficiently than the *Hinde*. Hayman thinks, *Only if the tiller and rudder hold, and we need water and food.* They had not provisioned for a long trip to the north, so a few hours will be needed for them to gather food and water and make another inspection of the steering gear.

One other item of business requires immediate attention. The bodies of Cowrites, Adden, and Peter are lashed to the deck of the barque, and the smell is almost overwhelming. They must be buried without delay.

As the anchor drops close to the northern shore of the bay, Hayman selects four crewmen to prepare graves. Whyte hastily constructs three crosses, and Gallawaye gathers his prayer book. Leaving no one aboard the ship, the seventeen survivors climb into the pinnace, and with the sailcloth-wrapped bodies, they row silently to the beach. They select a site east of the claim pole and at the top of the embankment. The graves are dug quickly and the bodies lowered and covered. It takes but a few minutes, and the crew gathers over the graves, each marked by a cross with an engraved name.

John gives a brief eulogy and prays for their souls. *Should I be the one doing this?* he thinks. *I have all but lost my faith in God, and here I beseech that spirit for the delivery of their souls. They deserve better, but there is no one else. Say the words, pay respect, and be done with it.*

The decision to chase the *Hinde* rather than remain at New Albion is made between the officers and Watkyns hurriedly and without dispute, as if the three of them already agreed that a more southerly location will serve them best, whether they overtake Drake's ship or not.

"What about the silver?" asks Watkyns.

Hayman shrugs. "No time to recover it. Besides, the general and his gentlemen know where it is buried. It isn't going anywhere, and we, or they, can dig it up when the time is right. It is a good incentive for their return as well as ours. Now let's gather provisions as quickly as possible and be on our way."

---

Although the westward journey through the Strait of Elizabeth requires tacking against the prevailing northwesterly winds, the weather remains fair, and progress is swift. Three days after leaving Nova Albion, the *Hinde* passes the Muh-kwa village. The ship skirts the coast to their north, well off from the facing shore to the south, but they observe a few canoes and some natives on the beach scurrying about like ants. They sail past the inlet a few minutes later, and no canoes pursue them.

"I suppose they might be disappointed that we didn't stop and exchange pleasantries," Fletcher says to Hawkins, observing the shore from the port rail.

"Aye, but we are only one ship now. How to explain what happened to the smaller one? Best they be left guessing."

Indeed, the council discussed slipping past the village at night so that any guessing would be eliminated, but the moon was relatively new, and the water was dark enough to render navigation risky. There is talk by more than one of the crew members who desire to socialize with the native women. The general and the chaplain suppress any notion of revisiting the village, and the issue is put to rest. The *Golden Hinde* now carries a compliment of sixty-three souls including eight boys under the age of eighteen—John Drake will soon turn from boy to recognized man—and four blacks including Diego and Maria.

Late in the afternoon of the next day, facing a brilliant setting sun behind an incoming bank of clouds, the *Hinde* passes the strait's entrance and turns south to follow the coast. They stay far enough offshore to avoid the perilous rocks and small islets that dot the coastline. As before, a magnificent, snow-covered mountain can be seen to the east projecting above the thick green forests. They make good progress from a steady onshore breeze that fills the sails and gladdens the hearts of all aboard. Darker clouds form far on the horizon to the north and west, but the ship maintains a safe distance from the gathering tempest. Fletcher has time to record his observations.

*Tuesday, 28 July 1579*

*We are now in new territory on the northern Pacific coast. The crew has been alerted to watch for a suitable harbor to acquire final provisions for the long ocean voyage ahead. The stopover will also provide a shore excursion for the crew. I asked our general if John Doughty might be permitted to stretch his legs on land. The last time he had the opportunity was at Port New Albion, but that was only for a few hours after unloading the flagship. He was transferred to the barque the same day, and although not put in irons, he was treated as if he was an enemy prisoner. It seems unreasonable that he would attempt to escape in such an alien location. I pray our leader will find it in his heart to be merciful and relax the severe restrictions imposed upon the gentleman.*

---

THE SEVENTEEN MEN OF THE *NORTHERN VENTURE* HURRY ABOUT the beach of Port New Albion to load the pinnace and depart. Graye and Cuttyll have been fortunate hunting game and come back with several rabbits, two deer, and a number of coneys. Franconi and Martyn fill several casks with stream water and bring them to the ship. Assisted by Huntsman and Whyte, Little Nele makes additional repairs to the tiller and whipstaff, reinforces the rods, and greases the access holes.

Accompanied by Big Tom and George Cooke, John Gallawaye and Christopher Hayman are obligated to deal with the natives. The Indians returned to the beach the evening after the *Venture* anchored, chanting and dancing with joy. Although Gallawaye is not as skilled at communicating with them as Crowley, he helps the natives understand that the crew is desperate to catch the larger ship. The Indians offer them baskets of vegetables and pine nuts, which Commander Hayman gratefully accepts. It is two days after they returned to the bay—more time has passed than Hayman wanted. Following a brief shipboard service on Sunday the twenty-sixth, the *Northern Venture* slips out of Port New Albion, again to the consternation of the observing crowds on the beach and headland.

As the barque sails down the strait and passes several large islands two hours later, Hayman's thoughts focus on their target. *I hope the* Hinde *makes stops at the Indian village and other nearby inlets in their search for a provisioning site. Do I risk sailing at night? The barque is smaller and more maneuverable, but sharp rocks just below the surface do not discriminate. One wooden hull is just as good as another for the devil's obstacles.*

The debate that evening aboard the *Venture* is animated but disciplined. Except for Little Nele at the whipstaff and Francis

Caube standing watch on the stern deck, the rest are gathered on the middeck around the New Albion Company's co-leaders. The barque is about to turn westward into the newly named Strait of Elizabeth and head for the open ocean. They will be approaching the Muhkwa village inlet in another day or so, and this forms the first topic of the lively discussion. Three soldiers and one of the workmen advocate stopping at the native village and seeking asylum.

"Would it not be right and proper for us to prevail upon our new friends and allies to let us join them?" asks Richard Graye. He is one of the respected and better-spoken soldiers in the group. He confided his plan to Emmanuel Watkyns the evening before, and the gentleman and leader of New Albion Company has encouraged him to bring it to the attention of everyone, acting as a council of the whole.

Thomas Cuttyll adds his support. "Instead of abandoning New Albion altogether, this would constitute a strategic but temporary retreat. We would be only three days sail from there to the village."

Hayman looks to Watkyns. The broad-shouldered Englishman attempts to retain neutrality, as has been his position on many occasions. He clears his throat and speaks carefully. "It is possible we will come upon the village and our general's flagship at the same time and place. That would be our best solution. If the *Hinde* is not there when we arrive, any delay at the village makes it less likely we'll be able to intercept her before they depart for the western ocean and home. We will need to decide quickly and decisively when the moment arrives. If we stop, we stay. Otherwise, we continue our pursuit until we catch our companions or fail."

John Deane raises his hand to speak and is recognized by the commander. Deane is one of the general sailors who often expresses a sour personality and tendency to shy away from others. He is a devout, albeit secret, Catholic who once thought about becoming a priest. Like the Basque pilot Morera, John has maintained silence during the raids on Spanish towns and wanton destruction of churches and sacred artifacts. He and the sailor Thomas Grige volunteered for the New Albion Company to distance themselves from aggressive and outspoken Protestants such as Tom Moone and Andy McGuane. None of the others on the *Venture* are religious zealots.

Deane has another reason for seeking asylum in the native village. "I also favor a request for consideration by our native friends," he begins. He glances around him, searching for sympathetic eyes. "A few of us might be inclined, if you permit, sir, to an entreaty to the same hosts for us to," he pauses, "make friends with their womenfolk. That is, those who might not be attached to one of their men and might be receptive to companionship that we sorely desire." He stops and judges the reactions of his companions. For the most part, their faces display neither repulsion nor encouragement. They are hard to read, as if afraid to commit to a particular course of action without further guidance from one of the leaders.

Nicholas Franconi grins and Thomas Grige enthusiastically seconds the idea. "It might work that we could enhance our presence and the aims of New Albion by marriage and family, expanding our numbers to compensate for our losses and more." He notices John Gallawaye's posture stiffening at his last words. Big Tom sits at the back of the group, with head down and eyes closed, unable or unwilling to communicate with the group.

Commander Hayman looks around the deck at the others, waiting for further comment. No one speaks, so he renders his decision. "If the *Hinde* is at anchor, the decision whether to join forces with the natives will be made by General Drake and his council. It will be out of our hands. If approved, we might request volunteers among you and the crew of the flagship. This would have the added benefit of providing more space aboard for the lengthy return to England. However, if the general's ship is not at anchor, we will move on and continue to pursue her proposed route southward as Mr. Watkyns has proposed. We will not make any attempt of our own accord to integrate our company with the natives." He waits for indications of protest or dissent, but there are none. His total command of the outpost group, abandoned or not, is confirmed.

A shout from Little Nele alerts them to a change in direction as they round the point of the land on their starboard. They enter the Strait of Elizabeth and head toward the great ocean. Now the *Venture*, like the *Hinde*, will need to tack against the prevailing wind, but the smaller ship maneuvers more efficiently. It is considerably lighter without the silver bullion but it has retained four cannons. The men on the evening shift scramble to their posts. They will sail until full darkness, employing narrower beating runs to avoid both shores. Unfortunately, the moonlight is still weak, and the risk of miscalculating and running aground is not negligible. The thought of a fourth grounding haunts every crew member's waking thoughts and dreams. Three hours after full sunset, the sliver of moon is obscured by an incoming bank of fog, and Hayman reluctantly gives the order to anchor in midwater.

A breakfast of tea and hard biscuits is distributed shortly before daybreak. First light sees the *Venture* underway in a light fog. John Gallawaye marks the morning with a brief prayer for the hope of reunion, and the crew returns to work. All sails of the three-master are deployed to catch as much of the light breeze as possible. Despite the skill of Little Nele and the other sailors, it requires a full day and half of the next to catch sight of the inlet marking the Muh-kwa village. It is shortly after high noon, and to their disappointment but not surprise, there is no sign of the *Golden Hinde*. The decision made previously holds. The barque passes the inlet just to the north of midwater. Whether the natives see the ship at all is unknown. The *Venture* sails on, and the crew is alert for activity from the shore and constantly searching for the full, square-rigged sails of the flagship ahead. It is now four days since the *Hinde* departed New Albion's bay.

---

THE *GOLDEN HINDE* SAILS AT A LOW-TO-MODERATE PACE throughout the night of the twenty-eighth, staying well offshore. At midmorning on Wednesday, 29 July, they see a large inlet, cautiously approach, drop the main sails, and make soundings at regular intervals. Prominent peninsulas guard the broad, shallow bay from the north and south, and they drop anchor a few hundred yards inside the entrance to avoid running aground on the sandbars and banks that project about the inlet. They can see the waters extend several miles eastward, and it occurs to more than one man that this is a candidate for the passage they have so fervently sought. They are just below 47°N latitude. John Drake makes careful notes and sketches of the bay, and Hernán Perez enters details of the soundings in the navigator's log.

At dinner that night, the council debates the merits of exploring deeper into the inlet. As customary, the general lets the gentlemen discuss it before he offers his opinion. His will be the last word in any case, so it is best to hear them out.

"The current is sluggish even at full tide run," observes Thomas Drake.

Gregory Cary nods. "Agreed, but the shores appear to close in upstream, if stream it is. It may not be a passage such as we seek."

The naturalist speaks next. "We seem to have left the larger mountains behind. In their place we have a broad valley or plain. If this extends eastward, perhaps it is navigable. We are still well beyond the reach of the Spaniards, and we have ample time to explore if we so desire." Lawrence Elyot leaves no doubt about his zeal for discovery. He has managed to collect and store representative samples of plants, birds, and the rodents and smaller game they have encountered. Several of his shipmates complained about the odor of the decaying animals, and he was required to skin and render the pelts dry and as scentless as possible. Processing also saved room, as space was high in demand but short in supply. Still, the naturalist wishes to take advantage of any opportunity to observe and collect flora and fauna from as many sites as may be practical.

Considerable discussion about the inlet follows until Drake clears his throat. The others become quiet. Some sip a mellow red wine, and others sit back to await the verdict of the ultimate authority. "I appreciate the considerable diversity of opinion expressed. Your counsel, as always, is most welcome and enlightening. All things considered, our preliminary observations weigh against this being the Strait of Anián. However, we have made careful note of its location. In any case, this bay may serve as a future harbor for our northern empire." He smiles as if the idea of a northern empire belongs personally to the crew of the *Hinde*. Until they return and announce their discoveries, the North American Empire *is* theirs by default.

"If we still had the *Venture* with us, we could prudently have her explore the back reaches. We will compromise. This is not a bad anchorage, but the approach to the beaches might be treacherous. Since our best time for departure will be from mid to late August, I suggest we launch a pinnace with a few armed men and journey inward, taking soundings. John, perhaps you would like to accompany them with a sketch pad?" John smiles and nods. "Lawrence, you shall have a chance to observe wildlife from the boat but no onshore excursions. I believe we already have a full stock of specimens, and we still have over half the globe to navigate before we arrive home." Elyot grins, happy to be included. When the gentlemen drift off to their beds, all seem satisfied but none more so than John Drake, who feels compensated for his exclusion from the *Venture*.

Carrying sixteen men under the command of Tom Moone, the pinnace shoves off shortly after breakfast. The low fog that came in during the night obscures the far shores and the way ahead. They have not seen any signs of natives from the time they passed the Muh-kwa village, but two of the men are armed with muskets, and several others carry swords. Two friendly encounters do not guarantee that the next will follow suit. Seagulls squawk overhead and follow the small boat as it moves across the bay toward the rising sun. Other waterfowl are abundant and many are familiar in form to Lawrence although of a different species. Herons, egrets, pelicans, fish hawks, and a variety of ducks greet them on all sides and on the many sandbars that line their passage. Georgie Kershaw has been anxious to join the group. He yields the sounding rope off the bow and calls out the depths as they proceed.

Two hours before noon, the clouds disperse and the waters reflect a greenish-brown hue, indicating a riverine source. The bottom is closer, with soundings half that of the flagship's draft. Farther ahead the river banks are closer and the confined current increases. At noon, they stop midstream and turn about to drift for a few minutes before continuing with the oar work.

Tom Moone is the first to notice a small party of natives on the northern shore, probably just out of arrow shot range. They stand in a line at the water's edge. There are about a dozen warriors; a few of them might be younger. No canoes are visible, so the crewmen sense no immediate threat.

Lawrence waves as if they are old friends he hasn't see in a while. They don't return the greeting. Lawrence contemplates the scene. *They seem like statues as the boat drifts downstream. Two peoples, two cultures, not destined to meet at this time. The astonishment must lie with the natives. It would be their first time to encounter such a strange boat filled with strange men. Even from that distance, we would be marked as foreigners, intruders on their lands, and for what purpose?*

The exploration party arrives at the ship two hours later to report that the bay is the mouth of a river without promise of a navigable path to the North Sea. Rather than leave with only a few hours of sunlight remaining, Drake decides to spend the rest of the day and that night in the harbor. He posts two extra sentries to keep eyes on the surrounding shores.

The next morning, they depart and continue their journey south, passing another large inlet at 46.5°N with the same output characteristics. Behind them, the storm clouds approach closer, and preparations are made to secure all items on deck. They sail on, passing an unseen large river during a night lit by the quarter moon but disguised by fog. The winds and waves increase, but it seems of little consequence compared to what they endured in the Strait of Magellan and the South Sea.

Dawn finds them running along a similar rocky shore of towering cliffs and intermittent beaches that are backed by dense forests of pine and fir. Occasionally they observe smoke curling up from inland fires, but they spot no natives or other direct signs of habitation. They pass between the coast and a large boulder offshore. John Drake and Fletcher stand at the starboard rail as they watch waves splash high up the rock face.

"What shall we name that?" asks John.

"It's all by itself, lad. A bare martyr of the sea. Perhaps Saint Bartholomew would be fitting." He means it as a joke, but John records the name and latitude of 46°N in the log and on his chart.

The weather remains blustery and threatening, but the height of the tempest is not yet upon them. The council that evening agrees to put ashore at the next uninhabited cove to weather the storm.

The next day, 2 August, they arrive at a large river opening at about 45.7°N. It appears to curve to the north, but there is a sizeable outflow, which indicates suitable depth. The *Hinde* anchors temporarily off the beach. An abbreviated Sunday service is held, but the seas are rough, and the tilting decks are to no one's liking, including the chaplain. Afterward, they launch a pinnace through rough surf with ten men aboard to survey the surrounding area with instructions to avoid contact with natives, if present. Instead of battling the outflow current of the river, the men row to the beach and walk along the water's edge to view the river and valley from out of sight of the ship. From the far side of a long, broad sandspit, the party sees that the river broadens as it continues upstream and north. A large cliff and low mountain frame its north side; low plains behind a beach face them from across the stream. Led by William Hawkins, the party hikes a mile up the spit until the river curves to the east and opens onto a cove surrounded by low cliffs and forests. A few sandy beaches line the cove.

"We'll need to get the launch upstream and make some soundings," remarks Will. "We'll start as soon as the tide turns."

The group returns to the pinnace, signals the *Hinde*, and waits two hours for the tide to begin its inward run. They launch and row up the river to the entrance of the bay while recording depths on the way. It is deep enough, even at slack tide, to permit entrance by the flagship. Furthermore, the spit provides shelter from the stormy westerlies assaulting the coast. They row back to the *Hinde* and report. Taking advantage of the inward tide, the ship raises anchor, enters the river, turns in the bay, and drops anchor in the center of the cove, again well out of range of any potential arrows from shore.

A scouting party of twenty men, mostly soldiers, is assembled to survey the area. John Drake, Thomas Drake, and Lawrence Elyot are not permitted to go ashore. The present objective is clearly military and caution is paramount. Francis Fletcher walks along the starboard rail clutching a bible as he watches the men disembark. Others also line the rails as sentries observe from the mast baskets for signs of natives. The dense forest makes it difficult to determine if there is anyone within miles of the group, but they wish to take temporary advantage of the location if they can. In addition to the river's navigability, the ship is effectively hidden from the ocean. Even the mast tops are below the raised sandspit that bounds the outlet.

Their visit does not go undetected. Eyes peer down on them from the mountain over their shoulders—other eyes watch them from the deep woods as they set foot on the beach and move along the forest's edge. The steady wind and movement of tree branches disguise any other sounds that might have been detected.

The men signal to the ship that all seems well, and they post guards at each end and in the middle of the hundred-yard strip of sand. The pinnace transfers several others ashore to hunt for vegetables and fresh meat. The pilot's cedar bark and needle tea has proven effective in reversing the ill effects of sailor's disease, so a special party is dispatched to gather the precious materials. It has the added advantage of enduring months of storage at sea, unlike fresh fruits and vegetables.

The hunting and gathering parties return to the ship in the afternoon, and the guards withdraw from the shore. The *Hinde* is made ready to sail at first dawn with the outgoing tide. Some bark has been located and collected, but very little game and only a few onions were added to the ship's stores. Evergreen forests do not provide the diverse natural larder that open plains, valleys, and coastal flats offer. Freshwater collection has been more successful.

"It seems our business here is done," remarks William Crowley as he paces the deck in the late evening. He is relieved he hasn't been needed for dialogue with any natives since New Albion.

Fletcher stands beside him. The logbook in his hand covers the secret journal that he wants to update when the topside is mostly deserted. The crew has become habituated to the chaplain's late-night writing and desire to be alone. They accord him that privilege despite the cramped quarters.

Fletcher looks kindly toward the large, muscular crewman. Although he is part soldier and part general ship's laborer, Crowley has a gentle tone about him. He is growly in voice but usually soft spoken, slow to anger and thoughtful, as if he was born to a higher status and received an education. In fact, the man can barely scrawl his name and only read a few words. "You have a fine temperament, Mr. Crowley. It was good work you did to seal our friendship with the people in the strait and at our harbor."

"They were different from many of the others we've met in the southern waters. They could have had us if they wanted, I have no doubt. Your prayers must have made the difference."

The priest smiles. "Divine providence is always wished for and gladly received, but the behavior of man remains the most important determinant of our success or failure. We make war or peace, not almighty God. I hope we can continue to enjoy the benefits of good fellowship with those we encounter in the future."

"Amen to that. We have no need for further bloodshed." William gives a nod and walks away, leaving the priest with his thoughts.

Fletcher sits in an area of the deck well away from others and writes in his second journal.

*Sunday, 2 August 1579*

*Unsaid but implied, Mr. Crowley refers to the internal strife among the crew and the execution of one of our own. The tensions that accompanied the ships from Mexico to New Albion have largely disappeared. Hard work and new vistas, along with the unseen dangers that abound in this uncharted territory, help offset personal grudges and resentments.*

*Our general has exhibited the best of behavior this past month. His courage and leadership are on display, and the men follow him as well as when we first left Plymouth. His admonition to the officers to help with daily chores has been partially adopted. They do not soil their hands or break their backs, but they no longer remain aloof from the common sailors. More than a few of them take risks when going ashore, and with only two exceptions, all converse with sailors and soldiers as if they were of the same class. Even the blacks, all former slaves, receive signs of goodwill from the crew. I will miss Big Tom and Peter and will keep them in my prayers, seeking favor for their safety.*

*The exceptions to goodwill rest with John Doughty, the brother of Thomas, and the lawyer, Mr. Vicary, his friend. It is difficult to judge their withdrawal. Although both are welcome at the captain's table, they participate only on occasion and prefer to eat by themselves. John has been allowed off the ship only once when they were at Porto Nova Albion. Even then he was closely watched by a crewman assigned by our general. I have little doubt of their hatred for our leader, and their return to England does not bode well for General Drake or for those who supported the verdict against Thomas. I also have concern for the health and welfare of Nazario Morera.*

*The pilot has not completely recovered from his recent illness. He still complains of fatigue and soreness of the gut. He does not look well, and his manner is downcast. I have tried to console him, but he is barely polite in his refusal of my services and disregards my concerns as if they didn't exist.*

*Still, the weather turns warmer as we proceed south, and the promise of the homeward-bound journey lies not too far in the future. Our fortune could be worse. I pray for the mercy of our Lord and wisdom of our general.*

A quarter moon shines on the deck of the *Hinde* several yards from where Fletcher updates his journals. "The cove is as black as any pit in hell," remarks Tom Moone to Andy McGuane.

"Been there, I suppose?" The Scot grins. "Would the natives here be the denizens or devils of that mystical region?" They have seen no signs of habitation so far, not even a footprint on the beach save their own.

"Nay, but ask the preacher if it might not be so. He be better educated in those places than myself, a humble, ignorant sailor."

"Not so sure about the humble, but I guess the rest of it is right."

---

THE NEXT MORNING REVEALS CONTINUING ROUGH WEATHER, and the general and his council decide to find a better location in which to reprovision. They sail out of the river with the midmorning tide and turn to the south. The seas remain turbulent, but the ship handles well at half sail. The *Golden Hinde* passes latitude 45°N and a large, exposed inlet when they round a rocky peninsula and discover a snug cove. It is small and requires a tight entry, but it offers protection from the strong northwesterly winds. It has a beach and appears deep enough to enter. They drop the mainsails, deploy the pinnace, and take soundings as the rowboat slowly tows them behind the protecting headlands and into the quiet inlet. They have found their secure anchorage site well north of Spanish incursion. They have ample time to give the hull a last scouring, repair any seams reopened or were missed at Nova Albion, and stock food and water for the lengthy Pacific sojourn.

Later that evening, Francis Fletcher notes the event in the official journal of the voyage. He also writes in his secret account.

*Monday, 3 August 1579*

*Praise to our Lord who watches over us and provides all our needs. We have reached what appears to be a fair haven in which to rest and prepare for the arduous journey ahead. Finally, after many trials and misfortunes, we will be blessed with the knowledge that we will be homeward bound to return to the comfort of those we left almost two years ago. How we have changed. The younger lads such as John Drake have become men. Men have grown older, and some are no longer with us.*

*We beseech you, Lord, to watch over us and keep us safe. Bless our general and guide him in his decisions so that no further harm will come to our righteous crew and good ship. Let us remember the friendly peoples of our northern journey and the hospitality they bestowed. May that encounter give us the wisdom and temperament in our future encounters with whomever and wherever they may be.*

*The climate is still brisk but bearable, and we know that within a few weeks, we shall be entering tropical waters and all the warm attributes they entail.*

CHAPTER 8

# Shipwreck

On the morning of Thursday, 30 July, the *Venture* passes out of the entrance to Elizabeth Strait and turns to port. As they pick up a favorable wind, their speed increases. They stay close offshore, and two men watch constantly for any sign of the *Hinde*. Hayman believes Drake's group will probably not take extraordinary precautions to hide from the Spanish at this latitude and that the general will try to push farther south before securing a longer-term anchorage. When they encounter the large bay at 47°N latitude, they pause and enter briefly. The flat inlet and its bordering plain reveal no sign of the flagship, so they depart and continue south. Behind them and to the west, storm clouds are gathering and will be upon them soon.

The storm delivers its promise the next morning. They reef the mainsails, leaving enough cloth to continue steering while they seek any harbor that can provide temporary shelter. A large bay appears in the afternoon, and they enter, turning around a large northward-pointing peninsula that blocks most of the gale. They inspect the barque, and damage appears to be minimal—all the masts, yards, and sails are intact. There is no sign of the *Hinde*. They have passed it, or as Hayman believes, the flagship is farther ahead. If the storm catches the *Hinde* in the open sea, it might force them to also seek shelter. The officers decide to weather the storm that evening and try to overtake their companions the next day.

The next morning, they discover the damaged rudder that was probably compromised during entry into the shallow bay. Fortunately, most of the tools and materials they need for this critical element are kept aboard ship. Chrystopher Huntsman and John Deane detach and repair the rudder, although again not as satisfactorily as they wish. Another day anchored in the bay is not to the commander's liking, but he is at the mercy of his damaged ship. He describes their surroundings in his new log and sends a few men out in the pinnace to kill ducks. The rudder is repaired by dusk.

Gallawaye conducts a brief Sunday service on the deck before they depart the shallow bay. He harbors thoughts of his inadequacy for the task. The continuing damages and repairs to the *Venture* do not reassure him that they are sailing under divine Providence. *Is this our just punishment for imposing ourselves on this land and these people? The attack in the north I can understand, but the repeated groundings and steering damage is disproportional to chance alone. Are we cursed? If so, why? Should I redouble my prayers or abandon them?* A darker thought occurs to him. *Is there a Jonah aboard? Could it be me?* Without an answer, he returns to navigational tasks.

Late in the afternoon, they pass the mouth of a large river. They can see from the breakers and the color of the outflow that it is a very powerful stream. It doesn't seem a likely place for the flagship to seek refuge, but they make a note of its location slightly north of 46°N. The storm is persistent, and it appears the worst is yet to come. They need to find the *Hinde* or, failing that, a better harbor. Without worrying about obstacles, they sail through the night but farther off the coast.

The winds abate after dark, giving some comfort, but the next morning brings darker clouds and the full fury of the storm. While running with the current and the winds, they stare at the imposing cliffs and bare strip beaches that offer no refuge as they edge close to the shoreline. In the afternoon, the barque passes the outlet where the *Hinde* spent the night and departed a few hours earlier that morning. They are still running close to shore at dusk and the ship rounds a towering headland. Heavy rain whips the lines, making it difficult to see. Three projecting boulders—small islets—appear out of the gloom as they discover a river and beach south of the headland.

As they attempt to bring the rudder hard to port, it snaps, leaving the tiller and whip useless. The ship drives into the largest and most southern of the three rocks, smashing the bow and swinging the hull around so it faces north. With a resounding crack, timbers give way, and the ship drifts off the boulder past the river entrance and onto the shallow bars of the beach beyond it. The barque flounders and tilts to starboard. The men cling to whatever is available as the hull begins to fill with seawater.

"Abandon ship! Abandon ship!" Hayman's cry is barely audible above the wind and surf.

It is no use to launch the pinnace, which would have been difficult from the sloped and rocking deck. Using ropes, Big Tom and Little Nele jump from the ship and wade chest high in the water onto the beach. They secure the ropes to stout trees at the forest's edge and begin transferring men and supplies from the barque. A bow line is brought ashore so the ship can be lashed in place to prevent drifting—better on the sand than on the rocks. The pinnace will yet be needed and perhaps the *Venture* itself saved, although it doesn't seem likely at the moment. Night is closing in, and the clear priority is to save as much of the ship's food, hardware, and clothing as possible. Hayman and Gallawaye oversee the removal of items from the ship, and Watkyns takes charge of assembling materials on the beach.

Franconi lifts a cask over the rail to Big Tom. The water is chest high on the black but would be over the head of any other crewman. The wind lifts a large wave over the deck, and Nicholas loses his footing while thrusting the cask into Big Tom's waiting hands. As Franconi and the wave disappear over the rail, Big Tom reaches his left arm out to snag the smaller man's leg while balancing the cask on his right shoulder. With a loud grunt, the black wades toward shore, dragging Franconi by the ankle. On the closest sandbar, Franconi stands and sputters his gratitude.

Three hours later, the exhausted crew huddles under sailcloth stretched across the low forest canopy, watching as the wind and waves batter the *Northern Venture*. Gallawaye is thoroughly dejected and cannot muster a prayer or words of comfort for himself, much less anyone else. Hayman recognizes that the fight has temporarily, he hopes, deserted his second-in-command. He offers a few words of encouragement, but they are token assurances at best.

Richard Graye cradles his harquebus, shot, and a pouch of powder. "Well lads, let us hope we have something left in the morning to bring ashore. Looks like we might be here a while."

George Cooke has rescued his most precious possession—his six-inch flute—and holds it in his lap but is in no mood to play. The events of the last twelve days weigh heavily on all. They are wet and hungry and face a very uncertain future. They have no way of knowing that the *Hinde* is safely at anchor in a small cove fewer than twenty miles south of them.

William Haynes glumly summarizes the dilemma. "They could be around the next headland or a hundred leagues beyond."

"Or we could have passed them already," adds John Deane.

"Maybe the storm did them in as well," offers Thomas Grige.

"Enough of this, men." Christopher Hayman realizes he must once again, more than ever, take charge. "We are alive, the ship is not yet lost, and the morrow will be a better time to assess our fate. Mr. Cuttyll and Mr. Martyn will take the first watch, one at each side of our position. Mr. Grige and Mr. Deane will man the second watch."

When Deane and Grige awake to relieve the sentries, they find them both asleep. The night winds have slackened, and the rain has become a steady drizzle. Grige nudges the men awake and whispers, "There will be no harsh words or report of your lapse of vigilance. Get some more sleep, lads. We will all need it and more." The early morning darkness is quiet, and there appears to be no one to guard the group from.

The *Golden Hinde* crew greets the new morning with fresh enthusiasm. The picturesque cove is tight and secure. The weather has decisively improved; the sun is not yet above the high horizon, and only a few puffy clouds obscure a bright-blue sky. The hills above the enclosing cliffs are covered with grass, promising a landscape not totally composed of evergreen forests. A freshwater stream feeds the small bay at one end of the beach, and at least one trail leads from the beach to the cliff tops on the northern exposure. Man-made or an animal trail, the crew wonders. A special service is conducted on the deck, preparatory to a shore excursion. After Fletcher pronounces his standard blessing for their safety and gratitude for deliverance from the storm, the general addresses his men and the woman. Gentlemen, sailors, soldiers, laborers, boys becoming young men, and freed slaves stand, sit, and hang from low yardarms facing toward the inlet and sea beyond. Francis Drake and his council have met the night before and divided the party into work groups to ready the ship and its complement for the voyage home.

Drake reminds them they are not alone in the enterprise. They have left an able and willing company in the north to continue the search for the elusive passageway that will assure England's access to use the western ocean and right to conduct trade with Cathay and the rest of Asia. "Even if the search for the Strait of Anián proves futile, they will establish and hold an outpost for God, Queen, and country. We are now obligated to return home and organize a relief fleet to fortify and expand the fledgling colony." In his flamboyant manner, he expresses hope that many of them will be willing to sail again, with himself and others, to fulfill the promise made at Nova Albion. "Our plaque announces our claim, and Commander Hayman and the New Albion Company will be flying the colors of Saint George over New Albion, Her Majesty's first addition to the New World Empire."

William Crowley and Thomas Drake lead three rounds of cheers as the general steps aside for William Hawkins to announce the work teams and their immediate tasks. The first is to scout the immediate area thoroughly. Local natives and their reaction to the *Hinde's* visit constitute a primary concern. All depend on Crowley to once again provide a means of communicating with, and pacifying, any inhabitants. Evaluation of water and food resources will be the work of an exploratory team under the leadership of Thomas Hord. The masons and woodworkers begin construction of a crude, temporary barricade and fortress, something they hope they won't need. The sailors and other workmen inspect, clean, and scrub the *Hinde*, but they hope to avoid even a partial careen if at all possible.

Diego and Maria stand to one side along with Francisco and Mark. The four blacks form a working unit within a larger group of laborers. Diego has been a free man for several years and served Drake well, but he has another chore to pursue. The black men smile at the ensemble— their shipmates and expedition colleagues—as they pitch in where and when needed. Diego's awareness of Maria's pregnancy and his promise to help her and the other blacks has given him another source of loyalty. He knows he has to approach the general or the chaplain to confide in them and trust their judgment. The question is whether to prevail upon them before they set off across the Pacific or wait until they reach the East Indies.

Diego has been told that the voyage across the Pacific could take two months or longer. By that time, Maria's condition will be obvious to everyone on board. Francis Drake might be angry that he has not been informed earlier. That is part of Diego's dilemma. As merciful as the general can be to captives and as friendly as he is to the blacks he rescues from the Spaniards, Diego knows that a long ocean voyage is no place for a woman due to deliver a baby. *Who will assist? We've lost our only two physicians in the South Atlantic and at Mocha. There is no midwife. Maria will be on her own, aboard a rolling ship, possibly leaking as well, with over sixty men. It is possible that our general would opt to leave Maria here with one* or more of the other blacks. If that happens, would I stay with them or sail on with the Hinde? The local native women might assist in the birth. Maria and the other blacks were admired by the Muh-kwa and the Indians at Port New Albion. What should I do? Whatever it is to be, Diego realizes he needs to consult with his leader and the priest without delay.

Fletcher updates his secret journal.

*Wednesday, 5 August 1579*

*No natives have been sighted, but sentries were posted at several points on the ridge overlooking the beach. The storm has passed, and we are blessed with fine, brisk weather not unlike a summer day in Plymouth. Under the leadership of Thomas Hord, several men hiked above the beach and onto the headland forming the north finger of the cover. Mr. Hord reported back to the general and his council this evening that they found signs of natives in the woods and the fresh remains of a fire, which they estimate to be only a day or two old, possibly from the day before we arrived. The firepit was partly sheltered from the worst of the wind and rain, and a stockpile of branches and pine needles was placed nearby. I believe it only a matter of time, perhaps soon, for the local inhabitants to appear and we will need to prevail on the negotiating skills of Mr. Crowley to secure our presence here. General Drake has decided to delay cleaning the ship until we determine the nature of the local natives. He would like to begin the long voyage well before the end of the month if possible.*

*Diego and Maria indicated they wished to speak to me in private. She has learned a fair amount of English under Diego's instruction. In addition to sharing a semiprivate sleeping place near the general's quarters, they are often seen together during the day. A few of the men have talked about Maria, sometimes in an unseemly manner. My good apprentice, Mr. Kershaw, has kept me informed, but it mostly appears to be the loose, common talk of sailors who have been too long without women. The general and his officers display good moral leadership and maintain a high sense of discipline to the benefit of us all. It is good that Diego is a formidable man and the crew likes and respects him. I must admit, though only in private, I am also drawn on occasion to her pleasant features and manner.*

The next morning brings thirty armed natives. A warning call from one of the guards alerts the crew of eleven on the beach. The four armed sentries join and stand by their comrades, ready to flee if necessary. The natives walk carefully down the central beach trail without signs of overt hostility. They approach slowly as if curious about the strange craft in the cove.

The general, chaplain, and most of the officers are finishing breakfast aboard the ship. A watchman posted on the port rail alerts the crew, and many of them gather to observe the scene on the beach. William Crowley joins the general and chaplain on the aft deck. Much of the native attention appears to be directed at the ship, and several warriors stand along the water's edge staring at the *Golden Hinde*.

To the credit of the beach party, the men remain wary but calm. None raise their weapons. The soldier in charge of the group, John Mariner, had been wounded at Mocha, and his right arm is still wrapped in a bandage.

Everyone witnessing the drama, including Drake, notes Mariner's serenity among the natives. "Stand fast," mutters the general, quietly admiring the discipline and courage of all on the beach. The *Hinde* retains the pinnace beside the hull, ready for use as needed. "Mr. Hawkins, take Mr. Crowley and a few other soldiers to shore as quickly as possible."

"Aye, sir." William nods at three others standing along the rail and points to the pinnace. Hawkins grabs William Crowley by the

131

hand, moves to the rope ladder, and enters the launch, followed by four soldiers. Two sailors accompany them with the oars, and a few minutes later, the boat noses into the beach behind the fifteen crewmen gathered at the water's edge. The natives watch the approach of the pinnace but do not advance or retreat.

Crowley steps in front of his comrades and raises his hand. One of the larger warriors sports a two-inch scar across his left cheek. He steps out from his group and returns the gesture. They are naked except for a hide belt across their waists; pouches holding tools or knives are attached. Most of them carry short spears. Their long, dark hair is double braided, and most have the black and white facial markings. The entire exchange occurs by signs and mimicking gestures. During this time, the boat that brought the interpreter returns to the *Hinde*. Drake and several others climb into the pinnace to bring gifts ashore and join the conversation. This is Crowley's third tribe with which to communicate, and his experience serves him well.

As the sun approaches its highest point, the natives and the men from the ship sit in a circle high on the beach. Like earlier encounters in the region, the tribe seems friendly and curious about who the white men are, where they originated, and what they want. William isn't able to answer all of these questions satisfactorily, but he is able to get across the idea that the white men want to use the harbor for less than a moon cycle and desire permission to hunt game and gather vegetables. The gifts of blankets, coins, tools, and weapons make the negotiations simple. Crowley indicates to Hawkins that they can hunt on land and gather shellfish but not take animals from the sea including fish, seals, and especially whales. Although this particular tribe does not hunt the giant sea beasts, they are considered sacred. Since the men of the *Hinde* have neither the appropriate harpoons nor the experience to take whales, the prohibition is of no consequence, and they have already cured and stored an adequate supply of seal meat from Saint James Island, their first stop after leaving New Albion.

They had named the island after the patron saint of Spain and Portugal. Day of Saint James celebrations typically start on 24 July and culminate in religious ceremonies on the twenty-fifth. Fletcher was in a rare mischievous mood and suggested the name following a sumptuous meal. When informed they had visited the island on the twenty-fourth by the civil calendar, he smugly remarked that they had beaten the Spanish to the site and would be eating the island's harvest the day following. The fact that it was a formal holiday of the Catholic Church added to the irreverence Fletcher and some of the other Protestants enjoyed. The joke was duly noted by Nazario Morera.

During the next few days, Indians continue to gather on the beach and the cliff overlooking it. A small drainage pond exists at the top of the cliff, and several streams feed it, providing a source of fresh water. The native village is half a mile away, set back in the forest and protected from the coastal storms. Like others they have met, the women are mostly naked, but the older women wear a waistcloth tied by bark-woven strings. Some wear animal pelts about their shoulders. The women and children do not approach the white men when they see them but keep their distance and remain silent. This is in sharp contrast to the vocal displays and dances the natives at New Albion exhibited.

Crowley clarifies the limitations on fishing. Apparently, the prohibition extends to fish in the ocean and the cove but not to the streams despite the obvious presence of fish passing back and forth between freshwater and saltwater. From what he understands, the ocean fish represent the "undersea people," whereas the stream and river fish are provided as food by the gods for the land people.

To be on the safe side, Thomas Hord leads a small party two miles upstream to find a suitable spot for fishing. Mark, the youngest black, carries a medium-sized throw net that he uses with skill. Others have simple lines baited with wire hooks and clams, but their luck is poor to terrible. Mark's use of the net yields trout and many fish with red meat. The black man delivers them to the cooks as if they are trophies, which in many ways they are.

Thomas Blacolar, the *Hinde's* boatswain, shows several of the native men how to use a shovel to dig for clams, which are not forbidden. The tribe has apparently relegated these shellfish to the land. The Indians traditionally employ sticks and their hands and are amazed at how quickly and efficiently the shellfish can be removed from the sand by spade. A long beach on the northern side of the headland is the best source of shellfish, and the crewmen make several trips, accompanied by the natives, to gather clams and shore crabs. The metalsmiths make two shovels aboard the *Hinde*, and Drake presents these to the chief of the village.

Inspection of the flagship's hull reveals a few small defects that are easily repaired. Despite the recent storm, the ship fared well with no damage to masts, spars, or sails. Less need for repairs provides a rare opportunity for the crew to relax and enjoy brief sojourns on land before the long voyage ahead. It also leaves time for speculation about the fate of the New Albion Company and why the *Northern Venture* didn't reappear as scheduled. The general's council considers the questions and possible courses of action to take during the next few days.

George Fortescu expresses pessimism about the survival of the fledging enterprise. "If the *Venture* floundered or was otherwise destroyed at some distance from the port, what would the chances be for the crew to return to our good harbor? For that matter, if the ship is lost, they will not have the supplies and materials needed to construct fortifications or any other structures. They could be fighting for survival if they live at all."

Chrystopher Hals, at one time the designated captain of the *Venture*, offers a more positive view. "Now George, let us be more hopeful. The barque is a good, solid craft and should be able to withstand the short journey as well as any ship. She is commanded by two of the best. I would put my faith and my money on Commander Hayman and Lieutenant Gallawaye to see them through safely. Although I can't explain the delay in their return, I believe they will prevail, with divine guidance." He looks at Francis Fletcher as he finishes.

John Chester faces General Drake. "Is there any reason why we cannot raise a second claim post for England and Her Majesty? The first could mark the northern boundary, and this would be the southern boundary of our landings. Extending each claim in a hundred or two hundred leagues would carve out a sizeable territory for England."

A round of hearty agreements answers the proposal, but all eyes turn to Drake. He smiles, clasping his hands in front of his chin. The council knows he is giving serious consideration to the idea, and they are wise enough not to disturb his thoughts. Gregory Cary starts to sit forward and speak, but frowns from several around the table make him freeze with his mouth open. Drake drops his hands to his lap and leans forward. "Gentlemen, I see no harm in erecting a second post and plate detailed as before. Mr. Hawkins, will you have our metalworker, Mr. Cadwell, prepare another plate?" William nods. "Mr. Hord, please secure for us a sturdy fir tree like the one at New Albion, about the same length."

Thomas signals his acceptance, and the talk focuses on reconciling the two locations. What name to bestow on their present location? Should it also be designated New Albion? The small cove doesn't have the characteristics of a harbor; it is fit for only one medium-sized ship. An ocean-going galleon of several hundred tons would not be able to navigate the narrow entrance. General Drake reviews the military and political consequences of their actions. "We do not know what has transpired between England and Spain during our absence. I am sure that our shopping ventures," this brings several laughs, "will be duly noted by King Philip and conveyed to Her Majesty. If we were on the threshold of war when we sailed, we might well be in the midst of a full assault by the time we return. We must pray that our tiny island will fare well against the mighty forces of Spain and its allies."

The council shows signs of uneasiness that had not been present before. Discussion of an Anglo-Spanish war was not raised when promises of a speedy return to New Albion were made. Have they misled their friends and shipmates?

The general continues, "When we present our territorial claims to the court, it will be up to Her Majesty and her counselors to determine how to present these to Spain and other nations. Once Lord Burghley is informed, it will be a small matter of time before word reaches the Spanish court."

His reference to the Queen's lord high treasurer and former secretary of state—a chief advisor opposed to Drake's voyage to the Pacific—is intended as a rebuke to John Doughty and Leonard Vicary. When Drake accused Thomas Doughty of treason, it was because he had revealed Drake's expedition plan to Burghley, making it possible for the Spanish to learn of his secret route. Although Thomas was actually executed for inciting mutiny, the consequences were the same. John and Leonard again joined the council as members and ate with the general and his gentlemen, but there was no love lost between them and Francis Drake.

"We keep two journals of our voyage's progress. As you all know, one is mine, the log of the *Golden Hinde*. Mr. Drake, my cousin," he nods toward John, "has added numerous drawings and maps to enhance the value of our account. Señor Perez has recorded the soundings of the inlets and bays we explored. These will provide the material for cartographers, astronomers, and others"—Drake glances at Lawrence Elyot, who wrote descriptions of plants and animals and assisted John Drake with his drawings—"to assess what we have done for many years to come. The other journal that reflects the events of our travels is kept by Mr. Fletcher."

The chaplain stiffens slightly, hoping his secret journal is still that: undetected and unsuspected. He hides the manuscript among his sacred papers and priestly garments, hoping no one dares to disturb his personal belongings.

"The problem, gentlemen, is this. When a map of our claims is revealed to the world, the Spaniards will react. If we set New Albion at 50°N, it is unlikely they will soon mount an investigation much less an attack. The location is well out of the way, and we would not reveal the precise position in any case. A southern marker can be placed at this cove, but it won't be manned or occupied. Therefore, the claim is weaker and might not be recognized as such by other nations. If we go ahead with a ceremony and plaque, it will be for our own edification and pleasure. We may be able to identify it in the future as a means to establish a boundary between New Spain and ourselves. In the meantime, the less the Spanish dogs know of our presence, the better. This is especially true if the New Albion Company is intact and prepares the settlement we pray will be built and occupied."

Drake waits for the council to comment, but it seems each man is lost in thought, considering the consequences for the group and his own future endeavors. At a signal from the general, Fletcher rises and leads them in a prayer for their success and the safety of the New Albion Company. They have no way of knowing that the survivors of the *Northern Venture* are less than twenty miles north of them.

---

It is Sunday afternoon, and a number of the native men witness a robust service on the beach. They are particularly entranced by the singing of psalms. The remaining three musicians provide a brief concert, and the spirit of peace and cooperation is evident to the Indians and the crew. As arranged, Diego, Francisco, and Maria meet with Fletcher at a quiet spot overlooking the beach. A gentle ocean breeze rustles the needles of the spruce and cedar trees over them. Fletcher is surprised that Francisco has elected to join them, because the chaplain thought the meeting concerned only Diego and Maria. The priest is anticipating a request for matrimony, and he is prepared to guide them in the proscribed church procedures.

Diego assumes command of the gathering as Maria and Francisco sit close by each other, not touching but obviously paired off. "Chaplain Fletcher, we come to you in confidence, seeking your guidance in a most important personal matter." He indicates his two friends. Maria gives him a shy smile and lowers her head.

Francisco remains stoic with his shoulders back as he sits upright, his hands in his lap. Diego looks back at the priest and asks, "Can we trust your discretion in what we have to tell you?"

*His English is so precise, so educated, but why so hesitant? This is not what I expected.* "Confidence can be assured." The chaplain nods for Diego to continue.

"Maria is with child." Diego states it without preamble or equivocation.

Francisco watches the priest for a reaction, and Maria keeps her head down and turned away.

Fletcher sits up and back, confused and not sure what will come next. He has counseled other mothers-to-be, in and out of wedlock, during his previous parish duties, but this—one woman among sixty men aboard an ocean-sailing ship—is quite different.

"My first question is an indelicate one." The priest fixes Diego in the eye and is met by an unwavering stare. "Who might the father of this blessed event be?"

"Blessed event? Are you sure this is something to be welcomed?" Diego has a half smile, but whether it is humorous or intended to mock the priest's pronouncement is not clear.

Francisco speaks for the first time. "Holy sir, I can speak to that." He and Maria exchange looks. She gives a slight nod, and Francisco faces the chaplain. "Maria was subject to the pleasures of Don Zarate, her former master aboard his ship. She was required to lay with him for several nights. She has been with nobody since." He glances at Diego for confirmation.

Diego's eyes remain fixed on Fletcher. "It is so, Chaplain. I have been her protector aboard our ship. I have done so at General Drake's request. No one aboard has molested or acted with ill intent toward our black lady. I did not know about her relationship with the Spanish pig, or I would have killed him with my bare hands. The question now is what we should do."

Fletcher takes a few seconds to think before answering. "We freed her from Zarate in early April. She would be somewhere around four months…" He stops and looks at her. She is only three or four years younger than he is, but his voice becomes soft and gentle, the style to which he is accustomed when offering advice or providing solace. "Child, are you yet showing?"

Maria is perplexed by the question, a slight frown on her face. "Showing? What do you ask?"

Francisco takes her hand. "He means does your belly swell?" He puts his hand on his own stomach and gestures as if it is growing larger. This brings a smile to Diego and Fletcher, and Maria shakes her head. She starts to raise her skirt to show them, but Fletcher puts his hand out to stop her.

"That won't be necessary. I just wanted to be sure you are not further along." He addresses Diego. "We may be leaving here in another week or so. The general has not set a specific date, but most of the preparations for the voyage are complete. If she is less than five months of conception, she will be swollen with child by the time we reach the East Indies. I don't know what General Drake would have to say about having a woman in her condition aboard the *Hinde*." He turns to Maria. "Do you have a preference? Would you wish to stay here and put your trust in our native friends or to continue the voyage with us?"

Maria lifts her head and meets the chaplain's eyes. "I do not wish to be left here. I will not serve the Spanish again should they capture me. I will kill myself first." Francisco holds her hand.

The priest asks Francisco and Diego, "What about you two? Would you remain with Maria if the general decides that she is not to come with us?"

Francisco answers. "I will stay with Maria. I believe Mark wants to be with her and myself. If Big Tom and Peter, her friends aboard the Spanish ship, were here, I believe they would also stay with her." Maria smiles, and all eyes turn toward Diego.

"My place is with my general. Although he is no longer my master, I remain his servant. I follow him, my dragon, until he no longer wants me. I will also do everything possible to protect her," Diego

139

glances at Maria, "and to see that those who stay with her are safe." He looks at Maria and Francisco and then back to Fletcher. "Should we reveal her condition now or wait until we reach the Indies? There may be a refuge where she can find a place away from the Spanish, perhaps with people better disposed to offer a place to raise a child."

"Maybe other children, black children," adds Francisco.

Fletcher says, "You have my discretion, and I will inform the general only if you ask me to. However, I ask you not to let him know that you have confided in me. Otherwise I have an obligation to share the knowledge. He will be merciful, I believe, but keeping her condition a secret might allow you to choose where and when to leave the *Golden Hinde* and our company. I do fear that if he knows about this now, he may decide to leave you here. Are we in agreement?"

They indicate their acceptance and stand. Diego shakes the priest's hand and thanks him for his consultation.

Fletcher adds, "That's what I do, what I really want to do. There is more to being a man of God than delivering sermons on Sundays and saying prayers during meals. I wish all of you the blessings of our Father and Lord. Go with God."

They walk down the trail to the beach: Diego beside the chaplain, followed by Maria and Francisco. The two blacks will not show any affection or close relationship around the others, and Maria will keep her condition hidden as long as possible. Fletcher hopes it will be so.

The masons finish erecting a low wall several feet long on the northern bluff of the cove. It is more symbolic than protective and a way to mark the English visit. The natives continue to be receptive to their presence and silently observe the stone placement and the cleaning activities aboard the *Hinde*. Their curiosity about the pinnace leads Tom Blacolar and one of the crewmen to row several of the Indians about the cove. At one point, two natives gesture that they wish to try the oars, but they are familiar with the smaller paddles of the much lighter canoes. They have the strength but not the technique to guide the eighteen-foot pinnace over the bay waters.

Francis Fletcher and Lawrence Elyot watch John Drake drawing one of the warriors with charcoal. The Indian sits patiently on a driftwood log as John sketches his face, body, and the pelts about his shoulder. He takes additional time to render the details of the shell necklace that symbolizes the man's high status within the tribe.

"Very nicely done, lad," Elyot says to John Drake with a smile, and then he turns to the priest. "He has quite a portfolio of drawings of native inhabitants to show the court when we return."

Fletcher considers the drawing and the past few days. "It would be nice to have artwork to commemorate the granting of these lands to our general and to England. Our taking possession is all part of God's plan for these ignorant but innocent heathens."

Lawrence frowns. "You don't really believe they gave up their land to us, do you? According to Mr. Crowley, they and the other tribes might have simply been good hosts. The exchange of gifts and elaborate welcoming ceremonies appear to be typical of the region's culture and shared by many of the tribes along the straits."

"No, Mr. Elyot, not in the eyes of the church. Just as we make use of animals to feed us, these people serve a purpose. It is our solemn duty to enlighten them and offer them the benefits of our protective embrace. If we don't, the Holy Roman Empire will."

John Drake addresses them. "We can't talk to the animals. I am curious as to how you will make these heathens, as you call them, understand they have surrendered their lives to us and to a country they will never see. To what do we subscribe that rewards us with such arrogance?"

Elyot is too astonished to add anything, but Fletcher replies to the general's young cousin. "Mr. Drake, we subscribe to the general's directives and beliefs. Our ownership of the surrounding lands and its inhabitants has been proclaimed and approved by all attending, including our native friends. Do you doubt what you have witnessed?"

"I doubt it very much, Father Fletcher, as much as I would doubt that the salmon, geese, and deer in these lands have yielded sovereignty to our waving flags or feel enlightened with speeches about distant rulers and religious orders. However, I am only seventeen and have much to learn about subduing people and building empires."

Fletcher says no more but realizes that one more conflict has arisen, one more issue to interpret and resolve between members of the expedition. *Is the general aware of his cousin's thoughts on territorial possession? Are there others with similar objections? How should I represent the natives' reactions to our visit? Clearly we are welcomed, and we depart each village as allies. Hope is high that the same will happen here in our last anchorage in the New World. What harm is there in portraying native acceptance to English rule and compliance with the moral values of the church?*

CHAPTER 9

# Stranded at Three Rocks

A bright day dawns on the beach facing the three rocks. The men's clothes have only partly dried during the night, but it is warm enough for them to remove most of the outer garments and boots. They leave the clothes on the sand as they return to the ship and retrieve additional supplies. Big Tom recovers his composure and shows signs of returning to the joyful giant of the past. He and Little Nele work to remove much of the superstructure. They attempt to save wood and metal, including nails, to build shelters or a second smaller ship later. There is already talk among the men about New Albion South if they can't locate the *Hinde*.

By early afternoon, most of the salvageable items are stacked high on the beach near the river outlet. Hayman, Gallawaye, Watkyns, and Cuttyll walk around the point and proceed up the south bank of the river, which opens into a broad marsh and grass-covered valley. If they had crossed the river and walked up the wooded, higher north bank, they would have easily spotted the remains of recent fires and a large shell mound, but their purpose was to quickly ascertain the presence of inhabitants in the immediate area and whether they might be a threat while the group is vulnerable to attack. After walking a mile, they return to supervise the movement of the *Venture*.

The rising tide allows the broken boat to partly float between two shallow sandbars. With every man pulling on the bow line, they maneuver the ship along the beach to the river mouth. The inflowing tide helps them push it up upstream, but it is slow progress of a few feet at a time. The lightened vessel has taken on a large amount of water, but persistence and sweat allow them to move it a hundred yards inland from the river mouth. This will offer some protection to the ship as they assess what can be repaired and what else might be salvaged. They tie it off to the south bank, intending later to cross the river and tie it to the north bank as well.

For the remainder of the day, the crew transfers supplies and other materials from the exposed beach to a sheltered spot along the southern bank. It is protected from the sea winds by dense foliage and the towering cape looming seaward from the north bank. As the evening breezes arrive onshore, the men don their dry clothes and boots and celebrate their survival with the last of the sea beer from the barque's stores and some of the venison from New Albion. George plays a few numbers on his flute, and Big Tom hums along.

Commander Hayman is pleased to observe his crew recover their good spirits after the disastrous events of the past several days. *It's as if the surf and rain has washed their grief away and cleansed their spirits and bodies at the same time. Staying alive in the face of death will do that. I have seen it several times on the battlefield and at sea. Back to basics, but we survive and continue the good fight.*

The discussion after dinner focuses on whether to split the group or stay together. Hayman and Gallawaye want to use the pinnace that is essentially intact to journey south along the coast and continue the search for Drake's company. If successful, they can return and pick up the others. The group that remains can build temporary shelters. Whether the New Albion Company remains at this site or seeks another place will depend on the availability of food and the presence of natives. Freshwater is not a problem, as small tributaries flow into the larger river. The marsh and a visible grassy open area promise reasonable diversity in wild plants and berries.

Richard Graye and two other soldiers argue against the proposal. They don't believe it prudent to divide their forces. While mindful of the attack in the northern inlet, they make the case for maintaining unity, although they concede that seventeen men and a few arms are no match for a hostile tribe. Exhausted from the day's labor, the marooned band posts two sentries and turns in, foregoing discussions and decisions until the morrow.

---

Decisions arrive the next day just after sunrise. As the men wake and begin to prepare a light breakfast, Indians appear on the north shore of the river. The opposite bank is twenty feet higher than the south bank where the men camp. The sentries did not see the three natives approach from the thick woods. Two of them stand and watch as the third disappears from view.

Cuttyll and Graye quietly pick up muskets and ready them for use. Big Tom is out of sight, behind bushes taking care of his morning needs. Hayman and Gallawaye step forward from the group to the water's edge. The commander estimates the distance between the natives and themselves at less than two hundred yards, which is well within range of the harquebuses but barely within range of native arrows.

Gallawaye confirms the distance. "These are no English longbow men. I doubt they would find their mark at more than a hundred yards." The current is running swiftly with an outgoing tide. It would be difficult for either party to wade across without undue time and effort, so the standoff continues. Hayman raises his arm, open palm toward them, as they had done at Muh-kwa and New Albion. The natives display no reaction.

Several more of the natives arrive on the bank and line up, observing the white men. Hayman glances behind him, not sure whether to have the other men join him or to keep them back and partly hidden. None of the Indians display weapons, although they may have knives. Two of them part to allow a newcomer between them. From the distance, he appears to be older and have some authority. Hayman raises his hand slowly, palm out, hoping the gesture will be reassuring. The older native starts to raise his hand but stops midway and drops it to his side. His mouth opens in astonishment.

Behind Hayman, Big Tom emerges from the bush, buttoning his britches. One of the natives points at the black man, and several mutter among themselves. Tom stands on the bank, several feet from the officers. He is shirtless, and his ebony skin gleams magnificently in the morning sun, but there is no smile. The sight of several natives only a stone's throw away is a brutal reminder of the northern strait attack and the loss of his friend, Peter. He steps back and is about to turn away when Gallawaye asks him to stop. This is one of the words he understands, so he remains in place. George Cooke comes up beside him and speaks quietly.

The tableau freezes. No one wishes to break the delicate balance of caution and readiness. Gallawaye slowly raises and lowers his hand to imitate the Commander's gesture. Big Tom and Cooke stay where they are, and the other men scattered along the beach do the same. Those with swords or muskets note where the weapons are lying or standing. All eyes are directed toward the natives, now eleven of them, motionless and silent.

Hayman whispers to Gallawaye from the side of his mouth, eyes never leaving the band of men across from him. "Can you communicate with them?"

Gallawaye nods. "I can try sir, but I'm no William Crowley."

"I understand. Do the best you can. I expect no more or less." Hayman is firm but not unkindly in his charge.

Gallawaye indicates reluctant agreement. "I can barely talk with Big Tom," he glances back at the immobile giant, "much less discuss anything complicated. I only know a few of the gestures and signs that William used. I might make the wrong ones, and that would be the end of us." He watches the commander, hoping for a reprieve from a task he is certain is bigger than any he has hopes of accomplishing.

Hayman clears his throat and says quietly, "How do we get close to the brutes?"

Gallawaye looks upstream where they hiked the day before. "The river widens and slows where the marsh begins. I presume we could safely wade across at that..." He stops abruptly, and they watch a dozen natives cross the river to their side at the spot Gallawaye indicated.

The party of thirteen includes the older Indian they noticed earlier. They walk slowly in a dignified manner, as if officials welcoming visiting dignitaries. Four of the men carry medium-length spears, and several possess knives. The older man walking slightly in front of the others has a deerskin vest. Most of the warriors are bare chested; a few are completely naked. They wear their long hair in double braids parted down the middle. Several have red streaks in their hair lining the central part. As they draw nearer, several focus on the sight behind the two white men. It is the ship. Bereft of sails, the hull and tall masts dominate the mouth of the river as the ship rocks gently in the swift current.

The other members of the crew rise to their feet and form a cluster behind Big Tom. He attracts undisguised stares from the approaching natives. George Cooke's wind-blown, blond hair and John Gallawaye's flaming-red beard and hair are wondrous additions to the spectacle that has come calling on the natives' shore.

Cuttyll and Graye hold their harquebuses and have them ready to fire, although they are limited to a maximum two shots before the natives will be on them. Thomas whispers to Richard, "I take out the old bastard. You go for the big buck there at his side."

Graye nods, hoping that such a desperate act won't play out. Although there are only four spears among the native group and no clubs in evidence, he notices that each one has a large knife strapped around his waist.

Hayman and Gallawaye remain motionless while the natives approach. From the view of the men gathered behind them, Hayman stands on the left with Gallawaye at his right. The native leader faces Gallawaye and raises his hand, palm out. John looks at Christopher, and the commander inclines his head. "Go ahead and say something. Your red hair is a beacon for them."

Gallawaye responds with the arm movement. "Hello. We are English. We are lost."

Afterward, the greeting seems inane. Although there has probably never been any contact between this tribe and the Spanish, caution overrules common sense. The hostile reception at Mocha was interpreted as mistaken identity and the Mocha islanders' desire for revenge against the less-than-gentle Spaniards. The attack at the inlet was still not understood, although the Englishmen could represent any territorial invader. In the present confrontation, the open-faced smile of the white leaders is helpful, because the natives relax noticeably.

John moves forward, and the Indians' eyes follow him. For some reason, probably not known to the lieutenant himself, he bows and then looks into the leader's eyes. He points at himself and says, "Gallawaye." He repeats this and then points to the leader.

The leader looks at the large warrior at his right and then back at John. The warrior steps forward to face Gallawaye from eight feet away. "Kin-te-ash," he says, pointing at himself. He bows. This brings muffled chuckles from the crew standing twenty feet back, but Hayman turns and frowns, resulting in their immobile silence.

Gallawaye introduces the commander as "Chief" and himself as "Chief Two." He motions for Hayman to stand tall, and John lowers his head and body a few inches. Hayman quietly asks Gallawaye to fetch one of the gift knives. They keep a supply of beads, coins, and knives for trade and gifts. John signals to Grige and tells him to bring several gift items from their supply cache.

A few minutes later, Hayman presents knives to the leader, whose name they learn is Quin-at-che, and to Kin-te-ash. He passes a silver pence or sixpence to each of the others, and they examine the coins with interest. Another native comes forward and begins to gesture and speak with Gallawaye. Apparently, he is their spokesman. He and the lieutenant sit on the beach and begin an earnest dialog. The leader makes the greeting gesture, Hayman returns it, and the group walks upstream to cross back the way they came. After several minutes, Hayman and Gallawaye leave the spokesman and rejoin their men, who are now talking, laughing, and continuing with their assigned tasks.

"I'll be damned for sure if Lieutenant Gallawaye won't be the most useful of all of us," remarks Francis Caube. Most of the expedition's members hold Gallawaye in high esteem. He earned additional respect by the New Albion contingent after he befriended Big Tom and displayed decisive leadership during the Indian attack in the north. The others agree with Caube as Hayman and Watkyns circulate among the crew and give instructions on the preparations to make.

Emmanuel Watkyns starts to assert more authority with the shipboard phase of their mission at an apparent end. Although they don't have much surplus food at the moment, they might share something else that they no longer need in large supply with the natives. They can cut up some of the extra sailcloth and present it if a ceremonial need arises. They aren't sure about what the tribe might do next and hope Gallawaye gained some insight.

Hayman is still anxious to search for Drake, and Cuttyll wants to start building shelters. Richard Graye and three others explore the marsh for food sources. Hayman agrees to delay launching the pinnace until a few repairs are made to its hull and two of the oars. They organize the camp but decide against erecting any obstacles or digging trenches as wasted labor. Although they don't yet know how many natives are nearby, it is obvious to everyone that their best defense is establishment of a friendly relationship.

A partial answer comes that evening. It has been a slow and tedious process of interpretation, but Gallawaye estimates there are seventy tribe members residing in the village nearby and many others a few miles away. The number includes a dozen children and thirty women of different ages. He tells the Indian spokesman, Winash-at-kish, the white men number seventeen. John understands that the gifts they bestowed will be reciprocated the next day when the white men are welcome in the village. It is just over a hill and behind a dense stand of spruce and cedar, much closer than they suspected. Two warriors will come with Winash-at-kish in the morning to fetch them for the meeting and meal.

Hayman sorely misses the guidance of his general, the chaplain, Crowley, and others who represented the expedition in the Muh-kwa village and at the harbor. It proceeded so miraculously well that the New Albion Company hasn't given serious thought to the etiquette and protocols they will undoubtedly need to observe during their isolation in the New World. Every encounter with a new tribe is a unique experience, and the lessons learned can be applied only so far. The lieutenant made good progress in learning some basic words and information they needed, but a formal sit down with the tribe is different from two men talking informally on the beach.

Gallawaye has indicated that all the white men are expected to attend, and no one will be left to guard the camp or supplies. As a precaution, in case any are able to flee the scene, they bury the muskets save two and some of the food.

Watkyns sits on a driftwood log and stares at the three rocks. *Is it a trap, an invitation that leads to a quick massacre?* With Hayman's concurrence, Watkyns decides to keep Graye and Cuttyll armed, more for show than actual protection. Half of the men will have swords, and all carry a small knife.

After dinner, Hayman tells the men to show no fear and walk proudly but display no bad temper or impatience. His own observations of behavior in several groups of natives has taught him to be respectful guests in their land but, if they are to die, to fight well and die with honor. As might be expected, the soldiers accept this readily as the code they trained and lived by, the sailors a little less so, and the workmen more reluctantly. They did not come on a supposed "trade mission" to die at the hands of savage brutes halfway around the world from home, but there they are.

---

THE NEXT DAY ARRIVES WITH FRESH BANKS OF FOG ROLLING onto the beach and up the river.

"Reminds you a bit of Plymouth or Devon, hey, mate?" William Haynes laughs. "Many a morning I woke up to the sweet smell and taste of this." He muses as he stretches his long arms and legs next to the fire. He just came off of guard duty and would prefer a few hours of sleep, but the events of the day won't wait for him to dream of English lassies and tavern ale.

Thomas Grige looks at him and then around at the beach, marsh, and forest. "Fancy you'll stroll along the wharf and find some hot rolls and a bit of mackerel for a bite, do you?" He shakes his head and starts eating hard biscuit from the ship's stores and berries they gathered the day before. "The fruits aren't so bad. Willy, try some."

Haynes picks a few berries out of a cup and gulps them down with freshwater recently collected. "Seems we could live here a while if need be. Won't be able to get wasted on the waterfront like in our earlier days, but we can hope for some accommodation by our hosts."

"Might be they have some goodly women in the village. If half as comely as the ones in the strait, I'd be satisfied with our lot. For now anyway." Grige might not be the horniest man in the company, but he talks like he is, and Gallawaye has cautioned him about keeping his hands and eyes busy with other things.

The title of horniest man might rest on the shoulders, or other parts, of Nicholas Franconi. He makes no disguise of his desire to gaze upon the naked natives they have encountered. He walks up to Grige in time to hear his comment.

"The lieutenant thinks there might be as many as thirty women in the village. Do you think they'll be as undressed as their men?" Franconi displays an impudent leer.

Haynes regards him with undisguised disgust. "If not, Nick boy, there are always the men for your lecherous eyes. Who knows? Maybe one of them will fancy a nice lad like you." Grige gives a hearty guffaw, and they leave Franconi standing alone on the beach, gazing at the barque.

The *Northern Venture* has settled noticeably into the sandy mouth of the river as reversing tides swirl around the hull and the wind rocks it. Although the crew has not completely abandoned the idea of repairing and refloating her, it might be too late to extract her from the sediment if they don't act in a timely fashion. A good storm with wave action could render the idea impossible in short order.

At midmorning, the three tribal envoys arrive from the north bank. The New Albion Company awaits them at the crossing, and they traverse the river easily, wading up to their waists and Big Tom to his thigh. As before, the men remain silent and observant as they walk uphill on a well-used trail. At the top of a ten-foot bluff, they spot a large shell mound to their left. Most of the shells are oysters, although there are cockles and elongated clams of a generous size. They can discern fish skeletons and animal bones of various sizes among the rubble. The remains of a large fire with some unburnt pieces of pine and fir are seen several yards along the trail.

John Gallawaye walks in front of the group with Winash-at-kish; Hayman and the other two natives follow behind. Thomas and Richard, with the harquebuses, come next, and the others trail with George Cooke and Big Tom bringing up the rear. The commander wants to keep the big man as a surprise for the natives who have not yet seen him. Although they can't converse well, the black man has been instructed to stay by Gallawaye's side when they are at the village and fight for him if needed but otherwise remain silent and visible. He wears a sailor's blouse, but his arms and thighs are exposed and provide the image that impresses.

The village is simple but adequate. A number of lean-tos are scattered about a large clearing. These appear to be temporary, erected quickly and primarily open sided. One substantial building in the center of the clearing is comprised of large hewn planks. Roof holes at each end spew white curling smoke, presumably from cooking fires. A large bonfire burns in front of the wood building in the center of the clearing. A number of warriors sit around the fire, but whether it is all or most of the village men is impossible to tell. Women and children face the visitors from the far side of the clearing. As Franconi wished, they are mostly naked. Several well-dressed natives sit at one end of the assembly. Their ground blankets appear to be deerskin pelts similar to the coverings the Muh-kwa used in their village. Four blankets are unoccupied. Winash-at-kish, who the crew simply calls "Kish," motions for Hayman and Gallawaye to sit on two of them. Kish stands and waits for both to sit while holding up two fingers, an apparent reference to Gallawaye's identification of himself as Chief Two.

When Big Tom strides into the clearing, stoic decorum disintegrates among the natives. Most have not seen him before, although they were probably informed by those who had. He doesn't smile, but he seems at peace with where he is and who he is with. Cooke puts his hand on Tom's arm, points to a spot next to the lieutenant, and says, "Stay." Tom walks to the spot and sits with Hayman and Gallawaye.

Many of the members of the New Albion Company had not witnessed the ceremonies at the two strait villages, but they were told what transpired, and some aspects seem similar. Gallawaye is presented to the leaders of the tribe, but it is difficult to tell if there is one single person in charge. It seems more like a council that includes Quin-at-che, the older leader they met the first day, and Kin-te-ash, the big warrior, who stands six feet or an inch more. The warriors begin sitting on the ground, and the rest of the New Albion Company follows their example. The white men anticipate the ceremony will take some time, and most of them hope they will be included in the midday meal. Chrystopher Huntsman remarks that he hopes they aren't the dinner. Some jokes never die.

Hayman brought several folds of sailcloth to give the tribe. Cuttyll stretches the material on the ground, and two of the council leaders hold it up to examine it. They realize it can serve as a useful shelter covering and share this with the seven other members of the council. A few of the native women come forward carrying presents. The first gift, a knife made from the same black, glass-like material that Big Tom claimed during the attack in the northern strait, is presented to Chief One, Christopher Hayman. The lieutenant sits between the commander and Kish to whisper advice and translate what he can. Apparently, the natives did not see their stormy arrival and the shipwreck during the night. Whether they were aware of the white men's presence the day after the storm isn't clear to Gallawaye, but he is able to explain that the large wooden hulk sitting in their river is how they arrived from the sea.

This creates a stir in the assembled tribe, especially in the elders. As far as Gallawaye can determine, the western expanse of the sea is where souls go after death. To have them return is either a blessing or a curse, depending on who they were and what they want. Gallawaye's understanding of the death cycle is less than perfect, but it reminds him of what they discussed on the beach the day before.

Hayman regards his interpreter for a moment. "Do they think we have returned from the dead?"

"I'm not sure, Commander. Kish says we don't look like dead people, and we don't look like his people, so if we are dead, we must be from somewhere far away."

"Well, he has the last part right. Should we go along with this or try to convince them we are as alive as they are?"

"It may not be necessary, sir. They keep asking about Big Tom. I wanted him to sit with us, so I told Kish he needed to be with his guardians. I'm not sure what they want or think about him."

"They seem to be in awe, and that might work to our advantage. Since he can't talk with them directly, you can direct his activities and responses to how they behave."

"They might think he is some kind of a god. They haven't said so, but I believe they want to honor him or worship him. I'm not sure this is a good idea, but I could be wrong. Besides, my ability to communicate with him is not much better than with the natives. I'm afraid we relied too heavily on Peter's Spanish. The rest of us are weak in that tongue."

While Gallawaye and Hayman confer, women serve food and drink to the council and the two New Albion leaders. Watkyns remains with the others, keeping an eye on Graye and Cuttyll. The harquebuses attract curious glances from the warriors, but they are naïve about what the muskets represent. The soldiers hope to keep it that way. Watkyns stays behind the scenes while dealing with the natives, deferring to Gallawaye's ability to communicate and Hayman's general resourcefulness.

The leaders are well on their way through lunch that features large portions of salmon and trout along with a fatty, strong-tasting meat that Hayman indicates is probably a type of seal. The natives serve the other white men. The native audience drinks a brewed tea but does not eat, and the women are present only long enough to serve drink and food and retrieve waste. Franconi loses no opportunity to admire the breasts and hips that pass by, and he quietly indicates his preferences to Cooke, who pointedly ignores him. During the meal, several wooden cups and tightly woven baskets are presented to Gallawaye and Hayman. After the last of the portions of the meal are consumed, the discussion becomes serious and lengthy.

The warriors leave the clearing and begin working around the village. Some walk off in various directions including the trail back to the river and their camp. Hayman turns to Gallawaye. "Ask them if our men can return to camp while we continue the talks."

The lieutenant mimics walking and then points to his men and the river. One of the council members nods at Kish, and Gallawaye tells the commander that their men are at liberty to leave.

Hayman stands and addresses the crew. "Go back to the camp, and stay prepared for whatever happens. Some of their men may be curious, and you can show them the ship if they wish to approach it. Make sure none of them falls or gets hurt. You can show them rope or a few of our things, but don't get the arms or anything we buried. Be polite, and don't antagonize them. Smile, men, smile." He turns and sits down on the pelt as his men file down the trail for the walk of several hundred yards to the river. Big Tom remains next to Gallawaye.

Hayman stares at the giant. *Good God in heaven, I forgot he was told to stay with Gallawaye no matter what.* He starts to ask the lieutenant to dismiss him but then thinks better of it. *Maybe this will help us reach a favorable agreement.*

The sun descends over the headland, and shadows grow. Gallawaye consults with Hayman as Kish relays questions and preferences from the tribal elders. When asked how long the white men intend to stay, John tries to provide an indefinite answer. Finally, he feels forced to specify a time. He proposes one moon cycle, and the natives indicate agreement. They make it clear to him that their village is not a permanent one; it serves for summer shellfish harvesting and seal hunting. Their long-term village is twenty miles away, northward and inland for protection from winter storms. Sufficient food from the sea, river, marsh, and adjacent meadows is available for all of them, and they are prepared to share with the "White Gods from the Sea."

The black man is a topic that John Gallawaye is having difficulty resolving. The natives want to talk to him to see if he is like the others even though he is a different color.

John clears his throat and speaks in a low voice. "I believe, sir, they want to know if he is human. In particular, the warrior Kinte-ash would like to see him demonstrate his strength."

"Do you think they will be satisfied if he shows them that, perhaps by lifting or throwing a large boulder?"

"I don't know for certain, but it might be worth a try," replies Gallawaye, although he is still reluctant to have Big Tom participate in a demonstration or to verify his mortality. "The way I see it, if you'll pardon me for saying so, we may be damned if we do or damned if we don't. I'm not so sure what they will make of him if they find out he is just a big man and not some immortal hero."

"Yes, I understand your concern, but at this point I believe we need to offer our cooperation and have Tomas appease their curiosity. Will you arrange it?"

"Aye, sir. I'll tell him what we need."

Gallawaye rises and motions for Big Tom to stand. He smiles as John stands beside him and, with words and gestures, tells him what the Indians requested. Big Tom grins and nods.

The council and a few of the remaining warriors gather near the bonfire. The lieutenant points to a large section of tree trunk on the seaward side of the clearing. The piece is ten feet long and appears to be destined to become a canoe, but the hollowing and chiseling have not started. It must have taken four to six strong men to drag it from the forest to where it lies.

Big Tom straddles the trunk and lifts one end toward him, balancing it on end. He bends down to one side, swings his arm under it, and lifts the log to his chest so it is perpendicular to the ground. It is heavy even for him, but with a grunt and a bent knee, he raises it slowly overhead and then straightens his legs so that he holds it high and balanced. Stepping back, he heaves it away from him, and the massive log hits the ground with a resounding thud.

Gallawaye and Hayman watch the reactions of the elders and warriors. There is obvious fascination, but they say nothing and don't smile. Only the size of the pupils in their wide-open eyes show they are impressed.

Big Tom picks up a rock that weighs about twelve pounds. He hefts it for a minute and then lets it fly out of sight. This alarms Gallawaye, who hadn't asked him to do it. He can only hope the missile didn't hit anyone outside the village. John puts his hand on the black man's shoulder, a sign that he has done enough and may stand and relax.

Kish confers with the elders and then signs to Gallawaye their appreciation for the demonstration and the gifts. They are free to return to their camp and join their men. After expressing gratitude for the meal and being allowed to stay for the agreed-upon month, the New Albion leaders depart.

---

That evening, the discussion among the men in camp continues in earnest. Facing a one-month deadline, the two naval leaders believe it is imperative to continue the search for the *Golden Hinde*. They do not know how far or how long they will need to venture and then return. They know Drake's intention to sail will be soon approaching. There is no time to waste.

Several soldiers, including Graye and Cuttyll, express the opinion that their best chance of survival is to return north to the Muh-kwa village. They reason that when Drake or other English ships return through the Strait of Elizabeth, they will be able to make contact with the help of their native allies. The soldiers want to journey inland to seek a more direct route to the strait, which would avoid large river mouths and might provide a wider variety of foods. However, they are willing to wait the month for the return of the pinnace before setting out.

Lieutenant Gallawaye speaks next. He tells the group that Big Tom might make it possible for them to extend their stay at the camp for the summer and join the native band when they return to their permanent winter village. He informs them that the natives refer to themselves as Ne-Chess-Nee and he is willing to accompany the black man if the Indians accept them. George Cooke indicates he favors staying with the native village. Three of the Indian men had admired his flute playing that afternoon, and he noticed one of the younger maidens giving him curious looks.

This brings Nicholas Franconi to his feet to regard Watkyns, Hayman, and Gallawaye. "Sirs, I also volunteer to remain at the village."

Watkyns asks, "What in particular motivates your desire to stay with our native friends?" This brings a smirk and laugh from Grige and Haynes, but they say nothing.

"To assist in whatever way I am able to the benefit of the New Albion Company, if it please you, sir." Franconi sits with a content expression as he regards Grige and Haynes.

Gallawaye is not pleased by his answer but refrains from comment. Watkyns signals his approval.

After everyone expresses their preferences, Hayman, Gallawaye, and Watkyns rise and walk fifty yards from the main fire. A second fire burns near the mouth of the river in case Drake has yet to pass by the *Venture* and river mouth. The three men confer about the discussion and how to proceed. It doesn't take as long to divide the company as they had anticipated. The friendly reception at the summer village seems to be genuine, and the points the crew members have made are valid.

They return to the men around the main camp fire and announce their joint decision. The pinnace and oars are to be repaired, and a group of six will sail along the coast, travelling as many as twelve days to the south. This allows them up to eighteen days to return before the month expires, whether they locate Drake or not. The nearshore currents appear to be from the south, but the winds prevail from the northwest. Extra time and effort to come back to the three rocks will be required. Commander Hayman will lead the pinnace crew that consists of the sailors William Haynes, Thomas Grige, Richard Morgyn, Little Nele, and John Deane. They will need but a day to prepare and stock sufficient food and water so that they don't waste time on either leg of the journey.

The six who desire to follow the river inland will be led by Richard Graye. They will include the soldier Thomas Cuttyll, sailors William Whyte and Thomas Martyn, and laborers Chrystopher Huntsman and Francis Caube. Again, they agree to wait for the encampment time to expire in thirty days before setting out on what everyone agrees will be a one-way trip. Gallawaye tells them he has learned from Kish that there is a large river valley on the other side of the coastal hills. The valley river flows north, and that might expedite their trip to the strait. He also warns them that some of the valley tribes might not be as friendly as the coastal people, so the two soldiers will be armed with harquebuses.

This will leave five at the Ne-Chess-Nee village if the pinnace group is unable to return within one month. Emmanuel Watkyns and Gallawaye will be co-leaders. Nicholas Franconi, George Cooke, and Big Tom complete the resident roster. If arrangements to extend their stay or journey to the inland winter camp with the Ne-Chess-Nee manifest, they are to leave signs at the river mouth for the return visit of the pinnace group or Drake's men. They are not concerned about possible discovery by the Spanish, since their location lies well north of the usual Manila-Acapulco galleon trade route. As they turn in for the night, they post their usual sentries, but the general mood is relaxed and one of accord with the plan. Their survival depends on finding Drake's group or securing accommodations in the Muh-kwa and Ne-Chess-Nee villages.

The next day, the repairs to the ship's pinnace require four hours, and by midafternoon, the seventeen-foot launch is ready to sail. She has a single midmast, aft rigged, and a five-foot bowsprit that can tie a headsail or jib, although she usually employs only one triangular midsail. The boat has six pairs of oars and a spare pair. It is an open-air boat with a small aft deck in front of the tiller. They load an extra sheet of sailcloth and extra rope for emergency repairs.

Several of the natives watch the preparations with great interest. Kish is not among them, so Gallawaye is unable to provide them with information or answer questions.

William Haynes regards his shipmates on the beach as they survey the launch converted to search boat. "Lads, this is the biggest working ship left in the naval forces of New Albion. Isn't it proper to bestow a name and christen her?" Hearing comments of agreement, the veteran sailor turns to Commander Hayman. "Sir, what name would please you?"

Hayman looks at the five crewmen who will accompany him and at his second in command standing slightly behind him. "Lieutenant Gallawaye, do you have any recommendations?"

"I don't believe it should be a designation of mine, sir. I won't be aboard, at least not for this voyage. I would leave it to the crew." He faces each of them, admiring their bravery and fortitude. There is no way of knowing what they might endure in the days ahead.

Hayman turns to the pinnace crewmen. "Anyone wish to propose one?"

Little Nele takes one pace forward, and all eyes are on him. "I propose we remember our other Nele, Great Nele the Dane, and call our lovely craft the *Great Dane*."

Big Nele was a popular crewman aboard the *Hinde*. His death at Mocha was grieved by many. It requires only a few seconds for the other members of the pinnace party to give their approval.

Commander Hayman nods, smiles, and says, "I am afraid we have no liquor to sanction the name or a priest to say the blessing, so I will do the best I can." He lowers his head, and the crewmen do likewise. "We beseech you, dear Lord, to look favorably upon our mission, to bless this crew and this craft, the *Great Dane*, and to return us safely to our comrades and countrymen. Amen." Gallawaye gladly concedes the blessing to Hayman without being asked. John Deane carves the name onto the starboard bow. They will launch at first morning light.

---

GALLAWAYE HAS BEEN KEEPING A CALENDAR WITH INK AND paper since before the wreck, but now he carves the progression of the days on a piece of driftwood. It is 8 August and, if he is not mistaken, a Saturday. The departure day dawns with a light, rolling fog and a steady but gentle breeze. The remaining members of the New Albion Company gather on the beach, along with a few of the natives, to watch the *Great Dane* put out to sea and traverse the rolling surf. The mainsail unfurls. Several minutes later, the *Great Dane* and one-third of the New Albion Company disappear around a bend on the coast.

CHAPTER 10

# Drake's Anchorage

―――∞―――

Fletcher writes in his secret journal.

*Tuesday, 11 August 1579*

*At midday dinner, General Drake announced to his council that the* Golden Hinde *is fit and ready to sail. He said we should prepare to depart this coming Thursday. The word has spread to the crew that tomorrow will be our last day on these shores. Most men greeted the news with great joy, and several suggested that a special feast of celebration be held tomorrow. This would be another opportunity to commemorate the brave souls of the* Northern Venture, *wherever they be. The general will use the midday to post the second claim for New Albion with a plate and English flag.*

*As promised, nothing has been said to our leader about Maria's condition. Diego continues to stay by her side, although Francisco is more visible now than before. If our navigators are correct, we should be in the Moluccas by November at the latest. This should allow us time to locate Maria and her two friends somewhere safe.*

*Our native hosts do not seem to be despairing with regard to our imminent departure. Mr. Crowley has informed the council at the village. He says that they wish us good fortune on our journey, but they are still ignorant of who we are and where we came from. They have freely surrendered their sovereignty to us but are not concerned that we remain to rule. There has not been time to instruct them in matters of policy or religion. At Port New Albion, I had hoped to begin the conversion of the natives to our practices, especially because of the grief they expressed when we left their company. I will pray for these innocent souls and hope to return or send someone to enlighten them before the papists have their way.*

The claim ceremony proceeds in a similar fashion as the earlier one at Port New Albion. The current date and claim for Her Majesty Queen Elizabeth appears on the metal sheet along with the name of Francis Drake. The indication of the land as New Albion is missing—it is simply entitled "For the Possession of the English Nation." Hawkins leads three cheers by the assembled gentlemen and crew while a crowd of curious native men looks on from both sides of the beach. As before, the native women and children observe from the bluff and headland.

One other observer stands at the back of the assembled crew. Nazario de Morera realizes this is the night to take action. By deserting the crew on their last night, there is little chance they will search for him. He has spent the last few days reenacting his illness and complaining of stomachache and chest pain, emphasizing his relative uselessness as a pilot and crewmember.

In preparation for his exit, he has stowed food, clothes, an extra pair of boots, and a large knife in a bag, hidden in a rock crevice above high tide. He has a flint for starting a fire, a compass, and a hand axe. He debates about taking a long sword but decides it is too cumbersome. A shorter blade will be more efficient. He includes a water-resistant poncho and a sailor's cap. He knows he is many hundreds of leagues north of his destination, New Galicia or New Spain. It will be a long trek that he might not finish, and if he arrives, his welcome will be uncertain. *Can I convey enough of value about Drake and his voyage to compensate for aiding El Draque in his efforts?*

Despite his feigned illness, the forty-year old Basque is in good physical condition. He has consumed some of Hernan Perez's tea and knows how to make more. His complexion is swarthy, and he has some facial features in common with the natives he has met in the Americas. *Will I be able to negotiate with those I encounter? All questions will be answered in due course. Tonight I take the first steps to freedom and leave the heretical blasphemers to their fate.*

---

FIRES BURN BRIGHTLY ALONG THE BEACH AS THE CREWMEMBERS of the *Golden Hinde* enjoy their last night on land for many long weeks to come. A few natives sit at the periphery of the gathering, but most of the noise is the crew laughing and dancing, a fiddle, clapping, and the general merriment of all attending.

Morera is present to avoid any suspicion, but he maintains the appearance of illness. The general deploys a few sentries, but the pilot knows where they are, how to retrieve his bag, and the route to make his way out of the camp. Before midnight, the fires have burned low, and most of the crew is asleep. The outgoing tide will begin just before midmorning, and the *Hinde* will sail with it.

Morera waits an hour after the last celebrant falls asleep. Some have returned to the ship, but the majority elect to spend the night on the beach. Deck or shore, the fog will present the same wet cold, but land will be a memory after tomorrow. Hearing nothing but snores and noting the natives departed some time earlier, Morera crawls from his blanket, wraps it over his shoulders, and walks the short distance to the rock and his hidden bag. The moon is a few days past full, and there is sufficient light to see the trail up the southern slope of the cove. The Basque wears dark clothes and will be difficult to spot even if a sentry or other observer is looking.

A few minutes later, Morera is at the top of the southern headland, looking down at the cove and the flagship. He knows the next few miles of shoreline will be rocky and inundated by small coves. According to Hord's scouting party, there are no major rivers to cross.

Morera plans to stay close to the coast for most of his trek, especially during the coming winter. As the climate becomes more agreeable, he might venture inland, especially if there is a valley. Traversing the coast seems the surest path south, but large bays and river mouths present obstacles that require detours and add distance and time to the journey. He turns his back on the cove—his final *adiós* to Drake, the *Golden Hinde*, and the infidels. Morera is determined to put several miles between himself and any pursuers before daybreak.

---

No one notices that the pilot is missing until the last of the shore party and their belongings are loaded into the pinnace. Fletcher has been looking for Morera since sunrise, but in the hustle and bustle of preparing to leave, he assumes the Basque is aboard the ship. After asking several of the crew if they have seen him, Fletcher notifies Drake that the pilot is not accounted for.

"I saw him last night," reports Hawkins. Several others second the observation as Drake stands on deck watching the last crewmen climb aboard. The pinnace is attached and ready for hoisting on deck.

Thomas Hord listens to the reports and turns to the general. "Sir, should we send a party out for him?"

Drake gazes at the cove and surrounding cliffs. "We don't know which direction he might have gone. I presume it would be south to join his papist friends in New Spain. If so, he'll have a long, lonely trip ahead. No, we are better rid of the devil, so leave him to hell. We have little to worry about from him or those he reaches." The general walks away, muttering.

Blacolar gives the signal. The pinnace is brought aboard, the anchor is raised, and the sails are unfurled. As natives on the beach and headland watch, the *Golden Hinde* sails out of the cove and into the Pacific Ocean.

Morera gets a glimpse of the ship as he walks along the crest of a seaside cliff. It is far out to sea, but the morning sun over his left shoulder illuminates the unmistakable square-rigged sails, bright white against the ocean blue.

---

A FEW HOURS AFTER DEPARTING THREE ROCKS, THE *GREAT DANE* sails down the coast. After rounding a slight rocky projection, they find themselves off a long sandy beach that extends for miles southward. The beach is backed by vegetated sand dunes and low bluffs. There are no signs of habitation, and it is apparent that if they haven't already passed the *Hinde* north of them, it also isn't immediately to their south. Staying outside of the surf zone, they make rapid progress, and by late morning, they reach an outlet that breaks through the beach. In the distance, they can see many additional miles of the same straight stretch of sand and low cliffs.

Striking sail, they row into the stream and investigate. It is a river that turns sharply to the south from the ocean end of the northward-projecting sand spit. A shallow bay and extensive marsh filled with a variety of shorebirds greet them as they slide upriver. It is apparent that the *Hinde* could not have entered such a shallow cove, but Hayman recommends they take their lunch break while protected from the sea waves and a moderate onshore wind.

They pull onto the landward shore of the bay, intending to gather greens to go with the salted meat. By this time, most of them can identify wild onions and some other tubers. Bushes of fresh berries provide an added bonus for their midday repast.

"We'll be off by noon, lads, so be brisk about your business," yells William Haynes. He is now the second-in-command of the pinnace, and Hayman trusts him to keep things organized while ashore. "Business" refers to relieving themselves before lunch, which has an unforeseen consequence.

It is a beautiful seaside day with gulls circling overhead, and the salty smell is refreshing and welcome to any who love the sea. The crew members disperse to gather greens and relax from several hours of rowing and sailing. It is a peaceful moment to reflect on their mission and destiny. Contemplation of the latter is different for each man.

Richard Morgyn squats next to a large bush, distracted by his continuing desire for a woman—any woman—and a bottle of whiskey to go with her. He never sees the club that smashes his right temple, scattering bone and blood across the sand in front of him. He falls with a grunt and thud and dreams no more. His body lies out of sight from Haynes, who is walking along the silty channel looking for clams.

Haynes looks up just as two warriors burst from behind scrubby trees and run at him, clubs raised. He draws his sword and gives a warning yell as they close. His sabre runs one through the belly, but before he can extract it, the other warrior hits him across the forehead and knocks him to his knees. The Indian draws a curved knife from his belt and shoves it into Haynes' chest.

Several other natives emerge from the brush and charge at the other four crewmen. Hayman yells at them to return to the boat, but several of the natives have blocked the direct path to it. Little Nele charges toward them with a sword and cuts one of the Indians across the thigh, hobbling him. One warrior about the same size as Nele dodges the sword and hits him with a club between the right shoulder and neck, causing the boatman to drop his sword and sink to his knees. His end comes as clubs descend on his head and back. The natives make no sounds, no yelling or shrieking. It is all business and as fast as that.

John Deane and Thomas Grige, the two secret Catholics, die fighting back to back. "Our father…" are Thomas's last words. John feels Thomas collapse behind him and faces several warriors alone. He never finishes his own last prayer. Hayman is the last to go down. He cuts two of the attackers across the chest before falling with a spear through his gut. A knife across his throat ends a potentially prolonged death. Within five minutes, the entire crew of the pinnace lies bloody and dead on the shore.

Two Indians walk over to the pinnace and look into it. One grabs the meat and two blankets from the boat while the other uses a handled stone axe to puncture the hull bottom. The *Great Dane* shares the fate of its crew. Satisfied, the small band of natives gathers knives and swords from the dead crewmen, ignoring the two muskets that haven't been fired. Three natives are dead and one is crippled with a deep leg gash. The bodies are picked up and the cripple is assisted as the band walks back into the brush without a backward glance.

CHAPTER 11

# Ne-Chess-Nee

Life for the eleven survivors of the *Northern Venture* at Three Rocks settles into routine tasks. John Gallawaye assembles the men on the beach in front of the barque for Sunday service. He again assumes the role of the unordained preacher, a lay practitioner, but with no book of Psalms or Holy Bible. They were not rescued from the ship and have not been found in subsequent searches. Nevertheless, the good lieutenant improvises with what he remembers: a few proverbs and lessons on perseverance and maintaining faith along with words of encouragement to boost morale. The simple rites are needed as reminders of who they are and to help dispel the depression of hopelessness and abandonment that threatens to overwhelm them.

Graye and Cuttyll, the two best soldiers in the New Albion Company encampment, start exploration up the river past the estuarine marsh. Because of the abundance of fish, including the salmon that the crew and the natives relish, Watkyns proposes the stream be named the Salmon River. Gallawaye indicates the Ne-Chess-Nee have already applied a similar name. William Whyte, a skilled and enthusiastic fisherman, often travels with the soldiers carrying a line and net he fashioned from salvaged materials on the *Venture*.

Thomas Cuttyll and Gallawaye attempt to assess the seaworthiness of the barque as it rests at the mouth of the river. There is considerable damage to the portside bow where the ship struck the southern rock. Repairs might be attempted if the ship could be careened, but they have few men to bring the barque over. Watkyns suggests they might be able to recruit some of the native men to help, but Gallawaye indicates that they are engaged in summer hunting and preparing for the fall move inland. The retreat from the shore will take place shortly after the one-moon residency period expires for the white men, raising the question of what will happen at that time.

Gallawaye fully expects the pinnace to return with word, one way or another, of the *Hinde* and whether a different site for their occupation is possible. Plans for the six who want to return to Muhkwa also depend on the news Hayman brings back. In the meantime, Watkyns and Gallawaye wish to remain in the good graces of the tribe. They show some of the natives their techniques for trapping animals and fishing and how to harvest crabs and shellfish. The natives occasionally hunt for seals on the rocks north of the headland, but the white men are discouraged from accompanying them. Graye and Cuttyll watch them from the cliffs above, but Gallawaye cautions them to remain discreet and hidden in case the prohibition is a serious or sacred one.

The crew actively employs Big Tom to retrieve heavy objects from the barque and to assist with any duties that require his superior strength. The natives adopt Tomas for the same purpose. For whatever reason, he is the one member of the company permitted to accompany tribal hunters to the seal rocks, and he helps bring the heavy carcasses of the sea lions ashore and lifts deer and elk onto sleds for transportation to the village. George Cooke is often with the big black when they are in camp or at the village, but he is forbidden to go to the seal rocks. The native men are fascinated with Tom and often feed him separately from the *Venture* crew. They also feed Cooke when he brings his flute and plays, and this seems to delight the children and women. Within two weeks, Big Tom and George are spending more time at the Indian village than at the company camp.

"Can't be doing any harm, I suppose. Seems to be keeping goodwill flowing, and George isn't that handy with much else," remarks Whyte.

Watkyns is not sure whether he agrees. "Keep an eye on them, John. George is a good lad but not the brightest candle on the deck. Big Tom is friendly and means right, but we still don't communicate that well, and he might misinterpret what the natives expect from him. They seem to almost worship him at times by serving him and allowing him to participate in their seal hunts."

John turns to Whyte. "Let me know if anything changes, Willy. George told me the other night that one of the young girls smiled at him several times, but he doesn't know what to do."

Watkyns frowns. "I'll tell him what to do. Do nothing. We have two more weeks here at the most. We don't need anything to complicate the difficult decisions we will need to make." Watkyns is firm and uncharacteristically stern.

Whyte acknowledges their concern and walks away to find the young blond.

Gallawaye and Watkyns stroll about the camp, discussing what they still need to do. Both are increasingly worried about the absence of Hayman and the *Great Dane* crew. Although there are still several days before they exceed the time limit for their search, the fact that they haven't returned means the *Hinde* is probably farther from them than they hoped. The alternative—that tragedy has overtaken the pinnace and her crew—is one neither man wants to raise.

The temporary nature of their residency inhibits any efforts to erect structures, and their tents provide shelter. They still post two sentries every night, but this serves to maintain a routine and keep the men occupied more than for protection from the natives. However, the lieutenant has learned that the tribe a few miles south of them is not as friendly and has engaged in border disputes with the Ne-Chess-Nee during the past several years. A number of the Salmon River natives were killed or injured if they ventured too far south of the river. This does not reassure the members of the company, and they are told to be watchful and not to intrude in that direction. They hope the pinnace crew will avoid contact.

Watkyns sums it up. "We can't very well send out a search party for them, can we? We have no other boat, and the land is occupied by a hostile tribe. We have two muskets left, and they will need to go with Graye and his men if they leave."

Gallawaye sips a cup of herbal tea. "I hope we can talk them out of going. If Hayman doesn't return, that leaves us with only eleven men. Separating renders both groups that much more vulnerable."

Watkyns thinks for a moment. "Might be we should join them if they are so determined. There is some solid reasoning to their objective. If we can't make contact now, perhaps our best chance for reunion in two or three years will be near the last place the general thought we were. That would be the Strait of Elizabeth at the Muh-kwa village or the harbor of New Albion."

"Manny, are we sure they, or all of us, can make such a journey over land? It was several days' sail away from here, and we passed several formidable rivers and bays. There are bound to be any number of tribes between us and the Muh-kwa, some of them as unfriendly as the group to our south. I know our hosts talked of a northbound river in the valley, but it might not feed into *the* strait—the Elizabeth Strait—that we would need to reach."

"It is so, John, and I don't have any good answers at the moment. I may not be the leader you thought I was. I am not a soldier or a sailor, although I have spent some time at sea. However, I believe we are close to finding the fabled passageway that will lead us swiftly back home to our fair country." He sighs and looks out at the three rocks where breakers wash their sides. "I miss Devon and the marketplace. I miss my good Lutheran parish and my many friends. I should have married and stayed. I suspect I may never have that chance and might not see the true white cliffs again."

Gallawaye puts an arm on Watkyns' shoulder. "Let us not yield to despair, Mr. Watkyns. You are our leader, and your advice to Bill Whyte about George is a good indication of that. Let us keep the company strong and high minded while we wait for word from our companions. It will come, and then we will all decide our next course of action together."

Chrystopher Huntsman and Francis Caube have become good friends since joining the New Albion Company. Huntsman is a carpenter by trade but not a great one. He can handle a musket when needed, but the only two harquebuses left to the group are in the hands of Graye and Cuttyll. Chrystopher started the voyage with Drake at the age of twenty-two. It was his first, and he was often seasick after leaving land, but he was of good disposition and liked to laugh and play tricks on his shipmates, especially Caube. Some of the *Hinde* crew considered him worthless and volunteered him for the *Venture*, but Chrystopher took it in stride as "a chance to see the world." As much as he enjoys the company of his shipmates, he expresses contempt and revulsion for the natives. Even the women who are fair-skinned and attractive to others in the crew give Chrystopher no pleasure. He characterizes them as animals who are fit only to breed with others of their kind. By most measures, Huntsman is handsome and six feet one inch tall but not inclined to talk much about the fair gender, not even the lasses back home. "Never had time for them" is his only comment.

Thomas Martyn avoids the natives as much as possible. He is thirty and says little during the evening fireside chats. Although a sailor, his skill with a longbow is well known and respected. He demonstrated his prowess for the natives, comparing his weapon with the light ones they use for squirrels, coneys, and other small animals. Although accurate, their arrows travel less distance and cannot bring down a large deer or elk, much less a bear. During his practice sessions, Thomas refuses direct contact with the Indians. On those few occasions when he is close to them, he seems ill at ease and usually makes an excuse to withdraw. When Gallawaye asks him about it, he reminds the lieutenant of the attack in the northern inlet and the disaster at Mocha. "Never can trust those bloody bastards no matter how friendly they seem."

Francis Caube receives Huntsman's light-hearted harassment in good humor and returns it in full measure. He is also a merchant but signed on with the expedition as a general laborer. His hopes are to look, learn, and prepare for trade with the Far East if the hopes of a northern passage are realized. He is in his late twenties and, like Martyn and Huntsman, has little use for the natives.

Graye and Watkyns are puzzled why the three men want to return north to possibly live with the Muh-kwa if they have such disdain for the natives. All three have a similar response. They don't plan to live in a native village and aren't interested in having an Indian concubine or wife. "Maybe for a few minutes at a time" is Martyn's concession. Caube thinks that consorting with a dark-skinned woman might serve until he returns to England, but Huntsman will have none of it. "Better to mate with a bear and be done with it" is his retort.

One man in the company holds a different view of relations with the locals. Nicholas Franconi is in his mid-twenties and has a swarthy complexion and long, black hair. "Almost like an Indian," he brags. Although he is one of the secret papists among the *Venture* group, he knows the Lutheran rituals well and never lets on about his Catholic upbringing or inclinations, even to fellow papists Grige and Deane. He is a skilled shipbuilder, and assembling the pinnaces is one of his specialties. His other specialty is alcohol. By fermenting berries, he is able to produce a heady brew that wins him favor with the crew and several of the tribal men. The Indians occasionally walk into the woods with him, where he shares his beverages. They communicate only with gestures, but it is amazing how much they understand each other after several cups of the potent red liquid. After several negative comments from fellow crewmen, Nicholas no longer vocalizes his lust for a native woman or girl, but he has his thoughts and extended fantasies, and he spies on them when given a chance. To his regret, none of the village maidens have prevailed on him for a relaxing drink in the woods.

Gallawaye learns about some of the important Ne-Chess-Nee rituals including the critical coming-of-age ceremonies for young men and women. For each child becoming an adult, it is necessary for the initiate to seek a guiding spirit. For males, this involves several days of fasting and isolation in the woods until he receives enlightenment. For a maiden, her first menstrual flow signals her coming of age. The conclusion of her spirit search requires a single night in the forest, but she is not allowed to reveal her totem spirit until she reaches the end of her childbearing years and can help guide other girls on the ceremonial path to womanhood. To help the other New Albion members appreciate the depth and diversity of their host's culture, Gallawaye relays much of this information to them during their evening gatherings.

A bit immature and flippant, Nicholas receives the accounts with obvious enthusiasm. He remarks, "I could almost pass for one of them."

"Pleat your hair in braids, man, and paint your face." Huntsman laughs.

George Cooke thinks this is funny, and Big Tom chuckles in response to George, but Nicholas grins and announces, "Maybe I will. Maybe all of you will before this is over."

Martyn looks at Cuttyll. "Save a lead ball for Nick here if you will, Mr. Cuttyll. We may not be able to tell him from the other heathen bastards." Only Huntsman laughs.

---

The moon passes the quarter phase, and only a week is left before their permission to remain expires. The pinnace has not returned, and Gallawaye and Watkyns discuss their concern in private, not wanting to give their men cause for further worry. According to Gallawaye's notched stick for days and knotted string for months, it is Sunday 30 August. The morning service takes on a desperate note. Gallawaye pleas for divine guidance in the week ahead. The thirty-day encampment grant will be over on the day after the coming full moon, 5 September. Their next Sunday service might be held on this beach, but after that, where?

Graye and Cuttyll make it clear that they will journey up the Salmon River and cross the low mountains to enter the broad river valley the Ne-Chess-Nee spoke about. A survey the evening before of those wishing to leave or stay had not changed minds. Gallawaye does not want to abandon the site but realizes he might need to ask the tribe for refuge for the five who have decided to remain: himself, Emmanuel Watkyns, George Cooke, Nicholas Franconi, and Big Tom. Although Watkyns and Gallawaye consider joining the departing group and discuss the pros and cons at some length, both believe the chance of survival is better with a known, friendly tribe than with unknown tribes they would undoubtedly encounter before reaching the northern straits.

Big Tom acts like he has already been accepted fully into the Salmon River tribe. He occupies a place of honor at the village council to the right of Kin-te-ash, their biggest warrior. Gallawaye learns that the tribe regards the big black as a favorite of the gods if not an actual god. Cooke and his flute are also welcome, although he is not as favored in position or treatment. The other three men are treated cordially, but their future status is undetermined.

Gallawaye does not want to ask for extended hospitality unless it becomes absolutely necessary, but that time is rapidly approaching. The Muh-kwa party, as it is now known, is scheduled to leave on Tuesday two days hence.

As the departure day arrives, Watkyns and Gallawaye are still trying to convince the others to remain in one group. Not knowing what became of the *Great Dane* party has increased their sense of vulnerability. For some in the Muh-kwa group, it manifests as a palpable fear, and they have no desire to stay on the coast. Big Tom, George, and Nicholas are happy to remain with the natives, and it appears they have permission to do so, although it has not been formalized between Gallawaye and the tribal council. He will discuss it with them if he cannot prevail upon the northbound crew to stay.

Monday night, the Muh-kwa group packs food, shot, and powder for their harquebuses. They gather their share of the tents and other materials they need. They have no way of knowing how long they will travel, but they need to be self-sustaining after their food supply is gone, probably within two weeks. The Ne-Chess-Nee assure them there is an abundance of game and fish, plants, and nuts in the valley beyond the mountains. The tribe has trade relations with some of the valley people, and most are considered peaceful, although how they will react to the white men can't be predicted. Caube wants Big Tom to go with them as "a visible deterrent," as he expresses it. Big Tom is satisfied where he is: a former slave now feted as a king and admired and valued for the first time in his life.

On Tuesday morning, the six men say their farewells to the five who will remain at the coast. No one laughs or makes light of the moment. Led by Richard Graye, they hike eastward out of the camp and move into the woods in single file, with Thomas Cuttyll bringing up the rear. The remaining men watch them disappear into the high marsh grass and then into the coastal shrubs and trees as they follow the west bank of the river. They carry the last remaining compass and plan to turn north as soon as they reach the great river in the valley.

"Maybe our other companions will arrive late but safe and with good news," says Watkyns as Cuttyll disappears from view.

"Never coming. It is us now. We're all that's left," answers Franconi. There seems to be neither remorse nor anxiety in his manner as if all is going well and to expectations. He turns to Gallawaye. "Well, Lieutenant, will we stay with our Indian friends, or do we move on? If so, where to?"

It is a rhetorical question, because no decision has been made about another location. To stay where they are with the forsaken wreck of the *Venture* would violate their agreement with the natives. To go south means risking a potentially fatal encounter with the neighboring tribe. Traveling north along the coast seems to offer no advantages. The only evident option is to request permission for the five to accompany the tribe back to their winter village. This might enable them to return each spring to the coast and await a passing ship from the rescue and resupply expedition from England. For Watkyns and Gallawaye, two or three years now seems like eternity.

The same afternoon, Gallawaye and Watkyns talk to Kish and ask him for a meeting with the tribal council. Gallawaye explains as best he can the nature of their request. Kish tells him he will arrange the meeting for that evening.

It is a small fire at the New Albion Company camp in the evening while Watkyns and Gallawaye meet around a larger fire with Quin-at-che, the leader, and his council of seven warriors plus Winash-at-kish, their spokesman. The meeting does not last long. The tribe saw the departure of the pinnace a month earlier and the departure of the other six men that morning. Once Gallawaye clarifies that the five of them, including Big Tom and George, are the only ones remaining, the leaders confer briefly and tell Gallawaye they are welcome to stay at their site on the coast. The difference between five and seventeen foreigners on their land makes a difference. The prohibition against visiting the seal rocks north of the cape will remain in effect, but they are free to use the other resources of the area. Furthermore, they invite Big Tom to come to the inland village with them if he desires. The other four white men are not invited. Gallawaye and Watkyns thank them for their generosity and indicate that all five will remain at the seaside camp. The lieutenant asks for permission to erect some wood shelters to protect them from the winter rains and storms. They are given permission but advised to do so on the north bank bluffs that are well above sea level and near the rear of the marsh. This will protect them both from sea storms and from winter and spring flooding on the river.

Watkyns conveys the news to the other three in camp. Big Tom expresses annoyance at the pending departure of the tribe and Gallawaye's decision, without his knowledge or consent, to not follow the natives inland. The real annoyance is expressed by Nicholas, who indicates his displeasure that neither Gallawaye nor Watkyns pleaded the case for all of them to join the winter village. His hopes to establish an intimate relationship with one or more of the young women in the tribe will now be impossible, and with the remaining

New Albion Company, he will face many long months of winter isolation. He previously encouraged George to make friends with the Indian girl who smiled at him, but she was still considered a child and not allowed to be alone with the white man.

Cooke isn't sure what he wants. As the musician comprehends the reality of their seclusion, he begins to regret that he didn't join the other six. Life among the Muh-kwa would have been nice, but it's too late.

With little work to do and the cessation of sentry patrols, Nicholas enjoys hours of free time wandering the marsh and forest edge. He continues to ferment berries, but he is no longer joined by tribal men, and none of the remaining white men wish to imbibe. He sits at the river's edge with a cup of alcoholic juice, attempting to devise a plan that will allow him future access to the winter village. The natives are accustomed to the white men going in and out of their village, but now the last sea lion hunt has occurred, and most of the village is busy with preparations for their semiannual move.

Two of the native boys are undergoing spirit searches that will be completed before the tribe travels. One girl is also ready to initiate her search on the third of the month, a Thursday night. It is two nights before the full moon, and she has chosen a riverside pool a half mile into the forest south of a curve in the Salmon River. It is an unfortunate choice.

Nicholas knows the location, because he comes to the sandy stretch on the curve to fish and contemplate his future options. With little need for security at the camp, he chooses that night to wander away from the camp on a moonlit trail, unaware that he will not meditate alone. Sitting on the bank under a tree, he watches the water flowing lazily out into the marsh and sea. A gentle lapping noise comes to him, and he turns to his right to see a naked young woman bathing. She is immersed to her knees, and the light shines from her as if she is a magical apparition. Nicholas is entranced, hardly daring to breathe lest he disturb the beauty before him. Years have passed since he knew a woman in England, and his arousal is immediate. She is not aware of his presence and washes her chest and belly slowly. The water is cold, but it is a key component of the spiritual search, and she is in no hurry.

He creeps closer on hands and knees, not wanting to disturb her yet wanting to disturb her in the worst way. He can see she is young but with the blossoming features of a woman. *This must be her spirit night. If so, she is alone. Just her and me.* The excitement rises as he breathes faster. He closes the distance slowly and carefully.

A pine branch betrays him. The loud snap is magnified in the quiet forest, instantly alerting the girl to his presence. She gasps, covers the front of her body with both hands, and tries to crouch down in the water. He is in the water and beside her a moment later, his hand across her mouth, the other arm around her waist.

"Don't scream. Don't run. I won't hurt you, I promise." The words gush out but are spoken in a hoarse whisper. No matter, she wouldn't understand his words, but she recognizes his intent. He isn't sure if a guard or protector is standing near, although he was told the spirit seekers were almost always alone.

She starts to struggle, and her movements arouse him further. He presses her wet breasts against his shirt and holds her firmly, keeping one hand across her mouth. She fights furiously with her free arm, striking him in the forehead and across the ears. When she tries to bite him, he relaxes his hold on her mouth for an instant. It is all she needs to give a high-pitched scream, leap onto the bank, and start down the trail toward the village. Without hesitating, he jumps out of the water and chases, his longer legs closing the distance. A few steps later, he grabs her from behind and forces her to the ground. Although he tries to quell the terror in her eyes, his rough kiss on her lips causes her to thrash about, kicking and flailing. Twice she manages to utter a short, high-pitched scream, and twice he chokes it off.

He has his pants down and is about to enter her, not an easy task during her struggles, when two warriors run up the trail and launch themselves onto his back, rolling him off the girl. Gasping, she retrieves her clothing and runs back toward the village. One of the warriors draws a knife and is about to slash Franconi's throat, but the other brave stops him and motions for him to pick up the white man. His pants are still wrapped around his knees, and the natives easily drag him by the armpits along the trail. He is whimpering and asking them to let him go, saying that he is sorry and meant no harm. The natives say nothing. By the time they emerge from the forest, Nicholas is actively praying to his Catholic Father, Son, and Blessed Virgin.

The girl reaches the village, half-dressed and bruised. Two women help her to a shelter as a party of men proceeds to the bank of the river. Two carry torches, and they stand on the north bank, awaiting the warriors and their captive.

Shouts from the braves carrying Nicholas, his cries, and the answering shouts from the village party bring the four men at the camp to attention. They watch in disbelief as Nicholas is handed to Kin-te-ash, who starts dragging him back to the village.

Kish hurries to intercept the four as they cross the river to the village. He gestures to Gallawaye that they should go no farther—their companion has done something very bad and will be punished. Gallawaye tries to determine what has happened and explain that they will punish him. They did not see the girl running back to the village, but they saw that Nicholas was half dressed.

Watkyns comprehends the situation immediately. "Damn it to hell. That horny son of a bitch must have assaulted one of their women. I didn't realize he wasn't in camp."

George and Tom are dumbfounded and not sure whether to go after Nicholas or wait for orders from one of the two leaders.

"They might kill him," states Manny.

"No, they *will* kill him," Gallawaye replies. "Spirit seeking is a very sacred time for boy or girl, but for a girl, to be sexually attacked at such a time will have everlasting consequences for her. She will suffer for the rest of her life if my understanding of their ritual is correct. They will show Mr. Franconi no mercy, I am sure of that."

Tom understands just enough of what they are saying to realize his shipmate is in serious trouble. Without a word, he starts for the village and George follows, still holding his flute.

"No, Tomas, don't go. George, wait. You can't do anything about this." Watkyns screams at them, but they charge up the trail to the top of the bluff and disappear.

"Manny, grab your things. We are leaving now!" yells John. "They won't be coming back, none of them. We run to save our lives." He races toward the camp to get his sword, extra clothes, food, and stuff it in a bag. He turns to face Emmanuel, who is doing the same. The moonlight allows them to see the trail into the forest—the same path the six who left took two days earlier. They are almost out of earshot of the village when they hear a bloodcurdling scream.

---

When Big Tom and George arrive at the edge of the village, they witness a horrific sight. Nicholas is strapped to an upright pole in the center of the clearing. A bonfire lights the scene as thirty or forty native men stand in a circle around the white man. No women or children are present. Nicholas is still alive but barely. He might not be able to see his two companions, his would-be rescuers, standing outside the circle of light. His pants are down, and he is bleeding profusely from where his cock had been. It lies on the ground in front of him as three men hover near him with sharp knives drawn. The black and the blond hear Nicholas muttering through sobs and tears, "Our Father…Our Father…"

The agony won't last long. One of the men is about to run a knife across Franconi's throat when Big Tom lets out a yell, charges through the circle of natives, and throws himself on the three men with the knives. George starts forward, but an arrow catches him in the right temple. It is a weak bow and a small arrow, but at close range, it brings George down. His legs thrashing, he is dead in less than a minute.

Big Tom is enraged. His strength and the surprise of his charge scatters the three braves, bringing a brief reprieve but painful suffering to Nicholas. Tom takes advantage of the disruption to grab one of the fallen knives and slash at the strips that bind Nicholas. He falls to the ground and starts to crawl away. Five or six warriors tackle the giant and force him to the ground. A sharp blow to the head temporarily knocks Big Tom senseless. Franconi is still crawling and sobbing when a large rock crashes on his head ending pain, suffering, and all else.

At a signal from Quin-at-che, the two bodies are dragged out of the clearing and down the trail to the river. They are thrown onto the shell mound with the other waste and trash from the village. They securely bind Big Tom, still unconscious, to the pole. Several armed natives walk down to the encampment that is still lit by the evening fire. They search the beach and part of the marsh for the two white men. Finding no one, they take what they want of materials and supplies. They stack the rest on top of the two tents and sailcloth from the barque. One of the Indians picks up a burning branch from the fire and lights the pile.

By the next day, only embers of the camp remain. Two bodies lie rotting on the shell heap. Big Tom regains consciousness. He is bleeding from wounds to his head, arm, and chest. The native men gather around him, and a heated discussion ensues.

One of the elder women approaches. Quin-at-che talks with her briefly, and she walks back to the shelter where the girl is recovering. After several hours of torture and a painful death, the black giant joins his companions in disgrace, to be disposed and forgotten by the tribe that had once considered him near to a god.

As the tribe breaks summer camp and begins to move toward their winter village, a broken ship sinks deeper into the sands of the Salmon River mouth—the last remainder of the New Albion Company on the rugged coast at Three Rocks.

CHAPTER 12

# Into the Valley

---

The pathway over the coastal mountains—mere hills compared to the larger snowcapped peaks that lay farther east—is distinct and has been used by deer, elk, and tribes of natives since time immemorial. Led by Graye, the six men trudge methodically uphill, following the upper stream of the Salmon River. Knowing the trail might host human traffic, the men move carefully, stopping often to listen. When they talk, it is in whispers. The forest provides a canopy overhead and around them and is interrupted every few miles by a small glade or open meadow. The difficult choice is whether to stop and rest in the open areas where they might be visible and yet see what is around them or to remain secluded in the luxuriant growth of mixed conifer and leaved trees.

The two men pursuing them do not take the same precautions. They speed on through the night, not knowing whether pursuit by the village tribesmen is underway. By morning, they stop to rest and drink water from the stream. Their best chance of survival centers on catching the group with a two-and-a-half-day start. Occasionally, they see a boot print in the soft sand or mud along the river bank, and they discover the remains of a small fire, the burnt branches carefully stacked in a radial pattern.

"Careless," remarks Gallawaye. "They should disperse or bury all remains of their passing."

"We should be thankful they are careless enough to provide us guidance. We can be sure we are following the correct route. I for one don't possess the expertise to track men over such distances." Watkyns picks up his bag, ready to move on.

"Let us hope the distance grows shorter. When they reach the valley, the signs of their passing may be much more difficult to find." Gallawaye rises, shoulders his pack, and follows Watkyns up the trail. They spent two hours of precious time resting, but adrenaline has strange and marvelous effects, allowing humans and animals to exert themselves beyond their usual limits of endurance and strength.

They needn't have worried. Two days after running from the camp, four days after the six left, Gallawaye catches sight of Thomas Cuttyll ahead. It is late afternoon on the fifth of September. Suppressing the urge to yell, John looks back over his shoulder and motions to Watkyns. In a low whisper, he says, "Manny, we found them. No shouting, but we need to be careful as we close lest we startle Tommy Boy and get a ball for the effort."

Manny nods, and they quicken their pace. Five minutes later, John is close enough that Thomas hears his footsteps and turns, musket held across his chest. If it had been an enemy, there would have been no time to load, prime, and fire, but it could still serve as a lethal weapon. His face erupts in a grin as he recognizes the two hurrying toward him, but he frowns as he realizes something is wrong. He turns and tells Grige, in a louder voice than he intended, to halt and pass it forward.

Watkyns is panting, and Gallawaye is waiting to catch his breath as Graye's men gather around them. Cuttyll motions to a small clearing beside the trail, and the group moves behind some thick trees, while Caube and Huntsman remain alert and standing just off the trail. Manny and John relate the tragic events of two nights earlier. Watkyns brushes away tears as he mentions the last thing they heard from their shipmates: the tortured scream of Nicholas.

No one needs to say anything. Franconi was never the most popular fellow in the company. He was brash and immature and had been censored for being reckless on more than one occasion.

However, his fate was not something they would wish on their worst enemy. Big Tom and George were another kettle of tea.

Later that evening, when they can talk about it, Richard Graye summarizes their feelings toward the big black giant and his innocent, blond musician friend. "We never had a last name for Tomas. Big Tom seemed enough. It identified him, described him. It was all he, or we, needed. I don't know what he must have been thinking when the natives began treating him like their king or god. He smiled and endured it with good grace. Being fed, watched over, admired…" He pauses as several men smile and nod. Who wouldn't enjoy the attention that had been bestowed on the former slave? "Big Tom was an asset to this company, and we will miss him greatly."

Chrystopher Huntsman rises to his feet. "If I might, I'd like to say a few words about Mr. Cooke, our Georgie boy. He was a fine musician, and his flute could ease the troubled heart and calm the waters of the stormiest sea."

A gasp of amazement bursts from Watkyns. "Why, Chrys, you take me by surprise. I never suspected you had such words of eloquence in you. Please do go on."

"George was everyone's friend, but he seemed to be closest to Big Tom. No wonder he didn't hesitate to follow him to the village." He chokes a bit. "I hope their deaths, for I fear they are not on this good earth with us, were quick and with little pain. I fear the big man may have suffered more as he would be a hard one to dispatch. May their souls be with our Lord and they rest in peace."

"Amen" sounds around the circle of the moonlit company. Gallawaye tells them he will conduct a brief service in the morning.

"Ah, it be Sunday then. You still have your string and stick calendar?" asks Caube.

John holds up the string for all to see. "No pen and paper, but I can still mark the time. We shall be counting the months and then the years."

"If the *Golden Hinde* and our general have moved on safely and complete their voyage, as we all hope," says Martyn. He has just rejoined the group from guard duty.

The thought nags all of them. The series of disastrous events, not knowing the fate of the pinnace crew, and not knowing whether similar misfortune has fallen to Drake and his men, weighs heavily on everyone. As the lieutenant reminds them, there are only two options. They can surrender to the whims of fate and ill fortune or continue the good fight. Despite the pessimism of a few, they choose the latter with a determination to survive and remain the Queen's servants in her new land.

As they retire for the night, Gallawaye is visited by the persistent demon of regret. *There is no excuse for my cowardliness. After all my speeches, my words about fighting the good fight and dying with honor and bravery, I ran. Worse, I deserted my shipmates, my friends and companions. As long as I live, it will ever be my night of disgrace, my time of dishonor. Do I dare to claim the right to offer spiritual advice or Godly words of comfort to men again?*

---

Sunday morning is accompanied by a cool oceanic fog that burns away before noon, leaving a bright sky. The weather is becoming noticeably colder, and leaves on the trees are assuming the bright colors of autumn. Still depressed from his admission of inadequacy, Gallawaye offers a brief prayer to remember their fellows and ask for the safety of the *Golden Hinde*. John announces that Emmanuel Watkyns, the nominal leader of the New Albion Company on land, has asked to be relieved of the responsibility.

Manny stands before them. "I was honored that General Drake offered me the opportunity to guide our enterprise. That was many miles and many days ago. It seems like a lifetime to me, and I am sure you feel the same. Our job for the immediate future will be survival. If possible, we will return to our designated harbor or to the village of our native hosts at Muh-kwa. I am not the man to lead you in this endeavor. We have two experienced soldiers," he glances toward Cuttyll and Graye, "and an experienced naval officer." The last is directed toward John Gallawaye. "Any of these men will be more appropriate for us to follow. Men, it will be your decision."

After several minutes of discussion, a decision is reached. As they earlier admitted, Huntsman, Martyn, and Caube have little use for any natives. The tragic events at Three Rocks only made their reluctance to return to Muh-kwa more decisive. They support keeping the group intact, but the consensus is to nominate Richard Graye as the leader until a final disposition is imminent. Everyone, including Graye, accepts this, and the group continues its trek over the slopes of the coastal range.

A week later, they top the last rise. A broad valley of meadows and patches of oak and aspen forest spreads out below them. They glimpse a river running north and south of their valley entrance. Mountains starting with low foothills but culminating in snow-capped peaks rise east of the valley. Plumes of smoke are scattered about, indicating the presence of other native villages.

Save for inevitable twists and turns north and south, the upper reaches of the Salmon River and its trail run almost due east until they reach headwaters just below the crest of the coastal hills. Martyn carries the compass and gives readings with each bend. Now they have choices. The Ne-Chess-Nee told them the big river flows north. They can walk east to intercept it or angle northeast along the margin of the hills and intercept the river farther downstream. Believing they might be able to avoid contact with other tribes by remaining close to the hills, they follow that route and strike out diagonally across the valley. It is easier walking, and they make sufficient progress despite stopping for midday meals.

The evening after entering the valley, they question whether to light a fire, especially at night. They retain salted meat from the ship stores and additional meat prepared during their month at Three Rocks. They gather nuts, berries, and vegetables as they travel but have not cooked anything since leaving the Salmon River camp. They are clearly observable by day and have no illusions about being invisible to the valley's residents. Would an additional plume of smoke, day or night, attract undue attention? On their second night in the valley, they decide to risk it. According to Gallawaye, it is Monday, 14 September.

The warmth of the coals following a cooked meal provides a rare moment of comfort that night. They caught several quail in the grasslands, and everyone agrees the fat little birds make a pleasant repast. They have not directly faced any of the valley's natives, but they know they are under surveillance from the river and the hills on their left. Each evening, they post guards in three shifts of four hours and are not disturbed. They recede some distance from the foothills and face the grassy, forested valley running in a north-by-northeast direction. Cuttyll points to the line of larger trees in the distance. They no longer maintain silence, so he shouts out to Graye, "The river changes course, heading east."

As they near the tree line, they see that Cuttyll is correct. A sharp bend in the river has it flowing east toward the distant mountains, but it appears that it turns again to flow north. They decide to follow the river at a closer distance, walk toward the tree line, and move along the north-flowing stretch for over an hour. The sun is beginning to set when the river forms a loop to the north and proceeds again in an easterly direction. They camp on its banks, noting that its broad, fast flow is not easy to cross.

"Perhaps we won't need to. This river might continue eastward, but even if it turns again to the north, we may be able to stay on this side of it," ventures Graye.

Whyte is sitting on the ground, looking out at a large flock of ducks flying upstream. "How far north do you figure we've come?" he asks.

Although voiced to no one in particular, Gallawaye knows the question is directed at him. "I didn't have time to grab instruments before we abandoned the *Venture*. If I had, I would have given them to Commander Hayman for the search. I can only estimate our position roughly, but I believe we are south of our latitude at New Albion by four or five degrees."

Staying within a mile or two of the river, they walk eastward the next afternoon. As they are about to begin a more northerly course, the river dips in a broad loop to the south and curves northward and then northeasterly. Before they see it, they hear the rolling thunder of water crashing. They emerge from a thick forest and the sight of the horseshoe-shaped waterfall with a thirty-foot plunge causes them to stop and stare. Mist rises from the plunging spumes. They can't see the bottom of the cascade in front of them, but the rocks at the base of the falls are visible on the opposite side of the river where the arm of the U veers downstream.

The men discern two dozen natives lined along the upper cascade on their side of the river and other figures in the distance below the falls. Even from a distance of a half mile, they see that the natives are fishing. Some are using spears, and at least two wooden platforms project from the bank of the lower river.

The men walk toward the natives cautiously but in the open and spread out in two lines of four. Cuttyll and Graye are on each end of the front line. They do not arm the muskets but rely on Gallawaye to negotiate their passage. As they draw nearer to the group along the upper falls, the natives stop and observe their approach. A couple of warriors step forward with spears upright, and one picks up a bow but does not notch an arrow.

Graye's group comes to a halt several paces from the natives, and Gallawaye raises his hand, palm out, in the familiar gesture. The other men try to look relaxed and smile. John speaks a few words he learned at the Ne-Chess-Nee village, but the natives clearly do not understand. Behind the native group, the men can see a large number of fish laid out on the bank. One of the younger natives runs down the hill toward another group beneath the falls. The Indian facing Gallawaye points at Graye's group and then to the Indians below him.

"Seems they want us to go down the hill," announces Gallawaye.

The men continue smiling but fall in line, following several of the natives toward the lower group. They are greeted by several men with feathers in their hair and elaborate pelts around their shoulders. The other fishermen are mostly naked; some wear loincloths and belts. Gallawaye repeats his greeting, and the Indians listen intensely before gesturing toward a spot above the river bank. A plume of smoke rises from the spot he indicates, and the white men presume it is the site of their village. There is no sign of hostility, only curiosity directed at the oddly dressed strangers. Gallawaye's red beard and hair receive much attention as do the swords and muskets they carry. Most of the natives continue working, but a dozen of them accompany the company to the village.

Their settlement is a substantial one with a large number of cedar plank lodges and firepits. Drying fish fill several large pole racks. The white men observe that most of the fish are salmon, but they also recognize eels in baskets and skewered on poles over hot coals. In the village, the adults are dressed in tunics and leggings of animal skins and some woven vegetable substance. Some of the men and a few of the women wear elaborate necklaces of beads and shells. The sharp-toothed shells they saw in the Muh-kwa village are prominent.

Three older men meet the entourage at one of the central firepits. After the native escorts and village elders exchange a few words, the white men are led to one of the cedar lodges and motioned inside. The interior could easily accommodate thirty people or more, and they are asked to sit on pelts scattered about an interior firepit. It is lit, and the smoke drifts through a smoke hole overhead.

Cuttyll brought beads and coins with him for possible trade to the valley natives. Since this is their first direct encounter, he produces a few silver coins from his waist pouch and hands them to Gallawaye. John looks carefully at each item, as if appraising its value, holding it in high esteem. He polishes a coin on his sleeve and then hands it to one of the elders.

As he turns it over in his hands, the firelight gleams from the surface. The image of the queen fascinates him, and he smiles at Gallawaye. Several other natives enter the lodge but sit behind the elders and remain silent as do the white men. Only Graye and Gallawaye speak to each other as they attempt to communicate what they want and assure the natives they mean no harm.

Graye and Gallawaye did a rapid assessment of the village when they entered, and they agree it has the look of a permanent location and might be a substantial trade center. The inhabitants display a variety of decorations and implements, indicating they are familiar with resources from a larger area than they occupy. They are right. Not only does the village occupy a central location geographically, but it serves as a conduit between tribes from all directions. The white men are invited to stay within the confines of the village, sleep at the periphery, and eat with their hosts. Food is abundant, including the fish they observe. Nuts, berries, a wide variety of vegetables, and several types of grains are in evidence. Some of the latter are used to make breads and cakes on hot stone platforms.

Compared to the other tribes the white men have visited, this river group seems advanced. From what they can learn, hostilities between neighboring tribes are minimal. After Gallawaye extends his knowledge and communicates with two of their spokespeople, he learns that most disputes between and within bands and tribes involve domestic problems, honor resolutions, or minor infractions. Serious injury or death rarely results from these disagreements, and most are resolved by a special council appointed by the elders. He is amazed at the level of comprehension of native language and culture he has gained in the past few months.

Even the three members of the company who regard natives as inferiors or, in the case of Martyn, to be avoided if at all possible, relax and begin to enjoy the serenity within the village. It is an efficient, functioning settlement. Fishing appears to be the major industry. The men use spears for the salmon and catch eels with their bare hands. Women and children transport the fish and set them on the drying and smoking racks. Other men hunt wild game, usually smaller animals and birds, while women gather tubers, greens, and grains.

Grige is incredulous as he watches some of the eel men at work. "They are quite skilled at grabbing them from the moving water at the base of the falls," he reports. "Then they bite them in the back of the head, killing or stunning them before throwing them into a basket." The eels are slimy and difficult to hold onto. Biting a raw one is not something Thomas wants to try, although one native held one up for him to do so.

Ten days after they arrive, the fields to the south and west are on fire. Large plumes of smoke fill the valley and along the river. Graye's men express alarm, thinking that lightning or a neglected fire started an inferno, but they are assured it is a deliberate event. The fire was set and is controlled by tribal members who burn the grassy meadows to harvest seeds for winter bread production. They indicate it is the right time to do so, because the summer growing season is done, wildlife have raised their young, and the rainy season will soon begin. The burnt fields will be restored the following spring. This produces additional amazement among the company members. It is increasingly difficult to reconcile the organization of tribal culture with European prejudice toward ignorant heathens and savages.

Despite his internal torments, Gallawaye continues to provide Sunday prayers and lessons for his men, but these are done discreetly outside the village. The men help their hosts whenever they can by transporting fish from the falls, trapping animals along the river, and helping skin the pelts. The Indians admire their metal blades, and one of the precious knives is awarded to one of the leading warriors.

The eight men meet along the bank of the river to watch the last of the fishing operations for the year. "Part of their village will remain as a trading center, but many of them will journey downriver and to the west. There is a great river only a few miles from here. Much larger than this. A flowing body of water difficult to cross," reports Gallawaye.

"Could this great river be our Elizabeth Strait?" asks Cuttyll.

Graye reminds him that they should not be far enough north to be near the strait.

"Unless we have come well to the east, far enough to border on the large inland sea that lies south of New Albion," replies John. Graye asks John if the natives can describe what would be found to their east and north. John reassures him he will inquire at the next opportunity.

Huntsman looks at Graye. "Should we be moving on then? As pleasant as these folks are, the winter will soon be upon us. Do we want to spend more time here or try to find our good harbor?"

Graye considers it for a moment. "Some members of the tribe will be leaving here in a week or so. They indicate they will journey north to the Great River. If we go with them, we may discover our next course of action."

"So be it. Let us be on our way," says Thomas Martyn, still displaying caution and reluctance to mix with the natives socially.

---

TWO DAYS LATER, WILLIAM WHYTE MEETS HIS TRAGIC END. Always an enthusiastic fisherman, he attempts to catch eels with the younger men under the falls. Spearing salmon above and below the falls is the province of older men. In addition to the strength required to haul the large river runners from the water, a man needs to balance on large, wet rocks as he thrusts the lance forward and then pulls the heavy burden back toward him. The natives are always barefoot when fishing from the rocks.

Whyte lost a middle finger when younger, the result of an entangled line aboard ship in a storm. It adds to the difficulty of catching eels, but he wants to try his luck at spearing one of the larger prizes. He is lent a long, sharp pole with a wicked-looking blade made of the same black, shiny stone that Big Tom had taken from the attack at the northern inlet. William clambers onto one of the rocks, wearing his ship's boots. Poised over a surge of foam that has proven productive for many other fishermen, Whyte waits with undisguised glee for the appearance of a silver flash. Several of his crewmates sit on the bank, cheering him on.

The flash comes, and Whyte plunges the spear, but it comes up empty. He turns to his mates with a grin and a shrug and looks down at the rushing water, spear held high over his shoulder. Gallawaye notices that the Indians do not hold the spear as high but seem to stab toward the water with a shorter, controlled jab. He is about to shout an instruction to William when the spear plunges again.

This time it finds its target, and a large salmon is raised from the water, tail flopping frantically on the end of the horizontally extended lance. The weight is too much and unbalanced, pulling William forward. His left foot slips, and he falls off the rock, still holding the spear. An instant later, he is gone. The men jump up and look downstream, but nothing appears—not a head or an arm. It is as if he had never been. Two natives downstream see him slip, and they also look, but the rushing water reveals no trace.

Cuttyll and Grige race down the bank, trying to maintain contact in case there is any possibility of resurfacing, but they soon realize it is hopeless. This is confirmed by one of the Indians who consoles Gallawaye. "If they enter the water at this place, they never walk with us again," he says.

That evening, they make their preparations for the morrow. More than three dozen of the village men, women, and children will travel north, and the seven remaining members of the New Albion Company will walk with them. None of the white men eat fish that night.

It requires two days to reach the Great River. From the falls, the smaller river runs to the northeast and then turns northwest and north. They cross a number of streams that are shallow with the summer runoff. At several places, the river widens, and wooded islands dot the center. Ducks and other waterfowl line the shores, and the tribe stops occasionally to gather eggs or take birds by net or arrow. The white men do the same, making sure they have adequate food for whatever comes next.

On the second day, after following a northwesterly stretch of river that requires five hours to descend, they turn once more to the northeast. An hour later, they are staring at a mighty river flowing from their right to left, from inland to the Pacific Ocean. There is a large, sharply pointed island upstream to their right. The river disappears around a bend at their left, heading northward.

"What now?" asks Francis Caube.

Nazario de Morera has a string on which to knot months and a stick to carve days. He has been walking for a month along the quiet, sandy beaches and forested bluffs that overlook the ocean. He crosses several rivers: some by wading, a few by rafting, and one by detouring upstream before he finds a place to ford. He doesn't know how far he has come or how much farther to go, but the climate and forests are the same. It is getting later in the year, the cool summer is gone, and the full moon has waned. He stands on a low bluff looking out at a number of small islands. He estimates they are one to two miles offshore, but the wind carries to him the squawks of seabirds and hoarse cries of sea lions. He longs to reach a warmer climate. He has replaced some of his ship's clothing with pelts from animals he has killed, using twisted bark to thread through knife holes in the pelts. It is crude but better than nothing against the chilling Pacific fog. The food taken from their last anchorage is gone, and the roots, berries, and nuts he finds are supplemented by the small game he traps.

*Have I done the right thing? It seemed so easy at the time. Walk away and go south to the warmth to find those who speak my language or close to it.* He smiles. *I am not one of them either. Not English, not New World Spanish.* He sees an occasional smoke plume and discovers footprints on the high beach and some forest trails. *There are people here very different from me. What will happen when we meet?* His hair is longer, and he has a black beard with a few streaks of silver. He feels more wild than civilized, but he is alive and intends to stay that way. *I will have stories to tell to children and grandchildren to come.* He pulls the rosary from his waist pouch and recites the Our Father, ending with "Thy will be done." He doesn't ask for much—a few more days of life, a merciful death if that be his fate.

CHAPTER 13

# The Great River

The band of natives from the falls, the Guithlakimas, continues north along the banks of the Great River. The seven men who remain of the New Albion Company make camp at the junction of the two rivers and determine their next move. Their vantage point allows them to see the downstream flow that moves swiftly north by northwest. Their native friends confirm that the river pours into the great ocean without an end. They indicate the outlet is four or five days' travel along the bank. Gallawaye estimates it will be roughly one hundred English miles to reach the sea, and this river is probably the large one they passed when running before the storm two months earlier.

Once again, three opinions divide the group. Huntsman, Caube, and Martyn want to follow the Great River eastward. Although they aren't certain the waterway is the Northwest Passage, they reason it might be wide and long enough to serve the same purpose of dividing the North American continent—if not completely, enough for them to reach the Atlantic coast. They know their nation is beginning to explore the eastern coast of the continent and discussing locating colonies along its shore. By the time they arrive, English settlements might be in place to greet them. Another possibility exists, opines Martyn. The waterway might connect to the southern reaches of the inland sea south of New Albion. If the river doesn't lead directly to and penetrate the mountains to their east, it might curve northward and bring them to their fair harbor.

"This is where the next English expedition will expect to find us," Caube reminds the others.

"That is also where the silver is buried," adds Huntsman.

"If you lads are correct, we will need to cross this river to continue north," states Cuttyll. He and Graye are still intent on returning to the Muh-kwa village with the possibility of reaching New Albion later. "It will be easier by canoe from Muh-Kwa instead of walking hundreds of miles through forest." Graye believes the Indian village they seek is due north of their present location.

Watkyns and Gallawaye have something different in mind. The Guithlakimas tribe's acceptance of the white men encourages them to follow their recent hosts north along the river. Although they are informed that another tribe called the Klatsop occupies the land at the mouth of the river, the tribes live in peace, have similar practices, and observe similar rituals and spiritual beliefs. The tribes are materialistic and consider possessions such as shells and weapons to be attributes of wealth and status. Like some of the tribes to the north, both bind the skulls of their infants to small boards to produce forehead flattening, which is considered a sign of superiority and prosperity. Both tribes use cedar for building permanent lodges and consider salmon one of their major foods. Best of all, the coastal tribes share elements of a common language that renders communication much easier.

Gallawaye reasons the seven white men might be able to wait for an English rescue ship on the coast near the mouth of the river and he pleads his case with the others. The major debate, however, falls between those wanting to head east and those arguing to go north.

Huntsman turns to Graye. "You may be right, but if this is truly a river, it should get narrower upstream. There may be better places to cross. You might wish to come with us for a ways."

The soldier shakes his head. "Narrow doesn't mean better. Although the current is swift here, it is wide and flat. If the water is falling from the mountains, it may be like the falls we left behind—dangerous or impossible to cross. I recommend we all cross here and continue north."

Watkyns speaks next. "Mr. Graye, you are now the recognized leader of the company. However, I don't believe we have a consensus for any one plan. I suggest we sleep on it tonight and see if we can reach a compromise tomorrow."

"If we can't?" responds Caube.

"We may have to go our separate ways, hoping for each that they survive and greet Drake when he returns. Although we dilute our numbers by separating, we might increase our chances of discovery by choosing three different options."

Manny looks at John for support, and Gallawaye nods at him. "Tomorrow then."

---

They wake with the sun and eat a light breakfast. Gathered around a fire for warmth, they sit in a semicircle, divided in twos and threes by their proposed plans. It is Sunday, and Gallawaye gives a blessing for the three groups, invoking God's will for the men to receive His mercy and survive to see their loved ones again.

The three wanting to travel east will need to cross the river near a miniature falls flowing into the Great River south of their camp. "I can't pronounce the name of the river we followed here," admits Gallawaye. "Let's call it the White Falls River."

"Where do you want to cross the Great River?" Watkyns asks Graye.

"We can build two rafts—one for Thomas and myself for the Great River and one for Chrys, Thomas, and Francis to cross the White Falls River. We can leave at the same time as you start north toward your Indian friends."

"I wouldn't turn my back on them," remarks Martyn. Now that Gallawaye and Watkyns are no longer leaders of the group, the members of the trio do not disguise their distrust and revulsion for the natives.

Gallawaye pauses before answering. "I regret we are separating, but each of you will face the prospects of additional encounters. Some may be friendly and others not so. You will need your wits about you, and I recommend that you attempt a friendly overture as a first resort. Be wary, but you will not survive the hazards of this land without help from its inhabitants."

Huntsman is holding one of the harquebuses for the eastbound group; Richard and Thomas keep one for themselves. However, there is enough powder and lead only for a few shots from each musket. All men agree that they hope to preserve the precious ammunition for hunting rather than defense. Martyn made additional arrows while at the White Falls village and will rely on his longbow. Gallawaye and Watkyns indicate they need no arms other than their swords and knives.

The seven spend the rest of the day at work on the rafts. By cutting and lashing pine trunks together, two rafts are completed by sundown. The White River raft is larger to carry the three men, but the Great River raft is sturdier to withstand the stronger current. Rafting poles are trimmed to allow the first group to cross the White Falls River a hundred yards upstream from its juncture with the Great River. They will use crudely fashioned oars while in midstream. The early-autumn flow from the valley has broadened and slowed at the juncture. Martyn estimates they can easily gain the opposite bank before the water pushes them into the larger river.

They spend their last evening together on Monday, 5 October. The east bounders are in a good mood with Caube and Huntsman trading jokes and insults. According to Martyn, they hope to pass the visible mountains before the winter snows. They have no way of knowing that even greater mountains lie ahead on the river that will be impassable in a month or two.

"I wish we could have one more tune from Georgie boy," says Francis.

"May God have mercy on his soul and all the other souls of our once-proud company," answers Watkyns.

"We still be proud, just not as numerous," replies Cuttyll. "When we meet up in Devon or Plymouth or mighty London itself, I'll buy the first round of ale and not that goat piss they served for beer on the *Hinde*, you can bet." There is no disagreement, and the night ends on a cheerful note.

---

THOMAS CUTTYLL AND RICHARD GRAYE HAVE THEIR RAFT ready as well but wait until they see Caube, Huntsman, and Martyn safely across the smaller waterway. They shake hands all around. Caube apologizes for any differences that may have arisen between the different factions, and everyone acknowledges the somber moment of departure. The trio loads their bags aboard the raft, and they push off at midmorning. Poling and rowing, they reach the other side with shoreline to spare a few minutes later. They pull the raft onto the narrow, dark sandy beach, unload their packs, and wave farewell to the four on the west bank. A few minutes later, they disappear along the southern bank of the Great River.

Thomas and Richard announce they will make their attempt after lunch. Just before they sit to eat, a group of ten Indians from the White Falls village walks down the trail and stops at their camp. Gallawaye greets them but is unable to say much, because they don't have an experienced spokesman with them. He points to one of the older women and indicates that three of his party crossed the river and are headed east toward the mountains. This brings an expression of alarm, and when she speaks to the others in her group, several men indicate concern. One makes gestures of something like a hammer or axe hitting his head. It is not an encouraging reaction, and the four white men can only assume that one or more hostile bands of natives might lie along the path their companions have taken.

As the men begin their meal, two loud reports are heard from the east: the unmistakable sound of a musket shot is followed by another. The four men exchange nervous glances and listen for additional shots. The Indians look nervous but appear to be reacting to the white men rather than the gunshots.

"What do you think, lads?" asks Watkyns. He is standing, looking toward the east. "Should we wait and see if anyone returns?"

Cuttyll and Graye lower their heads. Gallawaye looks up at Manny and shakes his head.

Gallawaye motions to Graye and Cuttyll, to their raft lying on the sand, and to the other side of the Great River. The Indian men seem to comprehend what they are going to do, and no reaction of alarm is detected. The lieutenant signs that he and Watkyns would like to walk with the small native group. The Indians sit and begin to eat while the white men finish their meal.

Shortly after noon, Richard and Thomas shake hands and slap shoulders with Manny and John. Repeating the promises of beers to be bought and fun to be had when they reunite, they push off from shore with the help of their two shipmates and two natives. Several yards from the beach, the current pulls the raft downstream, and those on shore watch as the men row vigorously for the opposite shore. They are able to see them for some distance on the long, straight river stretch, but they do not reach the other side before they are lost from view.

Manny looks at John. "Just us then, is it, Lieutenant Gallawaye? Two out of twenty?"

"Mr. Watkyns, I propose that from this time on, we drop all formal titles and pretenses at leadership or authority. Let's see if we can make our way with these people and live long enough to tell our tales to others of our kind."

"Agreed, John. Let's walk."

---

THE GUITHLAKIMAS VILLAGE LIES TWO HOURS DOWN THE RIVER on a high ground surrounded by a broad marsh. The area swarms with birds, beaver, coney, and other game. There are also meadows of camas lilies, wild onions, berries, and various trees with nuts. When Manny and John enter, they are greeted by some of the men they knew earlier by the falls. The spokesman who previously communicated with Gallawaye is told about the destination of the other five men. The man frowns but says nothing when John tells him about the three who went east. John indicates that he and Manny desire to reach the ocean. Once again, he is reassured that the Klatsop people are friendly and might be receptive to allowing the white men to live on their land, or if the sea winds are truly favorable, they might live in one of their several villages. The spokesman teaches Gallawaye and Watkyns a few opening phrases to help the process of introduction and assimilation.

The river beside the Guithlakimas or Lakimas village flows north, but Il-tkit-at, the village elder, indicates it turns to the west after a half-day walk, at which time they will be in the land of the Klatsop. From there, he says, it will be another one or two days' walk to reach the water without end. Gallawaye and Watkyns decide to remain with the Lakimas for the winter, knowing that much more time will pass before any ships from England appear.

John keeps his stick-and-string calendar notched and knotted so they will have some idea of the days passed and special days to celebrate. Each Sunday morning, he and Manny spend several minutes in prayer and recite a few psalms from memory. They also use the event to remember their mates from the *Hinde* and the *Venture*.

At a point overlooking the Great River, Manny erects seven stone piles, one for each of the men lost from the New Albion Company: Luke Adden, John Cowrites, Peter, the black, Nicholas Franconi, George Cooke, Big Tom, and William Whyte. The fates of the men of the *Great Dane* and the two groups that parted at the Great River remain unknown. A stick with a pine cone mounted on it is placed in the soil for the eleven men they hope have survived. Gallawaye states it best: "As long as we live and keep their memory, they live."

---

MANNY AND JOHN ADAPT TO NATIVE WAYS QUICKLY. BY THE spring of 1580, they wear the minimal clothing of their hosts and have let their hair grow long in braids. John reasons that the more they look like the Lakimas, the more likely that they will be able to integrate with the Klatsop to their west. One thing Gallawaye doesn't change is the color of his hair. The bright-red mane and trimmed beard provide distinction, much to the amusement of many of the Indian men who move from one tribal village to another. The diet and strenuous activities work well for both men, and they are in good physical condition to assist the tribe in fishing and hunting. John is particularly adept at rowing, and his skill in the canoe impresses his tribal mates. The other major accomplishment is in their ability to communicate. John has always been a quick learner, but Manny surprises him in being able to vocalize some of the difficult names of people and places.

Manny is the first to be attracted to a young woman in the village. She lost her husband on the river the year before and has a three year-old son to care for. Manny begins sharing his food with her, and by late spring, they are sharing a space in one of the larger lodges. His adoption of the child and caring for the woman meets with the approval of the elders and seals kinship relations with several warriors and families in the band of forty people. When John indicates he is ready to embark on the journey to the ocean, he isn't surprised that Manny elects to remain.

"It is not a bad life here. We will be going back to the falls to fish in a month or so. We are fully accepted by the tribe. They know us, and we know them. I also know there are at least two attractive women, one who has not yet been with a man, who have their eyes on that flaming head of yours."

John looks at his friend and smiles. "Hard to imagine what a son or daughter might look like, heh?"

"Mine won't have red hair, but Lask-imsk-sta tells me she may be with child. My child."

"Already, Manny? You didn't waste time. I believe congratulations are in order. I propose we imbibe a bit of the berry wine to mark the occasion."

"Do you still plan to go? You won't consider staying and waiting a year or two before starting your vigil?"

"Il-tkit-at is ready to introduce me to the elders at one of the Klatsop villages. He wishes to do this before they leave for the falls. Perhaps I can find a comely maiden among them and settle into life. We won't be such a distance apart. A few days' walk, barely a country stroll." He laughs and puts his arm on Manny's shoulder. "The relations between the tribes seem to be peaceful and steady. I know about a few who have married between the two groups. When the ship comes for us, I'll come and get you. At that time, you can decide whether to stay with the Lakimas or to sail away."

Manny gives it some thought before answering. "It might be a difficult choice at that. Already I might not leave here. What would I go back to? I still have painful memories of the days and nights we lost our mates, the scream we heard when we fled Three Rocks. The memory of the attacks, the shipwreck, and the failure of our enterprise—all that is fading and will continue to disappear with time. I am not sure I want to revive that and the life I lived before. It's not me anymore. Can you understand?"

"Yes, I do, my friend. I have watched you carefully the past several months. I have never seen you happier, more content, as if you were born to all of this." He looks around at the forests, the Great River, and the village below them, bustling with adults at work and children at play. "By staying, I may find the same, but my heart is pulled to the ocean. I was a sailor all my adult life, and in my heart I still feel a kinship with the sea. I miss the tides and the eternal roar of the surf. We have some of the salty smell and fog here, but I need the sunset vista, and for as long as I live, I will need the hope of seeing sails blowing from three masts. I will leave with Il-tkit-at next week." What he doesn't voice is his need for the ocean to heal him and cleanse the residual guilt and despair of their flight from Three Rocks.

On Sunday, 24 April 1580, they hold their last prayer meeting at the stone-and-stick memorials overlooking the mighty river. "I will refresh the memories each year when we return from the falls," says Manny. "I will think of you and your passion for the tides."

"We should make the effort to meet here at least once every year. I will continue to keep the calendar and return on or near this date, before you venture to the falls. By then, I may have a family of my own. We can plan a reunion, and who knows? There is always a possibility that other members of the New Albion Company will find us. Some of them know where we are, and others may search this way. I will ask my native brothers to listen for any news of their presence."

"Should we recite a few psalms or proverbs?" asks Manny.

There is a long pause. John looks down at his feet and then across the river, taking in the vast view as if seeing it for the first time. "I don't think so, Manny. I have done this out of habit, clinging to a past that no longer seems relevant. Let's keep the memorial and the memories, but I will seek favor of the sea and winds from this day." He turns to study his friend. "How about you? Will you pray to the same God, our Christian deity?"

Manny smiles. "I stopped praying when I married Lask-imsk-sta. I only joined you out of friendship and because I thought you needed my support. The gods of *my* tribe are enough." His emphasis on "my" tells John all he needs to know.

Gallawaye's ancient calendar records the date as 25 April 1580, a Monday, for the morning of his departure from the Lakimas village and Emmanuel Watkyns.

Manny stands with his wife, holding their son, as Il-tkit-at and Gallawaye walk north out of the village and follow the bluff overlooking the Great River. Several tribal men and women see them off, and more than a few indicate they will miss the red-haired white man. No one will miss him more than the former leader of the New Albion Company.

---

THE TWO MEN JOURNEY WEST ALONG THE RIVER AND ENTER A great delta of islands and marshes. Once again, John is amazed at the abundance of wildlife, especially ducks, geese, and shorebirds. They pass through two small villages, each consisting of a few families, before reaching Konope, a larger settlement at the mouth of the Great River. They have to cross several small streams from the south before entering the marshes and shore of the river, but they enter the village before sunset.

As with other native communities in the region, most of the buildings consist of rough-hewn cedar planks. Some form longhouses for several families. The men are mostly naked, although many have breechcloths, and some still wear fur moccasins because of the cold ground. The women wear a pelt cape around their shoulders and have simple skirts of pressed grass or beaten cedar bark. A few of the adults have conical caps also made of cedar bark. Drying racks for salmon and other fish are scattered throughout the village, and the settlement is similar to the Lakimas village at the falls but three times larger.

Il-tkit-at indicates this is but one of several settlements for the tribe and that others are located along the Pacific coast south of the point where Konope stands. John recognizes some of the words and phrases as being similar to those he heard the Ne-Chess-Nee speak beside the Salmon River. After greeting four of the elders, for again there appears to be no single chief, John is invited to sit at their fire. He and Il-tkit-at describe the events of the white men at the falls and their subsequent times at the Great River. The Klatsop people acknowledge the marriage of Manny and his Indian wife, a recognition of tribal affiliation. They have the impression Manny is John's blood brother, a misconception the redhead doesn't correct.

John presents the last of his trading beads to the elders, telling them they are from a place far away but to the east across the mountains. He knows better than to indicate an origin from the sea in order to forestall a misinterpretation that he is a god or dead soul. They marvel at his red hair, and several men ask permission to touch it to see if it is real. He assures them it is natural and not a red dye, which some of them use to paint their face or hair.

The next morning, Il-tkit-at bids farewell to John and reminds him he is always welcome at the Lakimas village or at the falls.

As his native friend walks back toward the east, Gallawaye has a moment of regret while watching the last tenuous connection with his former life disappear behind a hillock on the bluff. *Now there is one. What is yet to come?*

During the remainder of the spring and throughout the summer, John learns as much about his new tribe as possible, engaging in chores from hunting and fishing to building lodges. He is not allowed to participate in sacred ceremonies and does not share a place at the council of elders but is highly regarded nevertheless. Two attributes are of particular note. As before in the Lakimas settlement, he excels in rowing and steering canoes, some of which are used for seal hunting. There is no prohibition against his participation. The other skill he acquires that surprises himself as much as his tribe mates is playing the bone game. He didn't learn about it at New Albion because of his absence during the northern strait expedition, but he quickly catches on to the objectives and the social ramifications of the contest. The most active and rambunctious events occur when several tribal settlements gather during the late summer. His red hair and beard earn him disproportionate attention, and he is often the object of their friendly insults as well as their praise.

Like Manny before him, it isn't long before a young woman captures his heart. She is not a widow but had been the consort of a brave, although they never formally united. Late that summer, they are joined in a ceremony and share a lodge space. The cultural differences in romance and courtship baffle John, but necessity breeds creativity, and he discovers ways to learn her customs and teach her a few of his.

During the year after his arrival at Konope, he makes several trips with hunting and trading parties to other villages in the south. When at another settlement, they speak a common trade language that is related to but different from their own or the others. He learns that the Tillamuck, one of the southern tribes, is related to the Ne-Chess-Nee. His biggest surprise is that one of the Tillamuck warriors had seen a very large canoe with wings that came from the sea during a storm. It stayed for one day and night in a bay at the foot of their sacred mountain. This happened a year ago.

*It could only have been Drake's ship*, thinks John. The description of the "great canoe" and the clothing of the white men, with their beards and the strange things they carried, leaves him little doubt. When he draws in the sand the outline of a flag with a cross on it, the informer affirms that he saw something similar on one of the tall trees of the canoe. John isn't able to determine the exact date of the native sighting, so he doesn't know if it happened before or after the *Venture* journeyed down the coast and wrecked at Three Rocks. It leaves him with a strange feeling. Although he has not started a vigil for seagoing ships, he instructs several of his village's warriors about the great canoes and draws pictures of them on a sandy beach.

When a large whale washes ashore a few miles south of their village, John helps to cut and transport meat. It provides food for their people and several other settlements in the region. The other plentiful source of food is elk. The larger deer are hunted by spear, but they are often wounded first with arrows, weakening them. The native men must follow the bleeding animal before wolves or coyotes claim it for their own. John still has his metal knife and is efficient at skinning the different animals they harvest for food and pelts. He admires the way they use everything and waste little.

On his calendar, unless he has missed a day or two, he notes the twenty-sixth day of September, a fine fall day. Geese are migrating, and he feels at peace.

---

NAZARIO DE MORERA STANDS ON TOP OF A HIGH POINT OVERlooking a large inland sea. It is late morning, and he can see the narrow entrance to the sea from the Pacific Ocean at his right. The sea has a northern arm that curls off to his left and behind him. The southern arm extends in front of him, defining a narrow peninsula similar to the one he occupies. The width of the inlet and the fury of the waves in it make the barrier impassable. He will need to go around. That will entail miles and perhaps days of backtracking, or he will need to find a way to cross the open water.

Moving down the hillside toward the inland shore, he encounters, only for the second time, a group of natives. They are short in stature and wear their hair straight but close cropped. They have canoes, and he presents himself for their inspection. Showing no fear, he walks up to the tallest of the five men and mimics paddling a canoe. He points to the far shore and to himself. They stand without speaking, looking at him and at each other. This is the time to trade his last precious possession: the extra knife he carries. That will still leave him a utility knife and the short sword. He hands the metal blade with a wooden handle to the warrior and again points to the canoe and himself. *Maybe they think I want to trade the knife for a canoe. Probably not a great bargain in their eyes.*

He points to each of them, mimics paddling, and then points to himself as he sits on a log. The man examines the knife, feels the blade, and passes it around to the other men.

*That's it, now they have it. They might just take the knife and leave me, or use the knife to kill me.*

They smile at him and move toward one of the canoes. The Basque gets in, and two men climb in—one at the bow and the other at the stern. The man holding the knife says a few words to his fellows, and they shove off.

A few hours later, having bid his boatmen farewell, Morera begins the next leg of his trek southward in a valley along the narrow sea. He estimates a date of September in the year of our Lord 1580, more than a year and one month after leaving the company of Drake and the *Golden Hinde*.

---

IN THE SPRING OF 1581, JOHN GALLAWAYE TRAVELS TO THE Lakimas village and reunites with Manny and his family. They are doing well, and John tells him he was also has a mate and is expecting his first child. Manny indicates his second is on the way. They promise to meet again that fall when the Lakimas band returns from the falls.

Two months later, the first Klatsop child with red hair is born. She has the fine features of her mother, but there is no mistake about the father's identity. Tosh-na-kish-na reminds him they will need a red-headed boy as well, and he assures her they will work on that.

During the summer, John notices in a tidal pool that his hair is no longer the flaming red of earlier days. Streaks of gray have started to appear, and he sees the fine lines that now circle his eyes. That fall, he decides to begin his vigil for the approach of a sailing ship from the north or south. It might still be too early to expect the promised help from England—that is most likely a year or longer in the future—but the sea offers, and he accepts, a message of comfort, a rhythm of serenity and familiarity he can share with Tosh and his infant daughter.

---

IN THE AUTUMN OF 1582, JOHN SITS ON THE SOFT DUNES OVERlooking the beach with his family. The evening sun sinks behind an incoming cloud bank, producing a sky of brilliant oranges and reds. A gentle breeze ruffles his wife's dark hair and his own reddish gray braids. Although his family doesn't fully comprehend the object of his seaside vigil, they give him the strength to endure the years of loss and regret. They also provide the warmth for a future he would have never imagined for himself three years earlier.

Lieutenant John Gallawaye no longer searches for or waits upon the arrival of a ship. The gods of the sea and the winds are what he seeks and finds. They were always there, but he just needed to know how to recognize them. His thoughts drift back to Manny and his decision to remain with the Lakimas even if the English should return. For the first time, John understands why. The English might or might not arrive, but he will stay. A brunette head rests on his shoulder, and a red-haired infant plays at his feet. The overhead reds and oranges turn darker, crimson and purple, signaling another New Albion sunset.

CHAPTER 14

# Historical Epilogue

This is the story of what might have been a forgotten but significant piece of history. *New Albion Sunset* is fiction. The names of many of the characters are real, taken from lists provided in the book by Zelma Nuttall (1914). A few I made up to complete the tale.

The following material is based in fact, recorded and documented by various sources from fifty years before Drake's voyage to events several hundred years later. Some of this, such as the later voyage of Cavendish and the testimony of John Drake during inquisitions in South America, provides tantalizing evidence for the narrative scenarios in this novel.

### SIR FRANCIS DRAKE:
### ENGLISH HERO, SPANISH PIRATE

The *Golden Hinde* departed the west coast of North America in the summer of 1579, purportedly with sixty-three people aboard, including Drake and his officers and crewmen. Four blacks were aboard: Diego, Maria, Francisco, and an unnamed black (designated in the novel as Mark). On 14 November 1579, three blacks, not including Diego, were left on Crab Island in the East Indies. The island or isle, a habitat abundant in giant land crabs (*Birgus*), was named Francisco or Francisca, leading to speculation that the feminine form might have been named after Maria. However, it is more likely named after the Negro slave freed from the Spanish near Peru. There has been much controversy among present-day scholars and armchair historians about Drake abandoning the blacks. Maria was pregnant and probably close to giving birth at that time, but there is no evidence that she or the other blacks had not freely chosen to remain on the island.

Drake returned to England on 26 September 1580, sailing into Plymouth with fifty-nine people aboard the *Golden Hinde*—one sailor died off South Africa. Drake's ship was laden with Spanish gold, silver, jewelry, fine linens, and many other valuables. Queen Elizabeth gladly received her half share of the treasure, and the backers and sponsors were paid their due plus. Drake and his crew were also rewarded for their contributions to the crown's treasury and for being the first Englishmen to circumnavigate the globe.

However, because of increasing tensions with Spain and the fact that the crown's financial gains were at the Spaniards' expense, the Queen impounded all the logs, charts, and other accounts of the voyage. Drake and all crew members were sworn to secrecy on pain of death.

Despite Spanish requests for Elizabeth to arrest Drake for piracy and hand him over for justice, Drake was knighted aboard the *Golden Hinde* at Deptford on 4 April 1581. To avoid further protest by the Spanish, Elizabeth handed the sword to a visiting French diplomat to perform the honor, and this also signified French support for the Drake ventures. Furthermore, the Queen allowed Sir Francis to adopt his own coat of arms.

Sir Francis Drake may have wanted to return and fortify the probable outpost of New Albion, but the increasing tension between Spain and England would be a deterrent to any further encroachment on the Spanish New World. Despite his share of the treasure, the ships and sponsors would be at the mercy of the court's political will. Circumstantial evidence suggests, however, that at least two attempts were made to return to Nova Albion: during the Fenton Expedition of 1582 and the Cavendish Expedition of 1586 (see below).

In 1589, after the defeat of the Spanish Armada, Drake planned to release his account of the circumnavigational voyage, including a description of New Albion. The complex political interactions involving the publisher Richard Hakluyt, Sir Francis Walsingham, and the censorship ordered by the Queen are detailed in books by Bawlf (2003) and others. The Queen's actual reasons for withholding public disclosure of the New Albion discovery as told by Drake are not known, but she refused to permit publication. It may have been due to Drake's inability in 1589 to crush the remains of the Spanish fleet in Spain, which earned her displeasure. Hakluyt published his great tome on English discoveries without an account of Drake's voyage, and he also omitted the disappearance of the *Content* from Cavendish's expedition (see below). In 1592, Drake tried again to persuade Elizabeth to allow him to reveal his exploits in the northern latitudes. She again refused, permitting only the release by Hakluyt of the portion of Francis Fletcher's log that indicated a New Albion location at 38.5°N.

## Relevant Voyages

This novel centers on one part of one specific voyage: Drake's circumnavigation in 1577–1580. However, the history of Drake's feat also pertains to other voyages that bear on his mission and the consequences of his voyage.

Juan Rodríguez Cabrillo (1499–1543) was the first Spaniard (some sources say Portuguese) to survey and map the coast of California in 1542–1543. He encountered autumn storms after reaching the latitude of the Russian River in California.

Martin Frobisher (c. 1535–1594) made voyages in 1576, 1577, and 1578 for England to search for a passage through the Arctic seas to connect the North Sea (Atlantic) with the Pacific. Many cartographers believed, without evidence, that the fabled Strait of Anián or Northwest Passage existed. Although he found ore that he thought was gold and attempted to establish a settlement on what would be later named Frobisher Bay, the ore was iron pyrite, and the colony failed after much discontent and bickering. Note that Frobisher's voyages to discover an eastern entrance to the passage overlapped with Drake's attempts to find the western entrance.

Edward Fenton had sailed with Frobisher's second and third expeditions to the Arctic of North America and was put in charge of a voyage around Africa and across the Indian Ocean to the Moluccas and Cathay (China). He was also instructed to inquire about or secretly search for the Northwest Passage. The man in charge of one of the ships, the *Francis*, was John Drake, the cousin of Francis and cabin boy/artist during Drake's circumnavigation. The group of three ships sailed to Brazil, but disputes with his officers and inability to trade with the Portuguese in Brazil led Fenton to abandon the expedition. John Drake fled with his ship and continued down the Atlantic coast of South America but was shipwrecked and eventually captured by the Spanish. During inquisitions in Paraguay and later in Lima, John gave testimony that Francis Drake arrived at 48°N latitude and left the Nicaraguan boat at New Albion when the *Golden Hinde* departed.

John Davis or Davys (c. 1550–1605), also an English navigator, attempted to find the Northwest Passage in 1585, 1586, and 1587. He sailed with Thomas Cavendish on his last failed voyage in 1591.

In 1586, Thomas Cavendish (1560–1592) followed the same circumnavigational route as Drake, raided Spanish ports and ships in the Pacific, returned to England in his flagship, *Desire*, and was knighted in 1588. One of Cavendish's three ships, the *Hugh Gallant*, was intentionally sunk to consolidate crew lost aboard the other two ships. The second ship, the *Content*, slipped away during the night in November 1587 while off the coast of California. Did it sink because it was overloaded from treasure seized from the Spanish ship *Santa Ana*? Did a disgruntled crew mutiny and leave with riches far more valuable than the contract salary they were to receive? Was the *Content* fated to search for the Strait of Anián and the colony at New Albion? Some people believe the *Content* may have traveled north in the Sea of Cortez (Gulf of California) and entered a river leading to the Laguna Salada in northwestern Mexico. The remains of a large ship buried in the desert near there were reportedly discovered in 1968, and the metal rigging and other artifacts from the ship are now in the Imperial Valley Museum in Ocotillo, California, awaiting expert analysis and a long overdue verdict.

Sebastián Vizcaíno (1548–1624) was a Spanish explorer appointed to survey and map the Alta California coast in 1602 and to locate good harbors for the Manila galleons returning to Acapulco. He sailed with three ships following the same route mapped by Cabrillo. One of the ships, the *Tres Reyes* under the command of Martin de Aquilar, became separated from the group in California and continued up the coast as far north as Cape Blanco in modern-day Oregon, possibly to Coos Bay.

## Morena's Deposition

N. de Morena or Morera (Nazario de Morera in the novel) purportedly walked from New Albion to current-day New Mexico, above the Rio Grande river (Rio de Norte) to Santa Barbara in Chihuahua, northern New Spain, and finally to the mines in Sombrerete. He told his story to Captain Rodrigo del Rio, the governor of New Galicia. He didn't arrive until 1583, four years after Drake left the West Coast and three years after Drake had returned to England. Either Morera provided a mixture of fact and fiction or subsequent transmittals of the testimony produced errors, because the location of New Albion was never clarified. Morera mentioned that he had helped guide Drake through the Strait of Anián and walked more than 500 leagues (1,300–2,100 miles, depending on which definition of league is used) before catching sight of an arm of a sea that divided the lands of New Mexico from other lands to the west. This has been interpreted by some as the San Francisco Bay area, which is obviously false, since neither an Oregon nor a Marin anchorage site would have required 500 leagues of travel. The other candidate for a sea arm is the Gulf of California, which divides mainland Mexico from Baja California. The distance between Lincoln County, Oregon, and Santa Barbara, Chihuahua, is 2,120 miles, but this is a straight-line distance. If Morera averaged 1.40 to 1.45 miles per day, he could have covered that distance in the time allotted. A more believable trip might be 3,200–3,600 miles, which is still attainable at a rate of less than 2.5 miles per day over a four-year interval. Morera's account wasn't published until 1626 (see Hanna 1979, 387–88 or Bawlf 2003, 330–31, for details). If the account is true, it represents the only direct testimony from any person left behind at New Albion. But which New Albion?

## Roanoke

Most historians regard the Roanoke Colony on an island in present-day North Carolina as the first documented effort to establish a permanent English settlement in North America. The first attempt was made in 1585, and the second was in 1587. The first failure was due to a lack of supplies and poor relations with the local native inhabitants. The second failure was abetted by the attack of the Spanish Armada near England in 1588 and delay in resupplying Roanoke. When finally revisited in 1590, the colony had been abandoned, and the fate of 112–121 colonists was never determined. It later became known as the Lost Colony. New Albion, therefore, was not the only failed attempt by the English to establish a claim in the New World.

## The End of Spanish Maritime Domination

The end of the Spanish maritime threat to England came in July and August 1588. The Spanish Armada of 124 ships attempted to engage the English naval forces and affect a landing near London by the Parma army forces based in the Spanish Netherlands. A series of engagements scattered the Spanish ships, and the landing never occurred. Other factors that defeated the Spanish were the weather (the so-called Protestant Wind), which exacted a toll on the Armada's ships, the greater maneuverability of English ships, and the tactical experience of the English admirals, including Sir Francis Drake. The English attempted to launch an armada of their own in 1589 under Drake's leadership, but it also ended in disaster. The undeclared Anglo-Spanish war lasted from 1585–1604. Subsequent Spanish attempts in 1596 and 1597 to destroy the English navy and attempts by the English and Dutch to inflict critical damage on the Spanish only weakened each other's forces. The standoff finally resulted in a truce established by the Treaty of London in 1604.

## The Deaths of Sir Francis Drake and Queen Elizabeth

Sir Francis Drake, the audacious mariner, pirate, and servant to the Crown, died off the Caribbean coast of Panama from dysentery on 15 January 1596 at the approximate age of fifty-five. Against his express will, he was buried at sea dressed in full armor and in a lead coffin. His final resting place in Portobelo Bay has not been discovered but may well be found in the near future.

Queen Elizabeth, the last of the Tudor monarchs, died at Richmond Palace on 24 March 1603 at the age of sixty-nine. She ruled for forty-seven years and led the transformation of England from an isolated nation to a global maritime presence. She remained unmarried, leaving no heirs, and was succeeded by her cousin, James VI of Scotland, who became James I of England. With her death, the veil of secrecy surrounding Drake's voyage began to lift, and various accounts were published in the following years. The most notable, *The World Encompassed*, was compiled by Sir Francis Drake, son of Thomas Drake, nephew of the circumnavigator, and heir to his estate. It was published in 1628 and became the most cited and authoritative account of the voyage, but it did not mention a New Albion colony or the fate of Tello's barque after the *Golden Hinde* departed.

## The Palace of Whitehall Fire in 1698

The destruction of Drake's confiscated and sequestered logs, charts, and drawings removed any further political considerations for England's claim to the Pacific Northwest south of the Strait of Juan de Fuca. The Palace of Whitehall in Central London had been a major home of English monarchs from 1530 to 1698. Until the completion of Versailles, it was the largest palace complex in Europe and consisted of more than fifteen hundred rooms. On 4 January 1698, a fire destroyed most of the residential and government buildings in the complex. It was accidently started by a Dutch maidservant who hung linens near a charcoal brazier to dry. The linens caught, and the fire quickly spread, resulting in a fifteen-hour inferno. The next day, strong winds reignited the fire, and it destroyed most of the remaining structures. Gunpowder was used to create firebreaks, but many of the explosions actually spread the fire farther and faster. Only the Banqueting Hall and a few smaller buildings were spared.

Many precious works of art were lost (some to looters who climbed the palace walls while servants were trying to save other items). It is believed that the official logs, charts, and drawings of Drake's circumnavigation were among the items destroyed in the Whitehall library. The Queen's map, a large chart prepared for Elizabeth presumably under Drake's supervision, had been on public view for several years. It was also lost.

## The International Boundary between England and the United States

The United States and Great Britain signed the Treaty of Paris on 3 September 1783, terminating the American Revolutionary War. The Treaty included provisions for establishing an international boundary between the northern limits of the United States and British North America. At the time, the United States had not reached west of the Mississippi River. The boundary was extended by the London

Convention of 1818 westward to the Rocky Mountains along the 49th parallel of latitude as the two nations grew. By this time, Lewis and Clark had completed their famous trek to the Pacific Ocean and established a fort at Point Adams, west of Astoria, near the mouth of the Columbia River. It was located close to the Clatsop settlement of Konope. The continuation of the 49th parallel to the Pacific was established by the Oregon Treaty of 1846, although the United States originally wanted to make 54°40' N, south of Russia's Alaska Territory, the northwestern boundary. Later surveys and negotiations completed the International Boundary that Canada and the United States observe today.

Drake's original claim of New Albion for England is lost in all of this. Until the nineteenth century, the presence of the name "New (or Nova) Albion" on subsequent maps indicated England's passive claim to North America, sea to sea, a colonial intent that included the "back side of Virginia." Part of the problem of recognition for an English territorial claim was the lack of an occupied presence and the establishment of a true colony, no matter how small. In 1585, Roanoke in Virginia was initiated but failed disastrously. How much farther away and isolated was New Albion? How could twenty or so men hope to succeed in maintaining a presence against all odds without timely reinforcement?

If the colony has been successful, would the Pacific Northwest (Washington, Oregon, Idaho, and Northern California) be part of the United States today? Indeed, the 49th parallel may not have been a negotiable boundary, and the United States may have been confined to a much smaller area, perhaps excluding any territory west of the Rockies. The result would make for an interesting alternate history, similar to speculations in the novel *If the South Had Won the Civil War* by Kantor (see references).

# APPENDIX 1.

# Essays to Document *New Albion Sunset*

---

THE FIVE ESSAYS INCLUDED IN THIS APPENDIX PROVIDE MATErial for research consideration on the New Albion outpost depicted in this novel. They might serve as evidence for the possible location of the anchorage site in British Columbia or Oregon and explain why Drake may have believed he had discovered the fabled Northwest Passage.

### The Strait of Anián (Northwest Passage)

Based on their limited knowledge of North American (the New World) geography, several European nations attempted to discover and navigate a sea route from the North Atlantic to the North Pacific. This commenced in the late sixteenth century. The objective was to shorten the passage between Asia and Europe and avoid the dangerous route around the southern tip of South America, which the Spanish controlled at the time.

Knowledge of the Arctic Archipelago, eventually to be the far northern lands of Canada, was poorly developed. In addition, the belief that seawater didn't freeze was widespread, leading to the conclusion that an open sea route must exist. Locations for the Strait of Anián were proposed as early as 1539 by Hernán Cortés when he discovered Baja California and the Gulf of California. The name of the strait probably derived from Ania, a province of Cathay (China) mentioned in an account by Marco Polo published in 1559. The Strait of Anián appeared on maps by Giacomo Gastaldi in 1561, by Abraham Ortelius in 1564, and on a 1610 map by Jodocus Hondius, labelled as "Anian Frenum" (opening). The discovery of the Bering Strait in 1728 between Alaska and Kamchatka provided additional evidence for a northern passage across North America, but attempts to successfully navigate the passage proved futile until the twenty-first century and only after sufficient sea ice melted as a result of climate change.

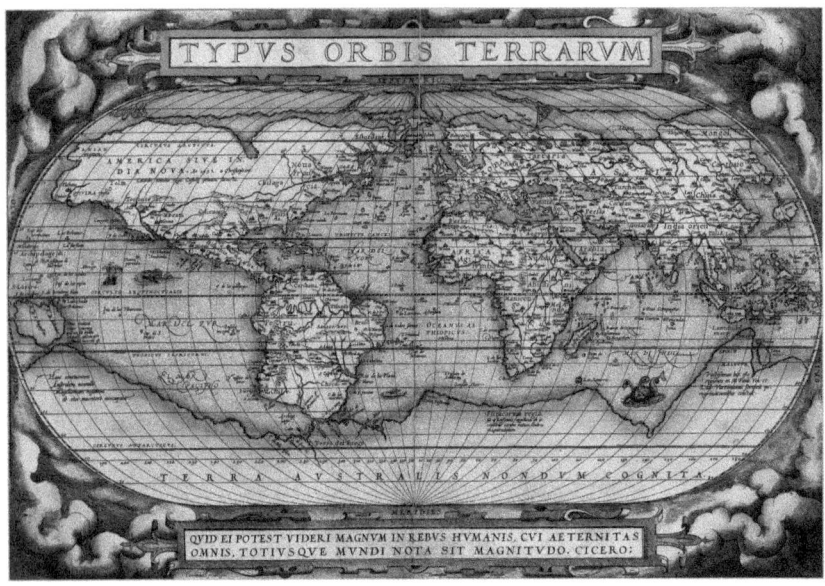

Figure 1. *Typus Orbis Terrarum* by Ortlius in 1564 showing Anián on the Pacific Coast of America and a passage north of the Arctic Circle to the North Atlantic (public domain).

Martin Frobisher, an English explorer, made three notable attempts of discovery in the 1570s. A 1578 map speculates that the Frobisher Strait, entered from the Atlantic side, connected with the Anián Strait on the Pacific Coast. Juan de Fuca, a Greek navigator, probably thought he discovered it in 1592 when he entered the passage between present-day Vancouver Island and Washington State.

One of the objectives of the Drake Expedition of 1577–1580 was to discover the Pacific entrance to the Northwest Passage and establish an outpost to be later fortified. After Drake's return to England, he attempted to finance an immediate return to the Pacific, claiming that he would be able to make the roundtrip voyage in one year because he had found a very short way. This novel describes the intent to found the first colony on the Pacific Coast of North America for the English.

In the novel, Drake's ships enter the Strait of Juan de Fuca thirteen years before its purported discovery by the Greek. The Fuca Pillar, on the coastal approach to the strait from the south, would have been a dramatic landmark and would have also been noted by the Drake crews as they emerged from the strait and turned south to follow the Washington coast.

Figure 2. Fuca Pillar on the Pacific coast of the Olympic Peninsula (photograph, National Oceanic and Atmospheric Administration)

## The Anchorage Site Map

No single aspect about the location of Drake's anchorage site, as described in the Fletcher journal, has raised more speculation than the inset placed in the Jodocus Hondius map of 1589. At the upper-left corner of the large map depicting the voyage of Drake and of Thomas Cavendish eight years later, an overhead perspective sketch shows the presumed cove or harbor where Drake spent six weeks. A number of authored references over the last one hundred years attempt to make the case for specific coves, bays, or inlets. The claims for California sites near San Francisco Bay are especially pervasive. Although recognition by the Department of Interior has been awarded to Drake's Estero in Marin County, this is based mainly on persistent promotion efforts by local business groups rather than serious studies by historians. Comparison of the Hondius outline with that of selected other sites are shown below. Note the last illustration of Acapulco, Mexico. Turn it upside down and compare to the Hondius map inset.

Figure 3. Hondius map inset, 1589 (public domain)

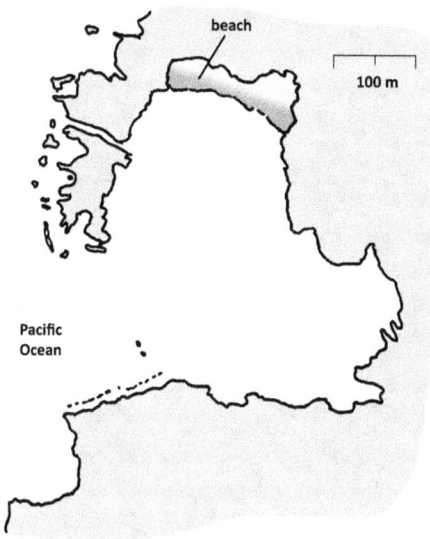

Figure 4. Whale Cove, OR
(Map by Dan Hawkes)

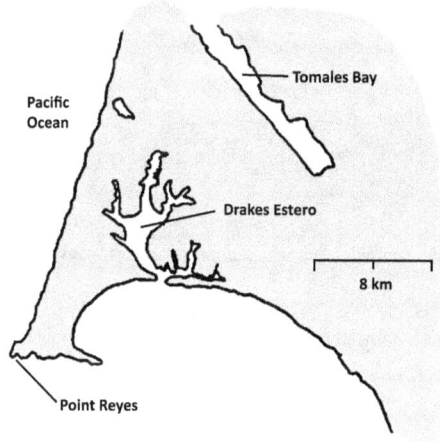

Figure 5. Drakes Bay, CA
(Map by Dan Hawkes)

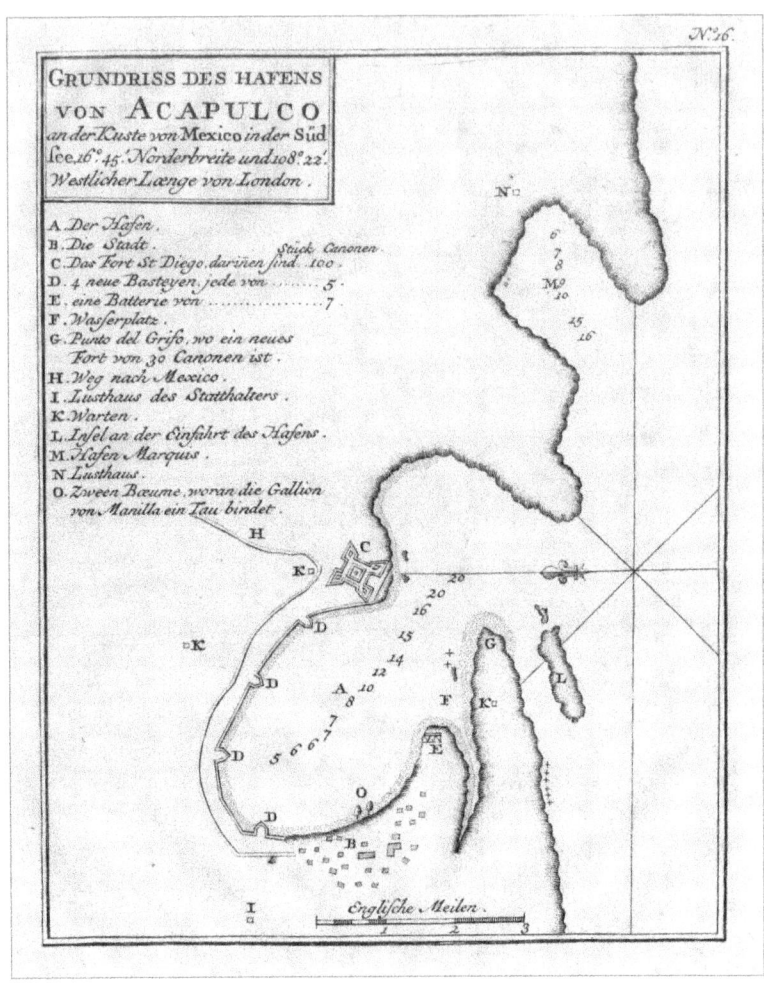

Figure 6. Acapulco, Mexico
(Grundriss des Hafens map, 1754, public domain)

No one prospective site accounts for all of the features indicated in the Hondius inset, and variations have been explained by: 1) the lapse of time and changes in topography over the four-hundred-year interval; 2) a deficiency in perspective accuracy from ground or sea level; and 3) attempts to disguise and mislead Spanish military investigations. Indications of anchorage latitude are definitely inconsistent, varying from 38 to 48°N by different accounts. Proposed sites include Boundary Bay and Vancouver Island in British Columbia; Puget Sound and inlets on the Pacific Coast of Washington; Nehalem Bay, Whale Cove, and Cape Arago in Oregon; and Trinity Bay, Tomales Bay, Drake's Bay, San Francisco Bay, and Monterey Bay in California, among others (see Appendix 3).

Melissa Darby's excellent book, published in 2019, reveals the repeated attempts to create history and suppress alternative discoveries and views in relation to Marin County anchorage sites. Much of the controversy centered on the discovery of a "brass" plate in Marin County during the 1930s—supposedly the one used for Drake's claim to New Albion. Although cleverly faked, subsequent analysis revealed that the plate was made of nineteenth-century brass, the inscriptions were not completely contemporary with the intended date, and the letters GC in the lower-left corner didn't stand for General Commandant or some such but for George Clark, the plate's originator. It was intended as a practical joke against a Bay Area historian but got out of hand. The hoax wasn't fully revealed until the late 1970s.

Although the actual plate was supposedly placed and dated on 17 June, as described by Francis Pretty (a second-hand source not with Drake's voyage), the plate was never found, and all records of its wording have been lost or destroyed. The date depicted in this novel, one month later than the "official" account, is in compliance with the altered dates and events that might represent the actual West Coast anchorages and New Albion claims.

## Coneys (Muskrats)

The account of Drake's voyage, derived mainly from the journal of Chaplain Francis Fletcher, described a large population of a medium-sized, rabbit-like animal that was hunted and used for fur by the Native Americans at the North Pacific anchorage site. The animal was characterized in *The World Encompassed* (Drake, 1628), as follows:

> ...*besides a multitude of a strange kind of conies, by far exceeding them in number [referring to an earlier comment on thousands of large, fat deer]: their heads and bodies, in which they resemble other conies, are but small; his tail, like the tail of a rat, exceeding long; and his feet like the paws of a want or mole; under his chin, on either side, he hath a bag, into which he gathereth his meat, when he hath filled his belly abroad, that he may with it either feed his young, or feed himself when he lists not to travel from his burrow; the people eat their bodies, and make great account of their skins, for their king's holiday's coat was made of them.*

Bob Ward of Newport, Oregon, indicated in his public exhibits and essays that the description fits that of muskrats, a species not native to California but abundant in earlier times from Oregon, Washington, and British Columbia. The single North American species, *Ondatra zibethicus*, is among the largest in the muskrat family, and it provides an underfur that is rich, dense, and waterproof. Bob was right and I was wrong. In my introduction to Gitzen's 2008 book on Drake at Nehalem Bay, I speculated that river otters might be the mysterious "coneys," but based on size and description, muskrats are the appropriate identification.

Figure 7. The common muskrat, *Ondatra zibethicus* (photo by D. Gordon E. Robertson, Wikipedia creative commons).

## Tello's Barque and the Missing Crewmen

As described by Fletcher and confirmed later by members of Drake's crew, a barque or frigate of about forty tons was captured from Rodrigo Tello on 20 March 1579 off the coast of Nicaragua (present-day Costa Rica) as the *Golden Hinde* made its way north along the Pacific Coast. The ship was refitted for an ocean voyage and sailed away from Guatulco with the *Hinde* on 16 April 1579. Mysteriously, no mention of it is made in any of the published contemporary accounts. When Drake left Guatulco, his company included about eighty-five people including a few Negro (freed) slaves, captured Spanish and Portuguese pilots, and underage cabin boys. By the time the *Golden Hinde* reached the East Indies in the autumn of 1579, only sixty crew members, excluding three black freed slaves, were present. What happened to the ship and twenty to twenty-five people? Interestingly, Fletcher's journal provides precise accounts of the fate of people who were lost at sea, killed by hostile natives, or lost by other means during the voyage. This includes details of freed blacks put ashore in the East Indies and a crewman who died of scurvy when the *Golden Hinde* rounded South Africa. N. Morera or Morena, presumed to be a pilot, was supposedly put ashore during Drake's northwest visit. There is no historical record of the fate of the other missing two dozen.

## Salmon River Discoveries

The mouth of the Salmon River lies a few miles north of Newport, Oregon. The outlet is guarded by three large boulders, Three Rox, but the river is shallow and not obviously navigable today. However, as late as the nineteenth century, the waterway served as a local shipping port for timber and delivery of supplies to communities several miles inland. The presumed size of Tello's barque would draft about six feet, more than adequate for a safe harbor site entrance during the fall and winter when prevailing winds turned southwesterly.

A number of Native American tales along the northern Oregon coast speak of visitations by white men in large canoes with wings, supposedly predating documented visitations by early Euro-American explorers and traders. Bob Ward summarizes findings of the white Calkins family that settled near the Salmon River in the nineteenth century. They sometimes caught their fishing nets on a sunken obstacle near the mouth of the river. On one occurrence, they recovered a piece of wood with metal bolts in it and identified it as ironwood, a tropical hardwood similar to teak and used in shipbuilding.

The biggest surprise came in 1931, however, when Elmer Calkins platted property along the river to construct a camping resort. An old Indian midden consisting of shell material had to be removed for the parking lot. On top of the midden was an old spruce tree. As they removed the shell material, they discovered the skeletal remains of three individuals buried haphazardly among the midden, an indication that the bodies were not of local tribal origin. Some of the bones were broken, and one skull had an arrowhead embedded. The bones were taken to Oregon Agricultural College in Corvallis (future Oregon State University) and examined by Dr. John Horner, a historian. Dr. F. M. Carter, a local physician, determined that two of the skeletons were probably Caucasian and not native. The third skeleton was as that of a large Negro, possibly as tall as eight feet, but this may have been an exaggeration. Horner tentatively dated them as about 160 years old. This would place their deaths in about 1770, but precise dating techniques were not yet available. The other finding of interest was the spruce tree, determined to be about 350 years old based on tree rings. Since the tree grew on top of the midden, this meant that the burial probably took place about 1600 plus or minus twenty years. Unfortunately, the remains were taken from the college, and their whereabouts are not known. Were the three bodies men from the missing crew of the *Golden Hinde* or Tello's barque? I based the character Tomas or "Big Tom" on this skeleton and ascribed him as one of the three slaves, including Maria, freed from Zarate's ship in Guatemalan waters. However, there is no mention of a black giant by Fletcher or in the other contemporary accounts. Surely such a figure would have evoked comment, but how else to account for the Salmon River discovery?

Because the site of the burials and the suspected shipwreck were only a few hundred feet apart, the Calkins family probed the adjacent mudflats near the mouth of the river during the 1970s and discovered a thirty-five-foot ship's keel with attached ribs during a very low tide. Attempts to rediscover the shipwreck during the past few years have been suggestive but not conclusive. Bob Ward used various instruments at the shipwreck site to confirm the existence of metals that conformed to a buried ship pattern, but ground-penetrating radar was not successful for detecting dense wood, because the salt-impregnated mud interfered with the signals. Ward indicates that archeological investigations should continue.

# APPENDIX 2.

# Reference Chronologies

THESE DATES AND EVENTS ARE CULLED FROM A NUMBER OF historical sources. They are offered as a guide to the sequence of events during the Age of Exploration, the Tudor Reigns in England, and important events of interest to Drake's life and legend. The dates are given per the Julian calendar as originally recorded. Add ten days for the modern equivalents.

## CHRONOLOGY A: EVENTS OF EXPLORATION AND POLITICS (1487–1698)

1487    Bartolomeu Dias (Portugal) rounded the Cape of Good Hope to discover the Indian Ocean.

1492    Christopher Columbus (Genoa), backed by King Ferdinand and Queen Isabella of Spain, discovered several Caribbean Islands while searching for Asia.

1494    The Treaty of Tordesillas was signed on 7 June 1494, dividing the New World lands between Portugal and the Crown of Castile, brokered by Pope Alexander VI of the Vatican. This agreement rendered the yet-to-be discovered Pacific Ocean to Spain.

1497    Vasco da Gama (Portugal) reached the Malabar Coast of India, opening trade to Asia.

Giovanni (John) Cabot of Venice, with license from King Henry VII, discovered Newfoundland but mistook it for northeast Asia.

1501   Amerigo Vespucci (Florence) followed the Brazilian coastline south to Rio de la Plata.

1508   Sebastian Cabot, son of John Cabot, followed the Canadian coast north to ice fields, convinced there was a northern passage west to Asia.

1513   Vasco Núñez de Balboa (Spain) crossed the Isthmus of Panama, became the first European to see the eastern Pacific Ocean, and named it the South Sea. He claimed the entire ocean and its shores for Spain.

1519   Ferñao de Magalhães (Magellan, Portugal) sailed five ships around South America in the service of Spain and entered the Pacific Ocean (South Sea) in November 1520. One of the ships, the *Victoria,* continued westward in the first global circumnavigation but without Magellan, who died in the Philippines. The ship and remaining crew returned to Europe in 1522.

1520   Hernán Cortés conquered the Aztec empire in Mexico, bringing Spain's full attention to America.

1525   García Jofre de Loaysa (Spain) passed through the Straits of Magellan with seven ships. Only two, minus Loaysa, reached the Moluccas. Only three of 250 men eventually returned to Spain.

1527   Cortés sent three ships from Mexico to look for Loaysa. One reached the Philippine Islands, but it was unable to return to Mexico.

1530   Pedro de Alvarado, a lieutenant of Cortés, plundered Central America south to Panama.

1531   Francisco Pizarro González (Spain) commenced the conquest of the Incan empire in the Andes.

1533   A ship sent by Cortés discovered the peninsula of Baja California.

Elizabeth, later to be Queen Elizabeth I, was born to Anne Boleyn and Henry VIII.

1534  Jacques Cartier (France) discovered the Saint Lawrence River and claimed eastern Canada for France.

1539  Francisco de Ulloa (Spain) explored the Gulf of California with three ships for Hernán Cortés but went only as far as the Isla de Cedros, about halfway up the Pacific coast of Baja California.

1540  Francis Drake was born in Tavistock, Devon, England, the first of twelve sons to Edward Drake, a Protestant farmer, and his wife, Mary Mylwaye. The exact date and year are unknown but could be as early as 1536 or as late as 1544.

1542  Juan Rodríguez Cabrillo (Spain) sailed from Navidad, Mexico, on 27 June with three ships. He landed at Bahía de San Miguel (San Diego) on 28 September and reached as far north as the Russian River in California at 38.44°N. They were reportedly searching for the Strait of Anián, based on Portuguese rumors. They missed the entrance to San Francisco Bay. Cabrillo died during the return trip.

1543  In January, Cabrillo's pilot, Bartolomé Ferrelo (Spain) reached 44°N (latitude of Eugene, Oregon) but abandoned the voyage due to the cold. He returned to New Spain in April.

1547  Henry VIII died in January and was succeeded by his nine-year-old son, Edward VI.

1553  Edward VI died at the age of sixteen and was succeeded by Mary I, age thirty-seven, Henry VIII's daughter by Katherine of Aragon. She was a devout Catholic and attempted to restore Catholicism in England.

First voyage of the merchant's stock group (later The Muscovy Company), attempting to find a northeast passage, discovered Novaya Zemlya at 72°N. One of the ships, under Richard Chancellor, arrived at the White Sea and established trade with Ivan IV in Moscow.

1556  Charles V, ruling Spain as Charles I, abdicated the throne and left it to his son who became Philip II.

1558  England lost Calais, the last English possession in France.

Mary Tudor (Mary I) died, and her sister, Elizabeth I, ascended the throne at age twenty-five on 17 November. She was crowned in January 1559.

1559  Catholic legislation was repealed in England.

John Dee, a prominent cosmographer, befriended Robert Dudley and became Elizabeth's astrologer. He advocated for the presence and discovery of a Northwest Passage.

1560  A treaty was signed between Elizabeth I and Scottish reformers.

Charles IX ascended the throne as King of France, and the Treaty of Edinburgh was signed between Scotland, France, and England.

1561  Giacomo Gastaldi (Italy), cartographer, published a map showing the Strait of Anián.

1562  War commenced between Protestant Huguenots and Roman Catholics in France.

1563  The Thirty-Nine Articles finalized establishment of the Anglican Church of England.

1564  French Huguenots established a colony at the mouth of the St. Johns River in Florida.

The Peace of Troyes was affirmed between England and France.

Abraham Ortelius (Belgium) published a map showing the Strait of Anián at 40°N in the Pacific (see Appendix 1).

1565  Admiral Pedro Menéndez de Avilés was sent by King Philip to eradicate the Florida Protestant colony; more than four hundred were executed. A fort at St. Augustine was established to prevent further colonization.

In June, Andrés de Urdaneta (Spain), one of the three survivors of the Loaysa expedition, sailed north from the Philippines to pick up westerlies at the latitude of Japan. He arrived at Upper California and in Mexico after four months. This established the Philippines–Acapulco galleon trade route, made once a year.

1566  Sir Humphrey Gilbert, acquaintance of John Dee, circulated a tract titled *A Discourse of a Discoverie for a New Passage to Cathaia* along with a copy of Ortelius' map. He advocated for the English to establish a colony near the "Sierra Nevadas." The Muscovy Company, granted a monopoly earlier, blocked Gilbert's petition.

1568  Netherlands revolted against Spain.

Mary, Queen of Scots escaped to England but was imprisoned by Elizabeth because the Queen feared a Catholic rebellion.

1570  Ortelius published the first atlas of the world, *Theatrum Orbis Terrarum,* showing the Strait of Anián and a large connecting Northwest Passage.

1571  The City of Manila was founded and became a Spanish trading center for the Far East.

1573  Elizabeth appointed Francis Walsingham as principal secretary of state for foreign affairs. William Cecil, now known as Lord Burghley, continued to serve as senior minister and lord treasurer. Walsingham and Robert Dudley (Earl of Leicester) believed that war with Spain was inevitable and maritime expansion was necessary.

1574  Henri III became King of France.

Richard Grenville petitioned Queen Elizabeth for a voyage to the South Seas. He wanted to found colonies on the Rio de la Plata and on the coast of Chile, below Spain's occupation. A license was granted, and Grenville assembled men and ships. Elizabeth later stopped preparations, probably under Lord Burghley's advice.

|  |  |
|---|---|
| 1575 | The Muscovy Company resumed northern explorations and issued a license to Michael Lok and Captain Martin Frobisher to look for the Northwest Passage from the Atlantic. |
| | Francis Drake arrived with plunder from Panama. This was reported to King Philip in Spain. |
| 1576 | Frobisher began his explorations and set sail on 12 June. At the end of July, sailing in the *Gabriel*, he discovered a large inlet on Baffin Island and believed it to be the Northwest Passage. He returned to England on 2 October. |
| | Grenville proposed a voyage to look for the Northwest Passage from the South Seas. |
| 1577 | England and the Netherlands formed an alliance. |
| | John Dee wrote in support of discovering the Strait of Anián, necessary for a completed Northwest Passage. |
| | Francis Drake departed England on 13 December (second sailing after repairs) with five ships and 164 crewmembers. |
| 1579 | Drake reached his farthest northern point, possibly up to Vancouver Island (50°N), but many historians place him no farther than 48° as stated in *The World Encompassed*. |
| 1580 | The Spanish assumed control of Portugal. |
| | Drake returned to England on 26 September with fifty-nine crewmembers. He presented his charts and journal to Queen Elizabeth. |
| 1581 | Mendoza, ambassador of Spain to England, wrote Philip II on 9 January that Leicester and Elizabeth agreed with Drake to sail ten ships to the Moluccas to be joined by six other ships near the coast of Brasil (see Nuttall, page 38). |
| | Drake was knighted by Elizabeth, using the French ambassador for the ceremony, aboard the *Golden Hinde,* on 4 April. |

**1582** The Gregorian calendar was introduced into Roman Catholic countries. October 5 became October 15. Britain did not change until 1752 and Russia not until 1918.

On May 1, Edward Fenton's expedition to the South Seas sailed from England, ostensibly to trade with China and the East Indies. One ship, the *Francis*, was commanded by John Drake, the younger cousin of Sir Francis Drake and cabin boy aboard the *Golden Hinde*.

**1583** Following a shipwreck near the Rio Plata, John Drake was captured by Indians.

**1584** John Drake escaped the Indians but was captured by the Spanish in Buenos Aires and faced an inquisition in Paraguay.

England sent aid to the Dutch Republic in its attempt to break free of Spain.

**1586** Drake sailed on an expedition to the West Indies.

**1587** Mary, Queen of Scots, was executed for treason after a Catholic plot to overthrow Elizabeth was uncovered.

Philip II, King of Spain, made plans to invade England and return the country to the Roman Catholic Church. He assembled the "Invincible Armada." Philip II of Spain declared war with England.

Francis Drake destroyed part of the Spanish fleet at Cadiz.

John Drake faced a second inquisition in Lima, Peru. He was acquitted after repenting and was held in a Jesuit monastery for three years. His testimony provided first-hand evidence of the northward progress of Drake's circumnavigation. He specifically cited 48°N as their anchorage location and the discovery Nova Albion and five or six good islands. He also stated that they spent six weeks repairing two ships.

| | |
|---|---|
| 1588 | The English defeated the Spanish Armada on 31 July. Lord Howard of Effingham, Francis Drake, John Hawkins, and Justinus van Nassau commanded the English forces. This ended the immediate threat to Nova Albion by the Spanish. |
| 1589 | Henri III of France was murdered, and Henry of Navarre ascended the throne as Henri IV. |
| | Jodocus Hondius (Flemish) issued a map of the world with the Portus Nova Albionis inset. |
| | João da Gama (Portugal) sailed from Japan to Mexico across the North Pacific, possibly at 45°N or higher. |
| 1592 | Sir Francis Drake petitioned Queen Elizabeth to publish the true account of his voyage. She refused. |
| 1595 | The Hondius map was reissued with text in Dutch, describing Drake's voyage (Drake Broadside). |
| 1596 | Drake died at sea, possibly from dysentery, off the coast of Portobelo, Colón, Panama. He was buried at sea nearby. |
| 1598 | The Edict of Nantes restored equal rights to Huguenots in France. |
| | Philip II died, and Philip III ascended the throne of Spain. |
| 1600 | Elizabeth granted a charter to the East India Company with funds from Drake's treasure. |
| 1603 | Elizabeth I died at Richmond Palace on 24 March. James VI of Scotland ascended the throne as James I of England. |
| 1628 | *The World Encompassed* compiled by Sir Francis Drake (1588–1637), son of Thomas Drake and nephew of *the* Sir Francis Drake (c. 1540–1596), was published. The report was based on Chaplain Fletcher's journal and an anonymous report from one or more crewmembers. |
| 1666 | The Great Fire of London burned from Sunday, 2 September to Wednesday, 5 September. The firestorm burned the medieval |

city inside the Roman walls, destroyed over thirteen thousand homes with temperatures reaching 1700°C., destroyed St. Paul's Cathedral, but spared the Tower of London, Whitehall, and Westminster.

**1698** Whitehall Palace, believed to contain Drake's logs and charts, burned on 4 January, destroying all original records of Drake's voyage. A smaller fire preceded this on 10 April 1691. The Elizabeth I library may have held the Drake logs, or they may have been stored in restricted archives or other places as documents in use. They have not been rediscovered and are presumed lost.

## Chronology B:
## Events of the Drake Voyage and Return
## (1577–1586)

### — 1577 —

9 Jul    Drake claimed funds to construct the *Pelican*, a bark of 140 tons (carrying capacity), 13 ft. draught (laden), 102 ft. length, 21 ft. beam, and 90 ft. mainmast elevation (based on replica construction).

15 Nov    Drake's fleet consisting of five ships and 164 men, gentlemen and sailors, sailed from Plymouth, supposedly for Alexandria:

The *Pelican*, 150 tons, commanded by Drake, later renamed the *Golden Hinde*.

The *Elizabeth*, 80 tons, a new Deptford-built ship, commanded by John Wynter.

The *Benedict*, 15 tons, later exchanged for a cantor of 40 tons, named the *Christopher*, serving the *Elizabeth*.

The *Marigold*, 30 tons, commanded by John Thomas.

The *Swanne*, 50 tons, a flyboat or canter supplying the fleet.

16 Nov  Drake's fleet was forced to put into Falmouth Haven (Cornwall) by a fierce storm. The mast was torn from the *Pelican,* and the *Marigold* was damaged. The ships returned to Plymouth for repairs.

13 Dec  The fleet sailed again from Plymouth on a Wednesday with the same ships and crew.

25 Dec  The fleet reached Cape Cantin on the Barbary Coast (Morocco).

27 Dec  The fleet arrived at Mogador Island, one mile off the coast (Essaouira, Morocco). They used a safe harbor to build a pinnace from ready-made frames. A group of natives approached and items were exchanged.

28 Dec  After a misunderstanding with natives, one of Drake's men was carried away, leaving 163 men in the fleet.

30 Dec  With the pinnace finished, they departed Mogador without the missing crewman.

31 Dec  The fleet spotted Spanish fishermen and captured and retained three caravels.

## — 1578 —

17 Jan  The fleet arrived at Cape Blanco, off the northwest coast of Africa, and discovered a ship riding at anchor with two sailors aboard. They took the ship into harbor and trained the men of the fleet on land warfare. They took supplies from the fishermen but left them the *Benedict* in exchange for one of their canters of about forty tons (named the *Christopher* by Drake's men).

22 Jan  The four original ships, one of the Portuguese caravels and the canter left Cape Blanco.

27 Jan  The fleet arrived at Mayo (Maio) in the Cape Verdes Islands. The natives refused to trade by edict of Portugal's king. The next day, Wynter and Doughty led sixty-two men into the interior of Mayo for food and provisions and obtained coconuts, meat, and milk.

31 Jan  The fleet departed Mayo and sailed by Santiago (Sao Tiago). They spotted two ships and chased, overtook, and captured the *Santa Maria*, which they renamed *Mary*. Thomas Doughty was assigned as captain. They captured a supply of wine and their Portuguese pilot, Nuño da Silva. The other Portuguese crewmen were sent off with the *Pelican's* pinnace. The fleet arrived at Ilha de Fogo (Fogo) and Brava in the Cape Verde Islands that night. They set across the Atlantic the next day. Becalmed for three weeks but with intermittent storms, they sailed for fifty-four days without sight of land.

5 Apr  The fleet arrived on the coast of Brazil at 33°S. Natives lit fires along the shore as sacrifices to devils for storms and shoals to wreck the ships.

7 Apr  The *Christopher* was lost during a great storm but found eleven days later.

18 Apr  All ships were reunited at Cape of Joy, and fresh water was taken on. They found large footprints inland. Anchored along the mainland and in lee of some rocks, they killed seals for food. The fleet sailed south to 36°S and entered the Rio Plata, anchoring in fifty-four fathoms of freshwater. No good harbor was found.

27 Apr  Returning to sea, they lost sight of the *Swanne* but found additional islands of seals and birds. After several days on an island, the natives appeared and traded.

17 May  After the *Swanne* rejoined the fleet, Drake and Thomas Doughty quarreled. Drake struck Doughty and had him tied to the mast.

18 May  The *Christopher* and *Marigold* searched the mainland for a harbor and resupplied food and water. Drake striped the *Swanne* and set it on fire to recover the ironwork. This brought to the beach armed natives, and one stole Drake's cap. They set sail sometime in June and lost sight of the *Christopher* for three or four days.

3 Jun  Thomas Doughty and his brother, John, were put under arrest and isolated from the other crewmembers.

19 Jun   Drake stripped the *Christopher* and abandoned it near the Cape of Good Hope.

20 Jun   The fleet harbored at Puerto San Julián (49.3°S in present-day Argentina). They found Magellan's gibbet on the mainland where he had executed some of his rebellious crewmen.

22 Jun   Drake went ashore with others and met two or three natives. A misunderstanding provoked the natives to attack, and the Englishmen escaped to their ships.

30 Jun   An inquiry into Thomas Doughty's behavior resulted in charges of mutiny and treason by Drake. Doughty was acquitted of treason but convicted of mutiny by an assembled group of crewmembers. Drake insisted on execution.

2 Jul    Doughty and Drake took communion from the minister, Francis Fletcher, and shared a last meal together. Doughty was beheaded at San Julián, after which Drake spoke passionately to his company for unity and obedience. For the first time, Drake took sole command of the expedition.

5 Jul    The *Mary* was broken up; the cargo and men were distributed among the three remaining ships. Some crewmembers were buried after dying of disease.

11 Aug   Drake addressed his men, offered a chance for dissidents to leave, and may have produced the Queen's commission. He restored order and discipline.

17 Aug   The fleet departed Port Julian with the three remaining ships: the *Elizabeth*, the *Marigold*, and the *Pelican*.

20 Aug   The fleet entered the Straits of Magellan. The *Pelican* was renamed the *Golden Hinde* from the crest of a sponsor, Sir Christopher Hatton, lord chancellor of England.

24 Aug   They arrived at an island with penguins and took over three thousand for food.

6 Sep   The fleet entered the South Seas at the cape or head shore.

7 Sep   Driven by a great storm southward about two hundred leagues from the strait, they continued during a lunar eclipse.

15 Sep  The *Marigold* with all hands (number unknown) was lost during the storm. The remaining two ships were driven farther south from the "Bay of Severing of Friends," reportedly to 57°S, but this must be an error since all of Cape Horn lies north of 56°S. They sheltered in a harbor among the islands and came into another bay where they met naked men and women in canoes with whom they traded.

3 Oct   They found the third of three islands filled with birds.

8 Oct   The *Golden Hinde* lost sight of the *Elizabeth* commanded by Wynter. Drake assumed that a storm had forced Wynter back into the strait, where he may have perished. Not being able to rejoin the *Golden Hinde,* Wynter sailed back through the strait and returned to England. The *Golden Hinde* passed the strait. They noted that Chili (Chile) did not run northwest as then reported on maps but rather northeast for many degrees of latitude.

25 Nov  The *Golden Hinde* cast anchor at the island of La Mocha, about 38.5°S.

26 Nov  Drake went ashore with ten men. He encountered natives who had fled the mainland from the Spanish and traded items for food.

27 Nov  Drake and a dozen men returned to the island for provisions but were met by a war party that killed two men, Thomas Flood and Thomas Brewer, and wounded all the others including Drake. Great Nele, a Danish gunner, died from loss of blood aboard the *Golden Hinde.* The ship sailed for the coast of Chile.

3 Dec   Bypassing Concepción and Valparaiso, they dropped anchor in a bay (Felipe's Bay or Quintero) at 33°S. A native from the bay informed Drake that a ship at Valparaiso was laden with treasure from Peru. The Indian guided them to the port of Valparaiso.

They captured the *Capitana* or *Los Reyes* on 5 December, looted the town, set all the Spanish prisoners free, but kept a Greek pilot, Juan Griego, to guide them to Lima. They retained the captured Spanish ship that provided wine, silver, and gold valued at 37,000 ducats, their first treasure score.

18 Dec  At La Herradura, near Coquimbo (30°S), Drake sent fourteen men ashore for fresh water. They were intercepted by three hundred Spanish horsemen and two hundred footmen. One of Drake's crew, Richard Minivy, was slain, and the others escaped to board ship. The Spaniards departed. Drake's men returned, buried their comrade, and obtained the water.

22 Dec  They next landed at Salada Bay (Chile, 27.58°S) where they constructed the last pinnace aboard the *Golden Hinde*. Although nervous about discovery, they were able to finish the construction ashore and completed it on 9 January. They had been successful at hunting and held a New Year feast on 1 January. During the next several days, one group prepared the *Golden Hinde* for careening and transferred everything to the *Capitana*, while Drake and some of his men used the pinnace to search for the two missing ships. They finally abandoned the search.

## 1579

14 Jan  Cleaning and repair of the *Golden Hinde* hull began and lasted five days.

19 Jan  The *Golden Hinde*, the *Capitana*, and the pinnace sailed northward to continue pillage. Later, they entered the coastal waters of northern Chile and visited the small village of Tarapacá. They confiscated thirteen bars of silver (4,000 ducats) and eight llamas packed with silver.

7 Feb  They raided three crewless barques in the port of Arica (Chile, 18.5°S) and confiscated additional silver. After setting sail for Lima, they encountered another small barque from which they took fine linen.

13 Feb   Drake entered the harbor of Callao (Lima) to find twelve ships at anchor. He raided the ships of silver plate, silks, and linen. He also learned of the *Nuestra Señora de la Concepción* or the *Cacafuego*, which had sailed earlier toward Payta laden with treasure. Drake cut the cables of the harbor ships to send them adrift and departed in pursuit of the *Cacafuego*.

Arriving in Payta (Paita, Peru), they found that the *Cacafuego* had sailed on to Panama. In pursuit, they boarded a barque carrying gold, a gold crucifix with emeralds, and ropes, which they took. John Drake earned a gold chain by being the first to spy the *Cacafuego* near Cape de San Francisco, about 150 leagues south of Panama (northern coast of Ecuador). After three shots, including one that broke the mizzenmast on the *Cacafuego*, they boarded her and claimed one of the largest treasure prizes ever taken at sea. They cast the ship and its crew loose after taking the treasure aboard the *Golden Hinde*.

20 Mar   They sailed to the island of Caño, off the coast of Nicaragua, to careen the *Golden Hinde* for repairs and to replenish water and wood. While there, they spotted a ship bound for the Philippines, a teak barque or frigate of about forty tons owned by Rodrigo Tello. They boarded and took some of the merchandise. Two pilots and a Spanish governor were aboard, but Drake kept only their charts.

27 Mar   Drake finished his repairs and refitted Tello's barque, placing six of his cannons aboard. He continued north along the coast and released Tello on 29 March.

4 Apr   They encountered another barque laden with silks, porcelain, and linen owned by Don Francisco de Zarate. The pilots were retained and the ship cast loose with its crew. Drake released one of the captured pilots from the barque, Alonzo Sanchez Colchero, but retained two black men and a Negress slave, Maria.

13 Apr   Drake sailed into the harbor of Guatulco (now Huatulco) at 11:00 A.M., landed twenty-five men to capture some treasure, and freed

three Negro slaves, one who decided to join Drake. They forced a local judge to warn the townspeople not to molest Drake's crew while they provisioned. They took silver and jewels from a fleeing townsman but let him go. Drake released the other Spaniards.

16 Apr   Drake sailed out of the harbor before dawn with Tello's barque and the *Golden Hinde*, leaving Nuño da Silva behind to face Spanish interrogation. They sailed five hundred leagues westward. Becalmed where they were, they sailed north to pick up a wind and continued northward for six hundred leagues until 3 June.

2 Jun    Wynter and the *Elizabeth* arrived in Devon, England.

3 Jun    After sailing fourteen hundred leagues, the *Golden Hinde* and frigate encountered very cold temperatures at 42°N and moved toward the coast.

5 Jun    *The World Encompassed* (*TWE*) noted that the shoreline bore farther westward, and their course and the prevailing wind brought them onshore to cast anchor in a "bad baye." High winds and heavy fogs prevented them from sailing farther north. They were at 48°N according to the journal entry.

Note: This latitude would not seem to be correct if they were at 42°N just two days earlier (at a latitude of Brookings, Oregon). One suspects that the June 3 entry does not imply that they arrived at 42°N on that date but achieved it earlier. If 48°N is correct, that would put them at or near the tip of the Olympic Peninsula. If they discovered the Strait of Juan de Fuca without entering it, would they have thought they had found the Strait of Anián? They departed, date unknown, and bore southward along the coast. During the way, they observed plains and hills, none very high, covered with snow.

Cold weather continued, and the overcast skies prevented sun or star height readings on most days. The journal, according to *TWE*, also cast doubt about the likelihood of discovering a Northwest Passage and indicated they turned back before finding such a possibility. The journal (p. 65) commented on the following: trees without leaves, ground without greenness, and birds that didn't leave their eggs on nests.

The journal stated (p. 66) that one reason for the coldness was the joining or approach of the Asian and American continents farther north. Their high, snow-covered mountains were the source of the north and northwestern winds. It compared their observations with those of the Spaniards that the prevailing winds were north and northwest in June and July and north only in August and September. It also mentioned that some sailors, having sailed as far north as 72°N in the Atlantic, did not encounter such coldness. On p. 67, *TWE* again states that they were at 48°N but found not one place where the coast veered to the east. Therefore, either a passage was not present or it was unnavigable.

17 Jun  At 38°30' N they came to a "conuenient and fit harborough." This is about the latitude of Bodega Bay in Marin County, California. They anchored in the bay.

18 Jun  Natives appeared on the shore, and a single person in a canoe rowed out a short distance to meet the *Golden Hinde*. The man in the canoe gave a lengthy oration with many gestures and then returned to shore. He returned a second and third time, lastly with a present of tied feathers and a basket of Tobah, an herb. He refused gifts in return except for a hat thrown into the water. He returned to shore.

Natives responded by gathering in numbers, carrying weapons but standing in submission (?). They were persuaded by signs to lay their weapons down. Men and women gathered around Drake's company. The natives were given clothing to cover them, and by demonstration of eating and drinking, the Englishmen tried to convince the natives that the sailors were men, not gods. They had houses over round holes in the earth with wood stakes joined at the top, covered with earth and protected from water entry. The door worked also as a chimney for smoke to exit on a slope of wall, and a fire was in the middle. Men usually went naked (despite the freezing weather!). The women wore a loose skirt of bulrushes and wore deerskin about their shoulders. Their village was about three-quarters of an English mile from Drake's anchorage. Upon return to their houses, the natives commenced whining and shrieking, especially the women.

21 Jun  The *Golden Hinde* was brought nearer to shore because of a leak received at sea. While anchored, goods were landed to ready the ship for repairs. Drake ordered men and tents ashore. The tents were pitched at the bottom of a hill. Drake's men still did not trust the natives and constructed entrenchments and a stone wall, his so-called "fort" (*TWE*, p. 70). According to Francis Pretty, Drake marched his men within their "fenced place." Pretty also stated that "there is no part of earth here to be taken up, wherein there is not some probable show of gold or silver."

23 Jun  A larger group of natives including women and children gathered, bringing presents. *TWE* described (p. 71) the fort at the bottom of a hill and the natives gathering at the top.

26 Jun  Additional natives gathered at the site, presumably brought in from upcountry by the news. The native chief with an estimated retinue of one hundred guards came to visit.

Ambassadors or messengers preceded the chief's (Hioh's) arrival with a half-hour proclamation. They asked for a gift from Drake, which he gave them, and they departed. Shortly afterward, the Hioh made his appearance with his guard singing. A man in front carried a staff of black wood. Two crowns of knitwork containing feathers wrapped in bone-like chains hung on the staff; apparently the number of links indicated the status of the bearer. The king wore a crown of knitwork and a cape of "conie" pelts. Guards also wore coats of other furs and had cowls of down and feathers. The common people followed, some with a single feather in their long hair tied behind. Most were naked. All had their face painted:

some with white or black, and some with colors. Each man brought a present in one hand. Women and children followed, each bringing one or two baskets made of rushes carrying tobah or a root (petah), from which they made meal and bread, broiled fishes, seeds, and downs. The baskets were mostly watertight and decorated with shell handles, some with bone-like chains. After their approach, they gave a salutation that was followed by silence as Drake's men stood in defensive postures. The man with the scepter voiced a proclamation, dictated by another man, for a half hour. After the native host gave a common shout of agreement, the king and the men descended the hill. At the base of the hill near the fort, the scepter bearer began a song and dance ritual, which was repeated by the king and his men. The women also danced but kept silent. The natives were allowed to pass inside the bulwark and continued to sing and dance.

The natives signaled Drake to sit, and they made several orations. The journal writer assumed at this point that the natives were asking Drake to take possession of their land and to rule them as his subjects. With the natives singing, the king set a crown on Drake's head, put chains around his neck, and called him "Hioh" (p. 76). Drake took the scepter crown and accepted the honor, presumably to enrich England and serve Her Majesty as well as facilitate the introduction of Protestant Christianity to the natives. After the ceremony, the natives dispersed among the Englishmen, especially seeking the younger men, but then crying out and repeating the facial mutilations of themselves. Even the old men joined the women in this (p. 77). Drake's men prevented them from this by showing their dislike, holding their hands, and finally resorting to withdrawal into their tents. Afterward, the natives asked for help in curing their wounds and illnesses, which the Englishmen did with lotions and other physical means at their disposal. The natives continued to seek help, especially every third day. The Englishmen's displeasure of their sacrifices (none were described other than the facial mutilation) finally caused them to cease, but they continued to seek help and sometimes did not provide their own food, requiring the Englishmen to provide for them. "Muscles" (clams, mussels, and crabs) and seals were among the provisions shared.

*TWE* commented on the native weapons (p. 79) being weak and more fit for children than men, yet the native men were exceedingly strong. The natives ran far and fast. They were very skillful at taking fish by hand near the shore.

Drake's men ventured upland and saw several villages, with many houses of the type first described. This area was described as far different from the coast, having fruitful soil, thousands of fat deer (might include elk), and multitudes of a type of coney (muskrat) described on p. 80. Drake named the country Albion because of the white banks and cliffs that lay toward the sea and because of affinity with England (old name is also Albion, based on the white cliffs).

Drake set up a monument with a plate of brass nailed to a stout post. A sixpence with the likeness of Elizabeth I was nailed to the plate ("brass" in the sixteenth century referred to a bronze-lead-tin alloy).

Drake's plans to depart became obvious to the natives, and they showed their sorrow by renewing their torments. The journal writer interpreted their behavior as an attempt to assure that Drake would return. The natives burned a sacrifice of feathers and chains. Their exhortations were broken by the Englishmen conducting another round of prayers and psalms. This distracted them, and they imitated the Englishmen's ritual motions.

23 Jul   The *Golden Hinde* departed from New Albion. The natives ran to the top of the hills to keep the ship in sight and burned fires (presumably with sacrifices) near them. Not far from the harbor were islands with great stores of seals and birds.

24 Jul   They visited one of the offshore Islands for food (p. 82). Although this is assumed by many historians to be the Farallon Islands off of Central California (named the Islands of Saint James in *TWE*), there is no undisputed evidence that these were the islands Drake visited.

25 Jul   They left the islands and steered westward across the Pacific. It was still cold and foggy, and the northwest wind prevailed.

11 Aug   King Philip of Spain requested King Henry of Portugal to intercept Drake in the East Indies.

16 Oct   Drake reached the Philippines.

4 Nov   Drake arrived at Ternate in the East Indies.

14 Nov   Drake arrived at Crab Island (Isla Francisco), provisioned, and left three blacks: Maria, Francisco, and one other. Maria was probably in the third trimester of pregnancy.

12 Dec   The *Golden Hinde* departed Crab Island.

## — 1580 —

9 Jan   The *Golden Hinde* struck a reef but was able to get off after jettisoning cannons and supplies.

26 Sep   The *Golden Hinde* arrived in Plymouth.

16 Oct   A letter from de Mendoza, ambassador to England from Spain, to King Philip stated that Drake had given the Queen a diary of everything that happened during the voyage (Breton, 1581, p. 5).

## — 1581 —

4 Apr   Drake was knighted aboard the *Golden Hinde* at Deptford by the ambassador from France in order to spare political embarrassment for Elizabeth.

## 1582

1 May — The Edward Fenton Expedition of four ships set sail from England, ostensibly on a trading mission to the Moluccas and China. After a layover in Sierra Leone, the fleet sailed for Brazil. (This date is also stated as 2 June 1582)

## 1583

27 Feb — Richard Madox died aboard the *Leicester* near Vitória, Brazil during the Fenton Expedition. His account also verifies John Drake's claim of a 48°N anchorage site for the *Golden Hinde*.

## 1586

21 July — The Cavendish Expedition of three ships sailed from England for the Moluccas via South America.

14 Nov — The *Content*, weighing sixty tons and commanded by John Brewer from Drake's crew, disappeared from the Cavendish ship during the night. A Spanish pilot aboard Cavendish's ship speculated that the *Content* had sailed for the Northwest Passage.

# APPENDIX 3.

# Geographical Considerations

### LATITUDES

Listed below are the latitudes for several, but not all, locations proposed by various authors as the anchorage site and gateway to Nova Albion. Those in bold are described but not identified by name in sequential order of discovery in *New Albion Sunset*. They are given a number corresponding to the accompanying maps.

> H = *Golden Hinde*
> V = *Northern Venture*
> GD = The pinnace *Great Dane*
> NAC = New Albion Company on foot

1. **Port of Guatulco (Huatulco), Mexico 15.7177°N**
   Current-day La Crucecita, Oaxaca, Mexico.

2. **Ucluelet Inlet at Barkley Sound, Vancouver Island 48.9232°N**
   The initial anchorage site on the Northwest coast.

   **Cape Flattery, Washington 48.3831°N**
   Entrance to the Strait of Juan de Fuco includes sites on Vancouver Island (identified as the Strait of Elizabeth in the novel).

3. **Neah Bay, Washington 48.3681°N**
   Inlet to the Muh-kwa (Makah) village.

4. **Boundary Bay, British Columbia 49.0047°N**
   The designated Nova Albion site in this novel.

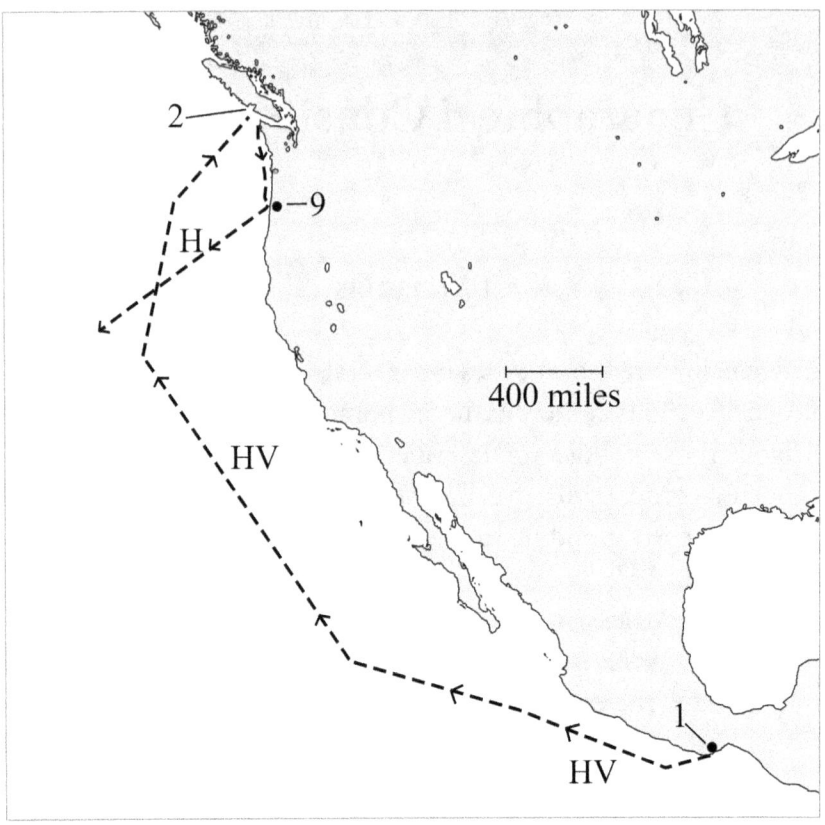

Figure 8. Route of the *Golden Hinde* and *Northern Venture* from Guatulco to Ucluelet Inlet. Map by Dan Hawkes.

5. **Stuart Island, Discovery Islands, British Columbia 50.3930°N**
   The *Northern Venture* entered the inlet of Evans Bay and passed Read Island, ran aground at Stuart; attack by Euclataws (Latch-Quill-Tak in novel).

6. **Saturna Island, British Columbia 48.7820°N**
   "Saint James Island" where the *Golden Hinde* stopped for seals and eggs.

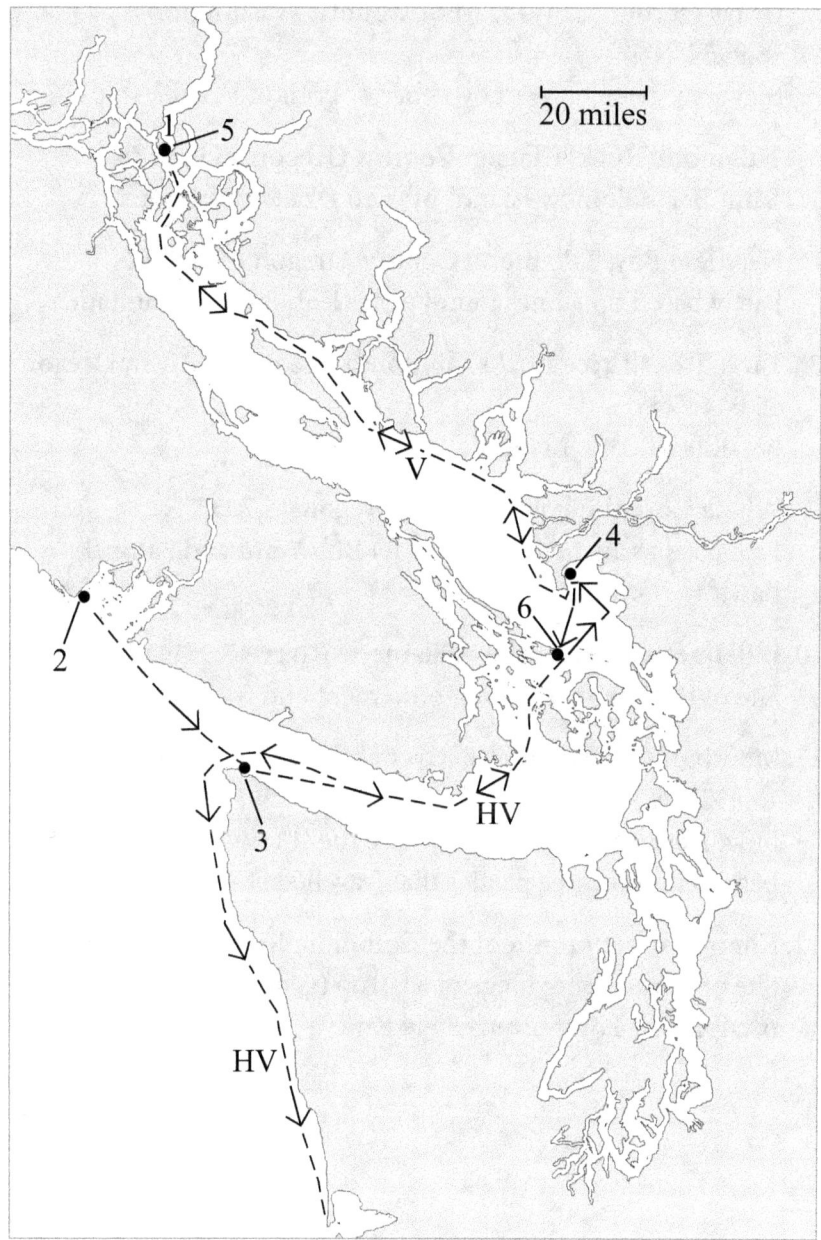

Figure 9. The *Golden Hinde* and the *Northern Venture* in the Salish Sea. Map by Dan Hawkes.

**Grays Harbor, Grays Harbor County, Washington 46.9954°N**
May have been entered by either or both of Drake's ships.

**Tillamook Rock, Clatsop County, Oregon 45.9376°N**
"Saint Bartholomew Island" of John Drake's testimony.

7. **Nehalem Bay, Tillamook County, Oregon 45.6959°N**
Partly based on stones found near Neahkahnie Mountain.

8. **Three Rox (Three Rocks) at mouth of Salmon River, Oregon 45.0446°N**
Possible site of remains of Tello's barque.

9. **Whale Cove, Lincoln County, Oregon 44.7333°N**
Proposed as an anchorage site By Bob Ward and Samuel Bawlf.

10. **Willamette Falls on the Willamette River 45.3511°N**
Site of the Lakimas fishing settlement and trade center.

11. **Mouth of the Willamette River at the Colombia River 45.6528°N**
Juncture at the Great River where the surviving seven members split into three parties that travelled east, north, and west.

12. **Konope at the mouth of the Colombia River 46.1994°N**
Site of the ancient village of Klatsop (Clatsop) Indians, now occupied by Fort Stevens State Park.

# New Albion Sunset

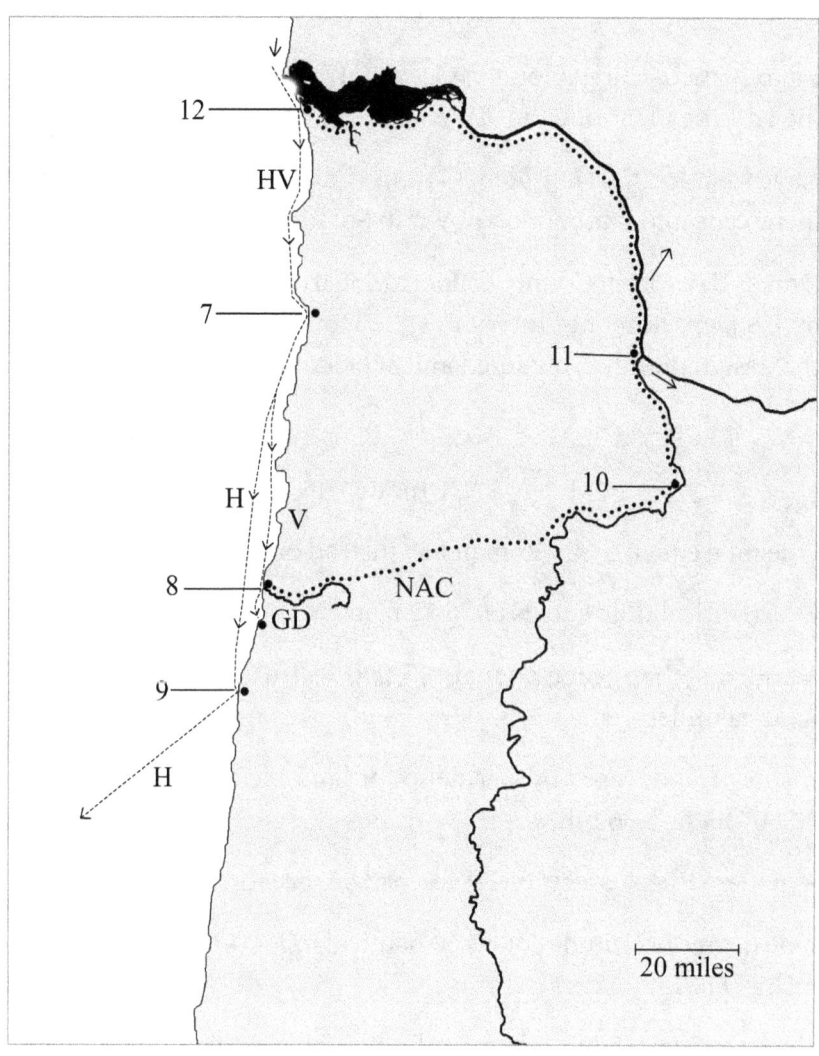

Figure 10. The Oregon coast and Willamette Valley. Overland trek shown as dotted trail. Map by Dan Hawkes.

## Other Latitudes of Interest: Drake Circumnavigation

Cape Arago, Coos County, Oregon 43.3065°N. Possible site for Drake to hunt seals and gather sea bird eggs.

Cape Blanco, Curry County, Oregon 42.8376°N. Corresponds to the latitude mentioned in *TWE*.

Cape Mendocino, Humboldt County, California 40.4401°N. Prominent cape and landmark, known to Spaniards.

Drake's Bay, Marin County, California 38.0138°N. This is recognized by US Department of Interior as the Drake landing site, although the designation was qualified and subject to further research.

## Measurements

One mile equals 5,000 Roman feet instead of the current 5,280 feet.

One nautical mile equals 6076.12 feet.

An Elizabethan league equals 15,000 feet or 2.84 miles or 2.46 nautical miles.

A short league, used by Cermeño for land measure, equals about 7,200 feet or 1.36 miles.

A modern league equals 18,228 feet or 3.45 miles or 3.00 nautical miles.

One degree of latitude equals 60 nautical miles (knots) or 69.2 land miles (111 kilometers).

Thus, the May 1579 journey in the Pacific from about 10–12°N to 42°N of about 900 leagues distance (2,550 land miles) was done in nineteen days, at an average speed of about 5.6 mph in favorable winds, well within the estimated speed of the *Golden Hinde* at 8 mph. The maximum speed of the *Northern Venture* is unknown.

# APPENDIX 4.

# Further Reading

THE FOLLOWING SOURCES ARE PROVIDED TO ALLOW THE INTERested reader to pursue the controversies about Drake and New Albion. The disputed reports of historians, professional and amateur alike, who have attempted to account for the location of Drake's lost harbor are included. There are many other books on the subject, but this provides an introduction to the historical basis of the mystery and the premise of this novel.

Anonymous. *A discourse of Sir Francis Drakes iorney and exploytes after hee had past ye Straytes of Magellan into Mare de Sur, and through the rest of his voyage afterward till hee arrived in England 1580 Anno.* (The Anonymous Narrative). London: British Library, Harley MS 280, Folios 81–90.

> Bob Ward (2003) believes, based on writing analysis, that the author is Reverend Philip Jones, who assisted Hakluyt with his historical publications including an account of Drake's voyage. As Ward relates, this account is based on the testimony of eight identified senior crewmen of the Hinde. The tract is about three thousand words and focuses on the voyage from Mocha to Guatulco.

Anonymous. *The Famous Voyage of Sir Francis Drake into the South Sea, and therehence about the whole Globe of the Earth, begun in the year of our Lord 1577.* (1580) aka Sir Francis Drake's Famous Voyage Round the World Attributed to Francis Pretty.

*Based on the account of Francis Pretty, who was supposedly one of Drake's gentlemen at arms but not a member of the circumnavigational voyage. This can be found in Voyages and Travels: Ancient and Modern, with Introductions, Notes and Illustrations. See: The Harvard Classics, C. W. Eliot, ed., vol. 33 (New York: P. F. Collier & Son (c. 1910).*

Armstrong, Erma. 2015. *The Labors of Sir Francis Drake*. Dallas, OR: Tanglewood Hill Press, 241 pages.

*Armstrong expands on the texts by Bawlf (2003) and Gitzen (2008), citing evidence for Nehalem Bay as the anchorage site and its relation to the purported treasure at Neahkahnie Mountain. She includes information on the triangulation surveys of the area done by Phillip A. Costaggini for his master's degree at Oregon State University in 1980.*

Bawlf, Samuel. 2003. *The Secret Voyage of Sir Francis Drake 1577–1580*. New York: Walker & Company, 400 pages.

*Bawlf is a geographer and archeologist from British Columbia. His book promotes the theory that Drake sailed as far north as Alaska and that his lost harbor was on Vancouver Island. He provides a nice overview of the anchorage site controversy. However, a number of historians and other Drake experts contest his findings and those of Bob Ward, a British historian from Oregon.*

Breton, Nicholas. 1581. *A Discourse in Commendation of the Valiant as Virtuous Minded Gentleman, Mister Frauncis Drake: With a Rejoicing of his Happy Adventures*. London: John Charlewood, 14 pages.

*The Elizabethan writer Nicholas Breton (1545–1622) published this short book dedicated to Francis Drake and his cir-*

cumnavigational voyage of 1577–1580. The address of Drake as "master" rather than "sir" suggests it was published before April 14, 1581, when Drake was knighted. Although it mentions Drake's triumphant return with treasure, it is discreet about where and how the treasure was acquired, reflecting the delicate political situation between Spain and England at the time. Likewise, there is no indication of territorial claims or the establishment of a New World colony.

Darby, Melissa. 2019. *Thunder Go North: The Hunt for Sir Francis Drake's Fair & Good Bay*. Salt Lake City, UT: University of Utah Press, 315 pages.

*Darby joins the recent efforts to place Drake's anchorage in the Pacific Northwest. Two major focuses of her well-written book concern the systematic suppression of Zelia Nuttall's research in the early 1900s and the creation, "discovery," and promotion of the fake plate of brass found in Marin County in the 1930s. She exposes the role of Dr. Herbert Bolton at University of California Berkeley in promoting the fraudulent evidence.*

Drake, Sir Francis. 1628. *The World Encompassed*. London: Nicholas Bourne. Facsimile reprint by the Hakluyt Society. Cleveland, OH: World Publishing Company, 108 pages.

*The narrative compiled largely but not exclusively from Chaplain Francis Fletcher's journal by Sir Francis Drake, nephew of the circumnavigator. The second part of the chaplain's diary was lost and it is not certain how much of his notes were used in TWE.*

Gitzen, Garry D. 2008. *Francis Drake in Nehalem Bay 1579: Setting the Historical Record Straight*. Wheeler, OR: Isnik Publishing, 245 pages.

Gitzen makes the case for Drake's landing at Nehalem Bay on the upper Oregon coast, reviewing evidence of stones with possible survey markings and local geography and ethnography.

Hampden, John. 1972. *Francis Drake Privateer: Contemporary Narratives and Documents.* University, AL: University of Alabama Press, 286 pages.

*This volume contains the full texts of the contemporary accounts, many illustrations and maps, and a reasoned assessment of Drake's personal behavior and motives. Mr. Hampden was the author of several books on Tudor maritime history.*

Hanna, Warren L. 1979. *Lost Harbor: The Controversy over Drake's California Anchorage.* Berkeley: University of California Press, 459 pages.

*As the title suggests, this volume provides evidence in support of Northern California sites for Drake's harbor but does not seriously consider evidence pointing to other possibilities. The organization is superb and allows one to review and quickly locate the assembled materials.*

Hayes, Derek. 1999. *Historical Atlas of the Pacific Northwest: Maps of Exploration and Discovery.* Seattle, WA: Sasquatch Books, 208 pages.

*Derek provides a nice compilation of early maps. Pages 11–15 feature maps related to the Drake voyage and maps of the later sixteenth century. Map 3B (p. 12) shows an apparent "correction" to the northward extension of Drake's ship to about 48°N. Also note the placement of Nova Albion on this 1589 Hondius map and compare it with Nova Albion on Van Sype's 1583 (p. 12) rendering, "The French Drake Map." Also note Carver's 1778 map (p. 33), showing New Albion north of Cape Mendocino and parallel with Cape Blanco in Curry County, Oregon.*

Kantor, MacKinlay. 1958. *If the South Had Won the Civil War*. New York: Houghton Mifflin Riverside Press (Forge Books), 128 pages.

*The historical theme doesn't relate to the Drake voyage, but the historical speculation on "what if" is well presented, allowing one to ask the same questions about New Albion.*

Kelsey, Harry. 1998. *Sir Francis Drake: The Queen's Pirate*. New Haven, CT: Yale University Press, 566 pages.

*Kelsey writes a comprehensive treatise on the life and times of Drake, exploring his personality and the mythology surrounding his character and exploits from early childhood to his death.*

Madox, Richard. 1976. *An Elizabethan in 1582: The Diary of Richard Madox, Fellow of All Souls*. Second series, number 147. London: Hakluyt Society, 365 pages.

*Madox was the chaplain aboard the galleon Leicester with the Fenton Expedition of 1582. His diary, encrypted to keep it secret, recorded information obtained from John Drake, the cousin of Francis Drake, about the 1579 visit to the Pacific Northwest.*

Nuttall, Zelia. 1914. *New Light on Drake*. London: Hakluyt Society, 443 pages.

*A 1967 Kraus reprint (Nendeln, Liechtenstein) of the original translations of Spanish documents by Nuttall is an invaluable source of notes from the reports, investigations, and inquisition of Drake's prisoners and captured crewmen. It contains a translation of the testimony of John Drake with regard to the Pacific West Coast visit by the Golden Hinde. Drake's confession provides the location and a brief description of the anchorage site. Nuttall's research was cited by Darby (2019) as one of the most important sources pointing to Nova Albion in the Pacific Northwest rather than California.*

Roche, T. W. E. 1973. *The Golden Hind*. New York: Praeger, 200 pages.

*The circumnavigation is compiled and related by a British descendent of Sir Christopher Hatton on his mother's side. It includes an index and twenty-four pages of black-and-white illustrations focusing on the ship and its voyage, but it also relates the earlier life of Drake. Photos include illustrations from Francis Fletcher's journals and the keel of the Golden Hind reconstruction being prepared in England. The book was nearly finished when Thomas William Edgar Roche died (1919–1972). Neville Williams completed the manuscript for publication.*

Savours, Ann. 1999. *The Search for the Northwest Passage*. New York: St. Martin's Press, 342 pages.

*This excellent account provides a brief summary of Martin Frobisher's exploratory voyages in 1576, 1577, and 1578 to find a northern route between the North Atlantic and North Pacific Oceans. This sets the stage for Drake's real mission, but he is mentioned only in a cursory fashion.*

Speck, Gordon. 1954. *Northwest Explorations*. Portland, OR: Binford & Mort Publishing, 394 pages.

*There are chapters on pre-Elizabethan voyages including the Chinese, Drake, and others. Includes an index.*

Sugden, John. 1990. *Sir Francis Drake*. New York: Henry Holt, 353 pages.

*This definitive modern biography of Drake includes an account of the circumnavigation, maps, photos, bibliography, glossary, and index. The volume contains extensive information on the Tudor court and the political intrigues behind the voyages. Sugden was a lecturer in history at Hereward College in Coventry, UK, and has been a researcher at the Newberry Library in Chicago.*

Taylor, E. G. R., ed. 1959. *The Troublesome Voyage of Captain Edward Fenton 1582-83*. Cambridge: Cambridge University Press, 333 pages.

*The accounts, based on journals and other documents, of Fenton's proposed trip to the South Sea and Spanish Pacific coast. Published for the Hakluyt Society as Vol. CXIII in their second series. John Drake, the cousin of Sir Francis, who had accompanied him on the 1577–1580 circumnavigation, was captain of the Francis, one of three ships in the expedition. Was this intended as a resupply of the New Albion group? The betrayal of the Privy Council–sponsored voyage and the subsequent capture of Drake and others by the Spanish are recorded as well as transcripts of the inquisition and letters between principals in England. Taylor was a professor emeritus of geography at the University of London.*

Wagner, Henry R. 1926. *Sir Francis Drake's Voyage Around the World: Its Aims and Achievements*. San Francisco: John Howell, 543 pages.

*Although somewhat dated and presenting some conclusions based on erroneous assumptions, this volume remains a valuable sourcebook of documents and accounts of the voyage. Wagner proposes a two-stop theory for Drake's coastal visit (the first in Trinity Bay and the last at Bodega Bay).*

Wagner, Henry R. 1937. *The Cartography of the Northwest Coast of North America to the Year 1800.* Berkeley: University of California Press.

*This valuable reference for the armchair historical geographer includes names and information on what was known from the earlier explorations of the Pacific Coast.*

Ward, Bob. 2003. *Whale Cove, Oregon: Francis Drake's New Albion, and Birthplace of the British Empire!* Depoe Bay, OR: Drake in Oregon Society, 20 pages.

*Despite the misleading title (the British Empire was not born in Oregon), this issued but not formally published manuscript contains valuable data and arguments supporting Whale Cove as a West Coast anchorage site for Drake in 1579. Ward refutes much of the evidence cited by the California contingent for a Bay Area landing and discusses material located in the British Library that support Drake's search for the Northwest Passage including the Anonymous Narrative.*

Wilson, Derek. 1977. *The World Encompassed: Francis Drake and His Great Voyage.* New York: Harper & Row, 240 pages.

*Well-illustrated with maps, drawings, and photographs, this book represents a nice amalgam of the voyage and the character of Drake from a British historian specializing in Tudor times. Not to be confused with The World Encompassed (1628)*

# ABOUT THE AUTHOR

L. WADE POWERS HAS PUBLISHED BOOKS AND ARTICLES IN THE fields of medical technology, ecology, marine biology, and animal behavior under the name Lawrence W. Powers, PhD. He authored a critique of *The Winter of Our Discontent* for *Steinbeck Review* and several articles for *The Oregon Encyclopedia Online*. He is a contributing editor for the *Journal of the Shaw Historical Library* and served as creative nonfiction editor for *Timberline Review* for two years.

As L. Wade Powers, he has published two novels, *The Home* (2017) and *The Party House* (2019), and two collections of short stories: *Falling in Love and Other Misadventures* (2019) and *Confronting the Boundaries* (2020). A revised edition of *The Home* was published in November 2019. This novel, his first historical fiction, is based on fifteen years of research on Francis Drake and his 1579 visit to the West Coast of North America. He is currently at work on a fourth novel.

A retired professor of natural sciences, Larry lives in Eastern Oregon with his wife, Alla, with the gracious permission of their cat, Mollie. He is a member of the Northwest Association Independent Writers Association (NIWA) and Willamette Writers. For further information about the author and his works, please visit lwadepowers.com.

www.ingramcontent.com/pod-product-compliance
Lightning Source LLC
LaVergne TN
LVHW011806060526
838200LV00053B/3679